A GOOD PLACE TO DIE

"Sooner or later James Buchan will be recognised as the top adventure writer of his time . . . He's a wonderful prose writer, vivid and romantic. In parts this novel is a love story, a modernist *Dr Zhivago* . . . But it's also a meditation on Iran and the lands around it, their religious culture, their heroin and their oil . . . I adored this book . . . It's a long time since I read a novel so brainy, so educational, and so genuinely sad"

JENNY TURNER, *Evening Standard*

"James Buchan writes like a dream . . . The first person story-telling is both paced and elegant, Buchan's prose cutting between action, reflection and rich description to bring alive both the exotic beauty and terrible brutality of the region . . . Buchan maps out the tragedy of modern Iran with sympathy and understanding and the ending has a perfect bittersweet poignancy"

PETER MILLAR, *The Times*

"James Buchan has rescued the [contemporary] novel with a masterpiece"   **SIMON FREEMAN**, *Herald*

"Superb . . . James Buchan was for ten years a foreign correspondent, so it isn't surprising that he should offer so solid a portrait of a world on the brink. What is surprising is the full-bloodedness of his inventions, the freedom of his drawing on English and non-English traditions of storytelling. The book is among other things a sort of apotheosis of romance, and even of that infinitely discredited form, the adventure yarn, but endowed with a startling emotional charge"   **ADAM MARS-JONES**, *Observer*

"Hyper-civilised, his sentences leave volumes unsaid . . . They are continually inventive, and they reflect a genuinely new tuning of the novelistic ear . . . the reward is complex and world revelation of a kind that none of James Buchan's contemporaries are offering"   **FRANCIS SPUFFORD**, *Guardian*

"A daring, phenomenally accomplished novel"

JOHN DUGDALE, *Sunday Times*

"Airy, graceful and big with truth, *A Good Place to Die* feels like a major statement of confidence, not just by an English novelist but by the English novel . . . There is really no word for it but 'masterpiece'" **PHILIP HENSHER**, *Spectator*

"Buchan's depiction of opium-addicted and world-weary Ryazanov is of the highest order and he uses his considerable knowledge of classical Persian references to orchestrate a courtly, ornate dialogue between almost all protagonists . . . there is often a precise and lyrical tenderness in his writing" **JOHN MURRAY**, *Independent on Sunday*

"This new offering is a high-class thriller concocted with Buchan's distinctive ingredients – passionate love, political intrigue, picaresque adventures and thoughtful comment" **SHUSHA GUPPY**, *Independent*

"The best new novel, I consider, is *A Good Place to Die*, James Buchan's love story set in the Shah's Iran. His tale is allegorical in its formality, his prose burns with an intolerable longing, rage and sadness" **FERNANDA EBERSTADT**, *Times Literary Supplement*

"On the surface it is a political thriller and as such provides exciting and believable twists of plot. A second reading shows it to be a profound study of the disintegration of Iranian society. As always in Buchan's fiction, the book contains pages of stunningly beautiful writing, and nobody – but nobody – tells a love story better" **PAUL BAILEY**, *Daily Telegraph*

"A really excellent, intelligent and poetic thriller-cum-novel" **NICHOLAS COLERIDGE**, *Daily Mail*

"Audacious, moving, often beautiful, and utterly compelling . . . It is written with love and tenderness and pity: and glows with beauty even in the midst of modern political horror. There is humour too, and in the midst of death and cruelty, a religious awe inspired by the unfathomable strangeness of life . . . Read it: you won't read anything new and more remarkable in a long time" **ALLAN MASSIE**, *Scotsman*

JAMES BUCHAN was for ten years a foreign correspondent of the *Financial Times*. His novel *A Parish of Rich Women* won four literary prizes, including the Whitbread First Novel Award. *Heart's Journey in Winter* won the Guardian Fiction Award. His most recent book, *Frozen Desire*, a study of the psychology of money, won the Duff Cooper Prize and has been translated into six foreign languages.

James Buchan

A GOOD PLACE
TO DIE

THE HARVILL PRESS
LONDON

First published in 1999 by The Harvill Press

This paperback edition first published in 2000 by
The Harvill Press, 2 Aztec Row, Berners Road, London N1 0PW

www.harvill.com

3 5 7 9 8 6 4 2

© James Buchan, 1999

James Buchan asserts the moral right to be identified as the author of this work

A CIP catalogue record for this book is available from the British Library

ISBN 1 86046 742 3

Designed and set in Stempel Garamond at Libanus Press, Marlborough, Wiltshire

Printed and bound in Great Britain by Mackays of Chatham

To Ali Akbar Barumand

PART ONE

❄ 1 ❄

Each night, says Molavi, the prisoner forgets his prison. Each night, he says, the tyrant forgets his power. Each night, when it seems the night will never end, when night appears to be the natural and unvarying condition of the universe, there is a breath of wind.

Invisible, the wind shows itself in a rattle of branches; and then, an instant later, in a coolness on my wrists and ankles, and where my daughter's cheek slithers on my chest. For that instant, I smell greenery and roses and water and methane and the scent of my daughter's hair to which I cannot give a name, except that it is the quintessence of sweetness, brought with her from wherever it is she came.

That breath of wind, which will not recur until this time tomorrow, is the only evidence of movement in my world: the sign that this house and garden, though I believe them to be stagnant and timeless, are subject to change. The wind, which originates out in the darkness, out beyond the town, in saltflats I have not seen, and passes through the town, blowing up sand at street-corners or flapping the tattered banners on the shrines of saints, exists both to make me happy and to remind me of the insufficiency of happiness.

The wind passes. My daughter, whose name is Layly, stirs against my chest as if she might recall the breath across her cheek and legs, as in a repetitive game, but it is gone: blown out through the curtained archway to the room where my wife lies sleeping. I sense, as I sense always at this time, that as the gust enters the mosquito net, passes over her as she sleeps, across her cheek that is creased by the rucked

3

sheet or stuck with a strand of damp black hair, or where the sheet has fallen away, and her skirt ridden up to her breast, for precisely this reason, that she might feel the wind over her sore belly; and as I hear her stir, open her legs so that the wind might cool the inside of her legs and dry the sweat that shivers in tiny droplets on the silken hair above them, I believe that a change is being worked in her. I believe that the pain of childbirth is receding from her, and in her sleep, which is not sleep as the world knows it, for it has no depth or freshness, she feels the impression of her husband. She stirs, turns, mumbles something from a dream. Her water cup tinkles. Something slides to the floor. I shiver. I kiss the child's soft head and whisper: Settle down, my darling, and then I'll put you in your crib, for your mother and I have something to discuss.

The child kicks out her feet, arches her soft back, sobs. My wife, whose physiology derives from Galen, says that Layly's stomach is cold. I believe that the baby's distress is caused by air that she has swallowed with her milk but yet may be dislodged by movement. I turn and continue my pacing across the floor, which is made of blocks of dead coral, smooth and warm with use and damp from my footprints.

For a year now, we have lived by window light. There is no moon tonight, only the flicker of a gas flare far out in the sea, and the premonition of dawn. By this light, and familiarity, I establish the room. Ahead of me is a framed print of the Shah in the character and uniform of Chief Scout of the Iranian Empire; and beside it, pendant to it, as it were, is a photograph of Stalin, hemmed in by country women wearing kerchiefs and carrying hay-rakes. Turning about, smartly, like a soldier, I confirm on my right a row of arches, closed by jalousies through which I can smell the sea; and in front of each pillar, a filing-cabinet, its drawers awry, spilling their contents. On my left is another arcade, and beyond it a terrace and a coral balustrade, a canopy of palm trees, a crazy wind-tower and a surging sun the colour of copper. Dazzled, and yet more sorrowful than dazzled, for

4

the night is over and our ordeal begun, I look along my copper footprints, to the door of my wife's room and beside it a table, covered in an old rug, and on top a coloured photograph in a frame that flashes back the yellow sun.

It is a portrait of a relation of my wife's, whose name she doesn't know, only his honorific: Amin ul Mulk, the Trustee of the Kingdom. What I know of him comes from a book he wrote or dictated called *Safarnameh*, or *The Travel Diary*, which was in the house when we came here, along with a Russian translation. I remember now that I look at this picture always at this time, so as to take strength to face the day.

In the spring of 1851, at about nineteen years of age, Amin travelled to Europe by way of Anzeli, Baku, Tiflis and Moscow. At St Petersburg, he stood for hours before the fountains of the Peterhof. He observed manoeuvres at Potsdam. Sailing on an English warship from Kiel, he noted how the Captain led the sailors mustered on the fore-deck for their Sunday prayers. At Windsor Castle, he was troubled by the décolletage. For three weeks, each morning and afternoon he spent in the Hall of the Machines at Crystal Palace, where he was sketched by both *Punch* and *Vanity Fair*. He visited the ordnance yards at Woolwich, attended a review at Aldershot, danced a mazurka at Londonderry House. As a guest of Professor Paget at Holland Park, he received a succession of ex-Army men, seeking exclusive concessions in forests, mines, telegraphs, the cultivation of cotton, tobacco and opium, river navigation and railways, which gentlemen he answered diplomatically. In Paris, on 15 March 1853, he was photographed in Nadar's studio in the Rue St-Georges. At the Brenner, his carriage overturned, but he sustained no injury. He stayed a year at Istanbul, then took service with the Tsar and at Sebastopol, on the Malakoff, on Christmas Day, 1855, he was blown to pieces by a British mortar.

In the photograph, Amin is seated on an ornate armchair in an embroidered robe-of-honour and the green turban of a descendant of the Prophet. He looks at the camera without surprise or curiosity, though I'm sure he'd never seen a camera or a photographer before. His left arm rests on a table draped in the kind of flat-woven rug called here a gelim; and though the photograph has been coloured by hand, it is certainly the same rug on which my wife has now placed the photograph. That congruence or echo, between the room that I am pacing with my daughter and the studio in the Rue St-Georges in Paris, never fails to unsettle me. Sometimes I don't know where I am or when or who.

With his left index finger Amin points at another silver frame, or rather this frame at an earlier period of its existence, which contains a piece of gibberish. At the end of each traverse of the room, I am drawn into that silver frame within a frame, am cast back and forth between them and between the centuries, in an infinite and darkling enfilade as when two mirrors are placed to face each other. In my vertigo, the writing is forever trembling on the lip of sense. I feel it struggle to take form as Arabic or Persian or old Turkish, and fly at me; and yet there is something hopeless about the writing, left-handed, disconsolate, dead, forgotten. When I ask my wife, she says: How can I know, being a poor ignorant woman?

Twelve paces up. Twelve paces back. I think that if I could read what Amin had written, it would help me, and help him, wherever he is. You see I think it is his message to posterity, which is my wife, and my daughter, and, because I have no other family, myself. I think if I could understand it, forget myself a moment and plunge into it, as into a mirror; of course you third-class English, it has been printed in reverse, you need a mirror, a mirror, a mirror.

My wife is beautiful, or so it seems to me, but she possesses no mirror. It is not that she isn't vain, for she is. She is absolutely certain of her beauty, intelligence, virtue, courage, piety, nobility of purpose and general superiority. I suppose she doesn't need a mirror. She possesses a knife, which she keeps clean, but she wears it on a string across her bosom and takes it off when I ask her. I possess a revolver, which I also keep clean and always with me, and, raising my Layly high up on my left shoulder, and taking out the gun and blowing on the barrel and rubbing it on her shift, I read off Amin's message to posterity.

It is not Arabic, but Persian, which is written in Arabic letters.

Daftar: ledger, notebook, exercise-book, desk, office.

Adamiyatra: humanity, can't be anything else, like Adam and Eve.

Khali: empty, void.

Didam: I saw

I turn and my wife is standing in the doorway. It always shocks me that she looks as she does and that she married me. Her dress and shawl are open on her breast and knife-belt and belly, her hair to her waist, her eyes slitted with short-sightedness and sleep. She smells of sugar and milk. The warmth of her body beats at me in gusts. She says:

"'I have seen the ledger of humanity and it is blank'."

It is strange for her to speak in English. Indeed, she refuses to speak either English or French and if, at a loss for a word, I use those languages, she looks at me without comprehension. I do not know why she has broken her rule or what caused Amin to lose his optimism. I feel if he could see her and our daughter, even if only for a moment of a moment, we would restore it to him, wherever he is.

She reaches out for the child and her breast trembles. She shakes down the right shoulder of her dress. The baby stirs and whimpers. I am winded by jealousy. I open my mouth to whisper something, about how much I also want her, that I too am hungry for her and have waited for her so long, and would wait some more, as long as necessary or proper, but not for ever, but I cannot make a sound and she is smiling at the baby at her breast.

As a child myself, I dreamed often of prison. Each time, at the instant that I felt I could not tolerate my existence, that it would be better to be dead than continue in that prison, my dream would lose its shape, become ragged or dissolve and reform as my familiar bedroom furniture; though traces of the dream remained, staining my desk or chair or in a pool in the corner by the wash-basin, acrid or caustic, even as the morning light re-established the room.

It is that sensation I have now, but in reverse, as in a mirror. My wife begins to lose her shape. She looks up from the baby's face and smiles at me, as if to say, as she once said: It's you I like in her, also, but she is retreating from me, perforated by a light that is not the light of the dream, but is none the less familiar. I reach out for them, but I have no reach for I too am retreating. Familiar sensations break in on me: grit against my cheek and bitter cold and the sound of doors banging, one by one by one. I believe I can save something of the dream, her scent or touch or at least that unmistakable sensation of herness, or the face of my little daughter, just as she looked at three months of age, but those, too, are going, going; and each crashing door shakes and shatters them, splinters them in the electric light, and, in a bang, in a burst of despair, I stand bolt upright, feet together, arms outstretched, head bowed, blindfold on.

❋ 2 ❋

In the spring of 1974, the year the price of oil went up and the British stayed at home four days a week for want of electricity, I went abroad for the first time. I waited for two hours at a drenched roundabout above the south-bound M1, and then travelled by car and truck by way of London, Dover, Ostend, Cologne, Munich, Klagenfurt, Belgrade, Salonika and Istanbul.

In a café called The Pudding Shop in Sultanahmet Square, I sat down across from a German boy in a Moroccan waistcoat. He was driving one of nine second-hand Mercedes diesels from Munich for a dealer in Tabriz. I joined the convoy, taking the driving with him in turns, although I had no licence. Tabriz was brilliant with electric light. After the darkness of the autobahns, there was something prodigal about the light, sweets, roasting kebabs, portraits of the Shah in splendour, wolf-whistles and long-winded jokes. I took a bus to Qazvin, where I drank a bottle of vodka with a traffic policeman and slept under a quilt with his sons. In Tehran, I cut off my hair, borrowed someone's degree certificate and, by pasting my name over his at a pavement photocopier on Ferdowsi Avenue, was taken on at a new school teaching English to Air Force cadets. That effortless achievement of my goals in existence – a university degree and a paying job – exasperated me.

I lived on the roof of a downtown hotel, where steel bedsteads were arranged in six straight rows, and overlanding junkies fixed each other up from plastic jugs of city water in the bathhouse. They stole my camera and binoculars and Miss Spenser's Persian Grammar. It was Ramadan, and my seventy pupils slept, or dug out their ears, or glared like wolves at the wrapped sandwiches they'd brought with them to eat at sundown. My second payday, the school's owner, a major, threw an onyx ashtray and pen-set at an Indian who'd shown me how to teach. I thought that for whatever reason I had come to Iran, it wasn't to support its military; and I had heard that Isfahan was beautiful.

I found a new job in half an hour.

"I have given you my best class, Mr John. The University of Bedford, indeed!"

This was Mr Jamalzadeh, a middle-aged man with the air and shape of an elderly village woman. He drank water without cease. His school, the Zabankhaneh or House of Language, was directly across the street from the Youth Hostel in Chahar Bagh. I was now entangled in my lie.

"Thank you, Headmaster. I shall try to be worthy of you." The sunlight across the peeling windowsill behind him delighted me.

Mr Jamalzadeh took on an air of intense severity. "You must be strong as a lion and cold as a molla's arsehole!" He spoke with the slow, clear vowels of a newsreader or poet. "They will slay you, my dear. Your predecessors went out feet first."

"I can handle them, sir."

"That, alas, you cannot do, John, or I shall dismiss you." He sparkled at his sally.

At break, I was led by a servant to the sunny staff-room. It fell silent as I entered. I did not want to disappoint my colleagues.

"I cannot teach them, Mr Jamalzadeh. They are too beautiful."

The room shimmered in delight. Mr Jamalzadeh was beside himself with water and laughter: "Ladies and gentlemen!" He waved his arms for quiet, but could not himself keep quiet:

> "'Je meurs de seuf auprès de la fontaine
> " Chaud comme fer, et tremble dent à dent.'

Villon, ladies and gentlemen." And he plunged his dipper into the water jar.

"You must marry, my dear," said Mrs Mohrabba. She took the infants in Persian.

"How can I, madame, if you are married already?"

"Oh, for shame," she said, and giggled.

"Take a goddam sigheh, man." Mr Parvin had studied in San Diego.

"What's a sigheh?"

"A concubine . . ."

" . . . a chick . . ."

" . . . for love only, not for marriage . . ."

"But not from the class, dear John, or I shall release you."

"Pauvre jeun' homme . . ."

"Aren't there any boys?"

The room disintegrated. I blushed.

"Enough!" shouted the headmaster, waving his arms. "We have embarrassed our dear friend." The klaxon rattled, and he led the way out and, as he passed me, I heard him mutter ". . . et tremble dent à dent."

The hilarity disgusted me. I thought the manners of the place were the natural consequence of oppression, of the seclusion of women and an autocratic regime, of all of which I advertised my disapproval. I hated the French tourists forever debarking from air-conditioned buses outside the Shah Abbas Hotel and the American officers picking fights at the Irantour on Thursday nights or sobbing for Indochina. I hated the Pahlavi crown picked out in fairy lights on the mountain to the south of the town. Boulevards had been smashed through the bazar, indifferent to rooms exposed in nude plasterwork and tinted glass, and I would collect fragments of a frieze under the eye of a cashmere-coated developer. In the vaulted alleys, the shopkeepers sat motionless within a musty mental quadrilateral of fabrics, money, iron weights and measures, and conjugal duty. Somewhere in there was God or rather God became manifest at those four corners; and it infuriated me that those men, cross-legged by their bolts of garish cloth or trays of banknotes, were unshakeably certain that they'd found the secret of existence.

I did not know what could bring the city to life for me, disrupt it, give it meaning and motion. Perhaps if I read more, learned more, spoke to more people, learned the slang of the city and four ways of writing it, I would pierce those veils of tourism and industry and military power to an Isfahan of my own. I suppose I knew that I had exchanged the solitude of home for the solitude of Isfahan; but the deduction, that solitude was a condition for life, was not something a boy of eighteen will easily accept. I was glad to be abroad, far from my generation in Britain with their girlfriends and record collections, where my personality and actions might take shape without witnesses; for I thought myself to be special.

I had never had much company and had learned certain disciplines of the single life. Mr Jamalzadeh had found me a room – at a hundred tomans a month – with a Jewish widow in Julfa, Mrs Mohandes; and in that tiny room, at the end of a cul-de-sac called the Bombast-e Parviz, with a small window looking into her quince tree, I broke up my day and arranged the pieces as sparsely as my possessions. In the afternoons after teaching, I visited the monuments, studied their architecture, drew them, and discoursed with the theological students in a dialogue of the deaf, as if I were an Elizabethan merchant at the court of Shah Abbas; took lessons in calligraphy and the classical drum; visited carpet and junk shops in the bazar. Mrs Mohandes disapproved of my way of life, since I had no family with me and associated with antiques dealers, notorious smokers of opium. I saw that she did not like me, and I was not used to making a bad impression except by intention.

I had to be careful with my money. With just five classes a week, I earned eighty tomans, of which fifty went on my rent and my own lessons. I had also three American Express travellers' cheques of £5 each which I had hidden under the gelim in my room, for I would need them for the ferry back across the English Channel, which had been £5.90, but would be more with the inflation. That left five tomans a day with which to feed myself. Breakfast I made in the kitchen in front of Mrs Mohandes' terrorised maid. My five tomans stretched to a picnic dinner in my room, and a glass of tamarind juice and a flap of bread after class from a stall that I liked outside the Hasht Behesht. I was thus always hungry, and eager to accept any hospitality; and in that I was fortunate in my town, because one cannot buy even shaving-soap in Isfahan without being offered tea and saffron ice-cream and salted melon-seeds wrapped in a cone of newspaper.

Worse for me was a sort of hunger of possession. Every moment of the day, I saw objects that I longed to own and whose ownership I thought would somehow transform my personality, yet cost the equivalent of £25 or even £100. What those pieces of glass or china or brocade had in common, I think, was not so much beauty and rarity as orientation. They were the relics of the commerce of a differently oriented world. In my mind, I made a map and marked it with cities, now unfrequented, centuries past their prime, their harbours silted, their khans quarried for building stone – Prague, Moscow, Baku, Bokhara, Kashgar, Bushehr, Muscat, Zanzibar, Isfahan – that I could inhabit in invisibility.

Fridays, when the monuments, shops and cinemas were closed, exhausted my ingenuity. I would stand on the rickety old bridges that marched across the river, hungry and light as air, repeating over and over, out loud, some lines of Forough Farrokhzad I'd been reading:

Oh how my life flowed, so calm and proud,
A foreign stream through the heart of those Fridays!

That the poet was a woman, bad and beautiful and dead in a motor accident in Tehran, who I'm sure never giggled and drew in her chador when spoken to, reassured me: if there had been one such person here in my lifetime, there must be another. Already by April, the river was turning to marsh. I would walk up the shore, turned away from the Pepsi cans, cold picnic fires, twists of newspaper, dried sheep's gore, fruit-skins and shit, or follow the paths that ran off between small melon fields or mud walls, where pomegranate trees were in flower and little boys would break from their games and run, puffing, after me to practise their Good-Mornings, while I affected some ulterior purpose. In one such village, there were three walnut trees and, beneath them, the tomb of a saint, shut in by green railings and bleached banners. I asked who he was, but nobody could remember and, though a name was at last mentioned, it was to please me; and I thought I would be glad to sleep through eternity under those immense trees and a succession of fanciful names.

Even on Fridays, I was not bored or lonely, because I did not believe in such sensations; and because I did not always feel alone. At times, say, picking up a letter from my old French teacher at the Poste Restante, and sitting down with it fluttering in the breeze on the bench beside the broken fountain, I was aware of my visibility: that somebody, not the gardener clipping the box or the postmaster at his transom, was watching me with interest. That was not a religious sensation, for I never thought about God; and the person watching me, for whom I made my gestures larger and more complete, was a person, a woman to be precise; yet was not my mother, or rather collected in her interest in me all the animation and wisdom that a boy ascribes to his mother, even when he never knew her. At times, say, walking beneath the oriental plane trees of the Hasht Behesht, if I saw a girl carrying a violin, threading the planes, absorbed in herself as completely as in her polka dot chador, then my existence became intolerable to me; and I didn't think I'd be able to endure it, even in this faraway town.

At times such as those, I would open the letter or turn for the river and, as it were, withdraw from a position too advanced to be defended, abandon the present and seek a sort of historic future. I sensed that I was a tough guy and that the sights and sounds and tastes and smells of Isfahan, that now meant nothing to me, would years from now convey the most intense sensations; and that I would taste happiness in the form of regret. I thought that certain formalities of the place, perhaps just a strip of three wall tiles surrounded by unfired bricks, or the blue of the sky and the domes, and a certain wintriness beneath the hottest afternoon, would return to me in the future and give me my fill of sadness and pleasure. Isfahan then had for me the character not of experience but of adventure: that is, it would gain its meaning for me only in its telling, back home, in my house, when I had one, before an audience of imaginary Britishers. One day, for sure, I'd say, Ah that, that is a minute repeater, made in Berlin for the oriental market in the 1890s, don't open the case if you're easily shocked. I got it in Isfahan, when I was a student in the '70s, from a fellow who had a shop in the upper arcade of the Meidan-e Shah, died of drink, poor man, name of Mo'in . . .

For such an existence within parentheses, Mr Mo'in would do. I called at his shop one day after class, intrigued by some Russian china in the dusty window; and I left in time for class the next morning. The place troubled me. Under its high vault, it was as dirty and chaotic as its master, who was sleeping on a pile of carpets in a drift of saffron filaments and rice, unshaven, drunk as a prince. I longed to organise them both, to separate the obviously good from the obviously bad, as once, shifting through a pile of chromate gelims for a couple from Ulm, I came on a baby's quilt spilling batting from its rotten chintz, whose blues and reds had probably faded before the 1750s; or amid the dirty objects on the shelves in the thick darkness, the brass jugs, bad Chinese porcelain of the type called *famille rose*, chipped pencases and mirrors of painted *papier-mâché*, an ante-bellum Smith & Wesson revolver with two brass bullets nestling in a box of cotton wool. For I saw those objects had to stand for the values I'd abandoned for lost, such as the experience of a great event, a war or revolution or a candid audience with the Shah, or the memory of the sight of a girl shaking off her veil. It occurred to me once that Mo'in might be right; that good and bad matter only to the solitary; and the Germans were more content with their rug that I stitched up for them in sailcloth and took to the Post than I was with the quilt, bought for a joke that made Mo'in laugh and a kebab dinner from the cook-shop. The gun I simply hid in a dish, for I didn't want it sold.

Mo'in found me comical. He used to talk about me under my nose, for he could not comprehend that a foreigner, pale as a girl, might understand his language or indeed know anything about anything. When one of his "brokers", as he called the numberless little creeps who brought things to him, staggered in under a cast-iron chandelier and I said it was rubbish, I overheard my word – "ashghal" in Persian – repeated for days in wonder and delight; or when I mended the selvedge of a rug in chain stitch, he laid the piece out on the balcony to gabble over with his friends. He trusted me with the key to the shop, but only because, left to himself, he would forget to lock up. I saw he liked me not for my white face and the reassurance it gave to European tourists, but for my novelty. I liked him, I suppose, because he always had vodka, and dishes of pistachio nuts from Kerman, and lunch cooked by his wife and sent in covered dishes by taxi (though he unkindly called her the Minister of War); because he did not proposition me; because we went on buying jaunts to Kurdistan and Abadeh; because he was so disreputable; because of his chequerboard teeth; and because I did not like to go back to Julfa and Mrs Mohandes during the day. I detected in his drunkenness and utter contempt for town opinion, in his anarchy and scorching blasphemies, the degraded remnants of an old, old cast of thought and conduct. Mo'in was a Khayyam, minus the gift and the jug of wine multiplied into a dozen of vodka; or rather – and this was a thought I could not have had in England – Khayyam himself was simply a mental habit and all the quatrains that ran above his name, and had been translated in Europe as the work of a single lonely genius, had in reality been dreamed up over the centuries by just such men as Mo'in and palmed off on Khayyam, for only thus might they be heard and repeated. While Mo'in snored away his lunch, I worked at my Persian on a tottering throne of carpets or tip toed barefoot between the soft canyons, effeminate, luxurious and insecure.

One afternoon, 19 April, 1974, 23 Farvardin, 1353, I fell asleep and woke to a shop full of angels. Their voices had the character of light in the dingy shop. I staggered up and saw, leaning against the high doorpost that separated the two rooms, a girl in a black prayer-chador. I thought: She thinks she's too tall, but she's not. Behind her, the bright voices of girls wheeled and swooped like the pigeons in the courtyard of the Shah's Mosque, but the person in the door was still. She had pulled her chador up across her face and where the hem had risen up I saw the edge of a light blue skirt, the uniform of the girls' secondary schools in Isfahan, and white ankle socks. Her eyes when I looked at them were black, so black they seemed to drain the room of all its light: their blackness was not an absence of light, but was itself a light, of a kind I had not up to that moment experienced or known to exist, beneath which the objects of the solar world took on a melancholy futility.

In the main shop, about twenty girls were seated in a circle on the carpet. Mo'in, in a flurry of elbows, thumbs and legs, was rolling out the tobacco from a cigarette into his right palm. My heart stopped; but there was her black chador, kneeling a little back from the circle, rigid with deportment. She's not popular, she's stiff or difficult, poor, or maybe rich, too clever or too dim, not pretty or too pretty, Bahai even, or Christian, and so very tall.

"Welcome, mamzils! My name is John and I'm from England. I am a teacher of English at the – ."

"Zabankhaneh, we know."

I inserted myself down by Black Eyes. I felt her gather up her hems and shift away a little. In that movement, in the friction of the carpet and the cotton of her skirt and chador, I felt her awareness not merely of her clothes but of her skin, as if she'd woken that morning under the weight of a bust and hips. She was drawn tight as a strung bow. I looked away into the ring and a girl, with glasses, bare-faced, was speaking to me.

"This is our club, sir . . ." She pronounced the word as "kloob".

"Not sir, John. John Pitt. I live at the Bombast-e Parviz in Julfa, with Mrs Mohandes . . ."

" . . . Mr John."

Mr Mo'in, stiff and frantic as some wind-up toy, was lighting his altered cigarette. I thought: Nothing for you, my boy, they'll tell your students, and you'll never hear the end of it.

"What sort of 'kloob', mamzil?"

"Oh, we are young and we have nothing and we want everything. We want to speak English and be friends, and smoke cigarettes and listen to music . . ."

"Black Sabbath!"

"Tom Jones!"

Mr Mo'in knelt down, took a deep pull on the cigarette, and kissed the bare-faced girl on the mouth, blowing the smoke into her lungs. I was shocked to the core of my nature. The girl took the cigarette, took a breath, and kissed her neighbour on the lips. I thought: Persian girls aren't like this, they're grave and timid and prone to put on weight. Mo'in was scampering round the ring, excavating kisses. The bare-faced girl now had a look of rapture, head in her hands, as well she might from what I knew of Mr Mo'in's hashish. I thought: If you touch the person beside me, I swear by God I'll kill you, Mo'in. I could feel her trembling on the rug.

"And what do you want, mamzil?" I glanced at her rigid black figure.

"I need to be free, sir."

Something in her look or posture immobilised Mo'in. She took the cigarette in her thumb and fingers, gloved by her chador, and passed it to me, tapping me with the butt on the wrist. Then she turned, and I felt cotton on my mouth, and through it her lips, and the radiating heat of her cheeks, and the damp of her eyes, and a scent like the scent of the rosebeds of the Public Garden after a rain shower. I took a deep breath from the cigarette. Waves of shock and misery and enmity and anger came rolling at me, passed and broke on Black Eyes, immobile as a rock. They passed on, as all things pass, as even the passing passes in the abolition of time, as said Our Master Jalaluddin Molavi in Book the Second of his *Discourses*, what I read at home in England, England.

When I looked up, my neighbour and all the girls were gone, Mr Mo'in was asleep and I was late for calligraphy. I ran the length of the warm Meidan to the gate to the bazar; men sprang from the stone benches and made gestures of astonishment; and the domes and palaces danced in my eyes and a voice sang in my ears some lines of *Khosrow and Shirin*:

> How often the Beloved stands, dishevelled, at your door,
> And you are bleary-eyed and dead with sleep!

"You will never be a calligrapher, sir."

I spun round. Before the arch into the brass bazar, ringing with hammers and gas jets, was a man in a bad suit and tie and a felt cap of the kind the Bakhtiari men wear. His long hair and limp moustache were turning white, before their time, as if scorched by the jets. His suit flapped about him. He did not seem to be Iranian, and yet was too poor and sad and badly dressed for a European; or maybe he was a Pole or Bulgarian, or someone like that, working at the new steel mill.

"I believe, sir, that hard work will sometimes mend the deficiency of skill." I breasted my pen and slate.

"But no, alas, it doesn't. Or I, too, would have succeeded."

Any comparison between us was ludicrous.

He said: "May I have the pleasure of accompanying you on your walk?"

"I'm afraid, sir, I have business . . ."

"Please don't worry. I am not homosexual." He smiled with a gentleness that touched me. "I have a vice, for which I hope you will pardon me."

"May I enquire with whom I have the honour of conversing?"

"The honour is mine. Ryazanov," he said, putting his arm through mine and steering us towards the boulevards. "And you are Mr John Pitt, student of oriental philosophy at the fabled University of Bedford in England."

I stopped. "How in heaven do you know?"

"Everybody in Isfahan knows. Also, I have nothing to do but wander. You see that, for all my stupidity and indolence, I am the Consul-General of the Union of Soviet Socalist Republics at Isfahan. I may not leave the city without written permission from the Foreign Ministry in Tehran, or receive any visitors or speak to anyone, for fear of the Savak."

"I am speaking to you with great pleasure."

"You are English, a fortunate race. Shall we walk in Chahar Bagh?"

"Why not?"

"Why not, indeed? You know, when your country and my country secretly divided poor Iran into two regions of influence, Isfahan was the frontier. Rather, our consulate on Upper Chahar Bagh and your consulate on Chahar Bagh Proper marked the respective limits of each country's dominion. We are now walking between them in a realm I consider to exist beyond politics and all its entanglements."

The Rex Cinema, which was showing a Western from Italy, appeared to me suddenly glamorous.

"Of course, every single greengrocer and nougat-seller and arak drinker and pigeon-fancier and pederast on this street sought to become both a Russian agent and an English agent, and gained an idea of his world importance that nothing in the past seventy years has been able to diminish."

We had reached the corniche along the river. The tarmac glistened in the warm twilight. Mercedes trucks bore down on us, burly as mountains. Mr Ryazanov stopped and turned on me.

"Why are you so happy, Mr Pitt?"

"I am in love, sir."

He clapped his hands. "God bless you!" Then he looked at me through sad and startled eyes. "And may I enquire, by the privilege of our brief acquaintance, the name of the Beloved?"

"You may, sir, but I do not know her name. Or where she lives. I am looking for her."

We stared, the two of us, down the pavement lit by roaring gas-mantles at a bevy of women, who drew their chadors tight around them to flatter their figures as they passed.

"And may I enquire, within the boundaries of propriety and disinterested advice, the attributes of the Beloved?"

"She has black eyes and lovely feet and is very tall."

Mr Ryazanov sighed. "All Isfahanian women are tall and dark-eyed and pretty-footed. That is why living here is such a torment to the spirit."

The generalisation offended me. "She is slender as a cypress in spring. Her lips are rubies, her teeth are pearls, her eyelashes are like the spears of the enemy in battle, her waist is like a hair. I haven't seen her face, but I suspect it is like the moon at the instant it escapes from a cloud. Her voice causes the rose to bloom and sets the emulous nightingale to song."

Mr Ryazanov pondered that a moment. "Well, that makes it much, much easier. You shall find her, Mr John. Do not doubt for a moment that you shall find her. And I shall marry you." He smiled in the gloaming. "I have always wanted to perform a consular marriage. Is your father here?"

"No, sir."

"I shall be a father to you." Then he slapped his head. "You are a Muslim, of course?"

"Church of Scotland."

"Scotland has a church? How unexpected. But the Beloved is a Muslim."

"Of course."

"So you must be."

"Why?"

"You must be, dear Mr John. For otherwise, how can you see the Face of the Beloved? Do you speak Arabic?"

"Nobody speaks Arabic. Even the Arabs don't speak Arabic."

"God speaks Arabic. Kindly say after me: la ilaha ila allah . . ."

"la ilaha ila allah . . ."

" . . . wa muhammadun . . ."

" . . . wa muhammadun . . ."

" . . . rasool ullah."

" . . . rasool ullah."

" . . . wa ali vali ullah."

" . . . vali ullah."

"There, now you're a Muslim."

"Is that all?"

"It's a beginning. And now, as the older man, I must initiate the intense pain of parting. Ey Hassan!"

We stared at a long mud wall topped by whispering plane trees, and a wicket gate from behind which something or somebody was grunting and grumbling. I was suddenly afraid I might not see Mr Ryazanov again, either.

"When shall I have the honour of calling on you, sir? I don't give a molla's fart for the Savak."

"Well said, Mr John, but not wisely. You are under their surveillance."

I spun round, and then regretted my silliness.

"Ey Hassan Hashash!" He turned half away from me. "Sometimes, I am in a bad mood, and I cannot attend to you as you have a right to expect. Also I believe that we should let this fortunate meeting rest a while, like the disturbed waters of a fish pool." He peered at me. "Do you like classical music?"

"Of course."

"I don't. Hosein, the tar player, is coming to me tomorrow night. He is a bore and a Savaki and claims to be blind, but it is better, for your sake, that we do not again meet alone. Unfortunately, he plays for hours and is quite offended if I so much as take a sip of tea."

An old man with a hennaed beard stumbled out of the wicket, and gaped at us with an air of ancient calculation, like the abacus on Mr Mo'in's desk. Poor Mr Ryazanov, I thought, is there nobody he can trust?

"I shall hear the concert with the greatest interest."

"Goodbye, Mr John."

"Goodbye, sir."

He dropped his shoulders to pass through the wicket.

❈ 3 ❈

In Isfahan, a town of at least a quarter of a million people, there are more than a dozen secondary schools for girls. Because of my class at the Zabankhaneh, I was probably more expert in that matter than any man in town. Of those schools, only two are within a mile of the Meidan-e Shah, which I thought to be the furthest distance girls would walk for a jaunt after school and yet be home before their mothers noticed. Of those two, one, the Islamiya High School, was a religious foundation and I could not believe that the girls I had met had been the Muslim equivalent of convent pupils; but the other, the Empress Farah Diba Secondary, was by all accounts the most fashionable in town. Why, Mlle Mashruteh had been there, and Mlle Bordbar, and no doubt others of my students who didn't speak up.

The street, which ran off Chahar Bagh, was clogged the next morning with chauffeured cars. An old man with a cane was harrying the girls through the gates. Fluttering by in their chadors, they took no notice of him at all. On the pavement, a police officer was shouting at everybody and everything through a loudspeaker. As I sauntered past, he started repeating himself, and I realised, with a flush of embarrassment, that he was shouting at me. As I made a circuit back to Chahar Bagh and the Zabankhaneh, I was disgusted with myself: that I had, in just a month, acquired the attitudes of the place and that I now regarded girls as a treasure, perilous and untrustworthy, which must be stolen from under guard. The notion that she, from behind the curtains of one of the Mercedes or gathering up her things and tripping out under the scolding of the porter or looking down from a high classroom window, might have seen me in this puerile reconnaissance, made me double my step. Somehow, in my long walk back from the Soviet Consulate last night or while I slept, this girl had displaced all my authorities. Her good opinion alone mattered or rather she had become the arbitress of what was good and right. My stomach gaped as if I were on a building ledge or precipice. Beneath the bland street and the closed-up villas, that teased me with the vines that spilled from their unscalable walls, I felt there was a deathly void which was a life passed without having seen her again. I thought: There are lots of girls in the world. Look, in a month or two, you'll have saved enough to leave this place and go to Afghanistan or Kashmir. Yet, as I reached Chahar Bagh, and its tumult of car horns, smelled tobacco and melon sherbet, felt the cold sun on my cheeks and the geometry of the seventeenth-century town beneath my feet, I still had not pulled myself together and did not truly want to. How often, as a child, I'd made a face and someone said: The wind'll change, lad, and you'll carry that face to the grave. It was as if one afternoon a wind from an unfamiliar quarter had blown through that dirty rag-and-bone shop in the Meidan, and I was myself no longer.

At least, I thought, I'm going out to dinner this evening.

Mr Ryazanov's garden was more beautiful than I had imagined a garden could be. Hassan gestured crossly down a tiled path, and padded back to his gatehouse. I walked between wrought-iron lamp-stands such as you see in parks in Paris. Light and shadow fluttered on the undersides of the box leaves in the breeze. I passed a raised tank and saw, down a right-handed path, a wooden kiosk which gave out flickering lights of rose and blue, as if there were a candle there and windows of stained glass.

Mr Ryazanov was seated against a bolster in striped pyjamas and a felt skull-cap. Before him was a brazier of polished brass from which he was selecting a charcoal with little tongs. In his lap he held a pipe with a long wooden stem and a porcelain bowl decorated with a transfer of some nineteenth-century Shah. He did not stand up or look at me. He spoke to the brazier. He said: "The search for perfection, in life and love, exhausts the personality. Beauty without flaw, kindness without hesitation, friendship without self-interest, religion without fanaticism, love without reserve, the Beloved without fault, those ideals make a laughing-stock of our natures, which are short-sighted, clumsy, distracted by appetites, deceitful from fear. For us, that is for the Iranians (for I have now lived here for thirty-three years and would seek to be counted among their number) the choice is between a life of perpetual frustration and a shameful suicide. For we find it more honourable, or as we say manly, to die in squalor with nothing achieved than to be satisfied with little; to pass the time in vain fantasies rather than give our hearts to home and shop; to live privately under a vulgar and cowardly despotism than publicly under an imperfect government of our devising; to mourn our murdered Hosein, not rejoice in our blessed Mohammed; and to while away history waiting for the Lord of Time to return and usher in the End of the World . . ."

He paused and then continued in the same remote and formal tone. "And so, as you suspected, I am a son of the pipe. Permit me to present the implements of my torment and delight. Here is the brazier; and the charcoal; the bellows; the tongs. Here is the drug, which we call taryak, 'the Remedy', and I buy in one-mesqal sticks from another addict who is registered with the Ministry of Health. This is the knife that cuts it. This is the pin, to hold the Remedy to the pipe." He took a deep pull. The opium crackled and bubbled on the porcelain.

"The virtues of the Remedy, sir, are these. The first pull induces a very slight depression of the spirit, which alleviates some of the pressure of reality, holds it at bay, so it can be experienced. Though the sensation is entirely without novelty, it never fails to gratify: it is more to be relied on than an old servant or an affectionate wife. Of its evil, well, the whole world knows of it." He looked fondly at the brazier. "It makes a farce of existence. Every night, the smoker dons the outfit of the idiot."

I grasped at the idea of a Mrs Ryazanov. "May I enquire about your family circumstances, sir?"

He looked at me viciously. "I am in the service of Lord Opium. He permits no other attachments. Have you understood me?"

I understood that I had looked forward to coming. I felt crushed by disappointment. I said: "Mr Ryazanov, I seek only your company when it is convenient to you."

"I seek from you a favour."

"It is yours."

That is the correct response in Persian. Had we been speaking English, I might have answered otherwise.

"Promise me, my boy, that you will not trust me. You will think that my purpose in this display is to authorise the Remedy for you, and you are right; but that is the will of my Master, whose will is stronger than mine. My purpose is to warn you. You must understand that though I love you, as a father loves an only son, more so, indeed, because you came to me when I had no more hope of love, yet you can repose no faith in me because I have no will."

"I do not believe that is the truth, Mr Ryazanov."

"Promise me, John."

"I promise."

He scraped the residue off the pipe and pinned a new piece, but I was distracted by something on the carpet before him, beside the book he was reading. It was a porcelain dish of tea. It sat in its holder, which was a gourd split down the middle and hinged at the base, cut on the outside with a fine pattern and lined inside with some silky animal-skin. At the tip of the gourd was a leather strap, no doubt to hang it from a saddle-bow. It seemed to me a perfection. I felt that if I possessed the cup and case, I would need nothing else: I would enclose my life in its self-sufficiency. The cup was the essence of fragility, and yet it had survived two hundred years, banging about

on Turkoman ponies between Marv and the ruins of Balkh.

"It is yours, my John, but not yet."

"Oh no, Mr Ryazanov, I wasn't admiring it! Please don't think I was admiring it!"

He smiled. He was calm now. "It was made by an Englishman, Gardner, in Moscow, which is my city. It therefore prefigured our friendship and is its symbol. I will leave it to you at my death."

"God forbid!"

He grabbed at his book and slipped it under his bolster. Out of the darkness came a rich, self-satisfied voice: "Peace be on you!"

"And on you! And welcome, Mashd' Hosein."

He was a tall old man with a pious beard. He slipped off his shoes and entered the summerhouse on bare feet. He wore a white robe such as Arabs wear, and carried a musical instrument with just a single string, a Kashmir shawl, a box of cigarettes and a wooden holder. Mashd' is short for Mashadi and means either that he had made a pilgrimage to the tomb of the Imam Reza at Mashad or, more likely, he was of an age and piety that such a journey would be superfluous. "May I present my young friend, John Pitt, an Englishman."

"Ah," said Mashd' Hosein, settling down on his bolster with a sigh of pleasure. "English intrigue. Is there never to be an end of it?"

"I am a student, sir."

"A student of intrigue."

Such conversations had ceased to surprise me, but they bored me. I said: "Mashd' Hosein, whatever was done by my country in Iran in the past, Britain now has only a commercial interest here."

"Britain is weak."

"Permit me, sir, but I do not believe that statement can formally be reconciled with your earlier."

Mr Ryazanov clapped his hands. "Our young friend is an expert in logic! He is a student of the University of Bedford in England!"

"I'm not."

"He is bewildered by appearances."

"Mashd' Hosein is right. England is responsible for all the evils of this country. For example, it is your fault that I am an opium addict, my son."

"My fault, sir?"

"Yes, your fault." He smiled with his wet eyes. "You'll recollect that when, after the Second Chinese War, the English gained new markets in China for the opium of Bengal, they cast around for other land to cultivate and found it in this unhappy country. Marx wrote on the subject, if I am not mistaken. Clever English, to see the weakness of the Iranian spirit, its melancholy and indolence, the tedium of too much history in a ruined and exhausted land."

He poured me a cup of tea.

I said: "Why does everybody always blame everything on my countrymen?"

"We don't. The Americans and also the Russians have done their harm. But chiefly it's the English."

Mashd' Hosein nodded through his wreaths of smoke.

"Why, gentlemen, might it not be your fault? Or God's will?"

"Ah, my dear John, you must understand that the Iranians believe themselves to be special. The Arabs were satisfied with the word of God as preserved in the Koran but we were not: we had to have the family of the Holy Prophet among us, if not in living and breathing form, then hidden from sight until the last days. Yet, look out at the world."

I looked at the lamplight fluttering in the planes.

"Look out at the world, and you will see that we are clearly not God's special people. How do we resolve this contradiction, which is the conflict of scripture with reality, of faith with phenomena? Easily! There is a conspiracy against us, a conspiracy of evil, like the conspiracy of wicked men that overwhelmed Hosein and his sister on the plain of Kerbela in the seventh century. Who is behind that conspiracy? The Yazid and Shimr of the latter day, of course, the lords and rulers of England! I once had the good fortune to attend the passion play we have here, that enacts the drama of Hosein and Zainab at Kerbela, and the evil characters wore the English red-coats and sun-helmets of two hundred years ago. Most gratifying."

I said nothing. I took a sip of my tea. It was vodka. Mr Ryazanov looked blandly through my shock. He pushed the teapot towards me.

"All nonsense, of course. Your country must be a happy place if it can spare you to us."

"Thank you, sir."

"Now," said Mashd' Hosein, fitting another cigarette into its holder, "perhaps our young friend will recite."

"I am ashamed to disclose my feeble verses. Anyway, they are in English . . ."

"What's the good of that?" said Mashd' Hosein, and blew his nose.

"I shall instead recite the ghazal of the immortal Forough Farrokhzad."

"Please don't, John." Mr Ryazanov glanced at the teapot. I did not feel drunk at all.

"A lady," said Mashd' Hosein, "of irregular habits, I believe, who died drunk in a Land Rover."

" 'And the Poets say one thing and do another'."

I had learned that conversation between men in Iran had some of the formalities of a game; and in that game, a quotation from the Koran, any quotation from the Koran, counted as a trump.

"Correct. Recite."

I recited the sonnet. It suddenly seemed to me no good at all.

"May I give my life for you," said Mashd' Hosein, without

conviction. "Her prosody is faultless. It is merely the sentiment that is trash."

"Well, at least it's sentiment. Aren't you weary of gazelles and willows and Rudaki's girlfriend who must be bit tired out after a thousand years of shaking musk from her tresses?"

"I felt," said Mr Ryazanov, "that the image of the penis as a fish lacked both propriety and precision."

"At least it's new."

"Pfu!" said Mashd' Hosein.

"I mean, look, when Qurrat al-Ain, a hundred years ago, spoke of the 'riches of Great Alexander', she would better have said, 'the riches of Greater Manchester', for it is metrically identical and conveys some meaning."

"On the contrary," said Mashd' Hosein. "Manchester will pass away, or, for all I know, has already passed away, but the empire of Alexander the Great is so embedded in the minds of men that it has taken on the character of a universal. God gave us poetry out of His great compassion, not so our age can chatter to itself, but so that all ages may converse."

"Point scored!" said Mr Ryazanov.

"I do not understand such matters," I said. I sipped my special tea.

"May we pass on, perhaps, from these women and heretics?"

"Our friend means, Mashd' Hosein, that he is in love."

"For heaven's sake!"

"And may I enquire of him the Name of the Beloved?"

"Her name is Shirin . . ."

"No, it isn't, Mr Ryazanov. I mean, I don't know what it is . . ."

"And will he recount the attributes of the Beloved?"

"He says she makes the rose to bloom and impels the envious nightingale to song."

Mashd' Hosein considered that a moment. "Good," he said.

"Mashd' Hosein, how will our young friend learn the Name of the Beloved?"

"Is he a Muslim?"

"He seeks to be."

"God willing. We must understand the words 'Name' and 'Beloved'." Having scored one conversational point, Mashd' Hosein now wanted the match. "When Khosrow saw Shirin bathing in a spring in the desert, he was struck dumb, not by her beauty or her attributes of femininity, but by the essence of beauty of which those were approximate forms. That is why he turned away, for phenomena had become to him enervating and futile. If our young friend now raves at the gazelle-like eyes and willow-slenderness of his Shirin, of her cruelty and tyranny, it is because they are aspects of the Divine Bounty and Indifference. The girl herself is interchangeable. He must learn to pierce the veil of forms, the 'Name', and contemplate the essence, the 'Beloved'. As Our Master Jalaluddin Mohammed Molavi spoke in the *Masnavi*, Book the First, Verse Three Thousand, Four Hundred and Fifty-seven:

'You seek the Name; but you should the seek the Object:
The Moon's not in the Canal, but in the Sky.'"

"What bollocks!"

Mashd' Hosein stiffened on his cushion.

"I mean, if I have understood you right, sir, you say we must seek Reality outside this sublunary world, which merely reflects it, dimly or in fragments, like the reflections of the moon in these irrigation channels. Mashd' Hosein, I don't give a fart for Reality. I want to find this individual . . ."

"Shame on you!"

"Mashd' Hosein, I will embrace the moon down here and now."

"You shall drown, boy. *Masnavi*, Book the Fifth, Verse Twelve Hundred and Four:

'The lovers of those pretty sluts
Were, in reality, in love with death.
Read Layly or Shirin ! You'll see

What those idiots did from jealousy!
Lover and Beloved came to nought
And so their passion, too, was nought!' "

"What do you or Molavi know about it?!"

In the silence, Mr Ryazanov spoke: "It is not appropriate that gentlemen should squabble over philosophy as children over toys. Apologise, John, to Mashd' Hosein for your intemperate language."

"I shall not."

Mashd' Hosein rose from his bolster, unstrung his instrument, gathered his cigarettes and holder. He looked at me with an infuriating compassion. I knelt at his feet. "Please pardon me, Mashd' Hosein, for my insufferable rudeness."

He put his hand on my head, and curled his fingers in my hair. He said: "Such conduct would, in usual circumstances, have been tiresome. But, in a young man, every action has its charm."

He took up his instrument. I squatted at his feet and put my head in my hands. Mr Ryazanov put his finger to his lips, and reached under the cushion for his book.

I woke with a horrible thirst. For a moment, I could not understand where I was. Mashd' Hosein was snoring by his bolster. Mr Ryazanov, whose arm I now remembered round my shoulders as I fell asleep, had gone, no doubt into the house. I drained the samovar of cold tea. My face burned with the drink, and I stepped out of the kiosk. I had an idea I would rinse my face in the tank where the irrigation channels met. The moon was full, and rattled in the branches or sprung at me from the channels. The water in the tank was clear and cold. I looked down the avenues and saw, at the end of one, that the wicket gate was open and Mr Ryazanov, in his felt cap, was bent down, as if listening to someone. Then a wind ruffled the trees, the moonlight flared, and I saw beyond him a man in military uniform and cap, heavy and impatient. Our eyes crossed. I took a step towards them, to show I wasn't snooping, but the officer went on talking, in his rapid way, as if I were of no consequence. Mr Ryazanov was not aware of me, or at least did not turn round, but his back conveyed a concentration and a vigour I had not imagined he possessed.

I stumbled back to the summerhouse with a thought the size of my hangover. So Mr Ryazanov's up to no good! The opium and dervishry is all for show! The villain! And now I come to think of it, what on earth's a Soviet diplomat doing in this backwater, unless to corrupt the Iranian military! Now that is a story I can tell, when I get home, with Mlle What's-her-name. Shirin means "sweet", she can't be called sweet; but sweet she is, in an Isfahanian way; not sweet like cone sugar, but sweet like dried mulberries and pomegranates and rose-hips and milk and opium. Shirin also means "lion-hearted" because this bloody language only has about six words to go round and each of them has a thousand meanings. Like the princess of Nizami, who was sweeter than all the canes of Khuzestan, and yet braver than a man. Shirin, whose bosom, when she bathed in the desert spring, caused the Dog Star to drop tears of jealous rage. Shirin, the torch that lit up the whole earth / Angels attend you in your sugar sleep!

❈ 4 ❈

The next morning I had a new student. She was seated at the back, her chador over her mouth, her books and pen-case piled on the arm-rest of her chair. I was out of sorts from Mr Ryazanov's tea, and did not feel I could accommodate another shy pupil.

"Good morning, ladies."

"Good morning, sir."

"... morning, sir."

"... darling sir!"

"Good morning, Mlle Bordbar."

I should have said that the name John, by a tiny lengthening of the vowel, becomes Jan in Persian, meaning "My love" or "My darling". The new pupil seemed uncomfortable.

"Good morning, mamzil. My name is John Pitt. Would you kindly tell the class your name?"

Silence.

"She is shy!"

I said in Persian: "Would the lady do us the honour of introducing herself to her fellow students and teacher?"

Veil.

"And if mamzil will not tell us her name, will she command us as to why she wishes to learn English?"

Our eyes met. I turned away. On the wall was a large photograph of a Canadian lake in autumn, which never failed to make me homesick.

The new pupil spoke in English. "So I may find a good husband."

Laughter and sympathy fluttered about the classroom. "Oh no, you must not say that! John will be angry!" They turned round and gabbled at the new pupil. "He will be angry, dear. Say you want to go to the university!"

"I am not angry. If it is true. We should all try to speak the truth."

"It is true."

My back and waist had turned to air. My mouth was dry, but if I took a drink of water, the girls would see something was up. They missed nothing. I said:

"This morning, I would like you all to write me a *thème* in English." I looked down at the glistening faces. "What subject shall we choose, Mlle Eftekhar?"

"Love."

"Yes, Mlle Eftekhar. Mlle Bordbar?"

"The Dam at Khashk-e Pol!"

"Iran: The Bejewelled Realm!"

"The New World Economic Order!"

"Isfahan Half-the-World!"

"The Shah-People Revolution!"

The new pupil shivered in her chador. I thought she was about to run from the room.

"Freedom," I said. "I want you all to write me a short essay in English on the topic of Freedom."

The laughter stopped. The girls looked terrified. One or two half-turned, as if they suspected, in their clever way, that it had to do with the new pupil.

"We do not understand politics."

"Nor do I. So don't write politics."

There was a moaning and dropping of pen-cases. Then Mlle Bordbar spoke:

"May we write about love?"

"Write whatever you like. How can I teach you if you will

not do as I ask? I hope you all marry Iraqis."

"Oh no, sir, never!"

There was a sigh of satisfaction, as they bent to their task; though Mlle Bordbar continued to look at me, searching my face for something. After a while, I went to the window, and heard through the screen the white voices of the infants in the hot playground.

I read the essays in the garden of the Poste Restante. Only the new pupil answered the question set. She wrote in capital letters, no doubt because she could not distinguish upper and lower cases, there being but one in Persian. There were no corrections or mistakes. She wrote:

FREEDOM

MY NAME IS SHIRIN FARAMEH. I AM SEVENTEEN YEARS OLD. I LIVE IN ISFAHAN, THE MOST BEAUTIFUL CITY OF THE WORLD, ONE SAYS. MR FARAMEH IS A GENERAL OF THE IMPERIAL IRANIAN AIR FORCE. HE IS THE COMMANDER OF THE HELICOPTER SECTION, HERE IN ISFAHAN. MY MOTHER IS A PRINCESS OF THE ANCIENT REGIME IN OUR COUNTRY. I HAVE A SISTER WHOM I LOVE. HIS EXCELLENCY TELLS ME TO MARRY HIS AIDE DE CAMP CAPT. TURANI. I DO NOT KNOW WHAT TO DO. I SPEAK FROM THE EXTREMITY OF DARKNESS. IF YOU COME TO MY HOUSE MY DARLING BRING ME A LAMP AND ONE WINDOWPANE SO I CAN SEE DOWN INTO THE GLORIOUS STREET.

After a while, I looked about me, and saw that I was standing in front of Mr Ryazanov's wall. I turned away and walked the breadth of the city. I walked all afternoon. The street lights came on, but I kept walking. You see, I wanted to be alone with her and I knew she could not visit me in my room.

* *

37

The next morning, her chair was empty. I understood then that I hated teaching: that from the first moment in Tehran it had been a torment to me; and that I'd now quit the school and try my luck as a broker for Mo'in. Whenever I looked up, I saw Mlle Bordbar's round face slack with misery.

"Sir is very kind today," someone said.

"It is to make amends for my rudeness yesterday."

"Did Your Honour drink too much hashish in the Meidan-e Shah?"

Excellent. "I'm afraid so, ladies. Not again."

Everybody looked relieved, though on Mlle Bordbar's face there were vestiges of suspicion. I thought: The world is not just, my dear.

On my way to the staff-room, Mr Jamalzadeh called me in. Beaming, he shut the door behind me. "I am very angry with you, John," he said.

That was patently untrue.

"Capt. Turani telephoned me this morning. Your new pupil, Gen. Farameh's daughter, will not be coming back."

"I am very sorry indeed to hear that, sir."

"John! You set them as an essay topic . . ." He looked down at a pad on his desk. "You set them as essay topic 'Love'. You cannot talk about love to Iranian girls. It is too perilous." He glared at me. "Didn't I warn you, John?"

"I didn't set that topic. I said they could choose their own topic. That all but one wrote about love is not my fault."

"No," he said. I wondered, not for the first time, what had brought a man of such ability to this dead-end place. Maybe as a young man he'd been in the Tudeh Party, or written an obscene sonnet about Princess Ashraf. She is right, the new pupil: These people need to be free.

"Do you wish to hold back my wages?"

"Heavens, no." He waddled towards me. "You are not my best teacher, John. In fact, you are a very bad teacher indeed. But you are a

38

graduate of Bedford University in England, and are very handsome, and I am neither."

"Nor am I, Mr Jamalzadeh. You will not forgive my deceiving you. Do you wish me to resign?"

"I wish you long life and happiness."

"Do you wish me to resign, Headmaster?"

He flared up. It was as if, by prodding him, I had found the sore place within. "No, I do not wish you to resign. I wish you to go and call on Gen. Farameh and apologise to him."

"I will not."

"You will, John. Farameh will snuff you out as a smoker a match, English or no. This isn't the age of Curzon, John."

"I know," I said, but Mr Jamalzadeh was away on the wings of his indomitable light-heartedness:

"'Says Agha to Meester,
I have a little seester,
And no one has ever keester.'"

He looked sheepish.

"I will not apologise."

"You will, John. Nobody may stand up to him. He took his cane to Molla Najafi right in the middle of Friday prayers."

"I will not apologise to any generals."

"You will, John. For love of me."

I dared not call on Mr Ryazanov without an invitation. I walked across the bridge, neither calm nor proud, just foreign. Julfa was sleeping through the blinding afternoon, the back lanes empty, even of children. I repeated to myself: It happens to all men, and particularly at this time of life, and I who thought myself so special ... I, who ... To my surprise, I found myself at the hateful door of my room. Then I remembered that I had something of hers there.

I knelt at my desk, re-reading the essays, or rather one of them.

39

Pigeons cooed from Mrs Mohandes' quince. After a while, I looked up at the door and saw someone standing in it, trembling. I sprang up. I needed to stop her trembling. And prevent her running down the stairs.

"Will you sit down, Mlle Farameh?"

She sat down on the floor.

"May I bring you some tea, Mlle Farameh?"

She put her right hand to her heart.

"A Pepsi?"

She touched her breast.

"May I get you a cigarette?"

Her fingers fluttered at her breast.

"Your essay was excellent, Mlle Farameh. You are a good student. You will be a credit to any university in Iran or abroad. I greatly admired the verses at the end. Are they yours?"

She spoke through her veil. "Sir?"

"Yes, Mlle Farameh?"

"My sister is in the shoe shop."

She stood up. It was a single sinuous movement, like a snake's.

"Can't she wait, Mlle Farameh?"

"It is inconvenient."

"If you go, Mlle Farameh, you will break my heart."

"No matter. You shall have mine."

I reached out to touch her. Her hand came out from the folds of her chador, long fingers, with the nails painted. I smelled a scent like geraniums in sunshine. I guessed she had made up her face and now regretted the presumption. She took my hand in hers, but didn't know what to do with it; or rather wanted to put it against her cheek or breast, for she suddenly dropped it, took a step back, sat down. I knelt before her and parted her chador. She lowered her head and wafts of scent came up to me from thick black hair. She raised her face. Its nudity filled me with panic; and its strangeness and unearthly pallor and unbroken Tartar eyebrows; and the little nose and helpless lip-sticked lips that sent a piercing shock of sweetness through my body to its tips; and the eyes that drew my spirit into them, as they had done before, it had worked before, perhaps it'll work again, so that I feared I'd lose not just the tatters of my self-control but also my very life, for all I cared. Our lips touched. I felt as if I were drinking from some unfathomable well of happiness; and also of security, as if in some other world than this one, which had preceded it and would succeed it, we had been used to kiss like this and been separated. My vertigo receded, and with it the impulse to suicide in my waist and groin. I felt handsome as a boy can be and ever was. I pulled her to me. She resisted and we became hopelessly entangled. Her bosom pressed my armpit. Her right arm had somehow become caught between her stomach and my groin. She yelped. Her face scorched me like the corn-cob braziers on the riverside at sundown.

"I must go to Layly in National Shoe."

"Mlle Farameh, I have to see your father."

She put her hand to her mouth, as if the thought were too much for her. She lowered her lashes, and lifted them quickly. "You are ill."

"It doesn't matter."

She put her hands to her head in frustration. "I am ashamed."

"It's doesn't matter."

"You'll visit another girl."

"I will not, Mlle Farameh."

"I am ashamed."

"It doesn't matter."

We were enclosed in circularities. I tried to break out, caught her, tried to kiss her on the mouth. She struggled against me, and also against something else, which must have been her own sensations. Alarmed, I let go, and she scrambled up into the doorway, scattering tears that spotted the madder red of the rug. In her black eyes was a look so forlorn that it seemed to hold us like a chain that neither she nor I could break. Through my agony and terror of her leaving, I felt buffeted by gales of pure pleasure. I felt I would burst with happiness,

41

which was not just the recognition that I was loved, but that there was such a thing as love in the world.

"I must call on your father, Mlle Farameh."

She broke whatever it was that held us and ran down the stairs.

The helicopter wing is at Shahinshahr, about ten kilometres down the Shiraz highway. I rode out in a rusty country bus. At the shadeless main gate, I waited half an hour among women until a cadet appeared to take me to Turani. Coming into his outer office, I heard shouting and then two scruffy airmen passed me, eyes to the carpet. A man appeared in the doorway ahead, tight with rage. He saw me, turned blank, said: "Yes?"

His hair was cropped short. His chest, neck and arms burst out of his battledress. As he stood in the doorway, I saw he was shorter than me, which was my consolation.

"I would be most grateful, Capt. Turani, if you would place this private letter in Gen. Farameh's hands."

He threw it in his adjutant's in-tray, turned, and I saw he now knew who I was. He looked slowly over me. I supposed he saw a boy in jeans with no money. Then, because I still stood there, looking at him, he said in icy English: "Had you further commands for me, honoured sir?"

A thought had silenced me. She thinks I want to marry her! She thinks I want to see her father to talk about marriage! She thinks I'm going to save her from this bastard! I am eighteen years old! I have no job, university degree, family or money! I can't marry a Persian schoolgirl! O heavens, what a mess!

"Indeed, I had, Captain." You can go and fuck yourself, that's what. "I need an escort back to the main gate, Captain."

"Jamal! JAMAL! Take the boy to the gate, arsehole."

Out in the bitter sunshine, I began to tremble. Stumbling after the little airman, I knew I had got it all wrong. I had taken too much trouble with the letter, which Turani was surely now reading.

Your Excellency:
After greetings your servant understands that Your
Excellency has received a report that I insulted the First
Class at the Language House, which includes a member
of Your Excellency's family. Nothing could have been
further from my intention. I deeply regret any distress
the report might have caused Your Excellency and
your family, and I seek the honour of calling on Your
Excellency at your residence in Isfahan, after prayers
this Friday, 28 Farvardin, to explain my conduct and
ask your pardon,
Your servant,
John Pitt

Isfahan – Julfa
Mir Fendereski Avenue
Bombast-e Parviz, 4
c/o Mrs Mohandes

And yet, who'd bother about a person who could write such a letter?

❈ 5 ❈

I had often passed the street in which she lived, fascinated by its shade and opulence. It was closed to traffic at both ends by square blocks of reinforced concrete painted blue and white. A canal ran down the middle of the street, planted with old acacia trees that made a canopy above both pavements. Along the length of one side was a plastered wall, broken by a solid black steel gate and a sand-bagged military police emplacement. The officer peered in disbelief at my business card, unhooked a field telephone, fawned into it, while I shivered in my best clothes in the shade. I did not possess a suit, but I had ironed my shirt and jeans and wore my tie.

I thought: How is it that this street cast its glamour over me even before I knew who lived here? How often, in a strange town, we've come on a district as by accident, because it's near the bus station or the last lift dropped us there, and yet in daylight and for purposes that are only subsequently established, it becomes the scene of our activity. Is that merely the sifting of innumerable chances? Or the person we love we are destined to love so she delivers a premonition of her existence? In a moment, God willing, I shall see her.

The gate opened noiselessly onto greenery, which was small orange trees, sunk into beds beneath a raised path, and so many of them they must have taken half the water of Isfahan. Before me was a large, new house with a flagpole and a limp Iranian tricolour.

Everything was clean and cool and extravagant, yet when I looked again at the house, I saw that it had two wings and a central block: that it was, for all its modernity, just another old-fashioned Iranian house with rooms for women and rooms for men and a place where they met in the middle: a house built as a speculation and sold for a fortune to the military. On a marble terrace to the right, a tall man in a white singlet was blowing water from his nose, while a soldier servant waited behind him with a towel.

Sweat trickled down my backbone.

The man, who had water in his eyes and shining on his arms and neck, and had evidently just been woken, was the man I'd seen that night in Mr Ryazanov's garden. The recognition burst in me not as thought but as cold which spread and engulfed me, carrying half-completed thoughts to every extremity of my body – You're history, boy . . . Her father's a goddam Russian bribe-taker . . . – till fear and thought collected in a single command: to wipe the recognition off my face.

The man blinked, looked down and recognised me. Rather, I should say that his eyes, which I searched in vain for something of his daughter in them, flickered. That tiny movement of the eye was the sole evidence of some mental displacement: to the gate, perhaps, or to the armed men outside or to something in the house, a gun, no doubt. It passed. I thought: He's been here before. He has a way of dealing with it. Beaming, I extended my damp business card.

"Your Excellency, may I present myelf? I am Pitt, the teacher from the Language House. I had the pleasure of writing to you . . . Am I addressing Gen. Farameh?"

I lost myself in harmless confusion. Bored, the batman shuffled off.

The man looked at me with interest. I hoped that the expected or repeated element in the scene, to which he was alert at every moment – Has someone tried to blackmail him? – had vanished behind my bland grin.

"You will recollect, sir, that I have the honour of teaching English to a member . . ."

He shivered in irritation. It was not just that I exasperated him, and everything to do with his family, though I saw we did; rather, he was vexed with himself for he was the sole inhabitant of his world. I guessed he hadn't read my letter or listened when Turani or someone told him of the business at the school, and those matters had now come back to bother him. He put his hands on his hips and barked with laughter.

"You think I give a damn, boy?" He spoke easy Texan English. "I've got an air force to run. It's Judge goddam Bordbar. Christ, I hate civilians."

Within my barricade of fear and self-control, I couldn't begin to accommodate Mlle Bordbar: that she had, out of mere spite, told her father and blown up my little world. I thought: It is not the end if he recognises me, just so long as he doesn't suspect that I recognise him. I forced myself to look at him, and from behind my servility, to search his face and squat, muscular form for the reverberation of my secret; and all the while I felt disabled by his English, lulled by the sirens of my mother tongue, enticed to share with him that secret that was beating at my smile. Why is he being so sweet? He could deal with me in the bat of an eye, and I'd be floating down the Zayandeh Rud, and nobody the wiser; and then I saw, with an embarassing clarity, why people try to have friends. People seek to have friends not for company or pleasure, but so that some day somebody will drag a Persian river for their bodies. Why is he so goddam cautious? In the midst of my fear, which was like acid in my guts and stomach, I now felt a recollection of pleasure, irresponsible and irrepressible and intoxicating, which I knew could only have to do with the girl. In my trembling heart I felt that what was happening here was bringing us together or even – and here, now, my intellect made a leap such as it had never attempted – was in some way a consequence of our attraction, of which she, though just a girl, might have a better understanding than I.

"I'm going to give you some advice, boy." He covered his face with the towel. "Don't mess with these people, and above all don't mess with their women. This ain't South Kensington." He threw the towel down. "Understood?"

"Yes, sir."

Something in me yearned for this complicity: two men of the world, modern in attitude, English in language, allied against non-entities such as Bordbar, medieval custom and an army of vengeful and dim-witted mollas. Yet in my mind, which I felt for the first time to be quite useless, slow and vain and childish, I knew I was succumbing to the force of his personality. I didn't know a man could be both violent and subtle. I thought: Just leave. Now.

"Thank you, sir. It has been an honour to meet you."

He was not ready for me to leave. There was something else he needed to do. "Aren't you going to say 'Hi' to your student? Ali Asghar!"

My heart fell out of my chest. "She's bright, sir."

The servant ran out with a shirt.

"Of course."

His answer was automatic. I don't think it had occurred to him to apply such a predicate to his daughter, or indeed to anybody but himself. As he pulled on his shirt, the soldier scampered past to open a door. I thought: be still, little heart!

The room ran at me in a shiver of silk and stockings, bare shoulders, cut glass, flowers, slippers, jewels, electric light.

She was seated on an imitation Louis XV sofa under an electric chandelier. Beside her was a much younger girl, who had to be her sister, Layly. In their adult make-up and prom dresses they seemed to me like terrified dolls. Their mother, who was very beautiful, sat in a matching armchair wearing a dress in the New-Look style with a wide skirt of grey silk. She was smoking thirstily, but without inhaling the smoke. Between them, above a Kashan carpet of spectacular intricacy and ugliness, was a glass table covered in tea-glasses in silver holders, silver bowls of confectioners' sweets and fruit glistening with water, and a spray of pink roses. I was stunned by my ignorance of things: that there existed, separate from my world and only touching it at such rare instants, another of a kitsch and tedious femininity.

"It's sorted out," said the General, pushing me into an armchair. He took no notice of the ladies: it was as if his family breakfasted like this. I stood up. The ladies stood up.

"For God's sake, everybody, sit down!" he said.

The girls resumed their postures. They wore identical sleeveless party dresses, also of 1950s style, Mlle Shirin in red, Mlle Layly in blue, white stockings and high-heeled shoes. The dresses had the air of having been home-made by a skilled dressmaker: it occurred to me the Princess might have been hard up at one time. Both girls had their eyes to the carpet. Mlle Shirin's hair had been put up in a thick coil on the side of her head; and while that showed her long neck, it seemed an act of violence on her, from which she was still bruised and resentful. The heavy red jewels around her throat she wore like a collar. I sensed she had fought her mother or the hairdresser, or indeed both of them; that she rejected her womanliness and exposure in the market; and that she carried somewhere with her secret proofs of her rebellion, a spot of ink, perhaps, on her right index finger or the wrong underclothes. Everything about her posture appealed to me not to look at or address her. I saw she hated me for being the cause of this parade; and also its witness for I thought that it was only in my eyes, or rather in the reflection of herself she thought to see in them, that she had lost her most precious and intimate dignity; and had I not been here, she might have borne it, had done so before, perhaps more than once.

The world had lost all reason. How could they sit here, father, mother, sister, before this piece of darkness in a party dress; who conceals in her black eyes the unthinkable and in her bowed eye-brows deserts and harnesses, arrows like hail, busted canals, snapped minarets, towers of skulls? I felt that I must spring up from my phoney chair and smash the room to bits for the agony of not looking at her.

The Princess spoke. "Vous êtes le bienvenu, monsieur. Vous nous faîtes un grand honneur."

"L'honneur est pour moi, Altesse."

She clicked her tongue at the title. "Jamais il ne m'appelle 'Madame' à la maison."

I sensed Mlle Shirin stiffen not so much at my gaucheness, or not much, but at her mother's indiscretion.

"C'est trés drôle, monsieur, mais nous pauvres femmes ne parlons que francais, et Son Excellence, grâce à son instruction militaire à Fort Bragg, ne parle qu'anglais. C'est absurde."

A kitchen servant padded in with two small plates of cake, but the Princess sprang up, took the plates with their little gold forks and napkins and placed them before us.

"Eat," said the General, eating.

The cake tasted of saccharine and fat. I said through a mouth of cake: "Je parle un peu persan, madame."

The Princess blew out her smoke and, though the cigarette was barely started, stubbed it out in a dish. "Comme je l'ai dit, monsieur, Son Excellence ne parle pas un mot de français."

I woke from my reverie. I saw that this rigmarole of money and nubility, of opulence without character and expense without taste, of provincial formality and nineteenth-century French and fathomless beauty and reckless virtue, was not unveiled for me, some little teacher of English as a foreign language, but, as it were, even for such an individual; and that the situation must be desperate in the extreme. I saw, in a flash that would have been far beyond my mental range an hour ago, that the whole thing – the regime, Iran, this family – was going to hell; and that I was a saviour of sorts, for them, or at least for one of them, the best the Princess could muster and the other must take her chance. I recognised, with an equal clarity, the true source of Mlle Shirin's rebellion: that she knew about her father and Mr Ryazanov, and it was killing her, killing them all, and now she saw it killing me.

Rather than look at her, I looked at Mlle Layly. She had been peering at me from under her fringe, and her eyes darted away. I thought that she was not ready for the world, was childish or a little simple, lived in the shade of her sister's care; and I was filled with such sorrow for the girls. I said: "Durant ma résidence à Ispahan, madame, j'ai appris à apprécier le mérite et le caractère de l'aînée de vos filles. La superiorité de sa raison, l'élévation de son âme, la beauté de sa personne . . ."

"Na baba . . ."

The plebeian Persian phrase, which means "Come off it, mate", or "Get along with you", caused the General to look up. I plunged on.

"J'insiste, madame, mes intentions envers votre fille aînée sont tout-à-fait honnêtes."

"Lui avez vous parlé?"

"Je lui ai fait part de ma profonde estime."

Mlle Layly giggled. The Princess glared at her and, then, turned slowly on her older daughter with a look of implacable vengeance. Mlle Shirin was staring at the carpet as if she wished to unravel each one of its million and a half knots.

"What the hell are you talking about?"

Mlle Shirin lifted her head and spoke. "We are speaking, sir, of the dam and hydro-scheme at Khashk-e Pol."

Her sister gaped at her and then at her mother.

"This goddam country is so backward. Come on, boy, let's leave these scatterbrains. I have something I want to say to you."

"At your service, sir. Permit me to take my leave. Madame, j'ai apporté des petits cadeaux pour les jeunes dames. J'espère qu'elles me feront l'honneur de les accepter."

Mlle Shirin tore at the wrapping. She pulled the bow into a knot and bit her lip in frustration. When she saw what the present was, her shoulders stiffened. It sat, untouched, in drifts of paper in her crimson lap.

"Très belle," said Mme Farameh, picking up the little lamp. It was of grey, unglazed pottery, with a tiny reservoir for oil and a handle, the sort of lamp you find in museums and at dealers all over the Arab world and Iran.

"Sassanian," said the General.

Greek, actually, by way of Mr Mo'in.

"I believe, my dear, it is Hellenistic. Such lamps were still being used in the villages when I was a girl."

"Or a Tehran fake," he said.

Mlle Shirin spoke: "Je ne crois point que ce soit truqué."

"Tais-toi, Chîru!"

Layly was enchanted with her present. It was a mirror frame of *papier mâché*, indeed made in Tehran, but at the middle of the last century, and painted with roses in the European style. Mr Mo'in had thrown it in to complete the bargain over the lamp. The silvering of the mirror had all worn away, and so I had had it replaced with blue window glass from a demolished house. "Ô maman, c'est adorable. Monsieur est très gentil."

I looked at her mother, who was once more smoking rapidly. In her beautiful face was a sort of exasperation at me, as if to say: Go home, young man, you simply do not understand, young man, go home to foggy England; and also a certain indulgence, as if she, too, had once been much admired.

I stood up and bowed. The girls curtseyed. I felt Mlle Shirin's eyes on my cold back, as I followed the General into his den.

There was no relief to the stifling opulence. Yet here it was expressed in heaviness and bulk and force and scope, in an immense desk of some dark tropical wood, a suite of leather armchairs, tables covered in bevelled glass, a cocktail bar, a bank of telephones, a big machine which must have been a teleprinter, another beside it for shredding paper into illegible strips. The walls were punctuated by framed photographs. One showed Farameh behind the Shah and the Crown Prince inspecting a guard of honour, no doubt at the helicopter base. Another was of the Shah alone, in an open shirt, at the controls of an airliner. The third, which was in colour, and must have been taken in the US, showed Farameh in shorts and a loud shirt on a jetty and beside him, standing on its tail, was a fish that towered over him.

"Scotch?" He had his back to me.

"No, thank you, sir." You prig!

He poured himself a small measure, but I sensed he would not touch it. He sat down behind his desk with a stifled groan. He smiled through a clouded face. "When I was Area Commander, running the F-5 program, I ejected at forty thousand feet." He arched his back. "I've been to every goddam doctor in the world. And you know the only thing that works? Right here, in Isfahan?"

The Remedy. Of course, the Remedy. That's why you have to call in the middle of the night on Mr Ryazanov, notorious opium addict that he is. You won't let me go, will you? I sank into an armchair.

"Isn't it dangerous? I mean I heard . . ."

He snorted and closed the subject. "Are you familiar with the name Khatami?"

Air force commander. Flew the Shah and Empress to Rome in the crisis of '53, married to one of the princesses, takes the Shah's discarded girls, they say, rich as anything. I thought: Was Farameh on that aeroplane to Italy? Does that explain all this money?

"Yes, sir."

He swivelled on his chair. I sensed there was something offensive to him about addressing me at all. He began again, quietly: "Do you know what keeps Saddam from bombing this little town back to the Stone Age?"

I was bewildered by the contrast with the guest-room, or rather the continuity: that, still dazzled by beauty and drunk with scent, I should now be exposed to this masculine blandishment, this dark wood and metal, high strategy, the Iraqis, violence, war; and all the while, his English, with its American accent that I recognised, with a start of disgust, was to me the true voice of power, kept leading me on and on.

"I don't know, sir. I am not expert in air defence."

He spun round. "I don't expect you to be. From nowhere, we've made this air force third in the world in mobility, after the US and Israel and ahead of the Soviets and you guys. I have 2,500 fighter-bomber pilots capable of assuming sole responsibility in an air sortie. We're doing seventy to eighty air sorties a day. Eighty per cent of my total force is deployed each day, which tells you a lot about the preparedness of my pilots and ground crews, rapidity of servicing capabilities and efficiency of logistical support. Before stocks are exhausted here, they are automatically re-ordered at our twin base, Fort Bragg, in Texas without me or any of my officers lifting a finger."

He looked at me now. "The fact is that I have more goddam airplanes than I have pilots. I have three hundred places every year at training centres in the US, a bigger quota than any other goddam country. I could have the whole of fucking Cranwell if I asked for it, but I can't and you know why?"

Because nobody can speak or read English worth a damn. I saw he was now going to offer me a job. What I couldn't tell was whether he wanted me near him, working for him, so he could watch me; or only wished to put me off my guard. I knew I exasperated him. My slowness of wit and my lack of ambition were to him an offence.

"I think, sir, it takes time for a whole generation to learn technical English."

"Time! How much time do you think I have!" His patience had gone. "Or will you guys defend us?"

I was overcome by homesickness. I saw the streets of Hull on rainy November evenings and my foster-mother fussing in her kitchen, and endless terraces and the big, fat Humber and all those

British things. I thought that maybe Britain wasn't what it had been, but it had laws and schools and soldiers living on their pay, and was a damn sight better than this place.

"I thought, sir, that it was His Majesty who so insisted that we leave the Gulf. The Arabs, as far as I know . . ."

"What do you want, boy?"

I want to marry your daughter, sir. If you permit me, I become your son and must keep your secrets. Yet I had only to form that thought to see that he had already considered that course and rejected it out of hand. I felt unsexed, and simultaneously enraged that this man, whose very family lied to him, should have power over them. Turani! What made him so special? What secret power did he have in the matter? An irresponsible chivalry welled up in me, and also a pride, that those women would confide in me what they would not confide in their master. And though I saw it was his intention, with his sudden questions and broken gambits, to provoke me to show myself, that he was a smart guy – else how would he have prospered under an arbitrary regime? – I didn't care any more.

I said: "I want your elder daughter to persevere with her studies, if not with me then elsewhere. You owe it to her."

Even as I spoke, I saw the extent of my folly. I saw that with that simple question, he had achieved what all the complex questions had not: he had uncovered the pattern. I knew he didn't care a damn for her, or her sister, would throw them to the cadets on their commencement night if that would suit him in the slightest; did not care for women in any way; and yet he understood that some men did, for he had heard those words, "I want your elder daughter", first from Turani and now from me. That was the pattern: Turani had found out his secret, and therefore so had I. And though I thought he disbelieved in love, he saw the possession of his daughter offered a man advantages – money, connection, influence – which, because they arose with him, had some meaning for him. And now I sunk out of my depth. This was more than just a military airman, alienated by the air and speed and America from his dull countrymen. I looked across not at a man but at a sort of god who was driven by a single impulse that obliterated love of women and children, loyalty to his uniform and homeland, opinion, decency, drink, pleasure, money. I saw there was no limit to his conception of self. I saw that he wanted it all. Starting with Khatami's job and not ending with the Peacock bloody Throne.

"Get out," he said and spun.

"I will take my leave of your family."

I saw, in his muscular back, a superhuman effort of self-control. He shouted: "Ali Asghar!"

The English language seemed to me crude and clumsy, and I took refuge in Persian at its most elaborate. "Sir, you may threaten me, but the ladies will certainly slay me if I do not take my leave."

In the guest room, the women had not moved. It was as if Iranian time were not uniform but had a sex, and the time that had unfurled next door and brought me to the brink of violence, had stood still in here. As I came in, the Princess started from her chair, as if I'd altered in a fraction of a second.

I said: "Mesdames, je vous ai dérangées."

"Pas du tout, monsieur! Prenez un moment de repos! Vous n'avez pas déjeuné."

She was appalled by the discourtesy. I understood that she was Persian through and through, had never seen Baku let alone Paris, had barely been to Tehran.

"Madame, souffrez que je prenne congé."

The Princess stood up. She was trembling with anger and mortification. "Allons, Layly!"

The girls stood up straight.

"Cher Monsieur, que votre ombre bénie ne dimin . . ."

"LULU!"

I sensed the room empty, slacken, come to rest. We stared, the two of us, at the carpet. I was aware of the brilliant crimson of her dress. I felt her nature spreading out to touch me, gently and against her will, like the ripples of a pool disturbed by a gust of wind. My fear began to drain away. I said: "Please come with me away from here, mamzil."

She shut her eyes and shivered. She said, "Excuse me, sir."

I reached out for her, but she took my hands, bowed her head and kissed them and ran with them and me to the door. We passed through a kitchen, where the Princess was smoking against a counter covered with dishes of delicious food. Beside her was an old Bakhtiari woman, with her back to us, chattering as she chopped herbs with a murderous knife: I suspected she was the only person that the Princess cared for. Mlle Layly was eating an eclair. They ignored us.

Mlle Shirin clattered to the end of a passage in her high heels. As her skirt swung, I saw she'd drawn her stockings only to the hem. The garden blinded me. She pulled me to a little gate, and drew back the bolt.

I started to speak, to ask her again to come with me, and felt her sweet hand across my mouth. Slowly, she withdrew it and stepped back to let me pass.

I felt the world had been condensed into this garden: it was acrid with sorrow and obstructed love. I was lost in a maze of objects and events, from which I could find no way out. I wanted to cry out: What is there here, in this corner where two walls meet, in the dry rose bushes and the cage of little birds and the parapet of barbed-wire, in your bare neck and shoulders and funereal eyes, that requires us to separate? We have chosen each other from across immense distances and towering obstacles so why must we separate?

Her face was bruised with sorrow. I thought if I spoke or touched her cheek she would bleed. I could see that she knew things I did not know and could not now tell me. I could see that she hated herself.

I could see that she did not wish to cry; that it would be an indignity; and that to leave would be a kindness to her.

She raised her hand, uncertainly, in the European gesture of farewell.

The gate closed behind me. I heard the stumble of her feet.

There was no sentry. When I could hear her no more, I started to run; but then, thinking that nobody runs in Isfahan, least of all a European boy at three in the afternoon, I dropped into a stroll, avoiding Chahar Bagh and the boulevards, following little streets and lanes to the river, where I jumped down off the Corniche and began to run again. Dogs sprang and snapped at me. I thought: If I'm bitten, that's an end of me. I ran and ran through sand and marshy places and clumps of esparto grass that cut my arms while the dogs circled and swooped; and all the while, I thought: We will not be separated, for our will to be together is stronger than the will of our enemies to separate us and we will obliterate them.

❧ 6 ❧

"Hassan, open up!"

There was no sound above the rustling plane trees.

"Open up! It's me, the English!"

There was a groan, and a sigh of bedding. "Master is sleeping. Go away."

"Open the gate, you dog-begotten hash-head, or I'll goddam kebab you!"

I heard the flap of slippers and saw a shadow above the hinges.

"Go away, boy!"

"If you do not open at once, I swear by God that Ryazanov will throw you and all your family into the street."

As he fumbled with the bolt, I kicked the door in. He had his turban tied about his jaw, as if he had a toothache. He gaped at me in superstitious terror: "You are like a mad, boy."

I put my thumb unsteadily to my mouth, a gesture of smoking and drinking. "I am sick, Hassan dear!" I started to shake.

He leered at me in delight and pain: "Ah, now it's over for you, too! You have become an addict! Alas!"

I ran past him towards the tank. At the end of the avenue, the summerhouse was lit in the gloaming. I thought: I wish the whole world could be like this, with paths that are straight and cool and invisible to the rest of humanity, and lead one to the place of one's trusted friend. As I ran down the tiles, that had been watered for coolness, and sent a flash of spray before my running feet, I said out loud: "We are saved. Mr Ryazanov will save us."

In the summerhouse, Mr Ryazanov was seated before his brazier. Beside him on the cushion was his book, which I now saw was, in fact, a xeroxed manuscript; a pencase; and the Gardner bowl steaming with tea. He did not look up.

He said: "I do not recollect, sir, that I issued you an invitation."

I heard something behind me. At the tank where the paths met, Hassan was hovering, anxious, uncertain, ridiculous with his toothache, deceitful.

I cried out: "I have found her, Mr Ryazanov! I have found the Beloved!"

He took up a coal with his tongs.

"She is Farameh's daughter!"

He placed the coal against the pipe, and inhaled deeply. He said, through garlands of smoke: "I am ravished for you, sir. She is said to be a considerable beauty." He looked at me viciously. "And rich, of course."

I realised, with a start of pain and loneliness, that Ryazanov was jealous and hated to lose me to some young girl. And yet, as I stared at him in my misery, at his cap and the brazier, and what he was reading – I deciphered its xeroxed title, *Islamic Government*, and the octagonal seal of somebody called Ruhollah al Musavi – I saw that it could not be so simple and unworthy; and that, in a sense that I could not begin to fathom, he was married for life to Lord Opium who was a demon from the depths of hell. Through his shirt and the bones of his bent back, I saw the source and origin of his sadness, which was the impotence that the drug had forced on him; that he could not bear to speak of women or think of them or to be in their company and be reminded of his shame and uselessness; and my face burned with the tactlessness with which, from our very first meeting, I had forced on him my preoccupation.

"No, please, no, Mr Ryazanov. In the garden. That night. He saw me. He saw that I saw him."

Mr Ryazanov dropped the pipe, which hit the edge of the brazier, and broke at the bowl.

"O my poor boy. What have I done to you?"

I was scrabbling on the rug to pick up the pieces, which were hot to the touch. I tried to piece together the scalding moustache of Nassereddin Shah. I lifted them up to him, but Mr Ryazanov was looking at me, eyes full of sorrow.

"Please forgive me, Mr Ryazanov. I'll replace it, if I can."

"What have I done to you, my darling son?"

I still held the pieces. "Will you give me asylum, Mr Ryazanov? I'll be your spy. I'm not a fool."

He smiled. "You are welcome here, but what protection am I and that hashish-drinker against Farameh?"

He shook himself, as if to clear the fatality of the drug. It occurred to me that it had displaced his will, and he was searching, a long way down, for the shreds of will that remained to him.

He said: "You will not go to Julfa."

"No, sir."

"You will not go to Tehran. You will not under any circumstances go to the English Embassy in Tehran. That is what he will expect you to do."

"Yes, sir."

"You must go where he does not expect you to go."

"Yes, sir."

He found whatever it was he was looking for. It was a small mortice key, of an old-fashioned sort, which he placed in my hand, and then closed my fingers on it.

He said: "There is a house in Bushehr, on the Gulf, on the sea-front. It was the consulate-general until it was closed at the time of Abadan, in '53. Rather, it was our residency, until Mr Beria made his move, you will understand one day. Nobody has been there but I since '53. The Centre ordered me to sell it, and I did, to myself, thanks be to God, against just such an occasion. Nobody at the Embassy knows of its existence and after you are gone I will destroy all record of it." He smiled in his mournful way. "As it were. You will take the Toyota cruiser, that will be parked at the Shahrestan Bridge at nine, key in the ignition, extra water and gasoline in the back. Have you a weapon?"

"A weapon?"

"A gun, John."

"A gun? Could you please lend me one?"

He smiled again. "Alas, I have but one and I need it."

"I know where there is a gun!"

"I said that you may not go home."

"No!"

"So go then, dear John, take your gun, go to the bridge and God protect you."

"The Beloved! I cannot leave without the Beloved!"

He sighed. "You must. You have a hard life ahead, and perhaps not a long one. You cannot ask another person to share it. Let her be, John."

"I haven't got a life without her!"

"Let her be, John. You are going into the night, and it is best that you be alone."

"I can't!"

"JUST GO! NOW! If she likes you, and she's brave, God willing you will meet again."

"But how?"

He was looking at the fragments of his pipe. He said quietly:

> "'You who came so late, and then so early went,
> You lit a fire and then like smoke were spent'."

I took a step backwards and found myself on the path. Mr Ryazanov did not look up.

> "'Like the hopes of desperate men, you lingered on the way,
> Like the kindness of the stony-hearted, vanished with the day'."

I had been to the Shahrestan once before, on the way back to the city from a Friday picnic with Mo'in and his friends. There was a dirty tea-shop just downstream of the bridge, with sticky wooden tables and a single butane lamp for light. While the friends plied Mo'in with tea and bread, so he'd be sober enough for the Minister of War, which wasn't very sober, and the tea-boy flitted with a cloth, darting witticisms at the libertine, I walked to the bridge and listened to the water roaring between its stone piers, while one of the party, a bore who'd attached himself to me all day, swayed and muttered, "Great Alexander made it, Great Alexander, by God!" – ignorant fool that he was, as well as a bore – then plunged into his jacket for his bottle.

I heard the water again through the darkness, and from the white light from the tea-shop door the snap of backgammon pieces. I thought: So bad it wasn't, my life. In my jeans, the Smith & Wesson ground into my hip. It scared me. I caught my breath from my run, and saw, beneath a ruined mud wall, the old-fashioned shape of a Toyota jeep: as if Japan were homesick for the 1930s. The boot was unlocked. There were two jerrycans, one with the smell of petrol on it, and a sand-shovel and what looked like a gelim and some bedding. The key was in the ignition, and there was an alien gear-stick that I knew would take me time to master, for I dared not turn on the inside light; and I smelt something, which was not the smell of plastic seats and petrol and dust, but something sweet and bland and feminine, like rose-water or confectioner's cakes.

Seated at the wheel of a car, I felt better; powerful even. So! Mr Ryazanov's been a-cheating on Master Opium! He has a girlfriend after all, the villain! The thought at once turned dark in my mind. I said: "I cannot leave without speaking to her for one last time."

I knew that she had given me a sense of the invulnerable, that in itself might cost me my life; but also that until the afternoon in Mo'in's shop, my life had been barely tolerable and few men, I think, could have tolerated it. In this flight and pursuit, I knew that all the demons I'd suppressed would fling open their doors and shriek at me till I went staring mad. When she kissed me in the shop, I sensed a quickness, in my limbs and heart and speech, in my very notion of my self, which I had not known existed or rather I had no doubt buried years ago along with my demons. Her kiss was the only thing that had happened to me in eighteen years: all the rest was sleep and blindness. It was the single, unrepeatable opportunity of my existence. To put it aside was to conspire in my own unhappiness. What life I had was at the Farameh house. If I was to be caught – and I was not certain that I would be caught – I wanted it to be at that house, not running from it. I started the engine and turned the car towards the city.

"NO SIR!"

To my left, a truck swerved into the road. The driver banged with his ringed hand on his door panel. I wrenched the gearstick. The jeep flew over the bridge. The truck passed me in a roar and gabble of insults. I looked in the mirror. I spun round. I could see nobody.

I said: "God Almighty, Mlle Farameh! I will love you and care for you as long as I live."

There was silence and the highway.

"Mlle Farameh?

"Mlle Shirin?"

"I am relying on that, sir. You see, I cannot now return to my school or my family or work for my living, except as a prostitute."

I don't know what I'd expected, but it wasn't that. I thought: I know absolutely nothing about this girl, except that she's come with me. We passed through the streetlights outside the helicopter base. Under their sagging rotors, the machines looked like ranks of bloated insects. "The situation is very inconvenient."

"Yes, sir."

"Do you know why?"

"Yes, sir."

"We are going to Bushehr. There is a house there where we can hide for a few days till everybody has forgotten us. Then we can get a dhow to Muscat or Bahrain."

"That's a good plan. Bushehr is so hot and pious nobody goes out."

"I have a weapon."

"I'm glad, sir."

I felt ridiculous. "But only two rounds, I'm afraid."

"No matter, sir. You only need two."

"Goddammit, girl!" I scanned the mirror for her. "You will not say such things!" I grabbed the box beside me, fumbled for the bullets, and threw one out of my window. "There!"

I heard a sigh behind me.

"Oh, Mlle Farameh, we must talk." Well, not just talk. "I'll pull over."

"I think we should go far away from here."

"Will you do me the kindness of sitting in the front?"

"I shall distract you from driving."

Her sentence ramified in my guts. Did she mean that she intended to distract me or that it was inevitable that she would distract me?

"Will you at least show yourself?"

"No, sir. They will look for a car with a passenger."

The road stretched before me, straight and tedious and celibate. Gigantic trucks bellowed past in a blaze of fairy lights, or bore down on our side of the road, forcing me into the gravel. I tucked in

behind a long-distance bus, with pleated nylon curtains closed on
the sleeping passengers and, painted on the rear window, the phrase,
O MASTER OF TIME! We passed a glimmering tea-shop in a flutter
of torn tamarisks.

"May I speak?"

"Please do."

"There is a police and Savak post at the Tang-e Shiraz. Every car
must stop there."

"We'll have to leave the highway."

"Yes, sir."

The Tang is a steep defile through which, suddenly, the road falls
down to Shiraz. So sudden is the view of the town, and so pretty the
towers and minarets and cypresses and orange-trees below you, that
if you come by day, you want to cry out. Indeed the place is called
the God Is-Very-Great-Pass. Mo'in managed a howl when we went
down on a rug trip. I was sure I'd recognise it in good time.

"May I speak, sir?"

"Just the sound of your voice is a delight to me, mamzil."

"The Russian gentleman gave me some things for you."

"What? What things?"

I heard a feminine rustle behind me. "I think some money, sir.
Quite a lot of money, I think. And a box with something in it, but all
wrapped up. And another thing."

"What other thing?"

"A paper."

"Is it important?"

"How can I know?"

Her voice cracked.

"Oh Mlle Farameh, please don't be sad. I'll stop . . ."

"Do not stop. It is, it is . . ."

She sobbed.

It is the licence. I thought: Look, lady, it's not my goddam fault. I
never wanted to marry you. I know absolutely nothing about you,

65

except that unless you'll let me kiss you soon, I shall unfortunately die. I'm not sure any understanding, other than that, is possible between people of such different origins. What am I do with you, my little millionairess?

I said: "I am extremely sorry, mamzil. I am sure that you looked eagerly forward to your wedding-day, but . . ."

"You are unkind. I did not know you were unkind. GOD ABOVE! Off the road! Now! Lights out!"

I stood on the brakes. The wheels locked, thank God, and we glided past the curtained back of the bus. The jeep stumbled off the black-top, sunk into a ditch, teetered, righted itself, and burst forward into utter blackness. I braked and turned off the engine. Through the side-window I could see car lights, white and red, strung out like a necklace for miles and miles. Over the ticking of the engine, I heard car horns, a door bang, shouts, laughter. In the far distance, the roof-light of a police cruiser turned round and round and round.

She was kneeling on the seat beside me, peering through the window. Her scent made me want to swoon. I fumbled for the gun, but she clicked her teeth. We waited and listened. Then she touched the light switch, made an angry face, and got down from the car. She gestured to me to follow her, very slowly. The engine fired like a gun-shot; but as I followed her dark figure, my eyes becoming accustomed to the moonlight, gradually the sound of horns and engines died away and the lights were extinguished by distance or a rise in the ground.

I felt humiliated as never before: that here, at the very first obstacle, I had lost my head, would have happily sat in the jam of cars, till our turn came and a police or Savak officer shone in his torch, shouted, yanked us out; and that the situation had been saved by this girl. In the bright moonlight, she was stepping carefully across the gravel, her chador pulled tight about her. I thought: Yes, miss, we all know you have a very nice bottom, that's why we're here. She changed her gait, began to walk on flat feet, like a village woman: it was as if my unpleasant thought had made its way to her.

And, goddammit, we're going in the wrong direction. We're going east! We'll have to make an immense circle round Shiraz, and come to Bushehr from the east. That'll take us days.

She had stopped and turned round. Her chador snapped in the wind. I turned off the engine and got down. She was standing on a wide track, churned up by wheels. Yet the marks did not run on top of one another, but spread out for twenty or thirty yards each side of her, as if the road were not used often and, when it was used, it was by groups of drivers in high spirits. Hunters, I thought, or maybe a herding people on its migration.

Her eyes glittered in the cold moonlight. I thought: This is the place where the road divides. I will follow the track east and she will return to the highway. This is also the last moment I can speak. I said: "I am in a land foreign to me, Mlle Farameh. Today is different from all the todays that went before it and which did not prepare me for it. All I know is that . . ."

"Excuse me, sir, but it is precisely because I am in my homeland and you are not that it is I who should speak. This track leads, after about three hours, to a place called Faisalabad. It is the winter quarters of the Qoyunlu people. I came there when I was a small girl with grandfather, who was a dear friend of Mr Qoyunlu. They were in Parliament in Tehran together until the Land Reform. Mr Qoyunlu was hanged in front of his people, men and women, in the market square of Faisalabad. The Qoyunlu are not on good terms with His Majesty the Shah. They do not speak to the gendarmerie or the Savak or admit them to their villages or pastures and if they find them they cause them inconvenience. Every few years the army goes
in and kills some of the youth and then goes away again."

"Shall we take asylum with them? I mean, you and I . . ."

"Excuse me, sir! Before this place, Faisalabad, about two hours from here, there is a pool. We camped there. The water is very sweet. There is a very old building there, from the time of the Sassanians.

It has a bad reputation. It is a good place to stop and rest."

"Yes, mamzil."

She turned away. She said: "Now, you must kindly tell me if you wish me to attend you at that place, I mean the pool."

"We're married!"

"Pfu! The paper means nothing."

"If you are willing, Mlle Farameh, I wish you to come."

"I have no property."

"Nor have I."

"I mean you have given me no dowry."

"Oh."

"To show you are sincere."

"Your dowry is . . . Oh, I don't know . . . All that I have I give you, my life, my head, my liberty, my blood . . ."

"Stop it! That's enough! You are silly!"

I stopped.

"Will you be kind to me?"

"Yes."

"You have made a promise."

"Yes."

She walked past me to the back of the jeep, picked up one of the jerrycans and, with her face averted, handed it to me. She seemed to me very strong for a girl. I took a long drink. The water tasted painfully of Isfahan. She drank nothing herself. She came into the front of the car, and sat as far away from me as she could sit, and still be in the car. The track was simple to follow even in moonlight. I sensed some of the elation of the young men who'd made it: racing down from summer pasture in their pick-ups, and the windows bristling with rifles, and the fat sheep bumping and grumbling behind the cab, and the flap of the women's scarves in the wind, and the dirty babies dozing in their arms. I wanted to say that, dug out the Persian words for it, but when I glanced at her, she was asleep with her head on the window-sill. I thought: We're going to make one hell of a couple. We've been married three hours and we're already at each other's throats.

I wondered what the girl was thinking, but could not imagine an Iranian girl's mind. Some verses of Sana'i stood in the way:

> Had it been up to me to come, I'd not have come;
> Had it been up to me to go, how would I go?
> If only I had never come into this dreadful place
> And were not here and did not have to go.

How is it that Sana'i, who lived eight hundred years ago, nevertheless describes the world I am experiencing; which because he too experienced it, or something like it – else he could not have written that quatrain – becomes not arbitrary and accidental and capricious, like the blow of a playground bully, but to some degree regular, if only I could find the rules? Or was it rather that he and the other poets invented love in Persian, the special torment of being in love in Iran, through which I must pass with this sleeping girl? I thought I could reach out, and perhaps touch the hem of her chador without her waking, but thought she would not thank me for it: indeed, it's why she's asleep in the place she's asleep.

What I do know is that the place that I set out from, and the place to which I am now driving, in this white moonlight, is loneliness; and this poor, impulsive girl didn't recognise that until too late, the night had come and we were in the desert. For the consciousness I have now of myself is the consciousness I have always had, but could not before now name, of a person standing alone in time, without predecessor or associate or successor. That solitariness, which is the counterpart of my sense of specialness or selection, attended me all through my childhood and schooldays, but has become intolerable to me as a grown man; and that is why I left Britain, and came to Iran not for any good reason, but precisely for no reason at all; really, as death without dying. And so bad a decision it wasn't, for I had found friends, Mr Mo'in and Mr

Ryazanov; and if one was a drunkard, the other an opium addict, it was perhaps natural that I should have such friends; and they would have been the adventure of my life, but for this other, who is sleeping.

She is frightened of the pool, for the same reason that I am frightened of it; not out of bridal bashfulness, which I've heard is customary in Iran; or because she probably knows as little about love as I do; but because she knows, as I do, that it is our last chance. Somewhere, in the secrecies of our wedding night, we must hope to find an understanding or amity that will not so much make good the disagreements of the daylight, but, as it were, give us patience to make them good. The consequences of failure are dreadful for her. She may wake tomorrow with a stone in her heart and her hopes in pieces; and know that she must either stay with me from pity, or leave, go to Tehran, pass herself off as just another mistreated divorcée, try to find work in an office or factory, and a man who'll take her. I now saw the inner meaning of Mr Ryazanov's warning: that to take her with me was to roll her choices into one; to take her choices, which God knows were few enough, and reduce them to just one. I must be kind to her. That's what matters, not this thing with not getting caught and the gun and all.

Something burst across the front of the jeep. As I jumped on the brakes I knew it was gone. In the fading image on my eyes, I saw not so much a deer as an essence of speed and wildness. It was if two worlds had accidentally collided, and that the gazelle had come out from the world of old things and was now long back there, leaving just the recollection of the coat on its flanks, bristling in the moonlight, and the indescribable scent of its wildness.

She was upright, staring before her. She turned a look on me of pure shock, and jerked her chador across her face.

"You don't have to do that for my sake, mamzil."

She peered, trembling, ahead of her. It occurred to me that she did not see well; and that at those moments in my room in Julfa and the guest-room of her house, when she had stood or knelt so close to me, it was not so much from liking as from short sight.

"I thought they'd all been long ago hunted to extinction."

"I thought so." She didn't look at me. "They need water. They don't go far from water."

I drove on across the illuminated desert. She peered through the windscreen. Then she raised her hand, in the Iranian gesture of "Slow down!" or "Wait a moment!" I stopped the jeep. She opened her door and, without turning, said: "Please wait for me here. I mean: Take your rest."

After a while, I stepped down, and saw the moon at my feet. The wind had dropped and the surface of the pool was utterly still. The halo around the moon, crystalline in its perfection, was confirmed in the sky above me. Beyond the reflected moon was an immense and vague dome, sitting on a massive cube. It was cold, and quiet as I had never experienced. The horizon was dark all around, and the only light was the haloed moon and the stars that struggled against it. Troubled, I filled the gas tank and radiator and took a long drink. She was standing in front of me.

"I have made you a bed. Please take your rest."

I followed her, stumbling on the stones. She had laid out the gelim and a quilt on a patch of sand. I said: "Will you do me the kindness of sharing it with me?"

"If you wish."

She lay down in her dress and chador with her back to me.

"Oh, mamzil, please don't torment me."

She sat bolt-upright. She said: "I am not tormenting you! I never wanted to come here." She snapped her fingers at the ruin and the desert. "I never wanted to leave Isfahan! One kiss and I must leave my home and my sister for ever, and run for my life with an English boy I don't know and don't like!"

"Two kisses, if I may disagree with you."

"Pfu! You are so silly. Couldn't you see I would have given you your heart's desire? Couldn't you see I would have had an illicit

71

liaison with you? Why, oh why, did you come to my house?"

Because of Mr Jamalzadeh! To save Mr Jamalzadeh from losing his school!

I couldn't say it: the earth had turned a full revolution. I stood up. I felt tired from the driving. I said: "Mlle Farameh, I will not hold you here against your will. Rest a little, then I will take you back to the highway where I will stop a Pullman for you. I am confident that, if I am not with you, your family will receive you."

"Who would look after you? You are so foolish, the Savakis would have you in a donkey's piss."

"God has protected me up to now, Mlle Farameh. I do not believe that He will now abandon me."

The darkness where she was turned cold and bitter. When she spoke, it was merely to herself. She said: "He does not like me."

"Oh, Mlle Shirin, please let's not talk. We were happy enough when we didn't talk." I knelt down and reached out for her. I touched her hair. "Will she do her servant the favour of taking off her dress?"

She turned to face me. Her face was cloudy with fear. "My dress?"

"Her dress."

"But I have no underlinen."

"Even so."

"Tomorrow."

"It is already tomorrow."

"There is a moon."

"And look there, the Dog Star! Even so."

🏵 8 🏵

I woke to bitter cold and woodsmoke. I did not know where I was or why I was there. Before me were black mountains, lined at the tips with yellow light. Below them, amid the ashy debris of the desert, and striped by long shadows, was a pool and beyond it a domed building so ruined that it seemed barely distinguishable from its surroundings, like a sand-castle the sea has been at. I thought something must have happened to me for me to be in this wild place; and then waves of fear and happiness engulfed me.

I sat up. Across the gravel, a girl was feeding thorns into a blazing fire. Her dark hair was wet, and fell down her crimson dress to the V of her chador at the small of her back. She rested lightly on the balls of her bare feet. On the fire, the jerrycan from the car was shooting steam. Beside her was an upturned sand-shovel and, on the back of it, four small rounds of dough.

I had thought she was my toy, some object of beauty and sexual happiness and oriental glamour, that I would carry home with me and cherish and display. It hadn't occurred to me that she had a will and existence of her own, that she'd got up, bathed in the pool, said her prayers and was now making tea in a jerrycan on whose sides she would soon bake sangak bread; as if she were not some pampered *nouveau riche* divinity but a village girl brought up to labour since she was five years old; and so light of heart, as she rocked on her bare feet, reciting something to herself over the roar and crackle of the thorns, that I was overwhelmed with the sheer luck of it; and recognised that, for the first time in my life, I wasn't alone, that I had an associate; or rather that I had ceased to be myself, vulnerable, intact, guarded and patrolled, but had become a new entity, that contained something of her. Then regret gained the upper hand, sweet and piercing as her wet hair and white shoulders and naked feet: that I would never see her in a swimsuit or tennis dress or at a party or see my own country again.

She was reciting a song in Turkish. It went like this:

> At the engagement I was shy,
> I didn't ask the how and why.
> They said that he was young and nice!
> Him! My husband! At that price!
> Don't let him come, O Granny dear,
> That awful man, don't let him near!
>
> His horrid hat, his hair like snow
> His skinny legs and his B.O!
> And what a cheat, we must be mad,
> He's even older than Our Dad!
> He's swindled us, O Granny dear,
> Don't let him come! Don't let him near!

She spun round. Her face, hot from the fire, composed into a private smile. At her white throat was a smear of ash. She sprang up, picked up the jerrycan, though it must have been scalding, and poured it from a height into a glass, which she brought to me. As she knelt before me, and I smelled the scent of her skin above the woodsmoke, I saw her smile was complicit, understanding, startled, under control: as if she had found something out about me, not exactly reprehensible but best not advertised, and I could rely on her discretion.

She handed me the glass. It was so hot I put it down at once. Also I wanted to put my arms round her waist.

She said: "It is risheh, a thorn which grows in the desert. It is good for the heart, the memory, the liver and . . .", she lowered her eyelashes, "the strength."

"I shall certainly need it, madame."

"You need a pound of cucumbers up your arse," she said. She restored her maddening smile. "May I take my leave?"

"Oh no, please no, madame. I am unwell."

"Unhappy man!"

I kissed the smile off her mouth.

"I have work to do."

"Indeed."

She spat at me; looked about her; and in a single movement, came out of her red dress. I had never seen a girl's waist, or bosom, or her face and armpits appearing, startled, from under clouds of hair and petticoat and taffeta. I saw she was now pleased with her beauty; or rather had discovered its delightful effect, which was to scare the wits out of her husband.

I kissed her bosom. It was cold and hard as a marble pavement. She sprang back. She looked down at my face, and it must have been a picture of sexual gluttony and awe, for she burst out laughing.

"Of course, I am at your service," she said and dropped her arms from across her breast. "But make it soon, for I am very . . ."

She looked round at the desert and shivered with laughter.

". . . freezing."

"Let me go! It will be dawn!"

She had turned her back to me, and managed to get her dress over her head, but I held her tight around the waist, and had twined my ankles round hers, and would never let go; for though she was strong, I was stronger.

"Please! Just a short time. The Savak always lies in. It is well known."

75

"You are so silly. And shame on you!"

I let go.

"Why shame on me?"

She turned round, and a shadow of doubt crossed her face, like a cloud on a summer beach. She wasn't so sure after all. "You understand me perfectly. You are pretending."

"I don't!"

She was mortified, but too obstinate to give up. "Is that the way you slept with the English girls?"

I felt it was better to get this over with.

"Madame, I have loved only one girl in my life. I believe I will only ever love one girl."

Her face went grey in the dawn light.

"And may I enquire if you are in contact with this person?"

"You may. I am."

Her eyes were ugly and savage.

"And may I enquire if you intend to see this person again?"

"You may. I do intend."

She sat utterly still.

"Is she English?"

"No, madame. She is Iranian."

"Was she one of your students?"

"For a while, yes, she was."

I caught her hands an inch from my cheeks. She whispered: "It's that goddam Minoo Bordbar, who is small and green and fat and stupid, all arse and bosom . . ."

"It isn't, madame."

"Let go of me!"

I let go, but kept her under surveillance.

"I demand that you tell me the name of this person. I am your goddam bride!"

"Her name is Shirin."

Her hand swooped through the air.

"You are strong, madame."

"And you are lucky to be alive. I sincerely regret marrying you and now, because of your recklessness and my lack of self-control, we will bring a baby into this world of misery."

"Oh."

I had forgotten about all that.

"Now let me go so I can do my tasks. Soon it will be hot, more hot than you have even experienced or believed possible, and then you will be angry and mistreat me." She had regained her smile. I sensed it was her protection against me, now she had lost her city and her family and her clothes.

"Don't regret marrying me!"

"Oh, there are things my heart misses: the sound of Mamdali watering the paths, and the smell of woodsmoke at the summer pasture, and grandmother's chador aslant in the doorframe in the early morning, and cutting sabzi with Jowhara in the kitchen and feeding my finches and crushing up geranium flowers to rouge my face and lying in bed in the summer afternoons, listening to the splash of water as Mamdali hoses the paths . . ." I felt she had ended up in a place other than she'd intended, for she blushed. She sat up and pulled her dress down to her waist.

"Mr Pitt, I regret only one thing in my life and that is the hours I was left alone by His Excellency in the guest-room of our house with Turani, whose notion of love consisted exclusively in pulling at my tits and grabbing at my . . ."

"Mme Farameh!"

" . . . when all the time he only wanted to be buggered by His Excellency, and every second of every minute of each hour I said in my heart, over and over again: One day, by God, the Englishman will find you and break every one of your goddam fingers . . ."

"You thought I . . . You already thought that I . . ." My world had turned inside out.

"Oh no! He doesn't understand!"

I said: "When I have you safe and outside Iran, I will address the question of Capt. Turani's rudeness to you."

"NO!" She had her hands in fists. I raised my hands, protectively, to my head.

At last, my slow wits comprehended. She thinks I won't let her forget him, or forget I got her away from him. She thinks I'll bully her about him. "Mme Shirin, I never want to hear that person's name again. It does not exist. It has never existed."

"You won't hear it from me." She lowered her head. "I have bored you. May I take my leave?"

"Please don't. Please tell me why you said 'the English'. You didn't know me."

"I saw you. Everybody saw you. We saw you in the streets and the gardens."

"What?"

She looked embarrassed. "All my classmates liked you."

I was bewildered. "And all the time I thought I was alone, you and your friends were looking at me, laughing at me behind your bloody . . ."

"Not laughing. The other girls liked you because you were the bread under the kebab. I . . ."

"I was the what?"

She blushed. "I . . ."

"Please say it, madame."

"You already are very self-satisfied."

"How can I not be! When I am married to the most acceptable girl in Iran!"

She turned away and whispered: "In Iran, only?"

"In the inhabited earth."

"More acceptable than Minoo Bordbar?"

My face must have answered the question. She sat upright. She said:

"I liked the way you walked with your head to the pavement and

78

yet always stopped to let ladies pass, and the way your mind never stopped thinking, sitting in the garden or with your papers or reading your letters by the PTT, and your wretched calligraphy and awful accent and clumsy manners, and the way when I stood behind you in the corner shop you were always robbed and still apologised to the shopkeeper and . . ."

"So it wasn't an accident! At Mo'in's!"

"I didn't want to go, Mr Pitt. I promise you I did not want to go. However, I could not permit the others to go without me."

"I suppose not."

She looked at me in defiance.

"And you kissed me so I would be your prisoner."

"I kissed you, sir, because I have no self-control."

"So all the while, when I thought God had brought us together, it was but one of His angels."

"Don't be vulgar." She looked away from me. "And anyway, angels are merely attributes of the Divinity, as any child knows. Excuse me, sir."

She stood up and I saw her legs and feet.

"O God, you're bleeding! What have I done to you?"

She laughed and laughed.

"The alliance of the poplar and the spear / Were too much for her ruby dear."

And laughing and reciting, she returned to her fire.

"Are you angry?"

"No. Won't you eat breakfast with me?"

She touched her heart and turned away.

I was not angry, just surprised. As I ate breakfast, for the first time I could remember that somebody else had made for me, I watched her step across the ash, rake out the fire, pick up the jerrycan and plunge it hissing in the pool, fill it and take it without exertion to the car, and then walk into the pool to her waist. I thought: While to myself, I seemed in Isfahan to be free and in command of all my actions, I was in reality at the end of a long thread pulled by a Persian ex-schoolgirl who is, at this moment, washing blood from her legs before the palace of her ancestors, the tips of her shawl in the water. I want her so much to turn at me, and smile, to record this moment, in this immemorial pool, before the palace of her ancestors, under the vanquished stars, but she doesn't and I suppose that's her way, and so I get up, and drain my bitter tea, and roll up the bedding and walk towards the palace.

Someone, years before, had placed planks of wood aslant across the arched doorway and there was a weathered official sign saying DANGER! DO NOT ENTER! I picked my way in and stood under the vault. The walls and piers were so crumbled that it no longer seemed a building made by human beings, but rather a geological accident. I tried to imagine it at the time of its prosperity, painted and furnished and inhabited and surrounded by gardens, with its poets and musicians and the morning draught of wine, but my imagination failed me. All over the walls, there were little prints of hands in faded blue paint and at the centre of the palm, an eye. The blood beat in my ears. The dome seemed to buzz like a hornet's nest that's been trodden on. I felt all the old things of Persia, all the devils and demons and ghouls, that could not tolerate the parades and boulevards of the King of Kings, had gathered here and I had disturbed them. I said: "Thank your for your hospitality. We are leaving now, taking with us nothing from here but water, without which we cannot live."

I fought my way out, and regained my breath in the warm sunshine, wondering: What is happening to me that I have become superstitious? Then I saw we had visitors.

Blocking the jeep was a long white American convertible, of a type I cannot name but famous as the car in which President Kennedy was shot. In the front, to the right of the driver, was a lady in a headscarf and dark glasses. Behind them two young men, with old-fashioned rifles slung from their backs, were seated on the doors. They looked at me without interest. Mme Shirin had put down the jerrycan and drawn her chador across her face. Her head was bowed under a torrent of kitchen Turkish. She was trembling with fear or rage. I forded the stream with a smile on my face.

"Get lost, boy." The lady, who was no longer young, did not look at me. The order, and the *tu*, infuriated me.

"May I enquire with whom we have the . . ."

She jerked her head. The young men dropped to the ground, and stepped towards me. I was trembling. I will not permit them just to pick me up and throw me in the jeep! I will not be humiliated in front of this girl! But, O Shirin, you must have known we could not go through their lands without them knowing. These are Qoyunlu, not teenage gendarmes missing their mums! I put my hand in my pocket. One of the boys smiled, came on more slowly. The other dropped back, shook down his rifle. Oh heavens, I've only got one round.

"PITT!"

The boy caught his step. I thought: I don't believe this, my goddam wife has forgotten my first name. The boys had their rifles trained on my face, but they weren't quite concentrating. I turned at Shirin, boiling with sorrow and fury. Her head was still covered and bowed. She had crossed her black arms at the breast. In her right hand was a knife: that same broad kitchen knife I'd seen the Bakhtiari servant using to cut herbs that afternoon in Isfahan. She must have closed the garden door on me and then run back and swept it into her skirt. The blade now rested against her black throat.

I looked at the lady. She sat impassive behind her sun-glasses. A bird began to sing: a high, sweet trilling sound above our heads, like a skylark in an English meadow. In the morning light I could see patches of green wheat. I thought: There'll be people getting up and going to their fields soon.

81

"Evidently, ma'am, there's more to Mr Bridegroom than meets the eye."

The lady stiffened. I turned on the young man, who was smiling at me down his rifle-barrel as if to say: Please don't take offence, sir, it's only a pleasantry, and meant with goodwill. Also, these women, you know, once they get an idea in their heads, they're into the saddle and half way across the district!

The other, to maintain parity, said: "I've heard, dear ma'am, that these English . . ."

"Please be quiet."

For the first time, the lady turned to face me. She was tanned from air and sunshine. She said, in good English: "You have God's good fortune, young man, that you came into my power and not that of the Government, otherwise you would certainly be dead. When, God willing, you come to your country, present my compliments to Miss Dot and tell her that I did this action for her sake. Now leave and do not return."

"May your eye be bright, ma'am."

The car spun away, the boys swinging themselves up onto the doors.

The lark piped above us. By the open door to the trunk, Shirin still had her head bowed, the knife against her neck. I said: "May you never grow old, Mme Shirin."

She dropped her chador from her face. There was blood on her lip. She stooped. I took her by the elbow and straightened her.

She said: "I am not too large?"

"No."

"Mr Farameh said I was too large. Nobody would marry me."

"I know. You are very brave, Mme Shirin. I am so proud we are married. For the future, should you have occasion to address me by my first name, may I inform you it is John."

"Yes, sir." She seemed relieved. She took a last look round.

"This was a good place to die."

"Please don't say such things. Anyway, what's it called?"

She blushed. "I don't know. The people call it, foolishly, the Castle of the Girl."

"Pretty name."

"The castle was supposed to be inviolable. But, as you can see," she spread her skirt and whispered, "it is in in ruins." She looked up. "Who is Miss Dot, if I may ask?"

I hadn't the strength to be slapped again. "Dr J. K. D. Spencer, professor emerita of Persian at the School of Oriental and African Studies in London. A great scholar."

"A great spy, you mean."

She put the jerrycan in the boot.

I said: "Will you do me the courtesy of riding in the front?"

"I shall distract you from your driving."

And she did. I had never seen such a fidget. She knelt on the seat, or sat cross-legged with her skirt and chador drawn up above her scratched knees, or rested her bosom on my shoulder or her feet in my lap, or put pistachios with her fingers in my mouth, or unbuttoned my shirt to examine minutely my chest, or rinsed my face with orange-flower water, or pulled at my hair to see if it was real, or changed gear for me, holding the lever with such delicacy between thumb and finger, that we had to stop to fill up the radiator and make love.

"Would you have really done it, Mme Shirin?"

"Done what, sir?"

"Stuck Mme Qoyunlu back there?"

"Heavens, no! Only your poor servant."

"O Shirin, please don't do that again!"

She laughed a mouth full of white teeth. "It was just a game, you know. Madame's late husband loathed my father. She just wanted to have a snoop at you."

"Did I measure up?"

"What can I say? I think not."

Our journey seemed to have lost its purpose: we were weaving like drunkards in the springtime across stony space towards mountains that came no nearer. Tracks that started with a flourish, petered out in no time, or branched, or doubled back. The sun blinded us and soaked us in sweat. A line of telegraph poles, shimmering with mirage, appeared for an hour before us and stayed for an hour in the mirror. We made a wide detour to avoid four black hair tents, and beside them a Mercedes truck, which she said were Qoyunlu but we saw nobody. All sense of danger and pursuit had evaporated.

I had heard in England of the Savak, that they pulled out fingernails and tied men to electrified beds; but it was as if our love made us invulnerable, threw deserts about us, raised over our heads a dome as hard and crystalline as the midday sky. I suppose all young lovers believe they invented love, else they could not love like this; yet it seemed to me, as she snapped the stopper on the can and hesitated for an instant, so I could enfold her waist and spin her round, scalded by the jeep's windows through my shirt, it seemed to me that our love made our enemies paltry, insignificant, three-parts dead; indeed, that every time she leaned back against the spare wheel – as if to say: If you have anything more to do, it is better to do it now – was somehow tossed in the balance of good in the world. The desert through the open windows was merely the projected arena of our privacy, across which we stumbled, bumping against garbled prejudices and unfathomable taboos, misunderstandings, mistakes of grammar, syntax, word order and Arabic, unconscious offence; offending, sulking, teasing and yet coming together under the irresistible force of our curiosity.

"Don't exhaust yourself with thinking, sir!"

I understood that up to then my notion of love had been pornographic, that I believed in a generalised femininity that could take away my pain but yet leave my loneliness intact, for I was not then aware that there could be another condition of existence. I did not know that I could, with her arms around my back, permit myself to feel more helpless than a child, and then look up and see her, a very particular female, still there, still Shirin Farameh, looking anxious or somewhat pleased with herself. I was astonished by this miracle, this device for generating happiness, that required no supervision or permission, but was entirely of our own creation, and seemed each time she leaned back and lifted up the hems of her skirt, to gain in objectivity, to take form between us, more permanent and shapely than our individual selves or than this high plateau scattered with oaks. I was awed, too, by the perspicacity of sexual attraction: that her glance in the doorway of Mo'in's shop concealed in its darkness not just this agony and delight but affinities that abolished all our differences of nationality, upbringing, language and possession.

I said: "I am glad I trusted my heart."

She was seated on my lap, learning to drive. She said: "Thanks be to God", which is really just a Persian "Yes", and then: "I never heard that noble part of the male body termed the heart."

The sun was coming through the window at my right. She shook herself like a dog and moved over. She said: "We are too slow. We must come into the town in the night. We must not talk or touch again. I will now go into the back."

"For God's sake, don't! I will concentrate on driving. I promise."

She was gone.

"Madame Shirin? What if it overheats?"

There was no answer. I drove on towards the hills.

"Madame Shirin? Why did you ask for a lamp and a pane?"

There was no answer. I tried one last time.

"How did you know to come to Mr Ryazanov's?"

I heard a gasp. "Because Mr Farameh ordered me to go! Because I always took the messages between the houses!"

"Ah. Of course." I thought: I am a fool and always will be.

"Didn't you know? Didn't he tell you? You see, the something made it safe."

"The what?"

"The covering. The modest clothing women wear. Nobody could tell I came from Mr Farameh." She sighed. "Yesterday, I brought your sentence of death. The least I could do was share that death sentence."

"No, madame. You didn't have to."

"Mr Ryazanov said the same. He burned the paper in his brazier. I forced him to tell me its contents. And anyway I knew."

"You didn't have to come."

"As you wish."

"I'm glad you came."

Silence.

"God, it's hot. We are going to stew like tea in Bushehr."

Silence.

We were descending at last down a dry water-course scattered with bushes. I stopped the engine so we could listen. From the top of the steep cliffs on the right, I heard the tinkling of a goat- or sheep-bell. She was beside me, shading her eyes against the setting sun.

"Is there a village?"

"No. Why?"

I moved off. After a while, the walls of the valley began to fall away from us, and then we burst into the open, to a still, purple sea radiating heat, telephone wires loping away to India, a stand of palms rattling in the wind, and an empty, shining, black highway.

"Turn right!" She crouched down into the well of the passenger seat.

"I'm not a complete fool, madame."

It was dark by the time we reached Bushehr and saw its brilliant lights.

"Please stop."

I pulled off the road into soft sand. She stepped softly down, disappeared and then beckoned me through the gloom. We seemed to be in some sort of scrape or depression in the sand.

She stood up on the wheel-arch, and said: "You must wait here till I come back for you. If I do not come back before dawn, you must go back to that riverbed, wait there until tomorrow night, and then come back to this exact same place. Stay in the shade and ration your water: just three sips every hour." She pursed her lips three times. "If I do I not come back by dawn in the second night, drive into town and buy water and gasoline and bread on the Shiraz highway. Then turn off, eastwards, towards the sun, and go to Pakistan and God keep you. Now please give me the key."

"You're mad, girl."

"I have wearied you." She jumped off the wheel.

"I mean, I'm sorry, I'm so sorry for my rudeness, please forgive me, but I must go with you. How will you find the house? And it's been empty for twenty-one years. We don't know what there may be there!"

"Only I can go, sir. Because of the covering. Stay here and take your rest. You will recollect that I asked the favour of the house-key."

"For a kiss."

"You're a child."

In my arms, she fluttered with excitement and fear. Then she vanished. I stared miserably into the darkness. On the road, eighteen-wheelers roared and hooted. The moon rose to my right. My head jangled with the day. Her face and lips, the way she carried the can and tipped the water in the radiator, the trailing of her chador, lost their clarity, became mangled, rough and indecent. I smelled her scent, of salt and roses and some quintessential herness, on my chest and fingers. I felt drenched in femininity. Certain words – *pushidegi* covering, and by extension the mental attitudes in girls that are the effects or counterparts of veiling, such as ambiguity, inversion, concealment, intrigue or deceit; *eish* meaning the delights of this worldly existence; *kamrani*, the attainment of a young man's desire – made maddening calligraphic shapes in my mind. I was depressed by missed opportunities: that we could have slept together one more time and still have reached here in the night. I thought: If we make it to the house, I am not going to stir from her bed for a year.

I woke with a burning, freezing groin. In my lap was a dish of chelo kebab, covered with metal foil, and a cold can of Tuborg wrapped in paper held by a rubber band. I jumped down, ran to the road, but there was nobody to be seen. I scanned the paper by moonlight, for some message, if only an XXX, and then realised, shamefully, that that was the English abbreviation for kisses. I ate with my fingers. In my gluttony, I could no longer distinguish between the delicious food and her: my appetites had all run into each other. I thought: It'll be easier in the city, easier to hide; and she can buy things, because of the covering. I'm not going to Pakistan on my own, whatever she says. I don't mind what happens now, as long it happens to us together. I got up to piss away my yearning for her and saw, in the back by the jerrycans, a six-pack of Saboo water and a sheaf of bread.

I woke with her hand on my mouth. She was trembling, but this time, I sensed, from elation. She withdrew her hand carefully. The moon was setting in the sea.

"Kiss."

She nibbled my ear and whispered: "We must go to the house. No lights. No speaking."

We crept into the silent dusty city, and every yard was a mortification to me, for she had walked it twice, to bring me my dinner. We came along a waterfront, at which rusty freighters sagged at their hawsers, while other ships bright as Christmas trees were strung out to the horizon. The houses were breathtakingly white in the moonlight, except where the upper storeys were covered in wooden fretwork or tracery. I thought: It is not possible for a city to be so beautiful. We passed onto what seemed to be a headland, with the glimmering water showing between the long walls of houses or factories on each side. A gas flare made a wash of yellow across the water and caused the whole town to flicker. She signalled me to stop and turn off the engine and got down. I felt the car inch forward. I sprang down from my seat, and led her, struggling and furious, and put her in the driving-seat; and then I pushed till I was drenched with sweat and my eyes sparkled and stung with salt and I wanted to die just to end the pain in my back and arms.

We were in a place of smashed palm trees. She was pulling a steel gate shut behind us. The hinges glistened from some oil or fat she'd put on them. The place smelled of dust and vegetation and sulphur and the sea. She put her hand over my mouth and pulled me stumbling up paths carpeted knee-deep in palm leaves. Up some broken steps was a veranda and a door and beside it a sort of mophead. Then my hair stood on end. She clamped her hand tighter on my mouth. She was rocking with stifled laughter.

I had planned in the jeep to carry her over the threshold; and explain that in some parts of Britain, that's what a bridegroom did to his bride when they arrived at the place where they would live together: it was so she did not trip on the threshold. I mean I was going to explain that later, when we were inside, but the snakes she'd killed with her hands in the dark while I slept put it quite out of my mind.

❂ 9 ❂

We stood in a room with a large steel desk indistinct with dust. On the wall above it was a photograph of the Shah in boy-scout's uniform and another of Stalin mobbed by country women. Shirin was shaking with laughter.

"It is very easy. I will show you tomorrow."

"How do you know how to do all these things?"

"Ssss. Grandmother. At the summer pasture."

She turned her back and minced out of the room. I caught her on a wooden stairway.

"Ssss. Stop it! I have made a bed for you upstairs. I mean, you must take your breakfast."

She slithered out of my grip, but I caught her on a wide landing, with a stone floor covered in rugs, a row of filing cabinets, their drawers all awry, spidery ceiling fans that flickered in the gas light. I could feel she was elated as never in her life: that she felt fierce and precious and wild. Yet within her power and independence was another impulse, that I'd never before experienced, and that must have been authentically feminine: that what she'd done she'd done not just for our lives, but for our honeymoon; and that even the pool in the desert had not been some providential refuge from pursuit, or not wholly so, but the Castle of the Girl, a place she'd selected for her wedding night, perhaps years ago; perhaps even, when she was little and had gone there with her grandfather and the Qoyunlu Ilkhan. I thought: This girl is completely without fear; or rather, so arrogant that she treats danger as she would a fool or bore.

She squirmed in my arms.

"After. After your breakfast."

I felt her personality was disintegrating: that her self-control, in which she evidently placed such store, was no longer intact and that she had dropped parts of herself in our struggle, which were now scattered across the stairs and floor like the slipper askew on the top step and her shawl spread out like a black sail across the white stone. I sensed that love might be a different sensation for girls, less painful and domineering and desperate, but also less local in its action, for it seemed to run all the way down to her little feet which I would kiss if I could just get them still without a nosebleed or a black eye and then, having secured them, advance, as it were, on a broad front.

She dragged me into a tall room, with one whole wall covered in wooden window tracery. There was no breeze, but I smelled and heard the sea beneath it. There was a bed draped in tattered netting, but she had made up another on the floor. I supposed that she had never slept in a European bed and wasn't going to start now. On the floor beside it was a felt mat covered in dishes. There was no other door; and yet I knew I was getting nowhere, for she was just so strong.

"My darling, please!"

She turned on her front with her face away from me, at bay. Then I heard the click of a loudspeaker and the hawking of the muezzin into it. Her shoulders relaxed. She stood up.

"I must pray. You must pray."

"Bona-fide travellers are excused the obligation of prayer, if the missed prayers are then made up as supererogatories."

"As you command." She began to wash her forearms in a basin on the floor. I recognised, as this was the second or third time, that though she was happy to use words about love that weren't in the Persian dictionaries, she hated any flippancy in matters of religion; and in that she was my reverse.

"God is very great! Prayer is better than sleep."

The voice filled the room, setting it trembling with sweetness and security: it was as if the voice were consolation for the sleep we'd lost, or rather was sleep itself in the forms of another world. Yet I was embarrassed to watch her pray. I wanted to thank her god for bringing us safely to the house, but I didn't know how, and could not be sincere; while her kneeling and standing and lip-moving, to the exclusion of all else and me, offended my self-regard. I looked down at the breakfast mat. It shimmered with glass. Condensation glimmered on the skins of apples in a metal dish. I felt famished. Then I saw something and it was as if the floor had risen to strike me.

She had both arms round my waist.

"He was my friend. My friend!"

"I will be your friend." She followed the line of my eyes and saw something she had taken from the Russian gentleman herself; unpacked it from its rags and box two hours before; washed it; put it ready on its carved half-gourd. The porcelain of the Gardner bowl was so thin I could see through it even in the faint light of morning: to Isfahan and Mr Ryazanov's last act of service to Lord Opium and the gun that he wouldn't lend me in his mouth.

"He died for me! So I could live. So he could never tell them we were here. You see, he thought he had no will. Because of the Remedy."

She was stiff and hard.

"What are we going to do without him?" I buried myself against her marble breast. "I am so frightened, Shirin. I don't want to die."

"No, sir. Nobody does. Mr Ryazanov didn't want to, but he died for you. God will forgive him."

It seemed to me that all that was left of him was this lifeless bowl. I could not tolerate the loss of his life.

"Please inhale."

I breathed in.

"And please exhale."

I breathed out.

She said: "Each breath you take, Mr Pitt, prolongs your life an instant. And each breath you make takes with it a fraction of your sorrow. Thus each breath confers a double benefit, for which you will, at the end, be grateful. "

I breathed out.

"Now come and lie down with me, my husband. Take your rest."

PART TWO

❖ 10 ❖

I woke in a blaze of sunlight. It was sharp, heavy, white, granular, smelling of sugar and methane. I jumped from bed and crouched naked on the hot boards. On three walls were windows blasted by the light through tattered wire netting. Where I had slept, a rag had been pinned to the pillow, with a message in Persian school copperplate: *Greeting and good morning your servant has gone to bazar take your rest be advised not to go into the garden nor the lane and by god not to touch any cupboards and doors and such because they will burn and god forbid injure you until we return soon I kiss your hands.*

I took the message to the scalding windows. I had dreamed of green trees, which embowered us where we slept, luxuriant and European and cold. I saw a muddle of palms, leaning at dead or dying angles or snapped at the bole, colourless with dust and splashed with bird-lime. The floor of the garden was a thicket of fallen branches, dry and grey, like the bones of large animals, beneath which I could make out the remains of paths that met at a raised tank smashed by a fallen palm trunk. The blue tiles of the paths were buckled into ridges or had come loose and lay in heaps. On each side were the stumps of what must have been box hedges. At the end of the path before me, in a patch of dirty sunlight between the blocks of shade, a brown snake lay coiled and motionless. To my left, beyond the garden wall was the ruin of a warehouse or factory, built of coral blocks and dripping with creepers, with arched windows shedding their glazing bars and pitched roofs of rusty corrugated tin. It had a churchiness to it that made

97

me think Europeans had built and used it. In a bush of creeper was a penthouse, tin panels hanging on by just a rivet, and a conveyor belt with an iron car jammed half-way. To my right was a cheap minaret with, at the tip, a string of cable and the loudspeaker that had deafened us that morning. I heard the slaps of the sea and the moaning of doves and, from a long way away, a jangle of undisciplined motor traffic.

It seemed to me that the condition of the world at rest was ruin: that sun and violence combine to annihilate any human enterprise, knock down the keystone of an arch, clog a canal, peel the paint off a wall, corrode a rug down to its web and take away the best people before they have even lived. I closed my eyes and tried to re-assemble the garden in its prime: Mr Ryazanov striding down the path, in shorts and a white shirt damp at the armpits, calling coarse greetings to the gardeners clipping the box on their haunches, and inside the whirr of turning ceiling fans, the smell of hot ink and soap, a clatter of teletype. Here there was no history, as I had learned to call the past in Britain, only the vestige of an old prosperity, of a civility so far superior to the present that it constituted its own order of legend. The Bushehr residency of the KGB was already as indefinite as those forgotten Persian dynasties whose shattered works are heaped together and given to Solomon and Alexander, Rustum and Shirin.

The garden door swung open. I scrabbled for my clothes and the gun, in that order, and then I saw it was Shirin. It was not just her black dress, and the black chador that hung from her head down to her toes, that I did not recognise; nor the groceries she carried in one hand, nor the pitcher she balanced with the other on her head, a pitcher of the cheapest sort that shopkeepers use to sell yoghurt or buttermilk, for I had never imagined those things and her together; it was a slowness in her movement and a drooping of her shoulders, as if she were weighed down by her luggage, exhaustion or poor spirits. I had not seen her in such a condition.

She flickered through the pools of light and shade, and as she did so, the garden lost its evilness; became, in each new picture of her, alive and teeming with possibility. I recognised that she was doing what she'd done for me in Isfahan: making each place not only as it should be, but also her own, as if she'd grown up in it. I was astonished that a girl so young should be so at home in the world. Then I saw the sleeping snake.

My mouth drained of spittle. I fought with the window catch, which came clean away in my hands. I waved my arms, but she was not looking at the house. Then she took down the pitcher, lowered her shopping bag, and straightened as if her back were hurting her; plucked up a spike of palm, as though for neatness' sake, and brought it down on the creature's head. She picked up her shopping, threw the branch and wriggling body off the path, and stepped towards the house; and as she came, she shook her chador off her head and with it, as it were, her bad mood; and her white face and the damp bangs of hair on the forehead made my heart stutter. I thought: She'll go into the kitchen, or whatever there is here, and then come up. I'll meet her on the stairs. I should put something on, but I don't want to.

She was standing in the bedroom door, with her finger on her lip. I thought: So Iranians really do put a finger to their lips in surprise, like in the paintings. I reached half-heartedly for a sheet. She whispered: ". . . and tore Zuleikha's chastity to shreds."

She looked down: "Hafez. No. 3 in the *Divan*, edited by Muhammad Mirza. You will recollect from the Holy Koran how Joseph's beauty caused the wife of Potiphar to throw all caution to the winds and her astonished friends at dinner to jab their fruit-knives into their wrists." She came forward, slid to her knees before me. She had a white shirt in her hands.

"Don't flatter me!"

The shirt felt warm and crisp. I looked at her. I thought perhaps I would see past all these things, her foreignness and the danger we were in and this bewildering heat, to some understanding between us or rather to a sort of future in which everything had turned out all right and we still got on well, considering. I fell into her strangeness.

"How are you, ma'am?"

"I'm well. Thank you, sir. How are you?"

"I'm well."

"Did you sleep well, sir?"

"I slept well. Thank you."

It was as if with our first goal reached, we had uncoiled like busted springs, not knowing what to do or why we were where we were. I did not know how to be a husband, and I doubted she knew how to be a wife or at least my wife. What was the rule of love in this country? How do husband and wife behave? I reached for her waist, but she shuddered, sprang up, stood by the window.

"Shame on you! You have not breakfasted. And I . . ."

She squinted through the blinding lattice.

". . . and I must make the orchard prosperous. Please take your rest."

I stood up. "What's the purpose, Mme Shirin? We'll be leaving tomorrow!"

"Yes, sir."

"At most the day after. It depends on the harbour."

"Yes, sir. When do you wish us to enquire at the harbour?"

"All right, tomorrow." I was ashamed of having ordered her. "If it is no trouble."

With a sigh, she shook out the sleeves of her dress. Two folded newspapers fell to the bed. I had never met a girl who read newspapers, and so thoroughly, that the ink was smeared and the edges dirty and frayed. I picked them up, for the sake of neatness, and half my face looked back at me.

As I unfolded them, first the *Kayhan*, and then the *Ettela'at*, the two main newspapers of Tehran, I wondered what I'd done to be famous: to deserve these photographs, vague and dizzy from enlargement across three columns. The photograph was that taken for my work permit at the Zabankhaneh. I remembered the studio in Chahar Bagh where it was taken, with a cut-out of an aeroplane for young men to pose in at high-school graduation and, on the other wall, a painting of a Swiss mountain in summer.

Shirin was opening and closing her hands. It was a childlike gesture, as if she wanted to grasp me but dared not.

I read: "WANTED by the Internal Security Forces for the violation and murder of an Isfahanian girl. Suspect is a British citizen . . ." I looked at Shirin. On her cheek was the glimmer of a tear. A thought that had been with me all the while, and been suppressed, moved to the front of my mind. It was that we'd both be dead very soon.

". . . 'Jan Peet' / JOHN PITT, believed to be carrying a firearm. Report any sighting to the nearest organ of the National Police or Internal Security Forces or Prime Minister's Office."

Shirin was looking at her hands.

I said: "They've taken away my good name."

"Not to me."

I had ceased to be myself. I tried to think of myself as somebody to hate and fear and kill. Shirin stirred, struggled up and peered at the front pages. "Your good name, sir! Your good name! And my good name, is that nothing to you, Mr John Pitt?"

"Of course it is! It's the same. They're indivisible"

"Goddammit, kindly pay attention: 'About 1.80m, skinny, clumsy in his actions, ill-favoured, stammering, wall-eyed, sinister, unintelligent'." She turned her swimming eyes at me: "What will they say in Isfahan? That I ran away with a donkey's arse!"

Dreamily, I read the caption. I said: "Jamalzadeh."

"Of course."

"And I was nothing to him! He didn't have to do anything for me, and yet he did it, took a risk for me! And even if it holds them up just half an hour, it was worth it!"

She looked away. "Indeed, sir."

I didn't know what she meant. I tried to kiss her. She pulled away. I felt as if a sticking plaster had been ripped from a wound.

"For shame, you have not breakfasted."

"You are such a fine people, Shirin." I think I meant Mr Jamalzadeh's bravery and kindness, but I was muddled by the touch of her breast and mouth.

"Of course." She kissed my hands, sprang up and tripped to the door.

"Madame, but you . . ."

"But I, sir?"

"It doesn't mention you! It doesn't name you! It says you're dead, I killed you!"

"But you have, sir!

'Tyrant, you have wounded me a wound . . .'."

"Please, Shirin!" Her spirit was light and slippery as mercury.

She continued to smile. "You see, sir, to Mr Farameh I am dead. When he finds me, well, he'll just bury me."

She was standing by the lattice, looking down into the garden. To be precise, that was not her sole or even primary intention. She was standing there to permit the sweat, mostly mine I'm sure, to drip from her neck and shoulders; and also to display to me her naked back and legs. I sensed that in neither was she being quite polite; and that her narrow shoulders, the hank of damp hair down her back, her pearly bottom, and her long tip-toed legs, expressed an indifference to my gaze. My pride began to drain away. Liquid, used-up, scalding, smelling of rosewater, I thought: Just when I'm beginning to learn not to elbow her in the eye, or tangle my shirt-buttons in her hair, or kneel on her thigh; when I sense in her, sometimes, a momentary affection; then she starts getting contrary with me, as if she cannot tolerate any intimacy.

"May I now put on my clothes?"

I treated that as it deserved.

She peered through the lattice. "They call this place the Russian Garden. It was the nest of Russian spies till they were all sent away at the time of Mossadegh and oil. It is very convenient. The sea comes up to the wall on that side and is both shallow and stony. On the east side is an abandoned factory. I think it was used to make sugar from canes. On the west is the mosque you know about."

"What about the minaret? I mean, Does it look down into the garden?"

"Just a loudspeaker. There is no stairway up."

"How do you know?"

"I went to pray to God and, while I was praying, I could not avoid noticing that there was no door upwards."

"Thank you."

"Why thank you? I went to give thanks for our safe arrival. You see, sir, it is too dangerous to make a gift to the poor."

"Let us wait a week."

"Until New Year, sir?"

"All right, all right, until after New Year. Until people have forgotten the newspaper." I confess that the idea was pleasant to me. I thought: Look, she's never been outside Iran. She's nervous.

She sighed. "Shall I have the honour, God willing, of being presented to your mother and sisters in England?"

"No."

She turned round. "Of course, you are ashamed of me, because I am Iranian."

"On the contrary. I have no mother or sisters."

"Everybody has a mother. Even Jesus had a mother!"

"I have no mother or father."

"You are an orphan?"

"Yes."

She laughed. "And I told my family you were the eldest son of a rich and honourable Lord. Old Pitt and Young Pitt, who fought Napoleon, la-la. Even His Excellency knew of them!" She came and knelt by me. "Of course, I knew it was otherwise." She touched my face with her hand and withdrew it. "I saw that you were like the mourners for Lord Hosein in Seddeh, bleeding blood and filth and sorrow from every pore. I saw the women of Isfahan, and the fathers, too, they all wanted to take you to their houses to reassure you. I knew that before an orphan marries he first orphans his bride."

"Shirin, I have said sorry."

"O what shall we do on New Year's Day!"

My hands rested on her hair, helpless and in the way. I felt infuriated by her loneliness. I saw that a husband was really no substitute for the family and friends that she had lost.

Finally, she said: "'It is what God determines that happens'." She pulled up her shawl. "The reality is, husband, that your servant is a weak and worthless woman and cannot bring water from the bazar. In truth, she can do so, but she would need to make three journeys each day, during which intervals she cannot serve you. With your permission, we will clean the well in the orchard so that we may bring you water this evening."

"I'll do it."

"Please take your rest. 'Where there are two cooks, the soup is tasteless or too salty'."

"You must let me help you."

She turned away. "You may recollect that in our letter we submitted to your attention certain advice the Russian gentleman imparted concerning the cupboards and drawers."

"Oh my God!" I threw off the sheet. Shirin frowned.

"This work requires a man of strength and experience."

"Please show me, Shirin."

Beside the office was a garage with an old black saloon subsided on four flat tyres, and a wall covered with mechanics' tools. I had always liked working with my hands, and took down far more of everything than I could possibly need. Shirin ran on bare feet in front of me, as if to make a breeze. In the office, beneath the portraits of the Shah and Stalin, there were three steel desks with a single drawer each. As I peered at them, Shirin sat on the floor with the tools in her lap, greasing them from a can she'd brought from the bazar. The division of labour delighted me.

Inside each drawer on the right, and just visible in the clearance between the drawer and the desk-top, was a brass needle, a quarter of an inch in thickness and tapering to a point. I thought: The needle is there so that, when the drawer is pulled open, it will touch something and complete an electric circuit. In other words, the desk is booby-trapped, except that there's no electric power in this house! And no battery could still be charged after twenty-one years! I reached for the drawer handle. Shirin sucked in her breath.

Perhaps the needle is designed to pierce or break something taped to the base of the drawer. I looked down. Shirin had arranged the tools in a row for me. I picked up a pair of pincers.

I felt the warmth of her lap and her excited breath on my cheek. With both hands, I pressed the pincers against the needle. I felt a rustle of skirts. Then she sat down on my heel.

A stab of pleasure pierced me to the fingertips. The pincers rang against the needle. I froze and counted: one, two, thee, four, five. Then I turned round, blackly, and Shirin sprang off me. She backed away from me on her knees, her eyes on the pincers.

"On the death of me, it was a mistake . . ."

I couldn't stand her whine. "STOP IT!"

She lowered her head. I thought: She wants me to hit her, and then she will do something unspeakable to me.

I said: "Madame, I must concentrate now. Inside the drawer is a vial containing a material element whose name in Persian I don't know, but is called in Greek 'phosphoros'. Its special characteristic is that it can only exist as an element in water. If exposed to air, it catches fire."

I sat back, astonished by my chemical Persian.

"That is why Mr Ryazanov put it here: not to hurt anybody but to burn the papers or whatever flammable is in the drawer. If I break the glass, the breath of air into the vacuum will dry the water and then make a sheet of flame that will burn off my face and set fire to your clothes, burn your hair . . ."

"I slipped, by God, I promise . . ."

"You must permit me to do something for us, to do the hard or dangerous things that men usually do."

"As you command, sir." I could see she didn't really believe me capable of anything.

I turned back to the drawer and reached in with the pincers. My hand was shaking, not from fear, but sorrow. I thought: I'll mess it up now and lose my sight and we'll have been quarrelling. I brought out the pincers and sat down on my haunches, breathing deeply. After a while, I felt her warmth beside me, that she was very close to me, but not quite touching me; and that she would, as it were, overlook my ill-bred conduct this one time. I thought: What have I done wrong?

"There!"

I eased the drawer open. The vial was screwed down with a brass band. In it, there was a piece of phosphorus the colour and size of my teacher's chalk at the Zabankhaneh.

"May your hand not pain you, sir!" She rested her bosom on my shoulder to peer into the drawer. "Certainly, sir, you must be a surgeon, so brave and skilful are you!"

"May we be friends, Madame Shirin?"

"Will he permit me to take my leave?"

She was gone before I could speak. I detached the vial and laid it in the cotton wool. Within the drawer was an old book, badly printed, called Kashf ul Asrar, or "The Unveiling of the Secrets", from which I shook out a blizzard of winged insects; a grey file and within it, bound by a spring-release, flimsy sheets of green and pink paper, covered in Cyrillic; five passport blanks, one Polish, one Indian, and the others Soviet; and a foolscap exercise book filled with manuscript Persian, prose and verse. I thought: Mr Ryazanov will not mind me selling or bartering this stuff to get us home. I'm sure the passports and the old code-book would interest the British Embassy in Muscat.

Why is she so mischievous? I mean she's very young and all that, but it's as if she finds everything to do with me comic: sleeping together, the Savak, the newspapers, my loving her so goddam much it makes me ill, my parents, the house. I guess she's lived such a cloistered life that she cannot imagine how vindictive the world can be. Perhaps if I ran after her a little less, she might take me more seriously.

The book was perplexing. It was much less my notion of a code-book than of a work of demanding Muslim theology. It was divided up into several chapters under such headings as "Unity", "Prayer", "Effort" and other classic topics, but those were not numbered, nor were the pages. The book was not dated, but bore on the first page that same seal I'd seen on the lecture notes Mr Ryazanov had been reading in his summer house: Ruhollah Musavi. The exercise book contained several ghazals and occasional pieces and a prose essay, neatly headed *Resaleh-e Hezrat-e Vafur*, which means "The Epistle of Lord Opium", and was some sort of blasphemous satire. Its leaden whimsy depressed me. I understood that even in 1953 Mr Ryazanov was an addict and had nobody to talk to.

The other drawer presented less difficulty. It contained two identical packages wrapped in velvet and oilskin. I unwrapped one. It was a block of brilliant pink copper, engraved on one side. I looked about for a mirror, couldn't find one, or even a piece of glass, and put it down. My guess was that it was for printing money, and that Mr Ryazanov had been up to no good after the war, maybe in the puppet republics the Soviets had tried to establish in the north, around Tabriz and in Kurdistan.

I came to the last item that she had pointed out to me: a door off the hall, covered in rotten cloth. It occurred to me there might be something of real value in there. Again there were brass needles which I cut through with wire-cutters.

The room was dark, stifling and empty, but for a Shiraz rug and some pillows, all rich in colour. There weren't even spiders. I patted the cushions, and no dust came up. Baffled, I went out and saw Shirin on her knees by a tray.

"Will you eat lunch?"

"If you will, madame."

She had spread out a mat and was laying it with dishes. Vaguely, she put her hand on her heart.

"Then I will not."

She raised black eyes at me. On the mat, a plate of rice and barberries steamed. I plunged on.

"Also, I understood that is usual to kiss your husband if you have been absent from him for a time."

"You were mistaken."

She stared at me from across the carpet. I could see she was angry, perhaps more angry than she had ever been, but she presented only surprise: that I of all people should ever think to cross her.

I wanted to fight with her, but was timid. I became facetious.

"'A woman who has been contracted permanently must surrender herself to any wish that her husband seeks and must not prevent him from having his wish without a religious excuse'."

"'A Muslim woman cannot be contracted to an unbeliever'."

I looked away, but there was nothing to look at, and so I turned back to her.

She gestured hopelessly at the food she'd bought. "Eat your lunch, sir." There was panic in her voice.

I ate my lunch. It looked beautiful, and tasted mild and clean. "You cook well, Mme Shirin."

"Of course."

She was angry. She had shown me something of her nature and regretted it. I thought: She doesn't trust me an inch. She thinks if she gives an inch I'll take a mile. She won't make the same mistake again.

"May I tell you a story?" she said.

"Please."

"In Isfahan, in the time of Shah Abbas, a glassmaker came to the town with his wares in two paniers each side of a donkey. At the customs post at the Khaju bridge, the officer shouted: 'What's in here, man?' and slapped with his cane on the right-hand panier. 'Do that on the other side, Your Honour,' said the fellow, 'and there'll be nothing.'"

"I do not understand the point of that story, ma'am."

"I'm sorry, sir."

"You don't have to fight with me. I'm not your father, Shirin."

"No, indeed, sir."

"May I for my part show you something, Shirin?"

She sighed. "I've seen it already."

"No! Something else. A secret room."

I opened the door for her and bowed. She looked around without great interest. I said: "It is a room from which no sound can escape. I suppose Mr Ryazanov built it so he could talk with his agents without being heard."

She revived. "So nothing can be heard outside? How admirable."

I didn't know what that meant.

"I'll show you," I said. "Please go outside a moment."

I shut the door and said what was in my mind. I came out, saw her face, and regretted it.

"How dare you!"

"I'm sorry, I thought nothing could be heard!"

"Even so! You are not to speak English ever! You must forget you ever knew a word of English or French! Do you understand, Pitt?"

"Please forgive me. I did not know you could hear."

She drooped. She was too hot to be angry. She shook her skirt out. My mouth went dry.

"I suppose that meant you want us to sleep together."

The walls seemed to be closing in on me. I thought: There is absolutely nothing to stop us doing what we please in this room, or anywhere in this house. It belongs to us. We are like squatters in the ruins of an ancient town, like the tribespeople who camp at Persepolis. The world of power and affairs and ambition and peril means nothing to us, for our concern is only with each other. I looked in her face as if by pure thought I could shrivel or scorch the dress off her. "Yes, please, ma'am."

She pulled her dress over her head. With her arm across her breast, she backed towards the cushions. I seemed to feel every filament of the wool beneath me, the scent of pomegranates and water from the dish, her musky hair. I followed her like a hungry cat. She knelt down. I tried to kiss her, but she turned her face and I had a mouthful of hair. I fought with my new shirt.

She unpicked my fingers from the buttons and whispered: "This room is convenient."

"But it is not soundproof!"

"It is. I know what you say before you say it."

When I woke, I searched for her in the garden. She was standing, bent double at the waist, beside the water pump beside the tank. She was rubbing her stomach as if it pained her. She straightened and placed both hands, and then all her weight, on the pump handle. She sprang and came down on her stomach. It gave and then whipped back, sending her flying. I ran to her, but she struck me away. Her big eyes were utterly dazed. She was breathing as if through a straw.

I lifted her skirt to her breast. A deep graze spread out in a bruise as far as her ribs. I fought the temptation to kiss it. I picked her up in my arms and walked towards the house. She fought me. As I climbed the steps, she closed her eyes; but not from her pain, or not just, but from the opposite. I saw in horror that she had never been carried, never been permitted the luxury of weakness, never been sick or exhausted, never been loved. Her pleasure ran through my arms and liquefied my heart. I felt my strength running away. I pulled at her skirt and buried my head in her lap.

She bit my arm, yanked a fistful of my hair. Something glittered in the tail of my eye. I dropped her on her feet and jumped back. In her hand was a sickle. She stood trembling with her back to the filing-cabinet.

I said: "I would be grateful, madame, if you ceased to threaten your husband with sharp implements."

"We would be relieved if you ceased to treat us like your whore."

"You are my wife! How can you be a whore?"

"You are our husband, and yet you are a pimp."

"I love you!"

"What do you know of love, except cunt and kebab?"

That's less inelegant in Persian.

I said: "You must lie down. That is a bad injury. I will attend to you."

"Go to Hell."

She turned and ran from the room.

The screws holding the pump handle were rusted. My soft hands were in weeping blisters before I had them apart, could polish and put ghee on the moving pieces, recut the stripped threads on the screws. I held imaginary conversations with Shirin.

I heard a ring and shiver of glass. She placed a tin tray of coffee and water on the edge of the tank, withdrew, and sat down on the step, her chador over her hair and half her face, eyes on the tray.

Ah, coffee, madame!

Yes. Coffee.

It was like a dream, in which one could speak without speaking. I flexed my back, shook the sweat out of my eyes, stretched, shook my stinging, rusty hands. After labour, refreshment!

I smiled sweetly: I understand that coffee was a speciality of your mother's family.

How well informed you are. To be precise, it was a speciality of the haramsarai or women's quarters, of the royal palace in Tehran in the last century. It was made only for very special purposes. I believe the ominous phrase "Persian Coffee" was current even in England.

You are right, madame. May I taste it?

Taste it, and may it take your soul to heaven.

I took the glass and made an exaggerated sip. It was very good: strong and sweet and strange from some spice she'd put in it, cardamom maybe. I think all Iranian women, and all but a very few Iranian men, understand the kitchen so that was natural. It is good.

Of course.

I sat down heavily on the tank. I shook my head to clear the sparkle from my eyes. Shirin half rose, sank back and, as I slid to the floor, ran towards me.

I feel . . .

"What? What do you feel?"

I . . .

"What?"

The coffee . . .

She grabbed the glass and drained it.

I closed my eyes. She tugged at my shirt, fumbled for the glass of water, dashed it across my cheeks. She put her mouth on mine, blew into my lungs. I thought: Can I get away with it? I closed my arms across her back.

She sprang back.

I shook the garden dust off me.

Kiss?

"I'll burn in Hell first."

She turned her back on me and sat down on the step. I went back to the pump, thinking: This has ceased to be a game. She cannot bear me after all. She came for reasons that I don't know about, to do with Turani, maybe. Goddammit, why did I promise not to ask her about Turani?

It took me an eternity to recut the threads and reassemble the pump. Shirin's idleness infuriated me. I pressed down on the handle.

There was a dry rasp and I felt movement beneath my feet. I turned and smiled. She threw up her hair, clicked her tongue against her teeth, looked away. Cow.

The light was turning to rose, but I began work on the pump chamber, tried to loosen the plate on the top. A rage had taken hold of me, beyond reason and balance and control, compounded of the pain in my palms and the Third World, this ancient Communist pump and the flakes of rust in my cuts and the sweat in my eyes and a Persian girl that I love, really love, as nobody ever loved a girl, but can't get on with. I sensed them suddenly all together in the half-light. I smelled her scent above the scents of vegetation, dust and sweat.

Take your rest. It is growing dark.

Please let me finish, ma'am. I need to grease the spindle. It is very important. You don't understand.

As you wish.

She sat back down on the step.

In my fury, the plate cracked under the screwdriver. I pulled clear the brittle semi-circles and squinted into depths. I saw two points of greasy light. A wet and fetid smell came up to meet me. I thought, O God, it's booby-trapped, too, and the lights hissed at me, a scalding liquid seared my cheek and lips, the snake was rigid as a stick, suspended on its tail in air, head arching back, it's going to bite me in the neck, I'm dead, I'm dead.

Metal flashed at my throat. Hot liquid splashed my neck. The snake coiled round the sickle, slipped, lost its strength or life, flew towards the palm trunks. Shirin spun her chador round her hand and plunged it into the pump chamber, pulled out a hissing coil, but my sight was going, must have been the venom in my eyes, she was grinding something under both heels. She jumped down on the pump, and it came, my God, a rasp of water, and then a stream, and I plunged my face under the pipe, tried to rub and scrub my sight back.

She shimmered before me. Her face was white and haloed as a full moon in winter. We've done it, Shirin! A bit of grease and it's silent.

Her hand flew back and she struck me on the cheek. I held both her wrists; and when she kicked me in the knees and thighs, trying to get my balls, the bitch, I picked her up and held her fast until she became slack in my arms. I carried her to the step and just managed to put her down, then stumbled to the house. I was utterly mystified. Why did she save my life, if it was only to kill me? I suppose she won't come in. She'll just walk out through the gate. I can't do anything about it now. I can't do anything about anything. I'm going to sick up my belly and shit out my guts, again and again and again.

I woke and she was putting a pillow under my head. A little later, she was sponging my eyes, face, chest, groin. The smell of vomit made me spin. "I thought . . ."

"Sss."

". . . I thought that we would have our own special LP, and kiss on windy street-corners, and sit together at lectures where I'd put my hand up the back of your blouse, or at pub corner-tables where I'd put my foot between your knees, and hitch-hike to open-air concerts in hay fields and wake in strange beds to tall windows and fog and your warm hair and an infinity of plough . . ."

"Be quiet, you donkey! I do not understand foreign languages."

❖ 11 ❖

Shirin Farameh had a liking for routine. The day began in the sugar light of dawn, with the slap, slap, slap of water in a tin jug, the pad of her bare feet on the coral, the click of a razor against a leather strap.

I resisted.

She sat back on her haunches. "He does not trust us."

"He does not trust you."

She tested the razor against her sunny wrist. "We are very skilful."

"Even so."

She leaned forward over me, lifted up my chin with a thumb, wet my face with the back of her fingers. "I must."

"You must not!"

She began to soap my face. "The truth is, Pitt, that at present you resemble Lord Curzon. You will not take one step into the lane without the children of the quarter running after you and crying, 'Here comes the Frank, the Frank from the newspaper!' all the way to the harbour. Unless, if you permit it . . ." She sat back on her heels and put her wet hand to her mouth. "Unless, with your permission, we dress you as a girl."

"Don't!"

"We will make you very beautiful."

"I absolutely forbid you . . ."

"He forbids us . . ."

"Excuse me. Please don't ever suggest such a thing again!"

She took my chin in her fingers. "Therefore, I will make you an Iranian boy. An Iranian of the third class. Crew-cut. Moustache. Cloth cap. Baggy trousers. Who walks along the street, not as you do, slowly, glancing from side to side as if you own it, but eyes down, hurrying, fleeing from cats and grannies."

"Whatever the Secretary of State for War commands."

That vulgar phrase, which Mo'in had used of his saintly wife, had entered our relations. The first time I'd attempted it, I braced myself for a slap, but when I opened my eyes, Shirin was smiling at the wall. It had not occurred to me that I might amuse her; or that my definition of her, as what in English might be termed bad-tempered or quarrelsome, might correspond to something in her notion of herself.

The razor slid down my cheek. She *was* skilful; and she smelled so delicious of roses and baked bread, that I closed my eyes.

"You are Ali Jan, Mrs Zahra's baby son, on the run from military service. You've had the call-up papers, but mama's heart-sore for her little boy, who doesn't cross the boulevard alone, and has sent you down to sister's husband's cousin's uncle's in Bushehr, which is, as everybody knows, so hot and pious that nobody goes out. Stop that! My hand will slip and you will bleed to death."

I stopped it.

"Sir?"

"Mm?"

"May we speak?"

"Mm."

"You are a Muslim."

"I am learning."

"God willing."

With the razor she sculpted the back of my jaw.

"Sir?"

"Mm?"

"In our privacy . . ."

That was one of her euphemisms.

116

". . . I could not avoid becoming conscious of something about you."

"Ah!"

"Keep still, you donkey's prick! Now, as is well known, that something is contrary to religion. Keep still!"

"NEVER!"

"Please permit us to do it for you. It will not pain you. We are very …"

I threw out my arms, but she was up on her heels, the razor flashing above her head, her white teeth glittering in her mouth.

"Shirin, I absolutely forbid you to ever raise the subject again!"

"Divorce me."

"Don't swear."

Meekly, she shut the razor in her hand. I thought: We could not be kissing now if the razor were open; so that by the closing of her fingers, and the click of the blade, and by what went before, step by step by step, she creates not merely her routine but its disruption. She had been brought up in the bosom of tradition, in which she did what other women did, and although she had thrown that tradition to the wind, she could not quite abolish the cast of mind, and so created obligations for herself and me from pure caprice. I kept imagining her as a woman in the house, with moods and habits and things in their own places, like my foster-mother; with a stewing samovar and pots and rolled up bedding, and son's graduation photograph askew on the wall, and a piece of calligraphy on tasselled velvet and a garage calendar of the Ka'aba in Mecca and grandfather's X-rays from Tehran. In truth, we had no *things*, only Mr Ryazanov's and the clothes she had made for us. Afterwards, she moved in the interstices of blazing light, busy with something, every part of her outraged by my clumsy kisses. From the garden, I heard the crash of falling branches. At those times, my head filled with her family and Turani and all my fears.

"Do you love me, madame?"

"You don't beat or sodomise one. What more can a poor woman expect of this putrid world?"

"But you find me handsome and amiable?"

"Let me bring your breakfast."

And as she passed, she whispered:

"'A pretty face, and a dress of gold brocade,
    Rose attar, aloe-wood, scent and colour of yearning;
    Those are the ornaments of women.
    But a man, well, it's just his . . .'"

The last word was lost on the stairs.

As I ate my bread and honey, and drank sweet tea, in the alcove where she'd spread a mat, she read to me from *Ettala'at*, first the Iranian stories, then the foreign; and with the newspaper held erect and at arm's length as if it were of great value, she looked like one of those professional readers you see outside the Central Post Office in Isfahan, but transfigured in age and sex; and I thought: Iran's not just Britain with salt deserts and an absolute monarchy and a script that goes from right to left, picturesque and benighted, but the utter confounding and destruction of everything I was taught was good and right.

Because Shirin Farameh had never been abroad, and because Persian words have neither capitals nor vowels, she often mispronounced the names of foreign cities – Vashanton, Sanjapur, Junev – and when I corrected her, as I thought I should, she looked at me evilly. Today, I corrected her pronunciation of the word "hang-glider" and talked about recreation in the West till she became impatient to go to the garden.

While she was out, I worked at my books, or rather at Mr Ryazanov's, on the Shiraz carpet in the balcony room with the filing cabinets. That, too, had been her idea.

"But you must!"

"What's the point? I can't go to university. I'm a murderer."

"Not to me." She sighed. "It is my duty to educate you. In our religion and culture, if you know something, you are as required to teach it as you are required to give water to the thirsty."

She came back white with coral-dust, carrying a pile of books to her chin. Above them, her face was transformed by black bazar spectacles. She flushed. I think she meant to whip them off, but her hands were full. She took refuge in the schoolmistress.

"In the name of God, the Merciful, the Compassionate," she mumbled. "I have brought the *Divan* of Anvari. I believe that you should begin with these early masters, from the sixth century, for otherwise you will find it difficult to comprehend the masters of the classical period, the seventh and eighth centuries, notably Sa'adi, as to form on the one hand and content on the other."

She knelt beside me. "The Persian lyric poets may be divided into five classes." She took off her spectacles and put them out of sight. "Those classes are: poor, average, good, excellent and sublime. Anvari belong to the excellent category."

"Which category does Mr Ryazanov belong in?" Her propinquity made it hard to concentrate.

"Mr Ryazanov's verses are very, very average." She blushed at her own severity. "However, you must remember that Persian was not his native tongue. And that he did not live to full . . . " She had her hands to her forehead. "He was, he was a sympathetic man!"

"Sss, Shirin. Please, my life, don't cry. Nobody is allowed to cry."

"Yes, sir."

The lesson was not a success. Each ghazal we came to, she would spring up and trip about the room, reciting it in her precise voice. It was as if she found print intolerable for fear it might impair her memory.

"Heavens, Shirin, how many couplets do you know off by heart?"

"None. Very few. Only ten thousand. Perhaps fifteen thousand."
I digested that.

"You learned fifteen thousand couplets at school?"

"At school? Why at school? Grandfather. Grandfather had the best library in Iran. I mean after Shah, the shrine at Mashad and Mr Qasim Ghani. At the summer pasture."

"Where are the books now?" I did not think Farameh was a reader of verse.

She touched her breast. "Here. And soon . . . " She came towards me on her knees and pressed her bosom against my chest. I could feel, beneath her sharp nipple, a slowly beating heart. "And soon, God willing, they will be here," she pressed against my chest, "in your heart as well."

That was the end of that lesson, and of all lessons. I bent to the poems, to violent or masochistic imagery, severe and monotonous rhymes, and then would find myself on the blinding balcony, squinting into the trees, till I found her, re-laying the tiles on her knees from a palette of home-made cement, or shinning up a curved bole, a sickle in her mouth, her skirt tied in a knot at her white hips. I could make out the garden's architecture. The worst of the palm trees she'd cleared and stacked by the kitchen shed to burn in the stove she cooked on. The snakes had gone, much to her regret, because they had been succeeded by rats; but those, too, we seemed to have on the run.

"What are those?"

She had brought back from the bazar rose-cuttings planted in rusted ghee-tins.

"That one is called *Gloire d'Ispahan*. And that one has another name. And that one is called something else." Her hands were covered in earth. "Mr John, the nomenclature is not in the least important."

"But we won't be here to see them."

"God willing."

"And it's not our garden!"

"'The Garden Belongs to the Cultivator'."

That was the slogan of the Land Reform that had ruined her mother's family.

"Also, sir, do you know whom I mean by the Zoroastrians?"

"I am not wholly ignorant."

"Well, you will know they believe that the universe is in a sort of equilibrium between opposing spirits, one good, one bad. That struggle is the force that runs through history. The good will be victorious, but human beings are required to tender assistance, which they do by good actions, not associating with women at certain times, please note, and by cultivating the earth, for it is only in uncultivated earth that the bad spirit can set up residence. Now, if you will excuse me . . ."

She turned towards the trees.

"I hate to ask this: Madame Shirin, will you cover your face when you go to the bazar?"

She stopped and turned. "Well said, sir!

'A veiled woman is a candle for the house,
While a flirt is a dreadful calamity'."

"Please be serious, Shirin. I mean it."

"You mean it? You mean it? How dare you!"

"Look a boy might see you in the bazar or lane, and follow you back here, and then it's the end of us."

"Why would a boy want to follow us?"

"Shirin, please!"

"Only plain girls go about veiled."

"That's unkind."

She sighed. "The veil is against the law, as you well know."

"Even here."

"Not so much as in Isfahan, but still against the law."

I gave up. I said : "Whatever the High Command decides."

She dropped her basket and stood in front of me. "You must trust us. We stand between you and death as timber stands between the sailor and the water. Have we ever failed you?"

"That's what I don't like."

"Of course." She turned for the trees. And as she went, I heard her mutter more of her infuriating poem:

> "'And if she shows her face, strip her naked
> And beat her till she cries aloud'."

Next day, she came back from the bazar with some black satinet, which she cut into a sort of dust-coat, tight at the throat and wrists, baggy elsewhere; and a shawl which she hemmed with a repellent nylon lace. It covered everything but her eyes. Black stockings and, for some reason, white shoes made up the outfit. As she stumbled across the garden to the gate, I saw her scoop up some dust to scrub her forehead and hands. I don't know what role she was playing to herself, but it looked to me like the adolescent wife of the neighbourhood boss, a bleeding throat on tottering wedge heels; best examine the pavement or bury yourself in a newspaper till she's passed.

"Sir, the butcher is very witty."

"I'm glad, ma'am."

"Oh, you are so unintelligent!"

"What! Was the bastard rude to you?"

"No! Gholam Ali Kassab is witty with all the ladies."

"Can't you go to another butcher?"

"Sir, Iranian butchers without exception are witty."

"Oh, it's too hot to eat mutton anyway. Don't you think, ma'am?"

"At your service, sir."

We now ate lunch together. Shirin was too obstinate to recognise any alteration, so we ate from the same Gardner dish and drank from the same Bohemian glass, which no doubt was a fault in point of hygiene, but I was too relieved to mind: whatever it was that disgusted her about eating in public – and I'd heard of young girls like that in Britain – it troubled her less now. After lunch, she brought coffee and flirted with me, or I think that's what she did. If she was forever coming into the room, had left her scissors on the table, fanned herself with her dress or pushed her hair out of her forehead or rubbed mercurochrome into a cut on her ankle or picked out palm splinters by window light; or if I heard her muttering to herself, "The bridegroom will go to sleep and then what will become of poor us? O Lord, why must you give to the jackal the sweetest grapes?"; if, each time I looked up, Shirin was appearing or vanishing in a doorway, then I saw that I was being invited to make my wishes known; or rather my duty, for, when one afternoon I thought to tease her, to make as if to restart my books, she gave me a look that said "Don't even consider it", and I fell into the routine. In truth, that was for me the best time of day, for she would sleep beside me for fifteen minutes of the stewing afternoon, without her clothes or a sheet, white and wet and scalding to the touch, and in postures that I had never seen reproduced even in European paintings: with her head stretched one way and her legs another, or on her back with arms and legs thrown wide across the carpet, or rolled up into a prickly cylinder. From the garden came the rustle and clatter of decay.

At such times, I could barely recognise myself. I had never imagined that a life that consisted exclusively of reading verse and making love could bring such understanding of the world and its inhabitants. I thought: Bedford University never had a student like me.

"You are so clumsy! You come to love as a village molla to his rice!"

She was washing in a basin on the carpet. Her splashing and sighing and grumbling, which I found offensive and hurtful, had a ritual character. I suppose its purpose was to cleanse herself not just of me, but of her own loss of independence. I thought at first that she found love-making a little indecent and disapproved of sexual affections; but, as in so much with this girl, it was not so simple.

"Why is it bad for women?"

"Because it weakens women and that is bad."

"And why is it good for men?"

"Because it weakens men. And that is good."

She found any discussion so disagreeable that I never got to the matter of contraception, which word anyway I did not know in Persian. That, like the boat to Muscat, was somehow none of my business, and anyway was in hand. Our love had no antecedents. Within minutes, our relations had reverted to their customary formality; and each day was the story of an acquaintanceship between persons of divergent character and experience. I had expected that we would become friends; or rather she would become the sister I never had or – if I had – never knew; and I could play the brother I never was or couldn't be. I did not know that I must woo her anew each day, and she me: that we were in a perpetual Isfahan in Favardin.

She dressed.

> "'Love seemed at first such a simple thing
> But now is full of pitfalls.
> The inky night and the waves and the dreadful whirlpool!
> How can they know our plight.
> Those careless watchers on the shore?'"

"You do know how to swim, ma'am?"

"Sir, it is what is called a metaphor."

"But do you know how to swim?"

It occurred to me that she might be frightened of boats.

"Of course."

I had learned by now that she hated to admit any incapacity; and that truthfulness was not among her particular virtues.

I said: "Please tell me, truthfully, madame, if you know how to swim."

"How can we know, being a girl!"

"I will teach you."

She looked at me with her look that meant: How can you teach anybody anything? She said:

"Where?"

"In the tank."

"But that is our drinking water!"

"So don't pee in it, madame."

"Don't be vulgar."

On the edge of the tank, she lost her nerve. I gestured to her to take off her dress, but she shook her head. I got into the warm water and handed her down. I thought that if she aimed for the diagonal corner, she could get in two or three strokes. I showed her how to put her head low in the water.

At the first attempt, she merely sank, with her black dress billowing like a balloon around her. She coughed, spat out water and looked blackly at me. I took the hems of her dress and lifted it off her.

"Chin down! Bum up!"

I was enjoying being a teacher again. Her face seemed to say: Your fate is already sealed.

She bent double to conceal her modesty and then, kicking hard against the wall of the tank, glided to the other corner. Gasping, she rested a moment and then returned. I made a gesture of congratulation, but she waved at me to go away and set off back.

I returned in half an hour. She was swimming along the sides of the tank. She went round and round and round. In the water, she was the colour of ivory. I thought: It is impossible not only for me to be more happy than I am now, but for any man to be more happy. She pulled herself up and crouched, without her dress, on the wall.

After that, she swam every day, sometimes often; but she always wore her dress, unless it was night and I was swimming with her.

There was no electric power and she said we could not use candles. The first nights, the moon was big, and we ate supper by the arcade over the garden. She had made herself a shirt and trousers of white Kerman gauze, which left nothing to the imagination; or rather seemed to send it scurrying down mysterious avenues of cloth and shadow and moonlight. As the moon ebbed, often she wore nothing at all.

"I very much regret that I cannot dance and sing."

"You dance? And sing?"

"Why not? I am your wife. However, we must be quiet."

So we leaned against bolsters and ate pistachio nuts and sweets, and talked, or did fortunes from Hafez or played old-fashioned French card games, one called *bazique* and one called *kanasta*, at which she was impatient and unable to lose; watched the moon fall into the sea; or she told stories or explained poems, and I drank juices of strange fruits – mulberries, unripe grapes – or from a bottle of pre-war vodka that she had found in the garage. At fleeting moments, I felt secure: as if Isfahan was a dream from which I'd awakened into this. Then she would wash and pray, and bring a sheet and pillows and we'd sleep wherever we were.

As the nights grew blacker, I learned something of Shirin's history. The year the Shah's father seized power, 1925, her family owned 172 villages in the country around Khomein, north of Isfahan. Grandfather was, she said, a progressive landlord, relatively speaking, built hard-top roads and maintained the irrigation channels, provided seed and tools to his share-croppers free of charge or interest, was the first landowner in the country to introduce American tractors. The crops were wheat, barley, rice, pulses, cotton, tobacco, oil seeds, melons and roses. The fame of the estate and its prosperity attracted the envy of Reza Shah. Rather than lose it to confiscation, grandfather handed over three-quarters of the acreage to the tenants. His enlightenment extended even to his family: his only surviving child, a daughter, Iran, Shirin's mum, was a Girl Guide and in the first intake of girls at Tehran University after the Unveiling Act.

In 1953, grandfather was active in the nationalist interest, was elected to the Majlis and was for a short time Minister of Agriculture under Mossadeq. With the return of the Shah from exile in Rome, grandfather was fortunate to escape into private life. Shirin, who was born in 1957 or 1958, spent each summer at what she called the summer pasture, which must have been some kind of country house, with her grandmother, who was the daughter of one of the share-croppers. (When the two of them took the government bus to Isfahan, the conductor ejected all the male passengers and made no stops.) In 1962, as part of the comprehensive land reform, the estate was confiscated, the summer pasture was burned by Savak agents, and grandfather was imprisoned in the Qasr in Tehran, where he died, officially of a heart attack, the next year. Grandmother stood for the Majlis in the election of 1963, and was returned, but was forbidden to take her seat on the grounds of her illiteracy. She died in 1970.

Shirin told the story without comment or regret, sitting quite still on her haunches in the darkness.

"But how can you bear to be here? That goddam, murdering bastard of a jumped-up Pahlavi . . ."

She clapped her hand on my mouth.

"Be quiet, donkey. You know nothing about anything."

"But your father?"

"My father, sir?"

"Couldn't he protect the family? I thought he was the Shah's friend."

She sighed. "No doubt, that was the plan. No doubt, Mr Farameh did what he could."

"But your family is still rich!"

"Oh yes. Mr Farameh, in conjunction with Mr Khatami, bought the land on which the Shah decided to build the helicopter section."

"Oh God."

"O God indeed." She came towards me on her knees. "Every kran that we have stolen from this country we will have to pay back. I and now you, unfortunate one."

Her family vanished into legend. The estate went back into the last century, when it was given by Fath Ali Shah to a girl from the Caucasus, captured in the Shirvan war of the 1820s. She was known as Qatilat as Saltaneh, "Slayer of the Monarchy", though whether her title came from her beauty or her ill-nature or her avarice or all three, Shirin was not sure. When she took the air in the streets of Tehran, grooms with sticks ran ahead of her litter and beat the lounging men until they turned their faces to the wall. She was passionate about hunting, wore a cavalry captain's uniform and boots, tied her veil round her forehead and rewarded the huntsmen who found her game from a velvet bag of Russian Imperials.

Her tyranny in the haramkhanah ended with a cup of coffee. She had borne two children to Fath Ali Shah, Amin ul Mulk, who studied at the Military Academy at St Petersburg, was received by Queen Victoria at Windsor Castle, and was killed in the Crimea in the winter of 1855; and a daughter, Fatemeh Azizeh, Shirin's great grand-mother. Fatemeh was reputed to have six fingers on her left hand. An Englishwoman called Feeta or Veeta Sackvil, who stayed with her when she must have been over eighty, described her in a letter to her husband, as "haughty, tall, ugly as sin, incomprehensible in six languages, never without a foul water pipe, rather sweet in a Persian way. As to the fingers, well, she wears silk gloves (none too clean), so one couldn't check." Her only son, Nasir ul Mulk, grandfather, was educated by American protestant missionaries in Tehran and early had a reputation as a traditional poet; but he was mauled in an exchange of verses with Nima Yushij in the pages of *Bahar* in, Shirin thought, 1933 and did not publish again. That autumn, riding home with his friends from a wedding in Isfahan, unused to French champagne, they saw a girl in a straw hat cutting rice in the gloaming, and they bawled extempore poems at her from the causeway till it was dark, the horses became tangled in their harnesses and they got lost. The next day at dawn, grandfather retraced his steps alone and got down from his horse and held the stirrup for the girl till she stopped work at sundown and brought him two hands full of water. That was grandmother.

As to my own history, Shirin found it ridiculous.

"Why?"

"I am not a good student."

"I will make you a good student."

"It's not that, Shirin, it's just that, in Britain, I couldn't concentrate. I could see no reason to do one thing rather than another. It – "

"Of course. England regrets its wicked past, but cannot yet select its future."

"I was good at mechanics and at sports, madame. Football, cricket . . ."

"Be serious!"

She saw I was offended.

"May I enquire, sir, why you learned Persian?"

"Oh, I don't know. I . . ."

". . . You wanted to be a spy!"

"Oh no, Shirin, not you as well! I am not, nor will ever be, a spy."

"Yes, sir."

"I wanted to be a hippie."

"A hippie! God take me to Him for I am married to a foolish man of the third class!"

I gave up.

"May we tell you a story?"

"Please."

She swung back on her heels, which was her posture for stories. She recited: "Through the famous city of Isfahan there flows a river. It rises in the mountain to the left of the city and expires in the desert to the right. If a river can be said to have a purpose, this one's is not to unite itself with the waters that englobe the inhabited earth but, as it were, to make possible a beautiful city: to make gardens of melons and quinces and fountains in the public squares, to wet the pavements of mosques and seminaries and run down channels by the thoroughfares in which Mercedes buses are forever breaking their axles and to be spanned by five bridges, their piers sinking into a fathomless antiquity. That is why the Isfahanians call it the Zendeh Rud, the "Life River". Its subsidiary purpose is to flow through your memory, bathing you in an insufferable regret.

"The river carries on its surface traces of an earlier existence, and may indeed exist to submerge them, like the plane leaves it carries down in autumn or the pieces of its burst spring dwelling. Let us now try to assemble that earlier existence, which is conducted on a smaller scale, in cold weather, under poor light. It is a boy squatting on the bank of a stream in England. In his hand is a toy of some description, let us say a motor boat of painted tin, brand new, made in Hong Kong, and he wants to see if the motor will hold against the current that runs under the acacia trees along the village street; or rather, to examine a secret fear, that he does not recognise, but is none the less his permanent companion: that something of his can be lost. He places the boat in the stream, lets go, stands up. For a moment, the boat holds its nose in the stream but then it turns and races away under the bridges and the boy is running after it and crying till it passes under the highway at the end of the village, where the dogs congregate to fight, and out of the boy's world.

"It is then, as he stands in tears before the station of the Jandarmerie, that the boy unbinds his imagination. He has heard of London and the sea; and for many years, at night as he rolls out his bed after his foster-father has comforted him, or on feverish mornings when the wind wafts in the scent of jonquils and the bickering of the pariah kites through the basement window, he imagines his boat on strange waters. It is at those times that the boy sets out on his journey, which will take him from there, which is England, to here, which is Iran; and all the while, he believes he will see his boat again, if only at that instant when his eyelids close for the last time, between the eye and the eyelid, his boat, jammed against a willow root at the foot of a damp garden or ploughing through tall seas, its red propeller still turning.

"You were that boy of three and four, and now you are a man of eighteen. You have found what you lost: not the boat – of course not, for that was, merely a toy – but what it substantiated. You see, this story has a happy ending. By God, it has a happy ending. And so farewell."

❈ 12 ❈

The next morning, I lay in. It had been my habit, as I woke, to move across to where she'd slept. I knew I was lazy and love-sick and risking our lives by not leaving Iran, but the hot linen smelt so sweet of geraniums in the sunshine. Through my closed eyelids, I summoned memories of yesterday afternoon as she passed into shade or white sun, muttering to herself like a crone:

"But what will the foolish bridegroom say? O God! That's the problem:

> 'Love seemed at first so simple,
> But now it's all over the place'."

I was listening for the distant click of the garden door. I recognised that every morning, as I lay in bed, I had an anxiety about her, which I cherished for it was merely the preliminary of the sound of the door and her flickering shadow in the trees; but, even as I lost myself in fantastic dreams of happiness and masculinity, so my anxiety grew until I found myself upright and dressing. I decided to make my own tea, as I had done before I met her.

In the sweltering kitchen, I found the fire had not been laid. On the step beneath the door was the steel bowl and knife that she used to prepare fruit and vegetables, squatting on her haunches, sleeves pulled up to the shoulder. On the rim of the tank was the cake of green soap she'd used to wash the clothes last night. Inside the house, the shade teemed like a headache. Pushing open a door, I had a picture of her reserved from some blazing afternoon, vivid and dishevelled and impudent and hot, so that I became more impatient than ever for her return.

"She's not coming back from the bazar."

I was thirsty. In each room, Shirin had placed porous jars of water that evaporated to keep both water and room cool. Each jar was empty. I walked behind the kitchen where two coral crocks, set one above the other, centuries old, filtered the tank water for drinking. I went past her wood-stack and ash heap and drying green, places where, if ever bored with the poets, I disturbed her, she hissed me away. Today, they seemed lifeless. Through the black glare of my sunstroke, the garden felt gritty and untended.

"She is not coming back."

Fear and loss made a tornado of the hot garden. I grabbed at little thoughts, that she'd gone further afield to shop or her bus broken down; but they were like sticks, caught, spun and submerged in the torrent of my fear. I thought that the Savakis had taken her, were coming for me too, were already on their way, and I must run or fight because I was too frightened to be captured. I ran to the jeep, parked in its dust by the steel gate, checked the gas and water cans, and then bent at the knee in uncertainty: what if she were merely delayed, and came back to find me and our vehicle gone? I had my gun with me, picked up the little paring knife from the step, took down the biggest adjustable spanner from the garage wall.

Behind the arcade outside the upstairs room, I stood in the hot shade, eyes on the gate. I estimated that if they came in through the garden gate, I could drop down through the window to the sea, and by the time they were up there, I'd be a head in the water, half-way out of sight. I breathed in and I breathed out.

I had no watch and there was no clock in the house: Shirin woke at dawn because, she said, she had always woken at dawn. In my mind's eye, I tried to construct the bazar of Bushehr from her description: low streets in colonial rectangles, contraband tea from India and electrical junk from Dubai, witty butchers among the carcases of flayed mutton, rope-makers, sellers of car batteries and vulcanised tyres, any number of reasons for delay.

"She is not coming back because she does not want to."

My head fizzed. I recognised, for the first time that I could articulate, that that was the sensation of madness. My nature simply could not accommodate her going and was about to blow like an overloaded electrical appliance; would, as it were, suicide to prevent itself dying. I recognised it because it was the companion of my life, sometimes forgotten or outstripped on the road, but always catching up by sundown. My mind twisted this way and that, sought some other reconciliation of events that would yet leave my pride and personality whole, that would keep me from the conclusion that leered at me: that the girl I was so crazy for couldn't give a toss about me, had gone off laughing and left me with only what I brought, which is an old-fashioned six-gun and a single round taped to the butt.

"I need a drink."

In the kitchen, there was still rice in the sack and so I lit the fire and cooked myself some. I burned myself and the pan. Everything I did was clumsy and messy as if I had fallen out of the habit of providing for myself. I found the vodka and carried it back with me to my post by the arcade above the garden.

I had respected her privacy; or, to be honest with myself, I was so grateful to her for her sweetness that I would do nothing to cross her. I suspected that she was deceitful, that she concealed the truth as a principle or habit, but that seemed to me the unavoidable counterpart of the veil; for if you don't trust a woman she will do something untrustworthy. Had she, in truth, not cared for me, needed me only to escape from a marriage she didn't want in Isfahan and my purpose was now served? I saw what I knew all along, and dared not examine: that by giving my word to her that early morning in the desert, I conspired in my own delusion; that she had to escape from Turani, it did not matter how; and I, a silly Englishman who, as everybody knows, are ruled by their pricks, take pride in their slavery to women and shower them with every indulgence, fitted the bill. I saw suddenly, with the eyes of an Iranian, my shambling figure turning into her street in Isfahan Abbasabad, vulnerable and spoiled, and knew that I must have seemed a game not worth the candle. She spoke the truth that night, though I was too love-sick to understand her: one kiss was all that was needed.

I took a gulp of vodka and my world went through one of its periodic reversals. I saw again Mr Ryazanov at his garden gate, felt on my hot face the breath of wind filtered through the fluttering plane-trees, in my throat the rasp of vodka, the soreness in my head, a mirage of cold water; but over Mr Ryazanov's shoulder is not a man in an Air Force uniform but a black chador, which fills me with an inexplicable grief.

"This life will destroy you, mamzil."

The girl says nothing.

"Mamzil, you must marry."

The girl says nothing.

"Is there somebody she cares for?"

The girl says nothing.

"Would mamzil accept the English boy?"

The girl says nothing.

"She should be aware he is a Christian."

The girl says nothing.

"Good, leave it to your servant, I shall investigate him, may I give my life for you, farewell."

So, as I knew all along, I was not the chief actor in this drama; but a mere instrument of change in a situation made brittle by violence, treachery and the veil; and he never loved me, why should he, when he had her to love? Chîrîn, le flambeau qui illumina la terre. And that's what killed him, poor faithful man. I suppose he had long ago stopped believing in Communism and the Soviet Union, but something kept him going: why not a girl who scratched on his garden door and drew secret messages out of her sleeves? Well, she is gone now, to Tehran I imagine, where a single woman can make her way in the world.

> "You came so late and then so early flew away
> You lit a fire and then like smoke you blew away . . ."

I wish I had not met her. Had I not met her, I would not know of happiness and would not miss it; could have got through my life in Britain, quietly, and without leaving a trace; would not be here; and would not have to go.

I capped the vodka. The action was reflexive; but as I turned the cap, I saw my muddled intentions. In the depths of my nature, I hoped she might return tonight, and I did not want to be drunk; and also I believed that I was altered, that I had somehow outgrown my self-pity and that if she, a Persian woman, could display such careless-ness and independence then how much more so a British man. I was stepping across the room, and with each crossing, I enumerated not what I'd lost but what I'd gained. I'd come safe from Isfahan, hidden for five whole weeks, learned more in that time than I'd have learned elsewhere in years, and not just conversational Persian, so that I would not die as a child. She needed her freedom, but she had done me more good than harm.

It is now too late to leave. I will get everything ready tomorrow, and leave at about eleven, not so late that there will be nobody about and the bakers and petrol pumps closed, but late enough for every-body to be sleepy. I will buy bread and gasoline on the Shiraz road and then, at a spot where I can see no lights behind or in front, turn right, to the east, towards Pakistan.

She will not leave Iran! At last, you understand, you British donkey! There is something about this country that she cannot leave; not merely her family, but something to do with the language or the customs or the feel of Iran that she cannot do without. She made that as clear as day, and yet I went on and on, and each time I mentioned the dhow to Bahrain or going to the British Embassy, I hastened her departure. Had I had the smallest understanding, woken if only for an instant from my reverie of Persian kisses, thought for a moment about her character and wishes, I'd have known what damage I was doing. The thoughts were so mortifying that I sat down, picked up yesterday's newspaper, held it to the moonlight, put it down again. Ah, of course, Gen. Khatami.

"What is hanjlaidar?"

"Hanjlaidar?"

"I will read another story. 'Prices of meat, vegetable fats and other essential . . .'"

"It is a little like a parachute. It consists of wings, attached to the shoulder. Another pronunciation is 'hangleider'. It permits a person to fly, or glide, in the wind "

"Why?"

"For pleasure."

"For pleasure? To fly in the wind?"

"Yes. It has many adherents in the United States."

"Certainly, sir, you are well-informed about all branches of human activity. 'Prices of meat, vegetable fats . . .' Tell me also, world-travelled one, what is inflation?"

I could read the splash headline by the moonlight. H.I.M. DECLARES DAY OF MOURNING FOR HOUSEHOLD MEMBER. 'ARCHITECT OF IMPERIAL AIR DEFENCES' KILLED IN ACCIDENT AT DEZFUL DAM. AIR FORCE C-IN-C, A KEEN SPORTSMAN, DIES IN SMALL AERO-PLANE CALLED HANG-GLIDER.

So, her father is on his way up. Not that it makes much difference to us how many stars Farameh wears on his epaulettes: he's still out to get us. For the life of me I cannot see why that could have caused her to leave.

The sound of traffic was diminishing. I went out into the garden to compose myself for five minutes before setting off, to bid farewell to Mr Ryazanov and the ghost of my wife. Somebody was seated in the middle of the path, a sack of dusty black, reeking of plastic, fag ash and diesel. She looked as if she had been seated there for some time.

"Thanks be to God!"

I stepped towards her, but she made no gesture to accommodate me. My joy stuck in my throat. I pointed to the house, so we might talk. She made no move.

"Sir, we have caused you trouble."

Her voice in the garden sounded like a bomb. Fear gone, joy gone, that left only rage.

"Have you been faithful to me?"

"Let me cease to trouble you." She got up, put up her veil. She could barely stand.

"You are not divorced, madame. You will answer my question."

"And you'll wake up tomorrow with your head on the pillow beside you."

"I will take that as No."

"You may take it as you like to Hell."

"I am extremely angry with you, madame, for going away without telling me your destination. I suffered great anxiety for you."

"But not for your belly and your honourable prick."

"Please come inside, Shirin. You seem tired. I will make you some supper."

"Lay a finger on me and I swear by God I'll cut your throat."

"Naturally. Now please take my hand and come to the house."

I led her up the path and into the kitchen. I brought her a bowl of yoghurt, and lit the fire for tea. She sat, head bowed, at the table. Her fingernails were dirty.

"I trust that your mother and sister are well."

"God willing. I have no information."

So where in hell has she been?

"Has His Excellency divorced Madame Your Mother?"

"Of course."

"And gone to Tehran and married the widow?"

"How can I know?"

"Please be aware, Shirin, that should you wish to bring Madame Your Mother and sister to this house and then beyond the water, I shall welcome them."

She shivered in impatience. At length, she said: "May I give my life for you."

She looked miserable beyond description.

"Please lie down now and take your rest. I have made up a bed for you."

"Your supper . . ."

"Please do as I ask." She went to bed without washing. She was asleep before I'd done the covers. She was asleep when I came in later, though she stirred in fury when I kissed her on the back; and she was asleep when the muezzin woke me, and I rose and prayed and made myself tea and went to my books.

The light was going out of the sky when she came in. Her hair was wet. She smelt of bazar soap. She knelt down beside me. She looked me in the eye.

"You may punish me."

I said: "Shirin, I won't question you about your journey. Only I would like to know why you are sad, so that I may comfort you."

"I am sad, sir, I am very sad because I am married to a slow Englishman who does not welcome his young wife after a separation."

"You said you'd cut my throat if I did!"

"I was not sincere. And, anyway, husband, were it not worth the risk?"

**

The next day, as we knelt down to lunch, I saw on the mat a bottle of Shiraz wine, uncorked, and dripping with condensation.

"Is it your birthday, Shirin?"

"Drink," she said and poured me a cup, holding the bottle in her palm and bending at the waist as in an Isfahanian painting.

The wine was golden in colour and tasted of dried clover.

"Won't you have some with me?"

She poured me another cup, then put her finger in it and touched her tongue. She laughed: "When you divorce me, I'll drink wine every day." She straightened and held the cup against my lips. She whispered:

"'Give me a fine wine to drink, that was old when Adam was
        created,
    A wine that was when nothing was but heaven and earth,
    That watched Time grow up, reach maturity and then become
        decrepit
    While it distilled to pure Spirit, freed at long last from
        contingency'."

"Wait a moment, Shirin. What's this all for?"

"Drink, sir. I'll tell you when you're drunk."

"I'm drunk already." I reached for her waist, but she swung away from me.

"After you're drunk. Let it be nectar to you:

    'The man drunk with wine wakes up at midnight
    The man drunk with the Cupbearer wakes up on Resurrection
        Day'."

The wine tasted of her. The afternoon light on the walls and rugs took on a heathen splendour. Her hair was an aura of light.

"Sir, you may be aware that each month a woman . . ."

O my God.

"... is in such a condition that she does not go out. I mean ...
I mean ... You understand perfectly what I mean!"

"You're pregnant!"

She beamed uncertainly. "Thanks be to the God."

Oh, you fool! That was why she came with you from Isfahan!
She was pregnant!

"We have, I believe, madame, been married six weeks."

Her face went black as night, and just as suddenly lightened.

"For you, sir, that is abundantly ample time. You would make
even your hand pregnant."

I could not speak.

"You appear to me not especially happy to be a father. That is
unnatural."

"If I am the father ..."

She made a violent effort at self-control. "You are the father, John
Pitt, as will be proved to you."

What could I say? I had no power in the matter. If I disbelieved
her, she would simply leave, as she had done before. I suppose I could
murder her, but I did not think that was my style.

"God bless you, Shirin. I am happy and thankful."

"We must make some provisions."

"Don't worry for a moment, a single moment. British doctors are
very good. Maybe the best in the world."

"I am glad, John. However, there are no English doctors in
Bushehr and though there may be such persons elsewhere, for
example in Tehran or at the military hospitals in the districts, that is
no help to us."

"What do you mean?"

"I mean what I say. I'm speaking Persian."

"But we're going to England!"

"You may go to England. But I refuse to travel while pregnant,
or if the child is born, until it is six months of age. The child will be
born, God willing, in this house."

My world caved in again. She had a look on her face such as I'd never seen before. It was as if she were in a corner, preparing to defend herself and her baby, as if she did not want to treat me as an enemy, but would do so if required. For the first time, I hated everything about her.

"Of course, if he wishes to put at risk the lives of his bride and daughter by sea and land . . ."

"You don't know it's a daughter." I couldn't concentrate. A homesickness for England, and for my solitude, and lack of attachment, surged in me to the brim. My eyes filled with tears.

"On the contrary, God willing."

"Are you happy, Shirin, for me to remain a prisoner here in this inferno of a house for another goddam year?"

"Fourteen months, to be exact. Eight add six. If necessary, sir, yes, I am happy."

"You don't care about my studies!"

"I am a better teacher than English professors. Also I think English professors do not sleep with their students morning, evening and night."

"You said in Isfahan you wanted to be free! Is this your idea of freedom?"

She looked away. "Every woman, sir, dreams of imprisoning a man. Every Iranian dreams of imprisoning an Englishman. Only I, of all the women of Iran, have enjoyed this double satisfaction."

"How can you be so nasty?"

"Were the situation reversed, that is, if you had imprisoned me, sir, it would excite no comment or rebuke."

"Good. I see. This was your plan from the beginning. Very clever."

She stiffened. I caught a glimpse of another Shirin: affectionate, faithful, doing her poor best. She was opening and closing her fingers, as if she wanted to reach out for me, but dared not. Then she put her face in her shawl.

"For God's sake, Shirin, pull yourself together!" She's done it again. She knows she's gone too far this time. She's trying another tactic.

She said: "It is to be expected that a boy who has received no kindness in his life will be himself unkind. However, I did not know."

Her face was wet with tears. I felt her nature reaching out, past her tears and the formality of her speech, to some essential part of me. Don't fall for it, mate!

"Forgive me, Shirin. It is merely that this life is hard for a man."

Weakling!

"Dear sir, it is precisely because you are so manly, because there is nothing weak or womanly in you, that you can tolerate such an existence. And I will make it sweet for you! I will serve you as no wife ever served a man. I will be more obedient to you than ever, more obedient than a corpse in the hands of the washer. I will cook you delicious foods, such as you have in England, all the sweetest foods and . . . and . . ."

Her imagination failed her; or rather, I think, became suddenly overfull. I did not believe a word of it. I had the sensation that I'd had once, on a train from London to Folkestone, when my pocket was picked: a sense of loss and irremedial foolishness.

"I'm not a man. A man is more than just a person who loves a woman, Shirin. A man serves his family and country and his friends, suffers for them, goes into battle and comes through it in one piece, helps his children when they go adrift . . ."

She clapped her hand over my mouth. "God forbid!" she said. Then she smiled as a woman of the world might smile. "Ladies are not greatly interested in those aspects of manliness."

❄ 13 ❄

After that, Shirin grew quickly, as if I had somehow been needed to authorise a process of nature. Having had no experience of women, I was fascinated by femininity; and it delighted me to witness the changes in her, the alterations in her shape and scent, the taste of milk on her breast, the faint line on her belly, the dryness of her hair and cheek, the dimples in her bottom, even her snoring (of which, for the moment, thank God, she was not aware).

I have said she was tall, but her grace was such that she never seemed large. Now, her bosom and her short-sight conspired to rob her of her balance. She was forever tripping on rugs, or bumping into me in the narrow door-frames or sliding on the stairs or treading in a dish on the floor or banging her head. She herself never complained of sickness or tiredness, or rather she had exhausted such words on the sensations of love: sick meant love-sick, tired meant satisfied, happy, replete. She was too proud to be other than well.

I thought often about her pride. She generally referred to herself as "we" or "us". That is polite Persian, for the self is insignificant, the wishes and opinions of the single "I" and "me" beneath consideration. It is also the Persian of the court and of the street and between the three, the oh-so-humble "we" and the royal "we" and the street-smart "we", her meaning reverberated down a darkling enfilade.

> The common man does not become noble
> from proximity to the great:

> The string does not become precious
> from being strung with pearls.

Whence did she, a girl of seventeen, derive her measureless arrogance? From her face, no doubt, but there was no mirror in the house. She wore ugly spectacles and no make-up and her clothes alternated from a black sack in the day to the diaphanous trousers of the evening. From her money? She'd left it in Isfahan. From her family? What, the late offspring of a lateral line of a royal family that had mulcted the country and long been dead of inanition when it was mercifully deposed? From her education? A jumble of languages she was doing her utmost to forget, the rudiments of accountancy and a few thousand indecent verses from her grandfather's library? Her liberty? Yes, perhaps that's what it was: she had burst the bounds of her femininity (of which I saw only the outside, as a passer-by sees only the walls and guard-towers of a prison) to be where she wanted to be.

I thought her irony, which was never far from her, even at those moments when I most needed her to be straightforward, was a gesture to her private self, to show that all this business of love and kisses was but a performance, from which, once completed according to contract or duty, she would return to herself.

> Master and mistress were at it all day long,
> From first light of dawn to blackest midnight,
> The Devil put his finger to his lip
> And the river ran back uphill.

I sensed that this irony, or ambiguity, or whatever it was, was a natural recourse for her as both a woman and a Persian; that it was, in truth, an accommodation to a history that was unkind or indifferent and anyway had gone on far too long; and that if she were ever to say, "Yes, this is what I want more than anything, I want you to know that"; well, that would be revolutionary.

Yet as the days and nights passed, and she settled into her pregnancy, her performance underwent an alteration. I ceased to be her doltish foreign husband, over whose shoulder, as it were, she would cast a glance, but a part of her complicit audience. The word "audience" is not quite correct, for it conjures a public performance such as a play or a concert: her performance was private and personal. The secret promise to herself, that her soul was kept intact from any taint of her activity, became a promise to me that I would find her as she was before. It is as if she had forgotten who or what it was all for. Sometimes, indeed, her whole manner would slip, and I would find her absently combing my hair in her lap, or standing staring through the window of the scorching kitchen, or lying with her eyes closed in the pool; and, when I kissed her warm hand, she'd turn, face burning with confusion.

"Do you love me, Shirin?"

"I believe, sir, you should take less interest in your wife's opinions."

"But are you glad you came with me?"

"Do you know the story of the old woman and the thread? It was the time that Joseph came to be auctioned, and all the ladies of Egypt were there, and the bidding opened and the old woman squawked: 'I bid this thread.' The auctioneer looked down and said, 'Come now, old woman, nobody will take that thread for this incomparable youth.' 'No matter,' said the old woman, 'at least the world will know that I was not content with my lot and that I tried.'"

Sometimes, indeed, I sensed her personality come off, item by item. Indifference and irony, deceit for the sake of it, duty, habit, caution, vanity, kindness slid down and dropped in a heap, till she stood before me in a sort of purity of spirit, tremulous, savage, white as paper. At such times, I lost my bearings in the world. Barbarian, implacably wilful, shameless, she seemed to be running somewhere, dragging me by the hands, as once in her house in Isfahan (which was, I now see, the promise of our intimacy had I but had the wit to have recognised it); she was stranger than I had ever believed possible: womanly, I suppose.

A coarseness had come into her speech. She, who had always spoken so beautifully, who would recite a quatrain of Khayyam and Mahasti so that I remembered it as sung, now talked like a barber's apprentice from Rasht. Persian sanctions all sorts of word-changes that sounded to me infantile. She aspirated every consonant, every vowel became a whine. Kerman became "Chermoon", Isfahan became "Esfoon", Tehran "Terroon", and even my name became "Joon", her voice rising in a plaintive screech. Once she stormed in from the garden, dripping with sweat and irritation, and spat out: "Kindly tell me, Pitt, where you put the dog-begotten divorce-me-three-times pick-axe?" She had taken to drinking her tea from the saucer, a disgraceful habit. I suppose the onset of her pregnancy had revived memories of some woman's world of which I could barely guess. Her education and her manners were no longer of any use or interest to her; and she was joining the main stream of Iranian women who have babies, over and over again. I thought that my beautiful Shirin, willow and gazelle, was gone, she'd never regain her figure, would take to sweets and cigarettes and dirty stories, or become a real, proper Persian lady, pious and severe.

"Dear sir, I have brought you a book to read."

It was called Advice to Newly-Weds, by Dr Reza Tabari, of the Medical College of Tehran University, and Hojjatulislam Ali Nabavi, lecturer in canon law at the seminary in Qom.

I was offended. "Am I so ignorant . . ."

Shirin looked down. "I am sure you will derive some instruction from the opening chapters. However, we wished to draw your attention to the later sections, notably the chapter entitled: 'The Blessed Event.'"

"Shirin, if you think I'm delivering any babies, you . . ."

"Excuse me, John. You must." She took my hands. "The Department has issued its Order. Now what you must always have in your mind is that it is more important for me to live than for our daughter to live. For if I die, she too will die, but if she dies, then, God willing, in the future . . ." She had a look of fathomless self-pity.

"I can't, Shirin."

"We have no choice. Or rather, there is another possibility, but it will not be welcome to you."

We sat in silence for a while.

"All right, what is it?"

"There is a lady here, in Bushehr, an expert and practised midwife, of good family, punctilious in her religious observances, refined in her manners, discreet in her conversation. Her name is Bibi Agha. It is possible she could come to the house. But it would be dangerous for her to see you."

"So I must hide again."

A look of pain crossed her face. "I have hinted to her that my husband is a merchant, wholesaler in cotton piece goods from India, importing through Bandar Abbas, and that he is now on business in that town. Perhaps, when she comes, we could impose on you to stay in the silent room. We will try to make it comfortable for you."

"What choice have I?"

"None whatever, sir. I am deeply sorry."

"And how much does this paragon charge for her services?"

"Nothing. Very little. One hundred tomans and expenses." That is, £8 and expenses.

"What expenses?"

"I believe that her wages are worth it. Unless, of course, you . . ."

"What expenses, Shirin?"

"Just a little opium. Two, perhaps five, sticks."

"I thought you said she was refined!"

"Madame Bibi is *very* refined! And also, occasionally, she smokes opium, for her rheumatism."

"Whatever Her Excellency the Minister decides, Shirin."

"Thank you, sir."

"What is this?"

She had something round her neck.

"Sss. Finish what you have started."

"How can I, my darling, with this thing round your neck?"

"It is a charm for childbirth."

"Oh for heaven's sake! That goddam woman's such a bad influence."

"You hold your tongue."

Everything Shirin said now had a minimum of two meanings.

"But what is it?"

"We call it in Persian: a necklace of rubies."

"Why?"

"Because it is an ornament for the neck and bust made from rubies, which are a kind of pebble, red in colour, glassy in form. They are very lucky. Now, shut your gob! You are supposed to love me as a husband, not interrogate me as an examining magistrate. Or perhaps I am too large for you?"

"Never!"

The moon was full again. She stood under the arcade. The stones around her neck flashed blood and moonlight at me.

"God above! They really are rubies!"

"Surely, sir, your wits are quite as sharp as your other vital organs."

"So that's why you went away! To bring the necklace!"

"I believe, Mr Pitt, that I heard you promise not to enquire about the purpose of my short journey. Are we to take it that your promises are meaningless?"

"No, absolutely not. Forgive me."

She knelt down and poured out some tamarind juice.

"May we tell you a story?"

I took the drink from in front of my face. "Please."

"Once upon a time, there was an Englishman, whose name was John Pitt."

Here we go again!

"He was a man black in heart, without culture or religion, violent, avaricious and cold."

"Shirin!"

"He was Lord of Landandirri. In those days, the English were expanding their power in India and this Pitt, Lord Landandirri, worked his way into the confidence of Tipu Sultan and extracted from him, at an insulting price, a ruby the size of a bitter orange. This Pitt, Lord Landandirri, returned to Europe, and carried the ruby round the royal courts, offering it to the Régent of France and the King of Poland and the famous Mr Law and the Prince of Saxe and the Tsar of Rus and who knows who, but none would buy it; for it had a fault in it, and none dared put it out for cutting, lest it shiver into a million million pieces.

"In despair of his money and desire, Pitt, Lord Landandirri, came to Iran, where at that time Karim Khan Zand was defending his kingdom of Fars against Agha Mohammed Qajar. Karim Khan Zand received Pitt at his camp in Bushehr, but he wanted money and soldiers and cannon, not a jewel for his aigrette, and so Pitt travelled to Tehran and sold it for one million tomans to the Qajar, who gave it to the heir apparent, Fath Ali Qajar, who gave it to Qatilat as Sultaneh after a night in her lap, who gave it to her son, Amin ul Mulk, who took it with him to Europe; where at Anvers, in the government of Holland, he found a Jewish boy of twelve thirteen years of age, who had never touched coffee or tobacco or wine (which is miraculous for I've heard the Dutch are inordinately fond of those products); and Amin put straw down in the streets and cloth round those church bells that wake the dead and hushed the chatter of the Dutchmen in their coffeehouses all one afternoon and night; and with God's help the boy cut it into a cabochon the size of a greengage plum, which you see here on this fat chest of mine and forty cushion-jewels for the rope round this gallows neck. Amin kissed the boy and rewarded him and took the necklace to London where he gave it to a girl who threw it on the ground; whence it was picked up by Lord Curzon, who loved Amin and sent it in a warship to great-grandmother, which was honourable and pious for a Christian and an Englishman, and she gave it to grandmother who gave it to me and I give it to you as my dowry and so farewell."

"I took you, my darling, without a dowry."

"Well, then, with your permission, I shall retain the necklace and wear it sometimes to gladden your heart."

"Who was the girl? The English girl Amin loved?"

"Tomorrow. It is time to sleep."

As it turned out, Shirin wore the necklace all the time, and it became as much a part of her as everything else. I was forever catching my hair in the chain between the stones. I suppose it was just another piece of armour against me, but more ingratiating than her dress or knife. She had brought something else from her journey, an old photograph of Amin, coloured by hand. It had been taken in the studio of a man named Nadar in Paris in 1853. In it, Amin is seated by a table covered with a rug, a vase of yellow tulips and a silver frame containing some calligraphy, which, try as I might, I could not read and Shirin refused to, saying it was none of my business. Also a present for me, a Russian-Persian dictionary.

It was now midsummer. It broke my heart to see her, standing in the garden, hands on hips, fighting the pain in her back. I found a rotten canvas hammock in the garage, and rigged it up between two trees, and made her lie there while I fanned her with the fan she'd woven of palm leaves and used to get the fire started each morning. She lay in prickles of hot sunlight, her gaze turned in on herself, in some inaccessible depth of maternity.

I heard a scratch at the gate.

Shirin blinked. "Aha," she beamed. "My sister in gossip. If he could kindly . . ."

She got up heavily and padded for the gate, while I hurried up to the sound-proof room – or "Bandar Abbas", as she called it – to stew in pools of sweat and samovar steam and stare at Sa'adi and the gelim. Every now and then, I'd open the door for a change of air and hear from the kitchen a coarse guffaw. A little later, Shirin would come in, flustered and anxious about me, and on her cheeks the faint blush of their hilarity.

"If that yellow Fatemeh makes a junkie out of you, I swear by God I'll kill her."

She lost her smile. "Poor boy," she said.

"What on earth were you doing?"

She smiled in recollection. "Spells."

"Shirin!"

"Will you fast, sir?"

Ramadan was two weeks away. It was our bad luck that it should fall this year in August. "Whatever you say, ma'am."

"It is not for a poor woman to say."

"Would it please you if I fasted?"

"It would please us very much, sir."

"But what about you, ma'am? It can't be good for you to fast, in your condition!"

"Alas, sir, a pregnant woman does not fast. However, I will display self-control in drinking water in front of you in the hottest part of the day. And at sundown, after you have prayed, I shall look after you. You seem unhappy, sir! That is not right."

"No, ma'am."

"I believe, dear sir, to abstain from food and sexual congress for the hours of daylight for twenty-eight days will help you to learn some self-control, of which you were not noticeably blessed by the Almighty."

"Yes, ma'am."

It happened on the afternoon of New Year's Day. As I stood by the green door to the quiet room, the silence seemed to be deeper than usual. Then I heard a small, tight scream, just as soon muffled, and the chittering of Bibi Agha. I put on Mr Ryazanov's suit and cap and walked smartly into the bedroom.

An old woman shrieked and put her polka-dot chador to her mouth. Her cheeks, beneath pats of sickly rouge, were yellow with superstitious fear. Beyond her, Shirin glowed with sweat and pain.

"Am I in time, madame? I have come with all despatch from Bandar Abbas."

"For shame, my lord, you are not welcome here with us. You will bring bad . . ."

"Be quiet, you disgusting old witch."

I knelt by Shirin. Her face glimmered in the dusk. It was as if she was sweating light and rose water. Her hand moved on the sheet and then stopped. At length, she said: "Welcome, husband. God willing your business trip was prosperous?"

"Thanks be to God."

Bibi Agha handed me a glass of tea and a sugar lump. I followed her to the window bay.

"God take me to my death now, sir. They, Their Ladyships . . ."

"Get on with it."

"They are too small. It were better you take them to the hospital."

"Can you cut her, madame?"

"She will die, God forbid!"

"If she dies, you die, you superannuated whore."

Bibi Agha giggled.

A spasm rolled through Shirin, head to toe. She was bolt upright, staring into her pain.

"I have brought shears and thread, God take me to His mercy."

"Are they sterile?"

I grabbed her hands and turned up her palms. They were cracked with henna and dirt.

"I have a primus and iodine. By God, the pain will kill her, and you will answer to Him."

I didn't know the Persian for anaesthetic.

"Kindly make us up a pipe of the Remedy."

Bibi Agha's scowl cracked in pleasure. "Bah, bah! The Remedy!"

I knelt down again. "My darling, Bibi Agha is going to cut you, so the baby's head can come out. I will give you a pipe of opium to diminish the pain."

Bibi Agha took an immense draw on the pipe – to get it properly lit, mind – and solemnly extended it to me. Shirin knocked it flying with her arm. Sparks climbed up the mosquito netting, caught, flared, unfurled in a sheet of flame. I tore the curtain down and quenched it with my chest and hands.

"Go away, husband!"

I turned. I was burned on my palms. My eyes were blind with flame. Through patches of darkness, I saw Shirin was pleading with me: that she had business at some other place, could not now attend to me, must go there now, was going, had gone. I felt terrified and superfluous. I stepped back to the door arch.

Bibi Agha was turning her shears in the gas flame. "In the name of God, the Merciful, the Compassionate . . ."

Shirin lifted her knees. I turned away.

"Are you certain it is necessary to cut her, old woman?"

". . . Lord of the Two Worlds. Now push, pretty . . ."

"By God!"

I closed my eyes.

"Ya'allah!"

Please, only this, only this matters, and You can have the rest . . .

"Ya'allah . . ."

The bed burst like a balloon of blood. In it, in the midst of the blood, something was wriggling that hadn't been there before, that didn't belong with Shirin or the bed or the blood or Bibi Agha, but was of itself, living, independent, coughing in a voice that had no sound. I was weeping.

"God is very great!"

Sobbing and keening, Bibi Agha cut the chord, and tied it, and wiped the creature's mouth and eyes, snapped something to the neck.

"Oh, the misfortune, the misfortune, sir. It is a little girl!"

I took the package from her, wrapped tight in white linen. Its face was red, with highlights of yellow in the cheeks, blond eyebrows, silky blond hair. It was very, very sleepy. Bibi Agha had put a blue bead on a thong about her throat, against the Eye. My tears splashed on my daughter's cheeks and made her start. I kissed her sweet-smelling hair.

"Oh you'll bring such sorrow to your father, my darling. You'll make his hair turn white with shame."

"Husband, please, please . . ."

Shirin was opening and closing her fingers. Her skin was translucent with pain and light. The midwife was grumbling over the afterbirth. I knelt down.

"O my wife, I am proud of you."

"Please . . ."

She put the baby to her breast. She closed her eyes, and then opened them at me. "I think she will be very plain, husband, and slow-witted, I am sorry."

"She has a squint," I said, "and will, I'm afraid, be small and clumsy. It is God's will."

"She is albino," Bibi Agha said. She had a curved needle in her teeth which jerked as she tittered. "She is not long for this earth. It was God's will."

"Poor little unhappy creature," said Shirin. The child was fast asleep at her breast. "She is not long for this wretched world."

* *

I walked with Bibi Agha under the trees. It was midnight. At the gate, she clicked her teeth at the banknote I held.

"Whatever you think, my lord."

"Good, then. Goodnight, Bibi Agha. Please don't trouble to return."

"Whatever Your Grace thinks right. It was very dangerous, sir. Eighteen centimetres of nylon. And people will ask me what I was doing, and the name of the family, and the registration of the birth and, what will we say, poor . . ."

I reached down and squeezed her fat bottom.

"Shame on you, Prince! With your poor lady lying half-dead indoors!" She shifted her legs a fraction the better to accommodate me.

"Madame?"

She hissed with pleasure.

"How do you imagine, Madame Bibi, that I came here from Bandar Abbas?"

She started. I gripped her more tightly.

"So that I arrived exactly at the opportune moment?"

She pulled away from me, but I would not let go. She was wobbling with fear.

"Don't be frightened, Bibi Agha." I stroked her softly on the inner leg. "I will take you home now. I am familiar with your district of town."

I opened the gate, and patted her through. The smell of dust and petrol made me swoon.

"Have mercy on me, poor woman that I am . . ."

I pulled her back into the garden, put my head close to hers, bit her ear. She stank of opium and pissy linen. I whispered: "You can gossip as softly as this, but I shall hear you. You can double-bar your street-door, but I can pass through doors. You can run away to Maku or Mashad and I will fly there after you."

I unravelled a banknote before her eyes, then rolled it up and stuffed it in her mouth. I opened the garden door. She scuttled away.

⁂

"You are a vicious bully. Poor Bibi! She was my friend!"

Shirin was too exhausted to be angry. I was walking up and down in the window, with the sleeping child in my arms.

"I also gave her another hundred."

"You did what!"

She was sitting bolt upright, face scrubbed, hair tied, in a fresh nightgown.

"I took it from your pen-case. I thought . . ."

"You thought! You thought! You gave her a second hundred toman note!"

"Yes, Shirin."

"Oh, sir, you don't know what you've done. Why did you have to interfere?"

"I needed to keep her mouth shut, Shirin."

"Of course. Forgive me. I am tired."

❈ 14 ❈

After the child's birth, Shirin let herself go. At sundown each evening, after she'd bathed in the tank and watered the orchard and pavement, she would sit down on the edge of the tank and smoke a Russian cigarette down to its cardboard filter. I had learned by now not to disturb her at such times, where she communicated with herself, embodied by the papperosse as other beautiful women enjoy their mirrors or their photograph albums or their jewels.

The garden gleamed. My world smelled of wet dust. I thought, as I watched her through the tracery, or between the arcade as I settled the child in my arms, that water was her extravagance, the incarnation of a generous nature under a mysterious restraint. The garden was to her not exercise or recreation, nor even the reward of a rose in a place where there had not been a rose, but the counterpart of her nature, of which I stumbled to grasp the elements. I saw this garden was but an expression of her privacy to which I alone had been admitted. The wet black trees and glistening paths and blocks of troubled shade vibrated with a perilous femininity. Then she came out from her reverie, tipped the embers of the cigarette into the flower-bed, stood up and took the filter into the house to return a moment later with the supper mat.

At first, Shirin was reluctant to give the little girl a name. I had come to partake of my wife's superstition; or rather to believe that, other things being equal, and anyway unknown, what reason was there to draw attention to our happiness beyond the necessary. A week passed and I began to sense that something was not quite right: that my wife had been knocked a few degrees off balance by her ordeal, and I must touch her, gently, like a watchmaker, to set her upright.

"My foster-mother was called Dilys."

Shirin shook herself awake. She said: "My sister is called Layly."

So Layly it was. Five minutes later, it seemed our daughter had always had that name and there'd been no other Layly in history. *Layly and Majnun* now seemed to me the greatest imposition on our privacy, and that Majnun better watch his step, for now he had me to contend with. I sensed it was a good name, for Shirin had watched her sister grow, had all but brought her up; and the baby restored to her some part of her lost Isfahan. As for me, I could not recognise myself. Holding Layly or changing her clothes or running with her to the sound-proof room when she was colicky, I seemed to be supplying her with something I had not had. My grievance with the world, which I thought must be eternal and would be handed to my posterity like some Olympic torch, would end with me, thank God, was ending now in this overpowering good fortune. Shirin and I did not talk much, and only about the child.

Shirin Farameh was strong. She regained her shape in a matter of days. I cut her stitches and her wound closed up. Whenever she could, wherever she was, she slept. In just days, I became aware of a rhythm to life, as if daughter matched mother in love her of routine. Yet sometimes I'd come on Shirin, sitting quite still in the darkness or standing under the trees, as if crippled by a spasm of pain, and I felt that she was troubled about something. I began to miss our old times very much, but did not wish to add to her duties; and thought, in moments of grandiloquence, that she must come to me as much as I to her.

"Who is Ruhollah al Musavi, Shirin?"

"Who, my moon-faced one?"

Shirin had lost all interest in the world beyond the gate. The Shah's announcement of the abolition of the political parties, or rather their amalgamation into one, called the Restakhiz or Restoration Party, which was in the newspaper that morning and I had hoped might be the basis for some conversation other than Layly's digestion, had not attracted her.

"A gentleman by the name of Ruhollah al Musavi. I am reading a book of Mr Ryazanov's. It is called — "

"Excuse me, John. He is a learned man, an enemy of the Shah and of all my family."

"Was he an agent of Mr Ryazanov?"

"God, no! He is an agent of no man, unless of the Lord of Time."

"Why is he your family's enemy?"

Here was something of the old Shirin.

"The Shah cast him into exile at the time of the Land Reform. He was teaching in Qom at that time, and had a great following of students. His people live in Khomein. Earlier, at the time of the Constitutional Revolution, when all the old quarrels were fought again, there was a dispute between two villages about water and his father was killed by a stone: Mr Khomeini blamed grandfather, because he blamed all landlords. I would therefore ask you, John, to keep out of his way."

"Where is this Mr Khomeini?"

She shifted Layly to her other arm. "In Najaf, in Iraq."

"Well, so there's nothing to worry about."

"No, sir."

She had her back to me, washing her arms in a basin. She was trembling in pure shock. She was frightened of her power over me. I desperately needed to touch her, to be sure that she was unchanged by what had happened.

"You are kind to me, Shirin."

"Of course. It is my duty."

"Are you sure?"

She was trembling, savage, white, slippery with sweat.

"Yes, I am sure." She did not look round, or try to dress. She said: "You do not think very much, John. I suppose it is not necessary for an Englishman to think, any more than it is necessary for an Englishman to pray. For that reason, your servant must think and pray not just for her poor self, but for the entire family. Our life in this garden cannot go on for ever. We will be separated, or some other misfortune will befall us. Your servant is a mere woman. When you order me to kiss you, I obey, and the pleasure it gives me arises chiefly but not exclusively in my obedience. For I believe and hope that out of those kisses you might remember one kiss. Or you might remember this doorway, and then my face in the doorway, the rustle of my skirt and chador, the taste of fresh herbs and buttermilk from a cold steel cup, the warmth of my bust and neck in the morning, the scent of roses from the orchard, the damp of my lap. Each one is a thread that ties us – or rather, though these threads must snap under the pressure of separation yet still there will be one intact – and you will coil it up around your wrist and make your way back to your poor bride and wretched child."

"I will never be separated from you, Shirin."

"We are relying on that, sir."

"What will happen, Shirin?"

"What can I say? How can I know?"

"I mean, in Iran. Will the Communists take over?"

"You asked me once about my ancestor, Amin ul Mulk, and the story of his broken heart. May I tell you now?"

"Please."

"You heard how he was in London."

"Yes."

"There was in the company that evening a young girl, the

most beautiful of the girls of England. Her name was Karulin and her father's name was Pitt, castellan of Landandirri." Her voice had attained a rhythm, as if she were speaking verse, but not in a metre I had ever heard. "Now when Amin ul Mulk saw Karulin Pitt, he was wounded to the recesses of his heart. Her black eyes and musky hair, her dainty foot as she tripped in the dance, her noble blood and her father's riches, her sweetness and gaiety robbed him of his native land and his religion. He prostrated himself before her, like a Hindu before an idol, like a prisoner before the executioner."

"Please stop, Shirin."

"Through the intervention of his bosom friend, Lord Curzon, he sought to be presented to the sprite; and in his robe-of-honour and turban, and wearing the Order of the Lion and Sun, bought with his wounds at Askhabad, he looked into the executioner's eyes and died."

"Please stop it!"

"The executioner laughed as if pearls were dancing on a necklace, and raised her sword. 'Dansent-ils la mazurka, Altesse?'"

I stopped my ears. Shirin unpicked my hands.

"And so they danced, Christian and Believer, executioner and victim. His robe swirled like the skirt of a dervish of Konya, and laughter fluttered to the chandeliers like pigeons to the rafters at a gunshot.

"Then up sprang from his place Lord Curzon and called out in his rage, He'd fight with steel or ball any man who spurned his friend.

"'Be still, my dear. What profit is there fighting for a corpse?' So spoke the prince and bowed and left the hall, and took a kalashkeh to Victoria, and Paris and Istanbul; and fought at Karabagh and Baku; until one day, at Sebastopol, in service to the King of Rus, what English eyes had started an English mortar finished. And as for Mees Karulin, through short days under cloudy skies she prospered in her debris of hearts. And so fare – "

"That's not true!"

"You, sir, naturally, know the story much better."

She stood up.

"No! Shirin, I mean, forgive me, she went to the Crimea! In '55! With Miss Nightingale."

"Naturally, with Mamzil Bulbul." She stepped towards the door.

"With the English nurses."

"Why not?"

"Caroline Pitt was a pioneer of photography. She made a famous panorama of the works at Sebastopol."

Shirin stopped. "A panorama."

"It's where you take a succession of photographs and join them together to give a complete picture."

"Of the battlements."

"I saw it! It's in the Imperial War Museum in Lambeth."

"Lambeth," she said to herself. "Not Lambas."

"And then, after the war, she didn't go home. She took a house at Bebek above the Bosphorus. People thought it very strange, an English lady, still young, of good family, living alone among all those Turks."

"Yes."

"And then, one day, in '60 or '61, I think, she went into her dark-room and, for no reason we know of, drank off a bottle of a substance called potassium cyanide."

"God will forgive her!"

She turned and I saw she had her fist in her mouth. She crouched down, averted her eyes and said: "May I enquire how you came to learn these things?"

"Oh, Shirin, it was just a fancy. You see, I was interested in anybody who had my name. You see, I thought that I might learn something about my own family, might one day, in some book or museum or family house, as it were, run into my father, stiff in his Church suit, or come upon my mother, in a photograph, wearing an out-of-fashion hat."

"Oh, you are so silly!" She walked forward on her knees, and knelt in my lap. "When God made you, His wisdom was notably hard to descry." She straightened, in the way I loved, for her breast brushed my cheek. "Can't you see?"

"See what?"

"That these events are linked by a chain that would stick in the eye of a sick infant?"

"What events?"

She took my hand, turned up the palm, took hold of my thumb. "These matters are hidden, or rather are indescribable in the language of appearances. The rubies." She pressed down my thumb. "Amin and Karolin." She pressed two fingers. "You and your servant." She pressed the last two. "In each of these events, a spiritual affinity becomes progressively more actual. An Englishman brings rubies to the Shah and takes away money. A century later, an English girl sees a man in a castle ballroom, dancing like a madman. Her eyes are still blinded by appearances. She cannot see through his strangeness. Or rather, she knew it in her heart but that was tarnished by worldliness. Yet what took her to Üsküdar? To pass her nights and days among the dying soldiers? To make the pano . . ."

" . . . rama . . ."

" . . . of the battlements of Sebastopol? To peer for hours in her dark-room at the pictures, lest she see him? And to drink the poison, God will forgive her? And as for you and me, a century later, well," she pressed my smallest fingers down, "you know the story."

"But she's nothing to do with me!"

"I think you are certain of that."

"No, I'm not. How can I be? If she'd been my relation . . ."

"She is your relation, in reality, if not in appearance. Human beings do not solve mysteries, they merely abolish them and exult in their ignorance. In reality, we were reeds torn from a reed-bed, perpetually homesick for the place from which we'd been separated. We were fashioned into flutes to make sad music at the weddings of handsome boys. But now, by God's grace, we are reunited." She burst out laughing. "You have broken the chains of contingency and found Union with the Beloved, O sultan of the soul."

"No. It's just that when I saw you in the doorway I couldn't help myself."

"Exactly! When I first saw you, in Isfahan, in the garden of the Hasht Behesht, when I was returning from my music class, I thought: What a strange, long, pale, unknit, moncyless, spoiled, unhappy person! Something about your shamble perplexed me. I could not believe you could be so helpless. Therefore I came back to that place the next day after school, to see if you really were so, and you were, but worse, far worse! And by then, it was too late, you were every-where. I couldn't buy yoghurt with Madame Jowhara except that you must be in the shop, muddling your tenses and dropping your change; or sitting in the garden by the Post Office, that was my favourite place, excuse me, and there you were, mangling Ghazali with some unbathed theological student. I sat at my geometry and suddenly, you were beside me, taking liberties; had stumbled right in through the open window, without asking permission or enquiring about my health or paying any regard to propriety. I was to myself so precious. I was the girl who was just mad about geometry! Who was learning the Koran by heart! Who had no friends and wanted none! And then one afternoon, at that time of a hot afternoon when everybody has forgotten the time, in Mr Mo'in's shop in the Meidan-e Shah, you introduced yourself – John Pitt, ladies, is my name – you introduced yourself to everybody, which was quite tactful by your standards, but the name was Pitt and was always and only ever for me, it pierced me like a blade, and I thought: Oh Lord, I am, after all, just a weak thing, I can resist this no more, my heart is in the sea.

"I tell you this story to gladden your heart and to pass the evening and also for another purpose. I tell you this story to make you think." She walked towards me on her knees and pressed both hands against my temples. "Think, John, why you learned Persian! Think why you came to Iran! Think about your poor mum and dad, though the pain of thinking scalds your heart! And then, God willing, perhaps you will come whole through the wreck."

❧ 15 ❧

It was Mordad again, the high summer month.

"Sir, may I speak?"

"Of course."

"The fish in the bazar is stale."

"No matter. We are happy with rice."

"I have no rice."

"No matter . . . "

"EXCUSE ME, SIR, I DO NOT HAVE MONEY!"

"Oh."

"John, you are so stupid. You never think. You just go on believing that God will provide. Oh, I have tried to make Mr Ryazanov's money last, to cook without meat or fish, to grow our own herbs and fruits, always myself to show restraint . . . "

"No matter."

"No matter what?"

"No matter, Shirin." I was teetering on the edge of a tremendous scheme. "For some time, now, dear ma'am, I have been considering requesting that you go to Tehran. It won't kill us to be alone for a day."

She raised her head. "I have tried. There is a problem."

"You tried!"

"Excuse me, John, you don't understand. In the old days, when Reza Shah was stealing grandfather's estate, he made a decree that the necklace was part of the national regalia and must be deposited in

167

the National Bank in Tehran to guarantee the banknotes. Grandmother hid it and swore on her father's grave she knew nothing of rubies, and refused to receive Teymourtash, the Minister of Court, who came himself to fetch it. That was before the Unveiling Act, so Teymourtash had to remount and set off and had nothing for his trouble except the Shah's suspicion and a rope round his neck in Qazvin Jail. But the bazar knows that grandmother was a deceitful person. No merchant in Iran would dare handle the jewels, not even Mosaffarian, whose father was grandfather's friend. I believe the stones could be sold in Junev, but only in the greatest secrecy and that does not solve our problem here. Sir, you are like a dervish, you never think about these things!"

"On the contrary. In fact, Shirin, you have something far more precious and marketable than the rubies."

She stiffened, as if she'd been shot.

"Speak Persian, please."

"We will go together to the American Embassy in Takht-e Jamshid Avenue in Tehran."

She relaxed. Slowly, she threw up her head. That always infuriated me. "What makes you think they will give us asylum?"

"You will say: I have something you need."

My plan dawned on her. I plunged on: "Please listen to me for the first time in your life. Can't you see it's immeasurably more valuable than the necklace. The Imperial Air Force Commander-in-Chief is a Russian bribe-taker! Mr Helms can either inform the Shah or turn him."

"What does 'turn' mean in this context?"

"Use him to pass falsehoods to the Russians. I go there, in the morning, in office hours, ask to see His Excellency the Ambassador, Mr Helms. I say, I have a secret of outstanding value and interest, but I will impart it only in Istanbul or Delhi, and with my family with me."

"Oh John, you really are a fool. You've learned nothing in this time!"

"Why?"

"John, they'll beat the secret out of you and then throw what's left to the Savak."

"They're Americans! Americans don't beat!"

"This conversation bears no relation to reality."

"So you agree?"

"You are free to go to the Americans and say what you like. We will not accompany you."

"Why not?"

"No doubt Mr Farameh is a bad man. However, I will not betray him."

"He's trying to kill you!"

"Of course."

"How could a person be as obstinate as you are?"

"I have inconvenienced you."

She stood up. If I offended Shirin, she simply went away. She had a sinister ability to hide herself, and because I could not call her in the day or light a candle by night or leave the child alone, it might take me an hour to find her, seated with her pen-case and account book by the compost heap, or standing quite still in the stripes of light and shadow on the balcony. I would kiss her hand and bring her the child for feeding. Those were our lovers' quarrels: silent, protracted, humilitating, more and more frequent.

"You should watch your tongue, Mr Pitt, or you will find it cut out of your mouth. I am not obstinate. I have another plan."

"Good. Please tell me."

She lost her poise. "There is a photography studio on Ferdowsi Avenue. I mean, it has a reputation."

"You are joking, of course."

"I am not joking. Do you think I will be glad to sit there without my petticoat . . ."

"How could you even . . ."

"I could get fifty tomans each game. Bibi said . . ."

"I should have killed that wicked old bitch."

"A perilous adversary for you, my dear sir! An illiterate old woman!"

"Shirin, I am sorry but, we really must now leave Iran."

"I will not."

"You must."

"I will not, sir."

"You must if you wish to remain with us."

Her head went down with a jerk.

"Shirin, how can you be so ... Can't you see there is no other remedy?"

She looked up. She spoke with the slowness of a nightmare. She said: "Mr Pitt, if you intend to take my Layly from me, you shall first have to kill me. For otherwise I shall kill you."

"I have asked you before, ma'am, not to threaten me."

"It is not a threat but the only solution to this difficulty." She snapped her head down.

"Oh, pull youself together, woman. I ..."

"Don't you dare address me like that, you ..."

"Madame, I have said before that I will not hold you against your will. Nor do I intend to separate you from your child! Never! Do you understand?"

"So he doesn't even care for his helpless little daughter!"

That didn't seem worth answering. Shirin Farameh sat down on the floor. She seemed puzzled.

I said: "In Britain, generally speaking, the child of a divorced couple remains with its mother, however wicked and ill-natured and unchaste and disloyal."

"Truly?"

"Generally speaking."

"How just!"

"As you command."

"We are not in England."

"Even so, we shall adopt the English system. Have you already made supper?"

She was nodding her head in astonishment.

"Will you kindly excuse me tonight, ma'am? I wish to go out."

"Out?"

"Yes."

"Alone?"

"Yes."

"But who will look after you outside?"

"I shall, God willing."

"Why are you going? Where are you going?"

"To breathe air."

Two boys were running down the steps of a lit confectioner's, Europeans, hippies. They were elated in the brilliant fluorescent light. One carried a box of cakes by its ribbon and a bottle of Saboo water. The other was looking at me.

His narrow chest was bare under an embroidered waistcoat. He wore pink Indian pyjamas tied with a cord at the waist, a money-belt, and sandals of automobile tyres. Over his right shoulder was a damp rag, also pink, also Indian. His hair was cut short. His face was extra-ordinarily handsome: dark and amused, the sort of face that makes you want to tell secrets, just to make an impression on it. He was looking not at me but past me; and as I walked up the pavement, I felt myself dropping my disguise. Heart spoke to heart, as they say in Iran: I longed for Europe and my generation.

"Hi."

He was French. His companion, with the cakes, looked pained. He, too, was in Indian homespun, tanned, muscular, perhaps a little unintelligent. Their nudity fascinated me.

"Where you from, man?"

"Oh, here and there."

He spat pleasantly at this hippie answer.

"Viens, Lachat." Lachat raised his finger to command his friend. "So what are you doing in this hell-hole?"

Same as you. "Hanging out."

"Do you want a smoke, man?"

"Sure."

"Merde."

Their hotel was called the Gulf. The porter looked at us carefully beneath his keys. We climbed a dripping stairway to the roof. On the way up, the friend, who was called Fan or Fann, seemed to spread himself across the steps, so as by pure mental exertion to exclude me from his world. I understood why when we reached the two bed-steads, drawn to face each other as if on a theatre stage with a minimum of scenery. He lit a candle, uncapped the water, drew out a spoon from his mattress.

Lachat smiled. "Are you cool about this, British?"

British?

"This is Iran. It's your funeral." I felt their aggression pass across to me. "People are shot for less here."

"Iran! Quel putain de pays fasciste!" There was panic in Fann's voice. He was now struggling with his sleeve. Lachat did nothing to help him. Instead, he was making a joint. I thought: He'll put some heroin in the cigarette, hope it'll knock me out, take my money, except I haven't got any, silly pricks.

"Where are you guys headed?"

Lachat looked up sweetly from his joint, licked the edge of the cigarette paper with his tongue, sealed it against his cheek. Fann was titivating with his needle. He seemed not to be there, or rather to imagine that he was alone and had locked the door on the world. They are out to do me harm, that could not be more obvious; but they are so absorbed in their private ceremonies, junkie slang, sentences begun and then nodded out, scoring, saving money, getting by, that they are to me quite unpredictable. The box of baklava was open, but nobody had touched it, nor ever would.

"Where?"

"Stop asking fucking questions, man!"

"Dubai."

Lachat pronounced the name with an elaborate foreignness, yet incorrectly.

"By sea?"

"By sea."

"'Tais-toi, Lass!"

Fann's face had fallen in. He looked more stupid than ever. Lachat lit the cigarette and, taking the smoke only into his mouth, passed it to me.

The hashish – from Afghanistan, I suppose – was leaden and sugary but beneath it was a searing bitterness: strychnine, perhaps, something like that. I put my head back and looked up at my familiar stars. I said through wreaths of uninhaled smoke:

"How much to ride with you?"

Lachat burst out laughing.

"How much to ride with you?" He made fun of my accent.

"How much to ride with you?"

"Too much, British." Fann was far out of earshot. He was lying on his bed, his sodden face flickering in the gas flares from the Gulf.

"I speak the language here. I can help you."

"You speak Irani?"

Idiot.

"Yes. And Arabic."

"Give me your hand." He was no more stoned than I was, yet I let him. His touch made me tremble.

"Don't be afraid, man." He looked down a moment at my palm, and then back up at my face. He ran his own palm across mine, all the while looking into my face. "You're messed up, man. You had a parent who died by violence." He picked up my hand again, tested it for weight, looked down. "Two parents, eh, but not at the same

173

time. Bizarre! And you're running away from something. And your girlfriend's fucking another guy. Maybe you should go home."

"Sure." I got up. "See you around."

My knees gave way. With an immense effort, I righted myself, made for the staircase, found myself looking down at the street, retreated, steadied myself on the stair rail. Lachat looked delighted. It pleased him to see me struggling, but he was too lazy or fastidious himself to rob or injure me. Now, perhaps, if I lay down on this tiled roof . . .

"British!"

I could see that he was not Fann, and that he had an interest in the world other than getting heroin. I wanted very much to understand what that was. He seemed at home on his roof in the starlight, like an old man in his garden.

"Man?"

"Midnight tomorrow night. At the Customs House on the dock. No baggage. Exactly at midnight, or we go without you."

Shirin was still up, playing with Layly. She had been crying. Her face and hair were smeared with dust. She had scratched her neck. I picked up the baby and hugged her to me. She laughed and put her finger in my mouth.

Finally, Shirin spoke. "Lion or fox?"

"Lion! God willing, I sail tomorrow night."

She was staring out over the sea. I turned with Layly and followed her gaze. I felt we were sailing together through an eternity of sorrow, accomplices in our own misery.

At length, I said: "What sustains me, Shirin, is the belief that a big change will come in this country, your father will lose his position and I will be able to return and live with you again."

"I shall be married."

The sea turned to ink. I kissed Layly. I thought: I must try to remember the touch of her warm cheek at three months of age.

I said: "Under the Family Protection Law of 1967 *anno domini*, 1346 solar, the Shah that you despise and hate nevertheless legislated that a husband could not unilaterally repudiate his wife by simply repeating the Arabic formula 'Thou Art Divorced' three times but must show cause in court of gross dissatisfaction. You have caused me no dissatisfaction, madame, gross or petty. I do not believe any eventual second marriage of yours will be legal or that Layly can legally be deprived of her father by any choice of yours."

"That law will not survive Mr Shah."

She has packed her bags already. I thought that we had one more day, but she is somewhere of her own. We have gone back to our first day together, in which everything is misunderstood. I turned and looked at her. Her filthy face was deathly pale and her neck was scratched.

She said: "The truth is, John, that your daughter will starve unless I take steps to feed her. Because you will not tolerate what I intend to do to get money for her, and have no suggestion of your own, you must now leave. For her sake, you must also release me to marry again by pronouncing the formula of divorce three times."

She was staring ahead.

I said: "Tomorrow. At the garden gate, when we separate. Will you excuse me? I want to put Layly in her cot." I didn't want her to be present at these discussions.

I put her down in her cot. She turned half on her side and began to purr like a kitten. After a while, I went out and sat on the tank. Shirin came out and sat down beside me. She had a cigarette in her hand.

May I smoke this cigarette?

Of course. You don't have to ask my permission.

"John?"

Sss. Someone will hear.

"It doesn't matter any more."

175

"Please don't torture me, Shirin."

"May I touch you only? To soothe not to hurt?"

"At your service."

She took my hands in hers. "During your absence in the town, I thought hard and regretted what I had said. It is because of me that you have suffered these misfortunes. Without me, you would be back at a workshop or college in England. I cannot abandon you while you still want me. Also Layly missed you while you were out. Please take us with you to England."

"Oh Shirin, I can't. It is too dangerous. They are bad, bad men. The dregs of Europe."

"They are Europeans? Why are they here?"

"Hiding, like I and you. They are drug smugglers. They are taking a cargo of Afghan heroin to Dubai for sending on to Europe. They are absolutely untrustworthy."

"What did you expect? Pilgrims? Pilgrims take the aeroplane to Arabia! I have heard about this trade, I mean narcotics."

"There'll be Navy boats out there. There may be a fight."

"Of course."

"My darling, I was not myself out there. They think I am a fool."

"Of course. You were homesick for your own people. That is natural."

"I was mad with anger and sorrow."

"It is precisely for that reason, John, that we must come with you. We will carry the gun. They will not expect that."

"You've never fired a gun!"

"I have heard that you point it at the adversary's face and pull the needle known as the trigger. Is that so very difficult?"

"But what about Layly?"

"She wishes to be with her father."

I hugged her. After a while, she lost her stiffness. She began to kiss me, and then to take off my shirt. I was determined to make her say she loved me, even if it killed me. I got her dress off and found her breast was wet. I thought it was her milk, but when I looked up, she was crying uncontrollably.

She kissed me before I could speak. "She missed you," she said.

Then we swam, until we heard a cry from indoors, and Shirin snatched up her dress and chador and ran in.

The next day we were busy. Shirin went through the house and removed all trace of our presence. She put back the books on the shelves and burned the clothes and bed-linen she'd made in the kitchen grate. She seemed even to restore the dust. In the garden, she dug up her herbs and flowers.

"Leave the roses for God, why not?"

"As you wish."

She sewed our last ten tomans and the passport blanks into her dress. I refitted the booby-traps to the desks. When I was done, night had come down and I could not find her. I feared that her resolve to leave might slacken; but as I wandered through the purple darkness and the first moonlight, I knew I could not compel her; that I was, as always, at the mercy of her will.

A bird was singing from a deep bush. I had not heard it start to sing, and it may have been some time before its voice infiltrated my thoughts. Its song was sweet and sad and fierce, but, in truth, those adjectives are merely descriptions of my own state of mind, of my sorrow and melancholy and excitement at leaving the garden and Iran. The bird inhabited a larger universe. It seemed to draw sounds and sensations from the recesses of the darkness and a world of feeling of which my melancholy and anxiety, my love for my child and grief for my dead friend, were mere samples.

"In spring in Isfahan, the nightingales won't let you sleep."

She was standing near me, her face striped by the blind. She handed me a piece of folded paper. It was taken from a lined exercise book. At the top, in her best calligraphy, she had written: FOR MY

HUSBAND. It was a sonnet, of the kind they call ghazal here, where every couplet has the same rhyme. I glanced down and then away. I refolded the paper. The intimacy appalled me. I felt as I had felt that afternoon in my room in the Bonbast-e Parviz in Isfahan, that I could not withstand the force of her concentration; and that indeed in all our long honeymoon she had never bared her modesty as she did now. The words I'd seen were just *ay jan-e man*, which means "O, my darling" which any poet might use to start a poem to her husband, except that it also meant "My soul" and "My life" and "My John" and so ramified into privacies I did not believe she could admit into her speech, let alone into verse. And I thought she was keeping accounts!

"You are a fine accountant, madame. I am much impressed by the books."

"Don't be silly."

It was silly, but I was disturbed by a new thought: she was a good poet, even by Persian standards, the best since Forough, for all I knew. I felt again the pressure on my nature: that I would, after all and against my will, be dragged into history. She had a gift from God, which it was my duty to protect for her people and all people who could understand poetry. Then, and only then, did I understand the true source of her pride, which was the absolute and unwavering sense of her gift from God.

"And all the while I thought you were counting money."

She blushed. "It's nothing. You see, since I met you, all the time, I'd be cutting sabzi or watering the orchard or embracing you or changing Layly's linen and suddenly I'd think: When I've finished doing this, I'll go and write a poem. I used to write in the new style, prose really, in imitation of Forough, whom I had the honour of meeting, in Tehran with mother, when I won the National Society of Arts and Letters competition; unfortunately she was not herself that day and when they saw I was just a girlie of twelve thirteen they made fun of my dress and ribbon. It was not their fault, mother said later,

Princess Ashraf was at the party and that had put everybody on edge, but I cried and cried and cried; but then when I met you I thought I should write in the traditional way for your sake, and indeed it has been good for me, for the old forms were not chosen accidentally and can accommodate new content, if only from a woman."

She stopped in embarrassment. The nightingale let out a sob. I thought: So in the end, in the last minutes before I leave this country, I am to learn the work of love. I had thought it was so easy, but . . .

"Excuse me, I have explained myself badly. I only ever wanted to be a poet. The question was: How could I be a poet and be a woman? You see, I thought I would be like Parvin and sit in a corner and send poems to the magazines that were technically flawless, in content conventional and cautious; and the poetic gentlemen would assume, as with Parvin, that they were written by a man for all poets are men, no? Then I met you and I resented you, oh how I resented you! Each moment of the day and night you were forcing me to be a woman, to be ruthless and long-suffering and affectionate. And in the end, I said, 'Good, all right, you win, for we have no more strength'. And that is why I do not wish to be separated from you ever again, or lose your shadow from across my cheek. I wish our dusts to be mingled until the Judgement Day. For your lily face and gentle heart I would go to hell and damnation, Mr Pitt. You made me happy, John. I mean you made me happy to be a woman."

The world had turned to sugar. I stood in drifts of sugar.

"Your compliments, Shirin, are all the more welcome for being infrequent."

"That's enough! All your nonsense about love, and if I loved you, and if I loved you how much did I love you, and if I loved you so much how much was so much, and would it make Little Ali a new cap, as if my opinion in the matter had any weight. It was not enough for you that I left my city and my sister and my prospects and my millions in money and who knows what. It was not enough for you that I am prepared to leave my country, which may seem to you a poor thing, but is my country; and my religion, which seems to you so backward, but is my religion; and it is not enough for you that I am leaving my most precious inheritance, this Persian, the same language that Mahasti and Tahereh spoke and Parvin and Forough – all these mad and bad women! – to live out my life in violent cacophonies, that will dislodge my language word by word, meaning by meaning, till there is nothing left of me but a half Englishwoman, standing dazed and sobbing in the aisles of Wolworth or Espencer! Even you must see that mine was no insipid or conventional attachment!"

She turned back to the window. The nightingale began its descent through a long curving valley of sound. Slowly, and with great difficulty, Shirin Farameh unwound herself from the bird's song.

She said: "It is time to leave the garden of union, my husband. It is time to confront these wicked men. It is time to die, if that is necessary. As Khaqani said:

'Grief is the highway: it's time to pack our things,
Roll up the bits and pieces of the will,
And set off for our destination, terror.'

I shall fetch Layly. God preserve you."

⊠⊠⊠⊠⊠⊠⊠⊠⊠

PART THREE

⊠⊠⊠⊠⊠⊠⊠⊠⊠

❧ 16 ❧

For years now, I have sought the sensation I felt, if only for a moment, one day during the Iranian Revolution. It was 5 November, 1978, the day they burned the banks in Tehran and paper money fluttered here and there in the hot draughts above Ferdowsi Square. The sun was dissolving in dirt and smoke when I set off, going nowhere in particular, except downhill, under the force of my own gravity. I knew I must be off the street because of the curfew. I came into Lalehzar and the reek of alcohol made me swoon.

Beneath a scorched movie poster, under the colossal bare pink legs of a trunkless woman, the beer bars had been sacked, their window grilles twisted as if by machines and tossed into the street. I crept down the hot tarmac, through drifts of broken bottles and window glass, and aluminium beer cans fused into sheets by the fire, where the chance sight of a bottle base still upright with a mouthful of vodka in it set me to maudlin reminiscence:

> Drunk beyond all reason once
> Nasser Khosrow took a walk outside town
> And passed a dung heap and a cemetery . . .

There was nobody about, because of the curfew, except sometimes I glanced through a sidestreet and saw a troop carrier plunge northwards between the dark cliffs of office buildings.

I walked on down. In beautiful Tehran, to walk downhill is to descend into past times. The streets were warm and dusty and quiet and smelled of horses, and after a while I knew I'd reached the nineteenth century. I thought if I went on I'd see Amin prance by on his grey and the flash of the cannons he'd brought back from Moscow to call the hours in Ramadan and the ladies passing in curtained second-hand kalashkehs and tulips and patched dervishes and heretics hanging from the gibbet in Artillery Square. I found that I could not walk straight and that I was drunk on air.

Before me were iron gates. I pushed and they opened on a breeze that cooled my cheeks. The moonlight flashed and flickered in little canals that criss-crossed the garden, lulling and soothing. A soldier with a rose in his teeth and a breast pocket stuffed with banknotes appeared smiling before me.

He scampered over the canals in plastic sandals, his rifle butt catching in the box hedges. We were moving towards a rickety building with a hall that broke the moonlight from a million stalactite mirrors, a stone staircase guarded by stone lions, and an alabaster frieze of soldiers with embroidered skirts and European muskets and stiff moustaches. I turned to thank the boy, but he wasn't there. The moon rattled in the branches of a weeping mulberry.

I lay down on the cut grass, and as I lay down, I felt I'd fallen out of my century; and falling, left behind the blazing liquor stores and swirling banknotes, the heat on my face and the clatter of helicopters and the women shrieking in their black georgette and the shield round my neck that read I AM IN SEARCH OF NEWS OF MY FAMILY; left cities behind and events and certainties; and in my solitude and shame found my way out of the world:

> Sweet cousin mamzil moon
> Hiding in branches
> Or bathing in a far-away canal!
> Too late!
> Sleep scatters us with this year's leaves.

* *

I staggered up. The sun scalded my face. On the pavement before the mirrored porch of the palace, in a space made by tended rose bushes, three well-dressed men were walking away from me. A fourth stood at a distance of about fifty paces, holding a clipboard and an open fountain pen. Further still, a high military officer stood rigidly to attention. They were clean and bright as angels.

The three turned; or rather the man in the centre turned, and the men on each side skipped a step to turn with him. All were tall, but I was surprised that the men on the outside were foreigners, Europeans or Americans. The man on the left as I looked at the group, whom I recognised as Burchill, the British Ambassador, was speaking softly, rapidly, with his head down, not just out of respect but perhaps for fear of the reaction to his words. The man on the right, who was no doubt the United States Ambassador, Freeling, looked straight ahead as if not fully a part of what his colleague had to say; as if, indeed, his mind were in America.

Between them, the Sun of the Aryans looked baffled. His handsome face, his gleaming hair, his well-cut suit, his patience and courtesy had seceded from his troubled spirit. I saw that he was wrestling with what Mr Burchill was saying so quickly and quietly or rather with a conception that was new to him and was this: that he did not trust the man, or the other, or their governments, which meant that he did not trust anybody. A pair of hooded crows flapped and fought on the pitched roof, plebeianly.

> We stagger up.
> The sun is high.
> Delegations scamper by.

I stood up. Had I stayed where I was and been seen, hiding, I would have been shot. In reality, I stood up because I was drunk on air and because I did not think it right to eavesdrop on other people's affairs. The Shah shivered. It is not just that he had been here before, I can't remember when, but as a young man, when a boy put five bullets in him in the garden of Tehran University and he survived and thought himself under the protection of Lord Ali himself. There was something about my wildness, and my strangeness, that suited the drift of his thinking, as if his very suspicion of the ambassadors had materialised me. He turned on Burchill in savagery. Burchill sprang in front of him, not so much to shield the Shah from a bullet as himself from suspicion. He was agile as a soldier. Freeling woke from his reverie, reached to his lapels for his weapon, thought better of it, made as if to push the Shah to the ground and then thought better of that, too: as if some aura of God's Anointed still radiated from the person of the Shah. The General was running at me tugging at his a side-arm as if it were a snake with its teeth in him. The official with the clipboard was stepping towards me on brilliant hand-made shoes.

I put out my arms to show I had no weapon. I smiled at the Shahinshah. He blinked at the presumption, then relaxed.

"Disarm the boy!" he said.

"It will be obeyed!"

The garden burst into life. The tin roofs bristled with riflemen. I could see that the General running at me was going to shoot me, just to be on the safe side, and then the other fellows would turn me into a colander, to earn their pay and expenses and at least to shoot somebody. I turned my back to them and rested my cheek against the hot mulberry bark. That was cowardice, but in those days I believed people had a compunction about shooting in the back.

"Who sent you? Where is your accomplice? Where did you drop your weapon?"

The official was standing very close to me, shouting so all could hear. His breath on my cheek was putrid, as if he were ill. I sensed he was fastidious, and anyway needed to conceal his illness, and stood so close only to keep me from being shot.

I whispered: "I have business with you, Excellency." And then, because the Immortals were all around me, peering down their automatic weapons, a hair's breadth from riddling me, I laughed and said:

"A dervish once came into the presence of the Sultan and began to make a commotion."

Which, as every Iranian knows, is a story from *The Rose Garden* of Sa'adi.

The first time I was in the Evin, after my arrest in the garden of the Golestan Palace, I was held in solitary confinement in the block that was later known as the Infirmary. It was bitterly cold and I ran in my cell to keep warm. The light bulb in the ceiling was never switched off, for which I was at first grateful: I was too frightened to close my eyes or take them off the door. Later on, I ceased to be able to distinguish day and night.

The guards kept pressing me for news and passed on their own rumours. I heard that the Imam had left the Holy Thresholds in Iraq and gone to France and that the Israelis had sent troops to patrol the streets in Iranian uniform. Every day there was talk of a new amnesty. Little by little the place became quieter until at times I thought I was the last political prisoner in all Iran. I would bang for hours on the door to be taken to the lavatory and even then nobody came. After one such humiliation, I preferred to go thirsty. I suffered agonies of hunger, till I learned to husband my bread and cheese and eat it only when the next meal was brought. I thought I had been forgotten and would starve.

One night, I was gently woken, told to dress. Suleiman hovered by the door, with his eyes averted, as if he expected a tip for having brought good news. As I passed down the corridor, the doors of the cells were open on unwashed dishes and eating-cloths still scattered with torn bread and cracked sugar. Outside, the snow sparkled in the floodlight and crunched beneath my feet. From the town I could hear a roar climbing up the hill as if to greet me: *God is very great! Khomeini is our leader! Free Ayatollah Najafi!* Suleiman was slap-dash, abstracted, clumsy as if he were no longer a guard with the power of violence over me but was already back in Uruj, his village near Tabriz, and did not know what he would say to his people when he got there. Under the arch of the main gate, a large white Mercedes had its engine running. Three motorcycle outriders looked away from me under their visors.

I sank into white leather as we rolled away. The car was curtained, warm and smelt of pomade and illness. I said: "Your Excellency, I am in your debt for my life a second time."

"A husband should keep an eye on his young wife, Mr Pitt. Or he'll lose her."

The reading light picked out a snowy shirt-front and cuffs, a gold wristwatch, diamond cuff-links, sleek hair parted in the style of fifty years before. I guessed he was Qavam, the Minister of Court. He looked much worse than that morning in the Golestan. He's well on his way. Cancer, I guess.

I said, also in English: "Sir, I did not lose the person in question but on the contrary she was kidnapped from me. I expect you to give me any information you have."

"Forget her, Mr Pitt."

"I do not understand you, sir."

"I mean, Mr Pitt, that you should cast your eyes elsewhere. This country is famed for the beauty and the kindness of its women."

"And you should take care what you say. Were you not already my creditor, and in poor health, by God I would help you on your way. Once again, do you have any information about her?"

"I believe Madame Princess has taken her daughters to Europe. St Moritz, I believe."

"Bollocks."

The car swung heavily to the right.

"Where are we going?"

His eyes were closed. He seemed to have overtaxed himself.

"Where are you taking me?"

"I am taking you to Mehrabad, Mr Pitt. Ambassador Freeling last night brought a message for H.I.M. from the President."

I waited while he coughed. "You know the Americans never really cared for H.I.M." He coughed out the initials. "It's only you people who like monarchy. The Americans want a military government. They want Farameh."

"Naturally. He'll shoot the people."

Qavam flashed. "H.I.M. will never permit his soldiers to fire on his people!" He changed course. "That's why we must have Farameh."

"And why you're taking me to the airport!"

He smiled like an old gallant. "I could never resist a pretty face."

"What do you mean? What is my family to you?"

He waved his fingers.

I said: "Mr Qavam, I am grateful for your kindness. However, I do not wish to leave Iran because I know my wife and child are alive and in Iran. Also, if His Imperial Majesty appoints Farameh prime minister with martial law powers, he will lose his throne. Farameh is not loyal. I would be grateful to you if you would convey that to His Majesty as my duty."

"You speak of matters of which you know nothing. It is done. Hoveyda goes to the Ministry of Court."

"And you, sir? Where do you go?"

"To my grave by way of New York Hospital. Do you know Hafez?" He was coughing uncontrollably, yet determined to get the couplet out: "'Darius, Alexander and all their hullaballoo' . . ."

On his lips there was a smear of red, as if he'd been chewing betel. We were coming up to the floodlit Shahyad Memorial.

"'Were all forgotten in a year or' . . ."

"Driver! Driver!"

I rapped on the thick glass. The driver craned round. He had eyes like a doe.

"You must take His Excellency home. Now!"

The car swung across the road, cracked through the flimsy median strip and accelerated back into town. I took Qavam in my arms, loosened his heavy silk tie, opened his collar button. He recoiled from my touch. The motorbikes had caught up and put up their sirens.

"Driver, do you have a telephone?"

"Yes, sir."

"Please call Mme Qavam and his doctor."

"Dr Bernard or Dr Plessis?"

"How the hell do I know? Call them both."

At the Niavaran Palace, we plunged through the gateway and pulled up before a toy house under floodlit umbrella pines. I ran up the steps.

"Madame! Come! Your husband is not well."

I heard a rattle of footsteps. A very pretty girl pulled wide the doors with both arms. She had on a white evening gown and a river of diamonds at her neck. She looked at my face, over my shoulder, and into the open car. I ran with her and the three of us carried her father in and laid him on the carpet. Her sister came sliding down the stairs.

"Téléphonez Bernard!" she cried.

The driver was already at the telephone. I walked to the door.

"Pitt!"

The girl who shouted had her father's head in her arms. She wanted to say something to me, perhaps about my wife, for all I knew. She opened her mouth to speak, but didn't have the words; or the words had lost their meaning, with her father dying and the old world going under.

I turned back and knelt by her father's head. His lips were moving. It was as if all his Europeanness and sophistication had fallen from him, and he was saying his prayers.

"What? I don't understand."

" . . . lawful . . . "

"What is lawful?"

"Please, Mr Pitt! Please! Dr Bernard is coming!"

"Make . . . it . . . lawful . . . to . . . me . . ."

"Goddammit, man, what? What have you done to me that I must . . ."

"GO AWAY, MR PITT!"

"Please, sir, you must go now. His Excellency is sick. Tomorrow. Or the day after."

❧ 17 ❧

I was imprisoned in the Evin a second time in the spring of 1980, on the day the Americans tried and failed to rescue their people from the Embassy in Takht-e Jamshid Avenue. At that time, I was living in the New Town: because that was where you went if you had no identity card and because there was heroin there. I suppose I was waiting like everyone else for Saddam to attack. The New Town seemed as good a place to wait in as any.

I remember there was a little street where the junkies smoked under veils of muslin that billowed in the hot draughts from passing cars. Sometimes, a gust would shiver the veil and I'd see a face from which all personality had vanished. I used to go among them, to ask about the Frenchmen, but could get no answer unless I put my hand between a man's lips and the burning crystal. Scuffles broke out, as among jackals at a carcass. Rumours scuttled up and down the street: that we were next, that now the universities were closed, Najafi was on his way down to us; but nobody imagined anybody could be bothered until on the morning of 25 April he appeared, a pistol at his waist, and two truckloads of Guards and even some foreign reporters picked up from outside the American Embassy. They rigged up a gallows from the lamp stands. I was making my way out of the New Town towards the bazar when something knocked me flying. All around me, the street was carpeted in box leaves. The smoke and the blaze and the smell of roasting flesh put me in mind of some antique festival. Somebody was firing over me. I craned my head and could see the remains of a Paykan saloon car engulfed in flame. It must have been packed with explosives. As I lay on the ground, a Guard ran up and tied my hands and dragged me into a bus.

To be an unemployed man without an identity card in the New Town was no particular offence, even when a car bomb had been detonated. I sat through the night in the Komiteh police station while the junkies groaned and sobbed. The Revolutionary Courts prided themselves on their speed – if there is speed, who needs justice? – and I expected to be tried and sentenced by noon. Instead, as I squatted outside the courtroom, Ayatollah Najafi billowed past and as I struggled to stand, to kiss his hand, he nodded at me and somebody took me by the hair. I was dragged down the steps into an old diesel Mercedes. As we raced uphill, my hands were tied and I was blind-folded: my last recollection was the garden of the Golestan Palace on my right. As we drove, it became cooler and quieter and I sensed we were going north, to the Evin. I thought I would suffocate for fear.

The car stopped and there was cold air on my wet face and back. "Take this, freemason!"

I had in my hand a roll of newspaper, which pulled me forward. I suppose they considered me too tainted to touch. We came into a place where there was no draught and something hard pressed me down against a wall. People stumbled against my feet, and I thought I was in a corridor. By resting my face on my knees, I pushed up my blindfold and saw a sight that broke my heart. I was in a corridor so long I could not see its ends and on each side, stretching out of sight, were young men and women in blindfolds. Each was absorbed in his own blindness, disconnected, submissive, ignorant that his plight repeated and repeated itself, dreaming, at rest. Every so often, a bearded young man pranced down, beating at feet with his rifle: "Don't raise your blindfolds! Pull your knees tight against your chests!" I thought: What has happened that so many have been arrested today? I didn't know then about the Americans.

I was picked up and pushed through a set of double doors. A soft hand pulled off my blindfold and vanished. Before me was a small man wearing a black hood slashed with eye-holes. The shock of the apparition made my hair stand on end. Before me was a chair with a wide arm-rest, such as the girls had had in my class in Isfahan, and by an inhumanly slow gesture of his head the figure indicated I should sit in it. For a long time, the eye-holes examined my face. The silence became intolerable to me.

I said: "Excuse me, sir, but . . ."

He struck me in the middle of the forehead, so that my chair tipped over backward. It was a blow of a violence I had never suffered, which simultaneously blinded me and filled me with sorrow. I picked myself up.

He said: "You are Pitt!"

He said my name, as if it constituted its own order of shame and disgrace. In truth, I was glad to have my identity, for I felt I would need it.

"Yes."

He punched me again in the same place. I thought that I couldn't take another such blow without something bursting in my head. I picked myself up onto my hands and knees.

"I have committed no crime. Why are you mistreating me?"

He came close to me. "Listen, Pitt. Listen well. We know a great deal about you, but we need to know some more. If you co-operate with us, we'll let you go back to Britain. If you do not, you will stay here till you do or until you die. I will let you think about this matter tonight."

"I don't want to go to Britain."

I felt the blow even when it was air. I felt, also, that the world had been knocked or twisted out of true, that the man did not see the same world I saw, was insane or was trying to mislead me. I stood up.

"And Pitt."

I turned to where I thought he might be. Something cold and hard touched my forehead. "Do you know what this is?"

"It is a knife."

"Correct. If for one instant you raise your blindfold or look me in the face, I shall cut out your eyes."

My cell, numbered 381, was on the third floor of the block known as the Infirmary. It was stifling and I had no means of turning off the light. When I banged on the door for the guard, somebody screamed the word "Forbidden!" through a metal hatch. A little later, a guard came round with soup and bread for supper, but I could not eat. I felt at any moment that the hooded man would be standing in my cell. I understood that up to then I had believed myself protected by a sort of invisible shield that had now been pierced: I was wholly at the prison's mercy. I tried to think, to go over the conversation, to organise it in such a way that my self might come out of it intact, but always there was something that could not be accommodated. I dozed, and was woken with the shout of "Time to wash for prayer!", and saw through the window high up in the wall a sky full of stars.

"Why?"

"I don't know!"

The blow incensed me. I said: "I don't know what you want, Mr Investigator, and cannot find out if you strike me every time I ask. I cannot see your face and you have not told me your name or your city. Under the Basic Law of the Islamic Republic, approved by referendum last year, I have the right of habeas corpus. I have a right to know the suspicions under which I have been deprived of my liberty and exposed to your tyranny. Therefore, it is for you not I to speak."

I tensed against the blow, but nothing came.

He said: "You are British!"

"Is that a crime?"

"Yes. All British are spies! Now, go to your cell. When I call you back, you will tell your story, from the beginning to the end, and then we will expel you back to Britain."

"I do not want to go to Britain. For the love of Ali, tell me what you need to know and I will do my best to tell you. I have committed no crimes and my conscience is clear. I have never heard of the British Intelligence Service. I do not know these people you speak of, McNee and Carrington and Major. I have not been in Britain for seven years, and in those days the Government was different. Madame Thatcher was just Minister of Schools, an unimportant position. There is no such person as John Major: it is not an English name. Major is a military rank, like colonel or captain. The name of the person must be Major John followed by the surname. Nobody knows me in Britain. You think they will take me in exchange for Mr Kasravi in Manchester or the boys in Dundee, but I assure you they will not."

At length he said: "Rape and murder are not considered offences in Britain, but they are in this society."

"Those false charges were invented by the former regime, as you well know. I did not expect the Revolution to prolong the crimes of the Idolaters."

I had gone too far; but I was probing for the limits of his patience and intellect, which, because they were no more invisible than his face or body, had taken on in my imagination a comparable form and substance. I sensed he was not experienced in the world, or consistent in his mental attitudes; and I would be hit many times more before I could make out the shape of his nature or instructions. Indeed, if the blows to my mouth or ear or forehead could be said to have a purpose other than mere reaction to frustration, it was to guard and protect the extremities of an injured personality. He had a smell of poverty about him. I imagined him a flunked seminary student, corrupted by the Savak in the 1970s, used but despised by Najafi, at the end of his tether.

I picked myself up and groped for the chair. Into the blind silence, the tannoy burst with the sound of the noon prayer. I thought that he must let me go now. I tried ingratiation.

"Mr Investigator, no doubt you suffered in the prisons of the Idolaters' regime."

"Of course."

"Then why in God's name are you persecuting your fellow prisoner?"

I felt he was standing close to me. "We are not the Shah, Pitt. We are not weaklings, like the Shah. We care not at all about what is said about us in England or Europe. We do not care about so-called human rights and other liberal chatter. If the Shah killed hundreds, by God we will kill tens of thousands. Now go!"

In my darkness, I had an inspiration. "Has the former Shah died?"

"Of course. They are stoking the fires in Hell!"

The news caused me an inexplicable anger.

"Which girl?"

"The girl you raped and killed."

"I raped nobody, as you well know."

"Where is she?"

"Who?"

"The Isfahanian girl."

"Which one? I taught a class . . ."

Once again, I knew I had gone too far.

There was no order to our meetings: not every day, nor every week, but sometimes three days in succession or ten days apart; not always in the morning nor never in the morning; not always stopping during prayers nor always continuing.

In contrast, everything in the prison was the same. I had been in the Evin four weeks before I made my first discovery: that the world of my interrogation was separate from the world of my imprisonment. Indeed, if there was any order to my life, it was that the hooded man might not enter my cell, was somehow bound up with the block across the yard, that the guards called the Ministry, and I was safe from him here with my red plastic bowl and dish and aluminium spoon and torn cotton gelim. I knew that I could return to 381, listen for the door to close, lower myself down on my mattress, bring my knees to my chest and be certain that for a while nobody could touch me. I cannot exaggerate the luxury of that certainty. The pain I felt, the sense of shame and taint as if I had lost all bodily self-control, gained an objectivity, as if I were saying: Yes, good, all right, time enough to suffer, now I will rest.

I delighted in my privacy. The modesty of Iranian society, that borders on prudery and that I had once found so laughable, now seemed to me the mark of the utmost civilisation. My solitude was complete. The guards announced their presence, with a shout of "FACE TO THE WALL!" or "BIND YOUR EYES!" or a pious variation, before entering the cell. I could shower and go to the lavatory alone while the guard waited in the corridor. I saw no other prisoners.

I began to lift my head and look around me. I asked to be taken outside for exercise. The guard grunted; but the next evening, quite unexpectedly, he brought in and left two books: the Koran with a commentary in Persian, and the Imam's catechism, *A Clarification of Questions*.

"You have said you will not tell me your name, Mr Investigator. Will you give me a name I can use?"

"I have no name, Pitt. His Holiness honoured me and my brothers of the Ministry with the title: The Unknown Soldiers of the Lord of Time."

"It would help me if I had a name."

I felt him come closer. He was a vain man. "What name would you give me?"

I said: "Shahid. May I address you as Shahid?"

The word means martyr. I suppose all I meant was that I wished his death. Yet for him to strike me now was to deny his readiness to die.

"It is unimportant."

On the contrary.

"Do not lift your blindfold!"

Beneath my fingers was a sheet of ridged paper. He whispered in my ear. "Do you know what that is?"

I could smell glue from my fingers and photographic chemicals. I ran my fingers over the tight ridges. A picture of Farameh's den, with its document-shredding machine, came into my head. Beneath my fingers, I conjured an embossed circle, and within it a striped shield and the raised wings of an eagle.

"No, Mr Shahid."

It was the Great Seal of the United States of America. My mind's eye conjured a row of girls in black prayer chadors, cross-legged on a thick carpet, and before them their pots of glue and heaps of shredded paper. I thought: Piecing together shredded documents at the American Embassy is no more painstaking nor skilful than weaving a Nain carpet. That is the genius of the clergy: for them this country's backwardness is not an offence, as it was for the Shah and Farameh, but an opportunity. That is what I must learn. I must become like them, if I'm to come through the wreck.

Shahid walked round me and yanked up my blindfold. On the photocopy paper, which had been cut into a thousand strips and gummed together again, was the seal of the United States and the words Central Intelligence Agency. I stiffened.

"Blindfold down!"

I welcomed the dark.

He whispered in my ear. "When we took the Nest of Spies,

they tried to destroy their secrets, but our devoted children have reconstructed them one by one. Each page will take each of our operatives many weeks. We know everything about you! Everything."

"I have no connection with the Nest of Spies."

"You are lying! Where is the Obliterated Farameh?"

"Who, Mr Shahid?"

"If you don't answer, Pitt. I will beat you so that you will never walk again."

"Wait! I don't know where he is. I once heard on the B.B.C. that . . ."

"The B.B.C. tells lies!"

"I have no other information."

"Where's the slut?"

"I know no such person. For God's sake! Stop!"

He came close. "At Jaleh Square, on 8 September, 1979, Farameh closed the streets going into the square and then brought over his helicopters. For three hours, we could hear nothing but gunfire and the engines of the helicopters. Fifty thousand people died that day and we have sworn to avenge each one. If you tell us where the slut is, then we shall have a means of reaching Farameh and bringing him to God's justice."

"I heard Gen. Farameh is in Europe. On the B.B.C."

"Do you know the penalty for fornication?"

"Yes. But I am innocent of the charge. There can be no fornication in marriage."

"You did not marry! You are not a Muslim!"

"Mr Shahid, you must distinguish between the laws obtaining in Iran since the Revolution and the laws of the monarchy."

"The Laws of Islam begin with the Revelation and last to the Judgement Day."

"Indeed. I became a Muslim by reciting the opening of the

Koran before witnesses. I was married by pronouncing the formula: I, John Pitt, accepted you . . ."

"What dowry was paid?"

"The question is irrelevant."

"Answer, or you will regret it!"

"The other principal accepted that no dowry be paid."

"Before which imam?"

"There were no witnesses."

"Then the marriage was not legal, but a mere whoredom."

"On the contrary. Please consult His Holiness the Imam's *Clarification* . . ."

It was high summer. My cell became infested with wasps. After a while, I stopped killing them, because it made no difference to their numbers and they weren't my enemies.

I began to look for an order or pattern in my interrogation. I don't think Shahid had been educated in the modern sense, or had even the most rudimentary seminary training. His mind was not easy to fathom. At one moment, he would speak of the unforgivable crimes of the Shah, or of Farameh during his twenty days of power, at another he would drop hints about far worse atrocities committed by his own side. He claimed privileged information about the capture of the American Embassy, the European and American hostages in Beirut, even the Abadan cinema fire (which I had thought the work of the Savak). He loved to mention the name of Ayatollah Najafi. Yet all the while, and never far away, was his depression: a blackness of spirit that tainted our sessions and filled me with foreboding even as the guard led me blindly across the hot courtyard to his ground-floor room.

I suspected that he had been set two tasks in my interrogation and considered them of equal importance. The first was to build up a legal case against me for the Revolutionary Prosecutor. At the end of each session, he gave me a sheet of lined paper and stood behind me dictating what I was to write. My blindfold was raised to my forehead and all the while I repeated to myself: Don't turn round! Don't look at him! We had puerile squabbles about wording: I remember writing "military" when he wanted "military-ideological". He kept trying to alter my Persian into an inert, verbless succession of Arabic malapropisms which was the new style of the hard-line newspapers.

"Mr Shahid, I thought there had been a Victorious Revolution. Why do I have to use all these Excellencies and Majesties and Holinesses?"

"Complete your confession!"

"I mean, Mr Shahid, I thought those honorific titles were a feature of the Qajar despotism and the Idolaters' regime. Now it is the age of Islam, why can't I just write: Mr Najafi?"

"Correct form is: His Excellency The Grand Sign-of-God Mr Najafi, God extend his Shadow!"

I gave up. I believed that the charges he hoped to bring against me kept diminishing in severity: murder, rape, espionage, fornication. His mind was so ill formed and inconseqential that it was impossible to tell what some new question presaged. His obsession with sex disgusted me, but it was easily put to flight: I doubted that he was married or indeed had ever had a private conversation with a woman outside his family. Anyway I knew from my reading in the Russian Garden and from the *Clarification* that though the penalties for any irregular liaison were severe, so were the laws of evidence.

"Mr Shahid, if you ask such a question again, I will seek to lodge a complaint with His Highness."

"It is relevant!"

"I had no girlfriends in England."

"You are lying! In England, there is free love."

"Naturally, you have been there."

He hit me.

I knew then that he had been to London, and he hadn't told me, not just because he did not trust countries abroad but because he knew there must be some record of him there. Whether I truly could get out of here and, in some file kept by the British Foreign Office or immigration department, establish his name was beside the point: the point was that he feared I might. Just the repetition of these words, "he feared me", filled me with hope. How was I to give up hope of my survival if my interrogator feared it?

Dispersed among all these questions about women and love and marriage and ritual washing was something else he wanted to know, something important to the regime, which I believed had to do with Farameh. I sensed I had his answer and that I must not think about the past lest I bring it to the surface. I had seen men kneeling in the showers, during my first imprisonment, who had been beaten on the feet with heavy electrical cable and I knew I would not be able to resist it. For that reason, I made no attempt in my cell to prepare for our meetings or to organise my life in Iran into a narrative or to remember my year of happiness or the night in Bushehr harbour when my wife and child were taken from me or my strange meeting with Qavam. I had nothing to hide. Every event was of equal innocence and unimportance. Shirin became just another of my pupils and Mr Ryazanov a mere acquaintance, disreputable enough by the standards of the Islamic Republic, but nothing more. Yet all the while between my interrogator and me there was a congruence of interest: for I, too, needed to find out about Farameh and gather any scrap of information that might lead me to his daughter. Shahid maddened me with his evasions.

"Where is that man?"

"Which man?"

"The accursed General Farameh."

"I heard on the B.B.C. outside that he was in London."

"The B.B.C. tells lies!"

"As you command."

"Where is he?"

"How do I know? He is my enemy and I am his."

"He is in Iraq with the other Royalist serpents!"

"First, Mr Shahid, if you know where he is, you do not need to ask me. Second, you should know by now that Farameh is not a Royalist. He is not an any-ist. He has no beliefs or loyalties, least of all to the late Shah. His sole concern is his own power."

That was how I phrased my questions. Even so, he recoiled.

"Is the woman with him?"

"Which woman?"

"The slut."

"I know no such person."

"The woman you claimed to marry."

"Impossible."

"Where is she?"

"I have told you I don't know."

"Pitt, do you know what the cable is?"

"I have heard the word over there from the former regime."

"Good."

I no longer believed in his story about the American Embassy. I thought instead that he was working from another dossier, originating perhaps from the time of the monarchy, for which he had a fearful respect; and that even the general questions he asked me threatened the security of that dossier. I used to write my confessions down on lined sheets under the heading *Ministry of Information*. One day, a sheet felt different, and when I had my sight I saw it was faded like a newspaper left in sunshine. It was headed *Office of the Prime Minister, S.A.V.A.K.*

"How dare you compare His Holiness with the Shah and our work with the Savak!"

"I did not compare His Holiness with the Shah. I merely said, Mr Shahid, that what you do makes the Shah and the Savak like lilies."

"Of course. Where is that woman?"

"Mr Shahid, I told you I don't know. I divorced her according to the Arabic formula in Bushehr in 1975. I have not seen or heard of her since."

"And the child?"

I bowed my head. I said to myself: If that was you, Madame Bibi, you God-forsaken Savaki, and if I come out of this in one piece, I swear by Almighty God I will remind you of your treachery.

"She took the child."

"She stole your child?"

"No. The child was still at the breast. You must understand that I took pity on them."

"You abandoned your child."

"Yes."

"Write that down."

"Pitt, if you tell us where the woman is, and she corroborates your story, then you are free."

"For pity's sake, I don't know where she is."

"What if you went on televison?"

My heart leaped but I beat it down. The thought had come in and out of my cell and been shooed away.

"To tell the world that I quarrelled with my wife and her father! Is that so interesting!"

It was almost a question. Shahid withdrew into his shell.

"How many times have you had illicit sexual relations with a man?"

"Never, Mr Shahid."

"Think! When you were a boy, in Isfahan!"

"Never."

"Pitt, you are lying again. We have evidence."

"Tell me the evidence, so I may defend myself."

"Why? You will only lie."

That goddam musician, what was his name? Or the doorman with the toothache?

* *

205

To be hurt again and again, without any power to resist, soon destroys the personality. I mean there is a violence in which the prisoner begs and pleads for death, and screams not so that he is heard but that the force of the scream might somehow injure him to death; and in the intervals of his torture, when the torturers are taking their tea, or he is carried blindfolded to his cell, seeks some method by which he might kill himself. That became my secret, the sole remaining shred of my identity: a certain window in the wash-room, the needles brought round one day each month for prisoners to do their sewing, or a metal spoon adzed each evening against the heat-pipe. Those were to me as a bottle to the drinker or heroin to the drug addict.

Even in the basement of the Ministry, where I was taken, strapped, beaten on my feet, I did not wholly lose consciousness. Sometimes, in the intervals, while the torturers were taking their tea or eating their lunch, or if a blow went awry, I would think: Why have they taken up torture? What is it that has scared them and given them this urgency? Has the war started at last? Then I would scream it.

"Yes! Go on! Curse the slut!"

I cursed her because she had told me nothing, and so I could not tell them now. I cursed her because she had not trusted me with the secret that they wanted, so that I could not tell them now. I cursed her because I could not find her and could not make them stop hitting me and hit her instead. I cursed her because she knew I would have to suffer this and still she married me. I cursed her because she had saved my life. I cursed her because I was cursing her.

"What? Whisper it."

I tried.

"I can't hear you."

I tried again.

"Where is this necklace?"

I don't know. I don't know anything.

I fell onto a gashed cotton mat between two rows of bearded men in pyjamas. Behind them, their shirts and jackets hung on rubber hooks. They were frozen in embarrassment. It was as if I had broken in on each of them in some humble and intimate occupation, like sewing a sock or washing underlinen. There was no space for me, so I squatted by the door.

The men shrank from me.

"Who is he?"

"God knows. Ask him, why not?"

"He looks foreign."

"Turkish, maybe."

"Greetings, gentlemen. I am Pitt. I would have wished I could have presented myself to you on some more auspicious occasion."

"What did he say?"

"How can I tell? Is he speaking Turkish or Persian?"

"My friends, he's Russian! I once knew an Armenian."

"It's the foreign spy. He has been tortured, poor man."

"No, that was another name. Pitt was his name, poor man. He was Russian."

"GREETINGS, GENTLEMEN. I AM PITT, THE ENGLISH SPY!"

The men flattened themselves against the wall. The door pushed into my back. I shifted. A man with long moustaches limped in and the door shut behind him. The other men relaxed a little, as if, even in his broken state, the newcomer would unravel the confusion.

"Who's the beauty?"

"We think it's Pitt. The foreign spy."

The man seated himself on his bed-roll. A little boy knelt before him with a cup of water and a lump of sugar, which he began to crack in his teeth. He was crazy from his interrogation. He said in English: "How's Dot?"

Seated with our backs to the walls, there was just room for eight men, or seven and the boy. The thought of sleeping in the place filled me with panic. I said in Persian: "It is some years since your servant had the honour of waiting on Professor Spencer, at which time she appeared to be in good health."

The man ignored me. He continued in Persian: "I'll never forget the first time I met her. It was in Isfahan, during the Shah. One Thursday evening, I was with my friends in the bar of the Irantour Hotel, not a care in the world. Siavush, the immortal painter was there, a tremendous drunkard, opium-smoker and lover of girls, who was telling stories of San Francisco, though he'd never been further than Seddeh; when suddenly, there in the bar, an apparition materialised. Miss Dot! In the bar of the Irantour!

> Last night I dreamed an angel rapped upon the tavern door,
> And held to me a cup fired from the clay of Adam.

She was dressed as a man, covered from head to toe in dust. Her clothes were white, her hair and hands were white. All was white but her ruby lips and her blazing eyes. She had come from Mashad, on foot, by Shah Abbas' old pilgrimage road, thirty-three days on the way, leading a female camel and all alone with only Haj Ali Borujerdi, who'd done the journey on his grandfather's back in the time of Ahmad Shah and was now plucking at her sleeve, saying, 'Come away, Your Ladyship, come away, come away.'

"We fell silent. Not a man dared touch his glass. She turned about the room and fixed her gaze on me. She said, so everybody could hear, in a voice of diamond-like clarity: 'There's more to life, you know, Abbas Khan, than drinking beer and spitting melon seeds!' She came and stood over me. Haj Ali brought her a glass of water in his hands. She took two sips, then set it down, like this, on the bar. Then she said:

"'Whose drink is this?'

"'Let it be yours, Mme Espencer.'

"'Why? You'd better drink it up. Then kindly go and tell His Excellency the Consul-General that that poor mistreated girl is dead!'"

I was banging with my fist on the cell door.

"Poor man, his heart is burning for his homeland."

"Incorrect! Our heart is burning for solitary confinement."

"Why?"

I was ashamed of my show of feeling. I saw that here, in the communal cells, a prisoner must not utter feeling, for it cannot be ventilated, sticks to him for life. I went back to my bedroll. I recited:

> "'For fear of the pain of separation
> I shy away from intimacy'."

"Why?"

The storyteller was looking at me. His wall eyes said: Fine spy you are, Englishman, if I can unmask you in a moment. He said: "A man of my acquaintance, a devotee of the pen, once said to me, in this very same house, under the ancient regime: 'The great penalty of prison is that a man is not free, by which I mean not that he is isolated from the outside world, far from his family and friends and the delights of existence or that he is delivered up to the boots of the guards and the gracious attentions of His Excellency The Lord Cable. Ach, a man whether he wills it or not will in the end submit to those torments for they are the price of his condition as a prisoner, as opposed to a corpse. The greatest torture and misfortune in a prisoner's life is that even in this little circle he is still not free.' For here each day his prison is renewed. With these people," he opened his hands to embrace himself and the others, "even though he has nothing morally or mentally in common with them yet he must exist with them, eat with them, answer calls of nature with them, live with them. Soon you will be weary of this monotonous existence, weary to death, and your only wish will be that for just one morning in your life you will wake and open your eyes and see something other than the grey, patched socks of Mr Mohajerani here. Or at meal times men much more unfortunate and wretched than you will be chewing and crunching their food, while scraps of food fly out of their mouths in all directions, and you won't have the guts to say, 'Would you kindly eat more slowly?' Or there'll be a time when you are plunged into a sweet and melancholy daydream, and the fellow beside you cracks a dirty joke and digs you in the ribs and you have to listen. Or a moment when you've closed your eyes and you're trying to pass beyond the window bars, to look down from a great height on snow and mountains, and a faint and haunting music keeps coming to your ears and disappearing; at that moment as you spread out your mountains and your snow beneath you, and try to catch that music as it whispers by, at that moment somebody lets out an imbecile laugh that sets every nerve in your body dancing, but you are obliged or condemned to listen. These pettinesses come every minute, and linger for years on end and Oh that the earth would catch fire or Mr Saddam blow us all to Hiroshima, so that we do not have to endure them for eternity."

He looked at me in pure hatred.

I said: "On the contrary, sir. I am honoured to be admitted to this company. It is merely that your story stirred a memory in me of my own first meeting with Miss Spencer."

"Of course," he said and shivered.

"Though I have been fortunate to live many years in Iran, I am, in fact, a child of Britain, of the town of Hull . . ."

"Son of Hull!" In Arabic that would mean, The Terrifying One or The Sphinx. The men were looking at me with shining faces, delighted with my novelty.

". . . in the north of England. I recollect one day, when I was a child of five six, Miss Spencer entered the house, without an appointment or an introduction, as if she owned the place (which, for all I know, and given the feudal conditions still existing in that part of Britain, she might have done). She was travelling to her brother's lands just outside the town, she said. She had brought me some books: her grammar of Persian, of course, and, if I recollect, the *Divan* of Hafez. She said she was passing by. My mother was quite, or rather very, offended."

"Oh yes."

Even by Iranian standards, the man was a know-all.

"Why?"

"Well, I imagine your mother was of the third, or working class. And Miss Dot is the Queen's father's brother's daughter."

"I do not believe, sir, the consanguinity is so close."

He threw up his hands at my quibble. He turned to the men. "You must understand, gentlemen, that Miss Dot Espencer is a tall lady, of prodigious beauty, powerful intellect, implacable will and unassailable chastity."

"Alas!" said someone.

"Do you like the science of hypothetics?"

"I do not, sir."

"But imagine a moment, if Miss Dot had not come that day, or mislaid the address or you had been at school . . ."

"Sir, with respect, that is mere talk for the sake of talking."

"We are in prison, sir. Talk is our consolation. May I be permitted to introduce myself and our company? I am Mr Baharmast, a notorious Communist, drunkard and homosexual. This gentleman here is my friend, Mr Mohajerani . . ."

"Religious fanatic, sir," he said. He stumbled to rise, but his feet were in bandages and he gave up with the sweetest of smiles.

"And Mr Dr Enayatullah . . ."

"Also Communist, Mr Pitt, but not homosexual." There was a faithful laugh, as to a beloved joke.

"And Big Ali Razavi."

"I am a thief and fence, sir."

"And the darling of our company, Little Ali, a drug smuggler."

The boy, who was no more than ten or eleven, sprang up and, with caution, shook my hand.

"I am extremely fortunate to make your acquaintance, gentlemen."

"Will you kindly introduce yourself and tell us your history?"

"Why not? As I have said, I am John Pitt, a child of Britain. My birth was low and mean. Yet, under the influence of Miss Spencer and others, I took to the study of Persian and some years ago came to Isfahan. In that famous town,

> 'Whose air is the breath of the angels of Paradise'

the scent one day of a barberry pilau converted me to Islam . . ."

"God bless you!"

"Congratulations!"

"Perhaps, Mr John, that barberry pilau was prepared with especial consideration for you."

Mr Mohajerani was beside himself: "Mr John, Mr John:

> 'Love is a condition quite unlike any other
> Love is the astrolabe of God's secrets
> Whether your love is of this world, or of the next,
> The end is the same, for it brings you to God!'"

"Dear Mr Mohajerani, I am not certain that our guest is burning with quite your enthusiasm for eternal life."

"Why?"

"Please, my dear."

Mr Mohajerani bit his lips. Mr Baharmast was looking at me. I sensed that he had heard some inkling of my story. To change the subject, he held out a crumpled packet of Ushnu cigarettes. "Won't you smoke? They bring a taper to light them."

The sight of cigarettes always caused me intense pain. I put my hand to my heart.

"We are divided about the merits of smoking. On the one hand, it provides pleasure which is completely to be relied on. Whoever heard of the smoker tired of smoking! On the other hand, it weakens the imprisoned man, makes him lazy and unambitious, displaces all goals in life but the achievement of a cigarette; causes him to fawn on his companions and the guards; may even provoke stealing and other wicked or improper actions. I am the leader of the smokers' party, Mr Mohajerani of the non-smokers. We are at everlasting war."

Mr Mohajerani smiled. Above our heads, the ceiling was brown from two dynasties of incarcerated smoke. I thought: Their actual dispute is in the realm of belief, but is here transferred to tobacco. I recognised that this was an elaborate and tedious joke, which yet preserved peace in the cell. I must learn like these men to be civilised and to pass the time.

"Young Ali!"

"Yes, Your Honour?"

"Please do me the favour of stepping over here."

He hesitated. I don't suppose he'd ever seen a European.

"Do you have a mohreh?" That has no name in English: it is a small octagon, made of pressed dust from the battlefield at Kerbela, on which some men rest their foreheads when they pray.

"Of course."

"Please give it to me."

With it, I wrote a word on the wall.

"Can you read that, dear Ali?"

"Of course. 'God!'"

"And that?"

"'Hosein!'"

"And that?"

He bowed his head in shame.

"Don't be sad. In a few weeks, you will read better than Mr Mohajerani."

That gentleman blinked up from the *Quintessence of Eloquence*. "You have shamed us, Mr John. And an Englishman, too!"

"I will not be responsible for algebra or geometry."

"Mr Dr Enayatullah!"

He was a bald, fussed man of the complexion known in Persian as judas-tree-like or purple.

"O for heaven's sake. I am far too busy with my proposal for Ayatollah Najafi."

I had never had much company, and at the beginning I found my life intolerable. Before I had been happy in the prisoner's conception of happiness: that is, returning from the Ministry in the afternoon, as the shock and shame receded to my walls, I had felt secure in my privacy. Now I had none. It was not just that I was observed at all times, especially by the little boy, but that my thoughts and fears were now available to all. Yet as I became accustomed to the cell, I began to learn something of their civility, and to become what Mr Baharmast termed *socializeh*.

His personality regulated all our intercourse. Whole areas of conversation and thought were placed irrevocably off-limits: women, of course, except Miss Spencer, who seemed to constitute a category of her own beyond sex and all its entanglements; time; our cases because of the Ministry's habit of placing stoolies, what they call antennas in the Evin, in each cell; and what passed or did not pass in the Interrogation Block. (It was our habit, when a man was called, to stand up and shake his hand at the door, but to say nothing on his return, only to offer him water and sugar.) Instead, we spoke incessantly of the war; the cost of living; and literature. In that last, I championed the New Verse, Mr Baharmast the traditional school. We spoke often of the wickedness of the British, the innocence of America and the irremedial stupidity of Russia.

They were engineers or technicians, and I learned many new

things. Mr Enayatullah was a town planner and had written a paper for Ayatollah Najafi on Reconstruction in the south once the territory had been liberated. He believed that there was great talent in the Evin that was being squandered at a time of emergency and which could be put at the service of the nation. Mr Mohajerani, who was a printer, and very well off, and had established a pious institute in Mashad called a Hoseiniyeh that had been closed down by the Savak, told me of a new technique where books would be stored on computers and transmitted at request down telephone wires into houses and schools. We disputed whether that was an advance over the present arrangement. He was a passionate opponent of the Imam's doctrine of clerical infallability, known as the Regency of the Jurist.

"I had expected you, Mr Mohajerani, as a pious and dedicated Muslim, to be an enthusiast of the Islamic Republic. I have heard that the turbanned classes are enjoying their best years since the time of old Shah Abbas in Isfahan. Why, all the best young men are taking the robe. The engineering colleges are empty, but the seminaries are full to bursting. The whole country has forgotten it knew a word of English. Heavens, even the guards here are spouting Arabic!"

"Is that what it is? I had been intrigued by some of the sounds. Dear John, if the Holy Prophet (Peace!) were to come among us and hear what purports to be his Good Book, the tears would roll down his blameless cheeks!"

"Yet, Mr Mohajerani, the clergy is leading the defence against Saddam in the south, in Khorramshahr and Abadan, while I and you are mouldering in prison."

Mr Mohajerani sighed. "Are you familiar with the Constitutional Revolution at the close of the Qajar era?"

"Of course."

"You will recollect that the clergy was greatly active in the Revolution and in the new Parliament. In short, they made of themselves such a pestiferous nuisance that the people became utterly sick of them. When Reza Khan took a stick to the prayer leader of the mosque in Qom, not a man in the congregation raised a voice for the poor divine. I fear, Mr John, that the effect of this Revolution will be to make this country sick and tired of the true religion."

"Now, now, my dear," said Mr Baharmast. "Do not agitate yourself."

I said: "I had the incalculable privilege of seeing His Excellency the Imam, as close as you are to me and to hear his melodious voice."

The men stiffened. Mr Baharmast closed his eyes.

I said: "It was in Tehran, in the Days of God, 12 Bahman of the year 1357, the day the Imam returned by air from France. I was always on the pavement in those days, sometimes at the University, sometimes at Azadi, here and there, not because I had any political enthusiasms but because I had no dwelling. Gossip flew high and low, that the aircraft had left Paris, was approaching, had landed at Mehrabad. I myself set out for the Behesht Zahra for it had become my custom to go there to consult the list of martyrs. I set off on foot from Artillery Square but buses were passing, picking up whoever wanted to travel without payment. The people seemed to me both giddy and sceptical, a strange psychological mixture. The soldiers at the cross-roads stared into the far distance or wore faint smiles. Soon the roads became clogged. I had never such seen crowds . . ."

"Like the Tehran Paradise when the great Mahvash headed the bill . . ."

"Shame on you, sir!"

"Mr Baharmast! Please permit our guest to tell his tale."

". . . of men and women and babes in arms. I got down and walked. Inside the cemetery, there was an open space where an Air Force helicopter was attempting to land. The people were running in every direction, I think because they had heard rumours of helicopters in the killings at Jaleh Square. The blades of the machine threw up whirlwinds of dust and sand, bent the little trees in two, stripped last year's petals from the rose bushes. Then the machine came down with a bump, the engine was extinguished, the door opened and the captain descended. He had taken off his tie and had his cap in his hands. I heard him tell the marshals that the machine and its crew are at the service of His Holiness and the Revolution and must above all be protected from damage, when there was a stupefying roar from the main gate. Imam has come! Imam is here!

"The crowd was surging forward then whipping back again like an oak in a high wind in winter. People were shrieking in fear and utter recklessness, when I saw the strangest sight of my eventful life. Above the heads, an automobile appeared, large, foreign, white, a Mercedes, I believe; and was moving through the air towards us. It approached with a funereal slowness. Then I saw that the Imam's car was resting on the shoulders of thirty forty young men before they laid it down, as if it had been glass, in front of the aircraft. The Imam stepped out, catching his robe about him. In the seething roar of the crowd, he seemed not in any way surprised as the Captain handed him up the steps into the machine. Haj Ahmad, his son, and two other gentlemen followed him.

"I was pressed tight against the burning metal of the aircraft. I saw the Captain kneel before Haj Ahmad, and though I do not exactly recall his words, his meaning was this: that if I fire up the engine, the tail rotor will cut the people to pieces and the main rotor in this confined space will anyway not have the power to lift the machine. The Imam looked up and asked, 'Is there a problem?' Then he turned to the Captain and said: 'Put your faith in God. Nothing and nobody will come to harm.'

"The Captain came back down the steps and lay down on his front. The marshals cried: 'We are to lie down.' Suddenly, the engine burst into life, the crowd scampered back and the Captain threw himself inside. The aircraft rose a metre in the air, two, three, but young men were hanging onto the landing-gear, and it crashed back to earth. Through the open door, I saw the Imam face-to-face. In his eyes was a look of complete indifference. I am sure he had never been in a helicopter any more than in a crowd of three million souls. It was as if over years and years he had extinguished every spark of fear and curiosity. The helicopter rose again, yawed, righted itself, the boys tumbling off the supports like blown litter, began to climb. It banked and moved off towards the Martyrs' Section and the crowd surged after. There the Imam made a speech that you know about."

"Mr John? May I ask a question?"

"The sentence first, Little Ali. Then the question."

"'The melons of Gorgab are exceedingly sweet.'"

"Excellent! You are a good student, Little Ali."

"You're just being polite. May I ask my question?"

"I am at your service."

"People say that England is the instigator of all intrigue in the world."

"So they say in Iran."

"And that Mr Khomeini is an agent of Britain."

"I am sure that is not true."

He looked at me in the way Iranians do, as if to say: You are entitled to say anything you please, however superficial or misguided.

"If England is the source of all intrigue, may I enquire: What intrigue are you, sir, at present engaged in?"

"Little Ali!" Mr Baharmast intervened. "That question is extremely rude."

I raised my hand. "No matter, Abbas Khan. My answer to your question is simple: My intrigue is to find my family."

"But Mr Mohajerani says that nobody loves his wife. Therefore . . ."

"Indeed, dear Mr John, I would go further: I would intrigue to lose my wife!"

"Excellent!"

"I also have a young child."

"A daughter, sir!"

"Ssss, my sweet boy. We must not speak of such matters."

Mr Baharmast tactfully steered the conversation to the safer shore of espionage. "You know, when you chaps kicked out Reza Khan in 1941, it was the middle of the night. Dot and Ismail Murtazaevich had the task of breaking the news to the Shah. The Americans in those days were all at sea in Iran, just did whatever Dot told them. At the Kakh Palace, the gate was barred and the guards asleep."

Stop fishing, Abbas Baharmast.

"'So! Kick the damn thing down,' Dot said.

"Ryazanov was far too delicate for that sort of work. So Dot just took a swing at the door – and it was heavy, studded with nails, you must have seen it – and that was that. That very night poor Reza Khan was on his way to Mauritius. Do you wonder that we Persians hate the English!"

Stop fishing, Abbas. That first day, I'd had a bad time over there, and you took me by surprise. It won't happen again. Also, why take the trouble? We're none of us getting out of here alive.

"Of course, not. I do wonder why, in spite of our wickedness to Iran over four hundred years, you Persians yet like us."

"Oh yes. That is obvious."

"You Iranians know so much, dear Mr Baharmast."

"Of course. Yet in all those years, we knew nothing of England, only certain Englishmen and English ladies. And what men and women: Browne and Curzon, Bullard, Miss Dot, Zaehner, and finally the seal and perfection of the series, your good self."

"Oh, for heaven's sake . . ."

"We thought that those men and women were samples of a race of heroes living under brief and cloudy skies! We thought there was nothing you could not do, no language too difficult, no script too vague, no problem too abstruse, that it would not yield to the force of your concentration. If sheer force failed you, then you used treachery, and if not treachery, kindness. What we did not know was that England sent us only its best: that Iran was truly the last outpost of English power in the world and with its loss England too would disintegrate. With the Americans it was quite different. When they started coming, about the time of the Kennedy years, but really only in large numbers after Nixon's visit in '72, we were baffled: for here were fools and criminals and drunkards and saints and the courageous and the cowardly and the utterly mediocre and the brilliant in the proportions you would expect in any large country. Also, you English always gave the impression that your minds were elsewhere: that while you said or did something, you were in fact thinking of something else. We spent all our time trying to understand the true motives of the Americans, and were very reluctant to take them at face value."

Big Ali spoke. "What is your opinion, Mr John, of the occupation of the American Nest of Spies?"

"My opinion is unimportant."

"Mr John thinks it was a mistake."

Mr Baharmast had spoken.

"Why? It was strong and decisive and taught World Arrogance a lesson."

"As you command."

"Don't you agree? They were helping the Idolatrous Shah."

"As you command."

Mr Baharmast interrupted. "If you wish to know, Mr John believes it was an error that will haunt us for years. Of course, dear Big Ali, you and I believe that it was a necessary operation so as to to embarrass the liberals and deepen and envenom the Revolution. Unfortunately, Mr John does not concur. He believes that fifty years from now, all our grievances against the United States will have been forgotten, the Revolution itself will have been forgotten but the world will remember that Iranians, of all people, mistreated seventy harmless men and women within their midsts. Is that so, John?"

"Yes."

※ ※

"Please go nearer, Mr John!"

"Is that better?"

Little Ali was on tip-toe on my head.

"Do take care, Mr John!"

"What can you see, lad?"

"I need something to scrape off the paint."

"I've a sharpened spoon. Can you try that? Pass it up, Mr John!"

"You are infants," said Abbas Baharmast. Nobody took any notice.

"What do you see, my love?"

"I can see . . . I can see . . . A tree."

"A what?"

"A tree."

"A tree! What sort of tree?"

"Together with other trees or on its own?"

"Alone. I don't know what sort of tree."

"Deciduous or coniferous?"

"*Meciduous vesiduous.*"

"Dr Enayatullah means, my love, does it have leaves or needles?"

"Leaves."

"It must be an oriental plane."

"It could be a box."

"Or a poplar."

"Or a cypress."

"Describe the leaves precisely, dear Little Ali."

"I am injuring Mr John."

"Not at all."

"Wait!"

"What?"

"There's something else."

"What something else. Quick, lad."

"A dog."

"A dog?"

"There's a dog sitting under the tree."

"A dog sitting under the tree!"

"It's asleep."

"A dog sleeping under *Platanus orientalis*!"

"What breed of dog?"

"It's a dog, that's all."

"Let me see!"

"Please be careful. I . . ."

"John, hold steady!"

"It's my turn."

"I have seniority."

"STOP IT!"

Ali slid to my shoulders and then to my hips and then to the ground. We turned, and Mr Baharmast was quivering with rage.

"For this work, John, I hope your hand will not cause you pain."

For a day and a night, nobody spoke.

I learned too about the Evin system. We were in a building called the Training Institute. Under the penal theory of Mr Najafi and the prison governor, any person who entered the Evin in custody was *a priori* sick and must be held in solitary confinement in the Infirmary so as to prevent contagion. If he were not incurable (in which case he was taken to the firing squad) he would then be put on trial before a clerical judge, sentenced and moved to the communal cells of the Training Institute to be taught the lessons of religion and the civilities of society. Once there, he was not supposed to undergo interrogation, though here we were exceptions – none of us had been tried.

In reality, as Mr Baharmast reminded us, the Islamic Republic had simply taken over the practices of the monarchy which went back to the nineteenth century: soften up a prisoner by torture and solitary confinement till he made a more or less coherent confession, and then drag what was left of him to execution or toss him into the stagnant society of an overcrowded prison.

One day, we heard that President Bani Sadr had been deposed and fled the country. As we entered summer, new prisoners were brought to the cell and then more and then more. The Training Institute took on a concentration-camp-like character. Sometimes, I would wake and a boy would be lying across my legs and, when I woke again, he would be gone. Once, glancing through the open door of the latrine, I saw a coffle of blindfold prisoners, young men all of them, who were what the guards called Hypocrites. I could not truly fathom their beliefs, but they combined the certainties of Islam with the certainties of historical materialism. Food had to be scrupulously shared. The "mayor" of our cell, by virtue of the beauty of his nature, was Mohajerani: he could cut a hundred-gram piece of sheep's cheese into twenty-four equal pieces with a sharpened metal spoon.

"Eat, my dear John, and may it be nectar to your soul!"

"Please give it to the young man."

"My dear son, the Englishman wishes you to have his portion."

"Keep it for the living."

I did not know whether to count, or to shut my ears. It began after midnight with a long burst of automatic fire, followed, a few seconds later, by individual shots. I thought if I counted the shots at least the life lost was recorded as a number. I thought, if I shut my ears, then perhaps someone would be saved. In truth, I could not close my ears, nor speak, nor move, for every shot was louder and nearer than the last, till I felt my head must burst. I thought that if I were dead then at least I would be spared having to listen. Even when the firing stopped, no one slept because we could not be sure it would not start up again. One night, in the month of September, 1981, I counted eighty-seven individual shots.

"Mr Mohajerani?"

"My dear friend!"

"Will you not lie down and let me stand for a while?"

"God bless you, John, but how can I rest when the sweetest children of Iran, our darling boys and girls in which we rested our hopes, are dying at the hands of these oppressors!"

There was another burst and then four single shots. Mr Mohajerani began to recite over the shots:

> "I have come from the Evin tonight, the house of
>   broken-hearted lovers
> of moths burned in the flame of the love of the Lord;
> of boys and girls who burned the harvest of their youth
> for a glimpse of the face of the Beloved.
> Let me speak of the murmur, of the prayers that rise
> through iron grilles at the hour before dawn,
> of the tears that run down the drenched walls.
>
> I have come from the Evin tonight, from the land of the
>   besotted, from the boundary of life and eternity, of dust
>   and the Kingdom,
> of an endlessly fought and refought Kerbela.
> And you, O traveller, should you pass by here one day,
> when all this is ruins, listen with the ear of soul
> to the stones as they murmur, This is the Vale of Love."

I was awake. Abbas Baharmast kept his hand over my mouth. He whispered in my ear: "John, I have some news for you."

I lost control. He pressed down hard on me. I tried to disconnect my mind, to hold my bowels, to choke the scream in my throat. He was strong.

"John, I want you to understand that women have a better chance of survival under this regime than men. Because of their upbringing

and because of the anonymity of the veil. You must take your consolation from that."

Gradually, I felt the convulsion subside. He lifted his hand from
my mouth.

"When, Abbas Khan?"

Mr Baharmast never answered questions of time.

"I alone?"

He smiled dreamily. "The whole company."

That changed matters. I had not expected to be allowed to die
with my friends. Then the sheer immensity of the slaughter turned
my stomach.

"I wanted to give you time to pray or whatever you do."

"God bless you, Abbas. That was considerate."

He sat up and played with a cigarette. "Was Her Royal Highness
worth it, dear friend?"

"I don't know. I'll tell you in five minutes."

His laughter disturbed the men.

"And you, Abbas? Was it worth it for you?"

He sighed. "Did you know that Ismail Murtazaevich was also
once in love! Mr Ryazanov in love!" He recollected himself and my
question. "I regret our stupidity and the unbelievable bad faith of
the Soviet Union. You know, Ismail Murtazaevich said to me once
in Isfahan, 'You must learn patience before all things. You must wait
your moment. Otherwise, that old man will make idiots of you all.'
Well, it has happened and we pay with our lives. That a revolutionary
must expect. Vivre et pas vivre est bien pire que mourir. What makes
my heart bleed is that my beloved Iran will have to suffer under these
pimps for fifty years."

"You never give up, do you, dear friend?"

He leaned forward and put his hand on my shoulder. "We knew
he worked an agent into the old man's household. In Iraq. And then in
Paris. And now in Tehran. You can tell me, John. It doesn't matter now."

I sprang back. His antenna's touch was like a scald. I should have known it was Abbas! He looked at me with eyes full of sorrow. There was a murmur from the bedrolls.

"What's up, Mr Abbas? What are you quarrelling about and the Englishman?"

He stood up. "I have some exceedingly disagreable news for us all. However, there is nothing I or you can do about that now. We should have considered this moment before embarking on our lives of wickedness. Please say your prayers, gentlemen."

The men rose together from their beds, white as ghosts. They dressed in a fumble, desperate to have their clothes on before the rap on the door.

"Nothing to be done about that, gentlemen. We are only men."

Mr Mohajerani cried out: "Hosein! We are ready! Please let us go out and die for you!" The men fell in behind him for prayers. He turned on me, smiling. "Won't you pray with us, Mr John? God is very merciful."

"I am relying on that."

Little Ali jumped out of bed. His eyes were smeared with sleep. "What's up! What's happening, Mr Abbas? Mr John?" He looked into my face and screamed.

The door opened and someone hissed: "ALL YOUR POSSESSIONS! MAKE IT QUICK!"

Mr Mohajerani threw open his arms. "I kiss the order of execution!"

"Brother, I protest at this injustice." I stepped towards the door. "The boy, Ali Rajavi, is a minor. Under the Constitution of the Islamic Republic, and the express statement of His Holiness the Imam, children under twelve years of age may not be exposed . . ."

"He had half a kilo of smack in the New Town, Mr John."

"The charges against him are beside the point. Under the Constitution . . . "

"SHUT YOUR FACE, JEW!"

"Leave it alone, John. You are upsetting the company."

"I would be grateful, Mr Baharmast, if for the few moments

remaining to me of my earthly existence, you would not seek to address me."

"May your eye be bright." He shivered and, to disguise it, turned and embraced the chattering boy. "Be brave, my lad, for it is not so very bad. Your friends are all around you, and will keep you company on the way. And your pretty mum and handsome dad are waiting on the threshold, their hearts have missed you . . ."

"What about my proposals for the reconstruction of war damage in Khorramshahr Town. We have drawn up det –"

"WHAT DO I CARE, HYPOCRITE? BLINDFOLD ON!"

In the darkness, I felt my hands being tied. As we shuffled forwards, I stumbled, fell against Big Ali's icy back, caught the blindfold on the seam of his shirt, gently pulled it up. The main lights were off, but in the light that came out from the cells I saw a file of men carrying weapons and wearing black hoods slashed with eye holes. I thought: They must suppress their humanity, otherwise they could not do this. My friends shuffled forward in a line, heads to the ground, in worlds of their own. A lassitude had taken hold of us all, as though we were almost there. Only Mr Baharmast walked upright, with Little Ali's head on his shoulder.

Ahead of us, a door was open. Snow danced and fluttered in the frame. A breath of mountain air nibbled at my face. It smelled of iron and granite and pure water. I was pierced by beauty and delight. I thought: If only I had known that one must live one's life like this, knowing it ends in a minute! I suppose we all learn this lesson at the end, but nobody comes back to warn the others. My chest was tight and bubbling with laughter. O God, may I see the mountains from the yard!

"Mr John! Shall we meet on Resurrection Day?"

"God willing, dear Mr Mohajerani." I stepped into the light. Before me were stakes, row after row of them: I had not known there would be so many rows! And so scuffed and cuffed and bitten by gunfire, and the wall behind, O God . . .

"Pull the band down, John. You haven't the courage. Nobody has."

"Go to Hell!"

"I believe that is my destination."

"SHUT YOUR FACES, YOU APOSTATES!"

"The donkey dies and it's a wedding for the dogs, eh Guards?"

Something hit my legs and, as they buckled, I was dragged by the hair and tied. The violence infuriated me, not because it was unnecessary, but because it robbed me of my will. To them I was already a corpse. I felt if I could keep some fragment of my will, remain alert to these last moments, to see the mountains when I lift my head, then I could send my love and blessings racing over deserts and cities to where they are sleeping, O my darlings.

I lifted my head. Across the snow, already stained with feet, a group of men were drinking tea. I say men, but they did not look like men, rather beings from a world of pure farce. They had their backs to me, hoods in a ruck at their necks. There was something taut about their uniforms, which was not fear, but a disciplined and secret hilarity. I could see that we must have been very wicked to have deserved death at their hands. They were drinking tea from the saucer, and chattering. Every sound and click reverberated. The rifles were stacked in two batches of four. I saw no machine-gun.

"John, I do not want to die at enmity with you. It is not as you think."

I turned my head to the left. At the stake beside me, they had tied them together: Abbas and the boy. My heart dissolved. They have orders not to shoot Abbas, and he's trying to save the boy! Is there no end to his effrontery in the face of these rifles.

"It is not for me to judge you or anybody."

"AT THE READY!"

It was quiet, or rather quiet enough to hear the first traffic at the Tajrish Bridge. A breath of wind scythed through my shirt. I was cold as I'd never been in my life. Something was trickling down my legs, but that doesn't matter, I am only a man. I looked up. The men were ambling into position, hoods on. A clergyman had appeared, in a clumsy greatcoat, and was peering through sun-glasses at a clipboard. A rifle sighted at me. I raised my head and saw mountains running at me.

"TAKE AIM!"

"Long live the Revolution!"

"Long live His Holiness The Great Leader . . ."

"Shut up, you cowards. John! Say something!"

The mountains will take me. And you, my darling . . .

"With one hand clutching a wine-bottle . . . "

". . . and another twined in the Beloved's hair . . ."

". . . I go dancing to the execution-square . . ."

"FIRE!"

I saw the smoke. I swear I saw the smoke; and heard the crackle of cold gunfire; and felt the splash of hot blood and shit on my face; and the lives punched out of them and the thump of empty bodies bouncing on the stake; and the creaking of cords and the reverberation around the mountains stopped dead in full career.

I thought that death was something other than we'd been told, and we survive, shaken out of our wits, for all eternity. I thought that there was no such thing as dying. I thought I was invulnerable. I thought that if I could open my eyes, which are gummed shut, then all will be explained.

I opened my left eye.

Abbas' chest had been dug out. I could see the white of bones amid his tumbling guts. The little boy's neck had snapped and he leaned back at a crazy angle. Mr Mohajarani was bent double to his toes. On the snow before him, the wind fanned the scarlet pages of his dropped Koran. O God, I got Abbas' blank! How could they be such imbeciles! I shouted: Shoot me! There's been a mistake! My friends are gone and I must catch them up! The sound came as a gurgle. Something was stuck to my teeth: I'd bitten my tongue through. I looked up, and one of the men was gurgling at me, gurgling and dancing, till they scampered laughing from the yard. The clergyman, white as the snow, followed them out.

My mouth was bursting with blood. Gently, I looked down and let it dribble through my teeth. I thought: It doesn't matter, I will bleed to death, or freeze in this bloody drizzle. In the back of my head, something had gone dead beyond all resurrection: rather as, in a theatre, a light goes off and plunges part of the stage into darkness. I was shaking so much, the ropes cut into my belly. My teeth jumped. Around me, the pieces of my friends grumbled and creaked in the wind.

"Shirin?"

"Yes, dear."

"Where are you?"

"Here."

"How are you?"

"How are *you*?"

"You see they have a spy in each cell group, because men like to tell their deepest secrets when they're going to die. When the time comes for the firing squad, they keep a blank for the spy, but they made a mistake, and it is I who survived."

"I'm glad, sir."

"You don't understand, Shirin. They are my friends!"

"Yes, sir. Your daughter misses you, she asks for you, 'Why is Dad's place empty? When will Dad complete his business and come home?'"

It was dark. In my hands and feet was a pleasant tingling. Men were moving heavily about me. Somebody was cutting my cords. He put his face close to mine. His breath stank of sheep's cheese and spring onions.

"Welcome, Mr Antenna. Welcome back from the threshold of Hell. The men know who you are. The days will be tedious for you, now, but not as tedious as the nights. You are going to regret you didn't die with your friends. You will regret you betrayed them. Oh yes, you will regret it, Mr English Spy."

❧ 19 ❧

I was moved back to the Infirmary, to a new cell: 396. On the wall outside was a loudspeaker, which blasted me with the call to prayer twice a day and the Voice of Islamic Iran. It was from that loudspeaker, one morning in May of 1983, that I heard the news of Farameh's assassination in front of the Royal Lancaster Hotel in Bayswater, London. For hours, the men banged on their doors and the guards did nothing to stop them. Sometimes, at night, somebody shouted so I could hear the lines of Persian doggerel: "The General's on his way to hell / Let's fix the son-in-law as well."

I did not move from the cell. I did not wash nor pray nor go to the latrine nor exercise. I kept my face to the wall.

"Why don't you eat?"

"Kindly go away."

"They were bad men, Bahais and Freemasons and Zionists and hypocrites, and also some real criminals."

"Please leave me."

"The authorities just wanted to scare you, so you would tell the truth!"

"Kindly go away."

"Mr John?"

"Please go away."

"You are a Muslim."

"Please go away."

"Yet look at you: hair uncombed, nails uncut, dirty clothes. I will

232

take you myself to the shower and stand before the door and then you will be safe."

"Please go away."

I was not summoned by Shahid. I did not consider why I had been spared execution, but I knew that now that Farameh was dead they could have no use for me. I was worth nothing, except a bullet. I knew that my depression would be the end of me, but I could no longer imagine any other mental condition. I lay on my torn rubber mat looking at the wall, where a prisoner had written the sentence "My heart is breaking for my son" and there was a stain as if from a bitter orange. I dreamed of the town of Bushehr on the Gulf coast. I dreamed of England, of playgrounds and seaside cottages that had an overpowering authenticity and yet were drenched in a merciless and unvarying whiteness which I knew from the vocabulary of dreams, and even as I dreamed it, was death. One night I dreamed of a woman who was not my wife nor my foster-mother, and knew too that she was death. I woke to the groaning of the drug addicts and the tap-tap-tap of the women prisoners conversing by code two floors below.

"Mr John, good news at last! The Badr offensive has been a total success! In one day, at most two, Basra will be ours!"

"Thank God."

"You must put on your blindfold. I am taking you to the Ministry."

"I will not go."

"Mr John, I must do my religious duty."

"I shall not go, Mr Kuchulu."

"Mr John, please. You have a visitor."

"Where is the slut?"

I was not sure if I'd heard that, or whether I myself had thought it. Seated, head-bowed, blindfolded, I had lost the objectivity of words or things. I smelled something new, Persian, bazar-like; musk, I think; and heard something new, like the swish of a skirt or robe on the gritty floor. I sensed, too, that the room was denser than usual, heavy and animate, as if men had slid in and squatted down against the walls.

"Where is the slut?"

The voice, which was not unkind, renewed the scent of musk and the swish of clean cloth. Sight is the master, for it is by pictures that we live. Without sight, the other senses struggle to bring order to the world. Weak and deceitful, thrown on themselves, they simply mislead. I fought to objectify the sensations of scent and sound and touch, to convert them back into movement and movement into persons.

It seemed to me an important man was standing near me. His cleanliness and calm and retinue suggested power: the Revolutionary Prosecutor himself, perhaps, or a high official of the Ministry of Information. Yet there was something confident and unofficial in his speech and motions. In my chain of blind supposition, where each link reduced the likelihood of truth, I thought that my interrogators despaired of making anything of me; that Farameh was dead and the rubies lost; that I must die now; and that this gentleman was here to approve or confirm that. For that reason, I must keep on to him.

"Excuse me, Your Honour. I do not understand your question."

"Where are the jewels?"

"I have told you. I don't know."

I was hit on my left ear: that is, not by the new man and his people, but by my usual interrogators.

"Where is that woman?"

By such triumphs is the tortured soul preserved! Now say her name which will sprout roses in your filthy mouth!

"Which woman, Your Honour?"

I sensed an unfamiliar motion. It was as if the man had raised his fingers to forestall my being hit. My time is up, it seems.

I said: "Sir, the jewels are the property of my wife and were returned to her according to the Law at our divorce. I do not know the whereabouts of either, after the events in the sea that I told you about. For God's sake, I can tell you no more, truth or lies, on that subject. There is something I wish to say on another topic."

There was no answer.

"Sir, I have despaired of my life. Yet I am troubled by an ancient secret, which I do not wish to carry to my grave."

"It is too late." The man's voice came from further away. He must be on his way out of the room. I felt a breath on my cheek from the cold passage.

"I merely ask leave, that the other gentlemen should withdraw."

I felt that same strange movement, but sharper. There was no blow. I paused. The breath from the door was extinguished.

"The brothers have my confidence."

For the first time, I felt an angle in the room: that I was not in confrontation with this man, but coming at him, as it were, from the side. A thought flashed at me, from God knows where: These people are losing the war!

"As you wish. Yet they have not beaten this secret out of me in all this time."

"You have not been beaten. Believe me, sir, you have not been beaten."

Who is this man? Could he be Ayatollah Najafi? No, his voice is too young. The Imam's son, could he be?

"As you command. If you knew what I know, the secret I've kept locked up in my heart for ten years, you would not wish them to hear it. You would not wish to hear it yourself. There is but one man in Iran with the humanity . . ."

"He's lying! We've investigated all this! He's trying to save his wretched pelt!"

On the contrary, I am trying to kill you. My little Shahid, if you go out that door, you die. There is nothing left for you but the Front. This is my gift to you in recompense for your stupidity and cruelty.

"I have said I am sick of life."

"To no purpose. I am not interested in ancient history."

"So be it. You speak of the Rule of the Supreme Jurist and yet you place no reliance in His Holiness the Imam. You are engulfed in uncertainties, that a word from His Holiness will scatter, and yet you seek no recourse there. So be it. You have done your religious duty. Will you please release me now to return to my cell?"

For a moment, my death took substance in the room. To have your throat cut in the Evin required no special aptitude. I sensed the important man was considering whether he really could keep me safe through the night.

"With your permission, brothers, will you kindly leave me alone with the criminal. You, brother, please stay."

"Is that my usual investigator?"

"Of course."

I felt cheated of my revenge, but startled by the new man's subtlety.

"Good. He is well informed about my case."

The draught from the door was stopped. When the man's voice came, it was from in front of me. He may have seated himself.

"What is this information?"

It is what you need it to be. I hope that is clearly understood. I am not intelligent, nor well-informed, nor brave nor truthful nor virtuous. I need to be taken through this with the utmost care. So I can survive ten minutes with the Imam. Or at least, so I can go on television. As my wife used to say, somebody must look after me.

"Your Honour, you will be aware that as a young man I had the good fortune to visit Isfahan, and to live in that celebrated city for a period of six months. That was the year 1352. In that time, I became acquainted with a sinister and reprobate spy, Freemason and drug addict by the name of Ismail Murtazaevich Ryazanov. Ostensibly, he was Soviet Consul-General in Isfahan. In reality, he was Resident for southern Iran and Khuzestan for the Committee of State Security of the Council of Ministers of the Soviet Union."

"Yes, yes. You have said all this before."

"I beg your patience, sir. The irregularities of Ryazanov's life rendered him repellent to the Centre of Spies in Moscow. But he was indispensable. As you know, the Soviets ceased to find Iranian agents after 1953. Their agents, if that term may be used for such worthless old pensioners, were military officers recruited in Azerbaijan and Kurdistan for pay during the chaos after the World War."

"We don't need a lecture."

"Please be patient, Your Honour. Ryazanov was indispensable to Moscow for he ran not one, but two agents of exceptional value . . ."

"Don't be taken in, Your Excellency! He is lying! Please look at his face and gestures, they have no reality!"

". . . and influence. One I have told you of. The Obliterated General Farameh."

"Did Ryazanov tell you of that man?"

"No, sir."

"How did you come on the intelligence?"

"My household informed me."

"Your household!"

"My wife, sir."

"Your stinking whore, you mean!"

I sensed the raising of fingers.

"The woman purporting to be the Accursed's daughter."

There! Was that so very hard?

"Yes, Your Honour. Farameh was shot by a team despatched from the Islamic Republic to London on the 2nd Khordad, 1362."

I paused. I felt Abbas's great spirit beating its wings above me. In the end, I said: "The second agent, sir, lives and prospers among you and has the sincere and intimate confidence of His Holiness the . . ."

My right eye flashed. Beneath the sting on my cheek was the sensation of softness and musk. On the hand was a heavy ring, which had caught my eye. Something sprayed my stinging cheek: "You shut your mouth, you snake! You'll take these lies with you to the grave. I will not permit you to drag your filth across Islam and the Revolution and the Deputy Leader, a man whom the People mention at Congregational Prayers immediately after their supplication for His Holiness the Imam . . ."

Ah. It appears the Imam does not trust Najafi. He knows he's dying, and he must get the succession straight. It is possible that what Najafi is doing, in Beirut and Nigeria and Yugoslavia and all those places, is bringing the Revolution into disrepute. That is nothing to do with me. What must be understood is that in return for my assistance in bringing Najafi down, you will leave my wife and child alone.

I stood up, swayed, steadied myself. "God's will be done."

"Did your so-called wife give you this poison, too?"

"Who, sir?"

"Your wife?"

"No, sir."

"Who gave you those lies?"

"Mr Baharmast, in the last breath he drew before he died."

"A notorious atheist and liar!"

"As you command."

He came so close I could feel his warmth.

"Yes, Your Excellency?"

"Do you fear God, prisoner?"

"Of course."

"Do you fear Him, prisoner?"

"Yes."

"God knows who you are and what you have done. You yourself know what you have done. Why do you not tell us?"

"I have told you."

"Everything?"

I lowered my head.

"I can't hear you, brother."

"No."

"Good, will you tell us now."

"Yes."

"Your soul is sick, wounded by its own vanities. With God's help, I can guide and assist you. Can't you sense the spiritual air that has descended on this room?"

"I do. Yes, My Lord!"

"Know that your shame and punishment, however terrible and intolerable they are to you, are as nothing against the fires of Hell! Forget this world which you have run through like a spendthrift. You have burned the harvest of this life. With God's help I can bring you to such righteousness and purity you will yet glimpse the gates of Paradise!"

"God willing!"

I sensed, were he not so delicate, he would have put his hands to my temples. He said: "You must imagine that God Himself is your interrogator and that this interrogation is your act of submission, your Islam, your creed. You must say now what you did not say to Savak for now is the epoch of Islam when all truths must be spoken."

"Yes, Your Holiness."

He pulled away. He sighed, as if relaxing after some intense exertion.

"We will pray together the sunset and evening prayers. Then, my brothers, set to your work, for the poor misguided criminal has much to say and his heart is burning to say it!"

"In the name of God, the Merciful, the Compassionate and Greetings to the Lord of Time (God hasten His glad advent!) and His deputy among men, the Sublime Guide, the Moses of the Age, Smasher of Idols and Exterminator of Tyrants and Liberator of Humanity, the Leader and Founder of the Islamic Republic His Holiness the Imam

Khomeini (May the Almighty extend his shadow!) the person before you is Mr John Pitt son of an unknown father and the late 'Miss Pitt' and I am making this interview for the first time and for the last and of my own free will and for the following reasons, that is, first to explain why action has been taken against me, and second to show the errors, mistakes and deviations that unfortunately both before and after the Victory of the Revolution took possession of me against the express line of the Imam who sagaciously described me as a deviant and conspirator. Thank God, since my arrest and during my time in custody I have had the chance to re-examine my soul under the fraternal teaching of my brothers the honourable interrogators.

"This interview is divided into two parts: the first deals with my errors and crimes before the Victory of the Revolution and the second with my errors and crimes since the Victory of the Revolution.

"Although I came into the world in Britain, my mother was an agent at the British Embassy in Tehran under the notorious spy 'Miss Espencer'. In the years of the World War and afterwards, my mother formed a shameful and illicit attachment with a member of the Soviet legation, which being discovered she was recalled to England and imprisoned in the ominous London Tower till I was born and given to another family to be nursed. It can only be surmised that the aforesaid Russian was my father. Certainly, from an early age I burned with the wish to visit Iran as though father's grave were here, and so in due course, and before I had completed my studies, I came to Isfahan.

"In those years, because of my haste and inexperience and immaturity, and because the line of the Imam was not as clear as it is today, I fell into a number of errors of which the chief were two. Primarily, intrigue and spying for the atheistic Soviet Union. Secondarily, sexual immorality. I soon gravitated to the circle of 'Mr Ryazanov', the chief spy of the Soviet Union in that district, and I engaged in some operations and plots against Islam and the independence of Iran. In those days the Imam's movement was gaining strength daily, and 'Mr Ryazanov' wished to prepare for the inevitable day of the victory of the line of the Imam, and bribed and encouraged gullible and misguided people to serve him. I did not personally become acquainted with His Excellency Ayatollah Najafi though I knew him by reputation as a wise and steadfast cleric and opponent of the Obliterated Shah. 'Mr Ryazanov's activities attracted the suspicions of the Savak and he was murdered and I was obliged to flee to another city. Also at that time, I became tainted by the immoral atmosphere that existed in Isfahan under the Accursed regime and I have given full account to my honourable interrogators of those illicit liaisons and activities.

"After the Victory of the Revolution, and particularly after the outbreak of the War Imposed by America and Iraq, when it was my clear religious duty to come forward and confess my activities and my connection with 'Mr Ryazanov' and the office and household of His Excellency Mr Najafi in Isfahan, yet I kept them secret to the great detriment of the system. My breast bleeds for the pain that my obstinacy caused to His Holiness the Imam. Finally, I wish to apologise to all brothers who had any connection with me and ask them to put aside their personal interests and in a spirit of obedience and without fanaticism to submit to the principle of the Leadership of the Jurist and use that always as a touchstone for their actions and opinions."

That was the version for the newspapers. In addition, a crew came and made two films of me, or rather what they call video, which is a magnetic tape that can be erased and re-used like audio tape but carries pictures rather than sound. One was a full version, for the Imam, Mr Najafi and the three service chiefs, and the other a briefer version without detail for the public. I read my prepared answers, and then was told that the questions would be dubbed in afterwards. The Lord knows what they would say.

"Will you watch, Mr Kuchulu?"

"Of course. We all will watch. It is the first time a criminal from our section has been on *Sound and Image*. You will be famous, Mr John!"

"God willing."

"Your family will see you!"

"I am relying on that."

Kuchulu held out the taper to light my cigarette. He could never get used to my not smoking.

"No, thank you, Mr Kuchulu."

He looked embarrassed. "I will tell you how you appear. Exactly. Your face, your collar, your eyes, your voice, your words. Exactly."

"No matter. Maybe there will be some of the interview on the loudspeaker." I gestured to the high window, through which the Voice of Islamic Iran invaded my cell.

"God willing."

But there was none of me that evening on the loudspeaker, or as I heard later from a baffled Kuchulu, on the television. I heard only that Mr Najafi had resigned his post as deputy leader and chief of the Bureau of Foreign Liberation Movements and retired to his house at Qom, and that the Council of Experts would be convened to elect a successor. I heard that the Russian leader, Mr Gorbachov, deeply affected by a letter from His Holiness calling on him and other world leaders to renounce their long and futile combat with God, the origin of existence and creation, and at last to embrace Islam, was sending his Secretary for Foreign Affairs, Mr Shevarnazi or Shevardnazi, to Tehran, arriving tomorrow to discuss the renewal of bilateral co-operation between the USSR and the Islamic Republic of Iran.

And I sat down in the prison cell and covered my head while the women tapped out their conversations on the heat-pipe that ran through the cell.

✵ 20 ✵

I waited for a small break, while someone pondered her answer to a direct question, and then tapped on the heat-pipe:

"O God!"

The metal fell silent. It was as if I'd thrown a stone into a shoal of fish. The men tossed and groaned or cried out in sleep but a part of the prison, a submerged storey of which perhaps only I of the men was at that moment conscious, had been put to flight, running headlong into the only cover that prisoners have, silence. The phrase I'd chosen, the Arabic Ya'Allah, had many layers of meaning. The topmost was that some stranger had broken the women's code and Heaven alone knew what risks that carried for them. At the next level down from that, it meant that that stranger was a man, for I had used a phrase these women would have heard as children in their villages or houses, shouted by a new male voice from the street door or courtyard, and each time an annoyance and degradation: Veil, women and girls, for a strange man is in the house. Deeper still, it meant that the man was cautious.

"Comrade sisters, I beg of you by the mercy of God a favour."

The pipe was silent. I sensed they had no back-up code, and could not confer; or seek advice from their leaders or committees of whatever they had down there.

"Dear comrades, my name is Pitt. I am seeking my family. Have you news of my family?"

Beneath the sobbing of the men, the silence seemed to deepen and extend. Time passed, I don't know how much, for in prison one no longer measures time, least of all in seconds and minutes and hours. I thought: They won't answer. They'll change their code. And if I break that, they'll change it again, and shop me to the Ministry.

The pipe rang. The person tapped so fast that I couldn't decode.

"Please, more slowly, comrade."

The pipe rang: "What are your crimes?"

"Spying and fornication."

"Are you dying?"

"We are all dying."

"Are your family Hypocrites?"

"They are private citizens."

"Are they fair or olive in colouring?"

I thought: Why is it that in this country every conversation between men and women, even in this hell-hole, soon turns into a flirtation. I was suddenly overwhelmed by a longing for women, for their sound and scent and sweetness which was conveyed without loss in the tapping. I felt below me a whole floor of the prison, three hundred cells though perhaps not all of those occupied, rocking with silent laughter at the silly, lovesick man.

"With your permission, neither, ma'am. One name is Shirin. Another is Layly, a young girl of about thirteen. They are Isfahanian."

"Not here."

"God bless you."

Silence.

The silence lasted ten days. When the tapping started up again, it was gibberish by the old code. I thought it might be Arabic, but it wasn't; and I cursed myself that I knew so little Turkish. My wife had told me that in the villages, women together had a sort of nursery slang, for saying things they didn't want men to overhear; and though I knew some words of that from her, they didn't occur in the code. Yet the rhythm seemed to have the character of Persian, or rather that ineffable peculiarity that each language possesses so that you recognise a hippie couple is French simply by the blur of their voices from across a crowded street. I believed that the women were still tapping in Persian and the old code, but had erected another barrier; that, for example, someone had made a machine of some sort, not necessarily a physical object, perhaps just a construct of an able mind, that jumbled the Persian letters; and that I was bound to break the code again. It was simply a matter of constructing that machine, which I thought of as a slide rule or two concentric wheels or, most likely in Iran, an abacus; and assign the most frequent groups of taps to the most common Persian groups of characters.

Yet I recognised that the new code and my inevitable decoding were also a flirtation: that in truth we were all dying, and the only thing left to us, even to these women, many of whom must have passed hard lives in prisons and safe-houses in fighting the Shah and then the mollas, is the delight that men and women have together, or rather the memory of it; for there was no hope of it, for we were all dying. I sensed, too, a certain reticence on their part, that arose in the very nature of flirtation; a certain gentleness with me; as if they knew that my searching for my wife sustained me in precisely the fashion that their code and what they said in it sustained them; and both must be protected from futility. So I listened with just half an ear, and gradually the words took on meaning, and it was phantom *coups d'état* and chains of command, theoretical disputes and disciplinary actions, food, tears, laughter: the everyday conversations of political prisoners. I hated to hear it, for I sensed I had introduced alien elements into a private language. Their awareness of me now caused them to perform. I had destroyed the prisoner's most precious possession, sincerity. I considered whether myself to tap in the new code, so that they changed it again; but I knew that I must eventually learn that code too; and the very sound and the pipe and the women became a sort of hell to me. I would ask Hassan Kuchulu to petition the Governor for a transfer to the Training Institute, where I would share a cell with other men.

The sound lapped against my shallow sleep each night, and what woke me up one night, when a cold moon was rising full over Mt Damavand, was a certain alteration in the sound. Through layers of sleep, I recognised that someone was speaking in the old code.

"Comrade! Comrade!"

I sprang up from my blanket to the pipe.

"John! Wake up, John!"

"At your service, ma'am."

"What is her family name?"

I couldn't say the name, though it thrust up from my guts into my mouth. There were antennas on the women's floor, I was sure of it; and if I tapped it, I couldn't begin to guess what risks that would bring on Shirin and on me.

"Idolater. Shirin Fereshteh Idolater."

She is the daughter of a high official or military officer of the Shah's regime, a Bahai or a Savaki.

"I must know her family name, comrade."

I sensed a change in the rhythm of the tapping. This was another lady, a cell-mate, somehow senior to the first tapper, perhaps a functionary in this phantom women's army. "You know it, ma'am. You do not need a man to tell you."

The word "man" reverberated round the prison, along the pipes and through the doors, and in the showers and across the snowy yard, running over the squatting women and unquiet men and coming back to me multiplied by a thousandfold in all its recklessness and folly. Oh God, you've betrayed these women who tried to help you! You don't deserve to live!

The silence filled the cell. Then the tapping started up again.

"You are not a man, my love, for it is off-limits to men here."

I shivered in relief.

"As you say, my love."

"A woman and a girl of your description were in the Adelabad

246

in '60." Your wife and daughter were seen in the gaol in Shiraz just before the executions of 1981.

I was overwhelmed with joy. With a few taps, the lady had given them six years life; who knows if a couple more taps could not give them another seven to the present? History itself seemed to be racing through my cell and dragging us towards a single place and single date.

"What are her crimes, dear comrade?"

"War against the Lord of Time."

"Is she dying?"

It was an idle question, given the charges. To obstruct the Messiah in his work of salvation is no misdemeanour.

"We must all die."

"God bless you, comrade."

"They say she's strong; and I heard somewhere that God is merciful."

"Indeed, ma'am."

Because I had come out of my mental depression, I was irritated by that of the guards. Even as they came in and I turned to the wall, I sensed averted faces. The routine had disintegrated. Nobody woke us for prayers, and nobody took me to the lavatory. I was told that my ration had been cut in half. Of the guards, only the older and simpler country men, such as Kuchulu, remained.

"O God, if only I could be martyred!"

"Now, Mr Kuchulu, don't be downhearted."

"Hosein, Hosein! Let me go out to fight and die for you! I do not fear the poison gas!"

"Don't be downcast, my dear."

There was a pointed silence. Then he said: "Make it lawful for me, Mr John."

"What do you mean, Mr Kuchulu? I have had no mistreatment from you."

"I have tried to do my religious duty."

"I'm sure."

"Please say you forgive me, Mr John."

"If you did your religious duty, there is nothing to forgive."

"Please, Mr John."

"All right, Mr Kuchulu, I forgive you! Enough, please! Please don't raise this matter again."

Three, four, five times a day, I heard the crackle of gunfire from the other side of the building. Some days, I heard ten or more explosions from downtown, and once from my window I saw an Iraqi fighter-bomber, a Sukhoi Su-25, according to Kuchulu, curvetting towards the west. Its bomb caused plaster to drop from the ceiling.

To connect the executions and the bombardment from the air, the short rations and long faces and the slow and gradual misfunction of the Evin system was not beyond me. From the radio tannoy, I heard of a breakthrough in the Fao sector, but not of any reinforcement. A little later, I heard that the combatants of Islam had taken new defensive positions at Majmun. I heard of a brilliant action at sea against the navy of the Great Satan America. A single overall commander, Rafsanjani, was appointed by the Imam.

With the shortage of hands, I reminded Kuchulu that I knew something of mechanics. I fixed the broken plumbing in the showers, the electricity in the prayer hall, the cooler in the Governor's office. Kuchulu came with me, chattered to me, and took back the tools when I'd finished.

"Will you stay working here while I eat my lunch, Mr John?"

I recited: "I can make bridges from light and ladders from shadow."

"Please give me your parole, John. You are not a bad man, only misguided."

"What if His Excellency were to return, Mr Kuchulu, and find me in his rooms?"

"He will not. He is at the . . ." He stopped, remembering that I was a dangerous criminal. He gave me his blandest look: "Mr John, what is a Rotarian?"

"I don't rightly know. I think he is a member of a private society."

"At war against Iran and Islam?"

"I think not only."

"But you are a Rotarian!"

"I am far worse than that, Mr Kuchulu. I am a Liberal!"

"Stop it. Don't muddle me. O Ali, life used to be so simple. There were landlords and there were tenants. There were Muslims and unbelievers. There were men and women, of course. And above it all, the Accursed Shah, except he wasn't called 'Accursed' in those days."

"I think we should all just concentrate on freeing our homeland of Mr Saddam."

"God willing!" He came forward out of the doorway. He said: "My brother works as a servant at the house of the Imam (may the Favour of God Almighty be with Him). One night, he heard the Imam in his prayer room, conversing with the the Lord of Time, God speed his coming! There is the war and Saddam and everything costs so much – rice that was ten tomans a kilo is now seven hundred tomans, tea is twelve hundred – I mean, is the world coming to an end, Mr John?"

"It is, Mr Kuchulu, thank God, but who can say when? Now go to your lunch and may it be nectar to you."

He hesitated.

I said: "Will you kindly inform the Ministry I wish to make a confession."

"God bless you!"

I had not seen Shahid for a year and a half. I knew my presence was poison to him. I said: "I wish to enlist in the army of twenty million of the Islamic Republic."

I have said that Shahid's first response to novelty was violence. I tried to relax but the blow across my ear knocked me off my chair. My blindfold flew against the wall. I crawled towards it with my eyes closed.

I said: "You must accede to my request, Mr Shahid. I wish only to give my life for my beloved adopted land and the glorious Islamic Revolution."

I had the blindfold on, but was so muddled by the blow, I had to grope for my chair.

"Never. You are a spy! You will spy on our military operations!"

There was something in his voice I had not heard before, but I was too shocked to identify it. I felt it had to do with the Front. My thoughts had been crushed together like a concertina and I could not see how to unstick them. Yet I knew there was a word which, if I used it, would cause him to lose control and I summoned my reserves of will to use it.

"In my honourable audience, His Holiness said that even the Blood of the Accursed will become Sweet . . ."

My right ear burst. A wind howled in my head. Something wet and warm was falling on my shoulder. I thought: He's shot me in the head!

"Never! You are sentenced to death!"

The phrase hung in the air, then settled on me. I sat before him on the floor, the liquid gushing out of my ear. The blindfold had come off again, but I didn't look at him, for I didn't need to look. I knew he was frightened, of the injury he'd done me – for I did not think I would hear again in my right ear – and the blood all over the floor and my clothes. I now knew why it was that he hated me and it was nothing to do with my character or history: it was that I confirmed he was where he was and not at the Front.

"I have not been tried, my darling, so how can I have been sentenced?"

In the roaring in my ear, I saw at last the shape of my sentence and imprisonment. I mean, I saw its architecture as I had seen the architecture of the mosques of Isfahan. I saw that I was of no use to the Revolution, now Farameh was dead and Najafi under house arrest in Qom, and Russia a friend. I was held in the Evin not for myself but for another. My life or death were of importance only in that it would provide the death of another. And at that moment, as I looked up and saw the face of my tormentor, I knew that that other person was Shirin; that for some reason that I could not begin to fathom they wanted to kill her but could only do so if I was there, buried with her to the neck in sand, while a truck backed up and dumped a loadful of building stone on the floor of the Meidan in Isfahan; or rather that they had had wanted to do that, but they goddam couldn't find the dog-begotten whore, and it was all too late now with the Revolution facing defeat in war.

I stared into his grey eyes, which shivered like pools under a gust of wind. I said: "Mr Shahid, I have placed on the Governor's desk a request to the Honourable Revolutionary Court to be admitted to the Patriotic Amnesty. I am an Iranian citizen and I have that right. I have committed no crimes, as you more than anybody know, and I have been described by His Excellency the Governor as cured of my deviations. I do not understand why you remain here in Tehran, filling yourself with rice and wearing civilian clothes, while your homeland is bleeding to death, but I am not like you. And now I must go to the hospital for you have broken my ear-drum."

His eyes said: You have chosen. You have forced me. Now take the consequence.

I put on my blindfold and stood up. I was taken to my cell. I staunched the blood with paper; and then, slowly, and in such pain that I did not think I could tolerate it, washed out my ear with salt and water. Then, because I did not believe my strength would last, I drew a picture of Shahid's face with my mohreh, of his wall eye and his straggly beard, and put it, the mohreh and my sharpened spoon into my underclothes.

"All your belongings!"

I had been sleeping.

"ALL YOUR BELONGINGS!"

However much you prepare yourself for the event you fear above all others, it counts for nothing. I felt every opening in my body go slack. The air burst from my mouth. My eyes gushed. Blood started from my ear. I went rigid to get control of my bowels and bladder. I was swimming in sweat.

Kuchulu was in the door, closed up like a pocket-knife. I looked at him: No Wild Thing, my friend. No Rotarian spy. No English Imperialist. I said: "I give them all to you, dear friend, as return for your humanity."

He turned away. "BLINDFOLD ON!"

I felt him bind my wrists with cable.

"Will you kindly comb my hair, Hassan?"

"WALK!"

I said to myself: Nothing lasts in the world. Even this moment will soon be gone. It does not matter at all how I appear to my executioners or to the world. It does not matter if I scream and shit myself. It does not matter.

"WAIT HERE!" He put my hand on something warm to steady me. It was one of the pipes. I began to tap with my little fingernail: SH-I-R-I-N. Then I stopped, because I did not want her to witness me, at whatever interval of time and hearsay, in this state. I felt something wet on my face. Kuchulu was swabbing my cheek and ear with a wet cloth. I supposed there would be a spectator or spectators, clerical or official, for this was an execution of sentence.

As I walked down, with my hand on Kuchulu's warm shoulder, I thought: In a sense, what is happening is happening by certain laws that are only now apparent to me. You see, we were a sort of group or "Kloob" in Isfahan, which is being picked off one by one. The founder went first: Mr Ryazanov. At a thirteen-year delay, I am killed. That still leaves her. And even if she is killed, there is still little Layly, and, if she lasts a little, she might have a child and that child go on; and so we will not vanish from the world.

I felt cold on my face and with it an intolerable regret: that my last moments of existence had passed in this foolish dreaming. I wanted very much to know where I was, which courtyard or space. It seemed to me the most important thing now in my life. Somebody with meaty breath was pinning something to my chest, on the side of my heart.

"Will you kindly take off my blindfold? I am not frightened."

He slapped me across the right cheek. My head rattled with the pain. I thought: I simply cannot tolerate more of this mistreatment! Put an end to it. Somebody kicked me in the arse and I sprawled forward into the snow. There was laughter.

"Shame on you, friends! Are you Muslims, or not?" I thought that was Kuchulu.

Someone picked me up and bundled me through a door. It had steps up, on which I tripped, and it smelled of plastic and petrol and sweat. I was pushed down into a chair covered with torn plastic. The cold wind stopped, and I was overwhelmed with claustrophobia. They're going to electrocute me!

"NO! NO! NO!"

There was a burst of laughter and then an engine started and the whole thing shook. A hand took off my blindfold and I saw a man with his back to me and a steering wheel and through the window the faint lights of the blacked-out city and I began to laugh. I turned round and saw prisoners like me with legends pinned to their chests, and a guard I recognised from the interrogation block, looking sour, and I knew what I had known in the secret depths of my being, all along and down and in the snow: that I was going to the Front in a bus! I looked down at the patch over my heart. It was clumsily written and anyway hard to read upside down. It said "O Master of Time!"

I laughed and laughed.

As we sped down the hill, on a motorway that had not existed the last time, with the cold wind racing across my wet face, I thought: I have missed movement so much; and the sound of horns in the Tehran traffic; and automobile dealerships sparkling and flashing with more mirror-work than an ancient-regime palace; and the smell of pastries from a late-night bakery; and the women tripping in front of the taped up shop-fronts in their sling-back shoes. I must control myself. It is in this euphoria that I could make a mistake. I sensed that Shahid was riding behind me, could feel his depression creeping forward to engulf me; knew that he, too, was going to the Front and that was why I myself could go there; or perhaps he would accompany me for the rest of my life. The new roads and the lights crawling up the distant hills saddened me. I thought: The mollas believe in progress!

We stopped in a large dark square. It was the square called Tupkhaneh, "Artillery Park", and through the slushy window of the bus was the Cental Post Office. I scrabbled for my blindfold, and the guards burst out laughing. Only we criminals got down, seventeen of us; and we were led up the steps of a tall building in the style of the Shah's father, which used to be the Ministry of Finance, I think, but surely wasn't now. Though it was the middle of the night, the building was a hive of light and people, most in military uniform. I fought surges of hilarity, which had splashed idiot looks on my companions' faces, and no doubt mine as well. We were taken into a room with a thick carpet and a metal desk covered with bevelled glass, and portraits on the wall of the Imam and Rafsanjani. We sat down in rows of armchairs arranged along the wall. An orderly brought in some cigarettes. The others, who must have come from communal cells in the Training Institute, chattered and smoked. Every now and then, clergymen or seminary students came in and looked at us unctuously. We stood up, but they just turned and billowed out. After a while, and one by one, my companions were called from the room. As each one left through the door, my fear increased. I thought: I have to be happy now, in these last few minutes in this room. In the end, I was left alone, staring at the dawn coming up over the snowy domes and pines of the bazar and, against the gold and crimson, a Scud missile which drew off great liquid streams of anti-aircraft artillery till it burst in the south of the town and set the windows rattling. I thought: War must be a lovely thing. A little later the sirens came on.

"Peet."

"Yes, sir."

I walked through double doors into a large room, fetid with long hours. At a desk were two clerics of widely differing seniority and, a little apart, an army officer. If they looked tired, he looked exasperated. On the desk, unopened, was my file. As I came forward across the carpet, another man, a civilian, unpeeled himself from the wall and skipped towards me. He looked kindly and officious. Yet what distinguished him was that he alone in the room had recognised me as a European; and that my education as an Iranian, begun by my wife in Bushehr and continued in the Evin, was now formally complete; indeed, that I had graduated at the moment when they kicked me down in the snow; and only this fellow recognised me, for he had read my file and been to Europe, perhaps often, and he'd better watch his goddam step.

"Bonjour, Monsieur. J'ai l'honneur . . ."

"Forgive me, Your Excellency, but I do not speak foreign tongues."

"Mais le tribunal dont vous . . ."

I turned to the senior cleric, for I sensed him to be the president of the tribunal. "May I speak, Your Honour?"

"You will answer our questions." He had a pleasant voice, though tired. It occurred to me that the other cleric was some sort of commissar from the Revolutionary Guard, and that he probably had first choice of the volunteers.

The president reached for my file, but then something, weariness, no doubt, got the better of him. He sighed.

"How many members of your family are Martyrs or Wounded?"

"I have no male relations, sir."

"How many men in your family are Militia volunteers?"

"I have no male relations, sir."

"Which mosque do you attend?"

"I am a criminal, sir."

"Do any of your relations attend mosques?"

"I have no male relations, sir."

He recognised the futility of his formulas, but continued. "Do any of the Prayer Leaders know you?"

"Sir, I wish to give my worthless life for my beloved country, for the Revolution and the Great . . ."

My head froze with the anticipated pain.

" . . . Imam, Smasher of Idols."

Nobody struck me. The junior cleric looked at me and then turned away. The officer snarled: "The wife-swapper's too old."

The word came at me like a fist. Old! My best years were gone, given to the Evin; and I am all but past military age! I felt such sadness that I bowed my head.

I said to the carpet: "I know how to read and write and to work machines and how to be quiet and to move in the dark and to take orders and . . ."

No good.

"Speak up, man."

" . . . I know how to die."

The officer snorted. I sensed a quietness in the room. Then the president said: "Look up, man."

I looked up. My eyes crossed with each one of them. As I reached the president, he said: "What was your sentence?"

No good.

"Your sentence?" He reached again for the folder.

"I don't know, Your Honour. I wasn't tried."

"Nonsense," he said vaguely. He opened the folder at random

and scanned it. He could scarcely read for tiredness. Then something piqued his interest.

"Wait! There is an illicit liaison."

"Look, I don't care if he fucked the entire Society of Muslim Housewives end to end. Are you a thief, pimp?"

"No, sir! Please consult the file, sir."

"Are you a queer?"

"A what, sir?"

The civilian giggled. The clerics looked pained. With tremendous slowness, the officer made a violent gesture with his right forearm.

"Do you like fucking men?"

"By God, no, sir! Never in my life, sir. Please consult the file, sir. It is all in the file, sir."

"All right, I'll take the motherfucker." He bowed to the Guard commissar. "Of course, if that's acceptable to you, Your Highness." The commissar fluttered his fingers. The civilian hustled up and untied my hands; and as he did so, he began to whisper something in my back. I cried: "WAR, WAR TO VICTORY! LONG LIVE THE GREAT IMAM! DEATH TO THE TRAITOR SADDAM! DEATH TO ITALY! DEATH TO GERMAN! DEATH TO . . ."

"Get out of here!"

The words that I drowned with my cheers were the French words Ça ne suffit pas, monsieur. It won't do you any good.

❊ 21 ❊

I think that for a solitary man a soldier's career is the best. I had
always wanted a profession and I was determined to succeed at
this one, but I knew that if I were to master it I must survive my first
day. It was plain that the military situation was desperate and that, as
a criminal and an Englishman and a spy I must have been the very last
soldier in the army of the Muslims, truly the bottom of the barrel.
Not for any fighting quality of my own but as the expression of a
mathematical exhaustion, I stood alone between my adopted country
and defeat.

We rode down in a convoy of British double-decker buses. The
other volunteers were mostly very young boys, but there were two
old men. We wore headbands and winding-sheets with the legend
I am ready for martyrdom. The others slept or stared at the desert.
On each side of the highway south to Qom, the bare hillsides were
covered in slogans marked out in whitewashed boulders. It was hard
to imagine that Rafsanjani's two thousand battalions of volunteers
were on the way to the front.

I had thought we were headed for the marshes, and the water
defences the Iraqis had dug and built and dredged to defend Basra,
but we turned south-west before Qom and somebody said "Central
Front". As we climbed into the hills and passed through towns and
villages, nobody came out to cheer or greet us. I could sense the boys
becoming downhearted. One asked me if I had experience of the gas.

We drove up into the dusk. Other vehicles, their sides plastered with mud for camouflage, bore down on us and drove us heedlessly off the road, or we waited for hours in sluggish traffic jams. We drove into rain. We stopped for supper in a the remains of a town called Qasr-e Shirin – Shirin's Fortress – which looked as if it had been fought over many times. For the first time, we could hear the thump of heavy guns. As we descended towards the Iraqi plain, I saw in the gloom gigantic castles of earth ledges, telephone wires undulating out of sight, parks of artillery surrounded by raised berms, tanks bedded down in deep scrapes. I felt I might be looking down at a campaign model at some army museum or staff college. On each side of the road were columns of weary men trudging forward, who did not answer our cheers. I had not known that the war had taken such a possession of the country, had, as it were, industrialised the villages and fields and draped over everything a layer of smoke and dirt. I was reminded of pictures of the trenches in the First World War in Europe. The bus was jumping in the bombardment. I thought, as I am sure the boys thought, I wanted to fight, but how can any one person make an impression on this monster!

We halted in the darkness. We waited and then were fallen out. Those boys who had had a month's basic training were each given a repeating rifle, a gas mask and two hand-grenades. I was given a small tank of water which was strapped to my front. Then we descended into a trench and waited. Gradually, the bombardment slowed.

The sun came up behind us and everybody was walking forward. Our line spread out as far as I could see in both directions. After ten minutes, we were no nearer, and then a shell landed on my right peppering my cheek with sharp stones. I could not see any officers with us. We were advancing simply because we had been told to advance.

Another shell burst. We began to run towards the Iraqi lines, shouting "God is Great". The boys, who were barefoot, were very fast and I couldn't keep up with them because of the water. Some of them threw their grenades, I think for fear of not having the opportunity later. I thought: I had not known that war was so sweet. Sand soared up in great spouts on every side, and I was ravished by effects of light and colour that I had never expected to see. Ahead, an artificial hill was rippling with flame from the enemy's heavy guns. I thought: If by God's grace we get to the lines, then maybe I can find a weapon and gas mask. My comrades vanished into the smoke. I ran up over a rise and saw Iraqi helmets and a .50 millimetre machine-gun, but we must have been still covered by the smoke of our shells. My momentum and the weight of the water on my chest carried me racing down and then somebody saw me and they opened up and I was flying through the air and down towards them.

Somebody was trying to wriggle out from under me. He had a red camouflaged uniform and a curved sword embroidered on his epaulettes. I screamed: "Give it to me! Give me the goddam gun!"

The Iraqi was much stronger than me, strong like a butcher or a farm boy, and smelled of hay and sweat, but I was on top, and holding him down. The water-tank at my chest had burst and we were soaked.

"It's belongs to me. It's mine, goddammit!"

My arms were entangled in the sling of the water-tank. I tried to hit him with the rifle butt, but he pulled his head back. Behind him, another Iraqi turned his head and pondered whether to help him. I pulled the rifle's trigger. The noise was deafening. Ten, twelve, twenty shots burst in the emplacement. Both of them scampered away along the trench, dragging the rifle. I shook off the water-tank and ran in the other direction. I was weeping with frustration: I must find a weapon!

I tripped and plunged into a large crater. Men sprang on me. Behind them, under netting, was a tank without its tracks. Then it bounced, and the noise knocked all my breath out.

"Where's your gas mask, Volunteer?" He was speaking Persian.

"I never had one."

"Goddammit, where's your rifle?"

"I never had one."

"Don't believe him, sir. The coward threw it away."

The tank fired again. The pain in my hurt ear was intolerable. I was reverberating with the shock.

"You see that weapon there?"

The tank fired again, filling my eyes with tears, winding me.

"Yes. The tank."

"You are going to fight and if necessary give your life to protect it."

"Yes. I am ready to die."

"If you turn your back to the enemy, or throw away your weapon again, I'll shoot you and if I'm dead, the Revolutionary Guards will shoot you."

"Yes, sir."

A Turkoman boy with slit eyes, dropped a rifle from his shoulder, threw off the old magazine, snapped a new one in place. I felt ashamed to be taking lessons from a teenager. He shouldered an anti tank weapon. He said: "Aim for the stomach. Gentle on the trigger. Two shots only. Another target. Two shots."

We ran forward together and climbed up to the edge of the berm. Half-way up there was a sand-bagged ledge with just enough room for us both. The boy shouldered his missile launcher.

"In the name of God the Merciful," he whispered.

From the top of the crater, men and vehicles were moving towards us with a methodical and ghostly slowness. There were three tanks in line, and fanning out behind them double that number of armoured trucks. For the first time, fear snapped at me.

"May I shoot?"

"Wait."

I heard the Captain behind me. Between the explosions of the tank, he said: "Gentlemen, unfortunately we must stay here. If we go back from here, the Chieftain will be lost and the line will be over-run. Please, gentlemen, if you love your families and your homeland, please stay and fight with me."

The rocket hissed and flew at the lead tank. I screamed from the

shock of it. It burst on the engine cover, and men came tumbling out.
I shot at one and he threw himself down.

"Ay!"

"Hold the barrel down, you donkey!"

Two shots. New target. Two shots. New target. The tank had spun
to the left, was churning up the ground. A second round burst on the
turret. I thought: How does he do it? How could a boy shoot so
well? I felt so proud to be fighting with these brave men. My rifle
went dead in my hands.

"Change the magazine!"

"What?"

"My God, didn't they show you how to change a magazine?"

The boy snapped a new magazine on, and as he did an enemy
appeared on the parapet. My comrade sighed: I knew then that his
helping me had cost him his life and my own. I threw myself at the
Iraqi's legs. His weight as he toppled onto my head blacked me out,
and then I sensed him convulse on me.

"Get up!"

The world was spinning. The Turkoman boy was covered in
blood. He held a bayonet in his hand. Dreamily, he turned back to
the front and shot a man before him. In the churning world, I stood
up and fired my rifle. Two shots. New target. Two shots. New target.

"Gentlemen, I beg you not to give ground. Please do not give an
inch of ground. There is nothing between you and your families."

The rifle went dead again.

"Shots! I have no more shots!"

I stood up on the parapet, prepared for I don't know what: to
run at the enemy, to try and capture another weapon, Heaven only
knows. Somebody tugged me down by the hair.

I shouted: "We need an airplane! We have them in a trap . . ."

The boy smiled behind his launcher. "Captain, the Volunteer is
calling for air support."

The Captain joined us on the ledge.

"Air support, Volunteer? You're proposing that we call up an F-4 sortie?"

"Forgive me, sir. I am ignorant, sir."

"Well, I anticipated your pleasure."

Above the bombardment, I could make out a clatter; and then two shadows shook and rattled over us, past their best, no doubt, but combat helicopters all the same, God bless you, Gen. Farameh; stopped dead overhead; bowed; and fired, four missiles apiece.

"They're regrouping, Captain."

The officer slid down to join us.

"What's your name, Volunteer?"

"John, sir."

"What?"

"John, sir. I'm a criminal, sir."

"Nothing to steal here, Mr John. Shall we counterattack, Mr John?"

"Yes, sir. Ready, sir. I need a magazine, sir."

The survivors burst out laughing.

The officer's name was Captain Toloui. The engine of the tank had broken down and the British would not send parts for it. So it had become a fixed artillery piece, which could be moved only with a tractor. The Iraqis had made use of a rise in the ground to fortify two positions about a mile in advance of their main line. These were known to the men as Lat and Uzza, after two heathen idols in the Koran. Toloui was incapable of resting or of letting the men rest, and gradually the notion took hold that we would mount a night attack.

I was in the Lat group and launched the grenade that sent the Iraqis scampering through the wire, and though nobody was hit, we blew up both installations and took no casualties in either party. The men were elated. For myself, I picked up a weapon that had been dropped in the fight: a silver-plated AK-47 made in Russia, with a beech-wood stock that I decorated with a portrait of Hosein. To Toloui's disgust, I wore a yellow head-band with "HOSEIN!" stamped on the forehead.

I still ate and prayed alone, but not so far away. The men fought as they played football: each was aware where all the others were. One afternoon, a month into my tour of duty, as the men dozed under the camouflaged awning, Toloui squatted down before me. He said: "I am your officer. Tell me your plan."

"I can get the tank moving."

"Bollocks!"

"I can and you know I can and so can you."

He nodded. I sensed he'd started at the problem in his mind.

"You do not understand the military, John. There are only two rules. One, do not seek responsibility. Two, if you have responsibility, do not delegate it."

"Yes, sir."

"Goddammit, if this tank moves, then the whole line moves, you fool. We advance, fool."

"Yes, sir." I saw that he had to speak his thoughts; that his mind was methodical and would reach its conclusion; but it preferred to do so out loud.

"It is known I was a regular officer of the army of the Accursed Shah."

"Yes, sir."

"You are an English spy."

"No, sir. I am an Iranian citizen proud to serve his adopted country."

"Bollocks! John, it's too late. It's coming to an end. Along the whole front, stocks are so low, in battlefield artillery we're down to just a couple of thousand .130mm cannon, maybe a thousand battle tanks most of them on their blocks, fifty operational aircraft, a few dozen helicopters. The Americans are sinking the navy. Rafsanjani promised a hundred thousand volunteers and what did we get: you and a couple of Second World War veterans! The Imam will accept Resolution 598. The only man who wants to fight on is Najafi and that's why he had to go. The Imam will drink the cup of poison. To save the Revolution."

"The Blood of the Martyrs will save the Revolution."

"FUCK YOU, JOHN!"

The words were in English: American English, I guess. I thought: Don't give me your secrets to defend, Toloui, I have enough, God knows. Yet I had to respond to the confidence.

"Because I was born in Britain, sir, I know something of the minds of the engineers who devised this tank. If you give me a stripe for the night action against Lat, I can order Golpayegani to strip the engine and power pack. Over the inlet and outlet valves we will rivet seals of small-mesh cloth painted with an incombustible that will keep out the fine sand: either what the French call *organdie* or, if we can't get that, chador-material from Isfahan. Then we will wash, grease and re-assemble the power pack and re-lay the tracks. Then we will train the other crews. It will take four to five days for our machine, about ten more for the sector."

"You are mad, John. It's too late. The Saudis are shitting their robes. The Americans will not permit another Iranian offensive. They'll bomb one of our towns." He looked at me. It was all too far and fast for him. He said: "Don't press me, John. Keep your mouth shut and your head low. I have the power to give you an honourable discharge. I don't want to lose you, but I will if your conduct justifies it."

"I do not seek discharge, sir. I wish only to go into battle with my comrades and distinguish myself for my country, the Glorious Revolution, and the Imam, to throw back the forces of world arrogance and drink the sherbet of martyrdom."

He squinted with concentration.

"You want to go on television, don't you?"

"Yes, sir. God willing, sir."

"And have your face in the paper and tea and melon-pips with Rafsanjani."

He had taken his time, but he had got there in the end. And yet there remained a small perplexity.

"Why?"

"Yes, sir. I want my family to see me on television, sir. So they know where I am, sir."

"I will inform the crew at prayers about your promotion."

"Yes, sir."

The delegation that came to see the exercise included the sector commander, Masoudi, a fat cleric with a half-mad stare in his eyes, I think Kola'i, a film (or rather video) crew from the television news and an air force officer, whom I recognised. How much more, my God, how much more, before you take me from these agonies!

They watched without enthusiasm, as we took the Chieftain up to thirty-five knots and fired two rounds. The men were whooping with applause and crying "God is Very Great". The display of the power and mobility of modern armoured cavalry left the visitors restless and embarrassed, which I thought at first had to do with the answering fire from the Iraqi lines. Afterwards, tea was served and Toloui introduced the crew. I held back, but Toloui was set on procedure. I kept my eyes down and my cap on, muttering apologies.

"I know the man," said Turani. "He is an English spy."

"Your Honour is mistaken, by God. I was born in Britain but have lived here with my Iranian family. I am proud to serve . . ."

"Lift up your head, Corporal."

I looked into Turani's stony face. The cleric was licking his lips.

"Goddammit, he's one of the best men on the crew."

"Why is he here?"

"He came out of prison."

The cleric smiled.

"Arrest him, Captain."

To my surprise, it was Kola'i who bound me. He had wire with him. He was muttering something in Arabic and stank of eau de cologne. I shook my head, quickly, to get the crew away from me; but I had reckoned without Toloui.

"Bid God-Protect to your comrade, men."

They came up one by one; and because they could not shake my hand, touched my cheek or neck, and then turned away. I tried to walk to the jeep, but somebody kicked me, and I had to crawl.

The problem in facing up to death, and I am sure this is new to nobody, is that a person cannot maintain his spirit indefinitely. I was prepared to die — indeed, was grateful that no further consequence would befall the tank crew – but not to stand all night in my shorts tied to a basketball post in the yard of an abandoned school.

The men were examining new weapons. They had broken out two boxes of rifles, from China or Korea from the writing on the side, testing the breaches, filling magazines. Suddenly, Kola'i spun and pointed the gleaming rifle at my chest. The burst went over my right shoulder. He struck a pose. The men fawned on him.

I was trembling with shock. "I am a soldier. I demand to die as a soldier."

The men laughed. Kola'i licked his lips. He dropped the barrel to my legs.

Shock shut out the light. I fought for breath, but my chest had been crushed flat. My head burst with pain where it had snapped against the post. I vomited air. As the light came back, I saw a baffled look on Kolai's face. The soldiers were laughing. My head fell down on my chest and I saw, lodged below my ribs, a triangle of pavement. It teetered, rolled off my stomach, fell to the ground.

* *

A bus was negotiating its way through the narrow entrance, and immediately being driven back. I suppose nobody was supposed to see me. In the confusion and shouting, I was being untied and a blue track-suit held out for me to wear.

"Give me some water, brother."

"Go to Hell!"

I dressed and my hands were re-tied. Strung the length of the bus was a banner with the verse: "And say not those slain in the Way of God are dead!" Around the door of the bus, boys in track-suits were milling in front of Kola'i, who held a large Koran in two hands. We kissed the edge of the Koran, touched it to our foreheads, and climbed into the bus. Last up was Turani. I suppose he wanted to ensure I reached the Front.

We passed through a succession of circular emplacements, spaced to give interlocking fields of fire. To left and right, the barrels of an anti-aircraft piece or a hull-down tank looked skyward out of camouflage netting. Scattered here and there were spiny trees, sometimes with groups of men dozing or making tea in the shade. We passed an anti-tank trench and a raised berm, where Kola'i got down or rather was pushed down, protesting and sobbing and calling on Hosein, by the Volunteers. The bus fell quiet, and I sensed we were now coming to the point of contact between the two armies. I glanced behind me and saw our plume of dust. Beside me was a pale boy with carrot-coloured hair.

"Give me water, brother."

There was a burst of smoke and dust through the window to the right. A string of mines crackled in sympathy. I was counting, three, four, five, while the boys cheered and whooped. Eight, nine. Turani's back stiffened. I twisted round to my left to face the boy.

"You must give me some water!"

Fifteen, sixteen, seventeen.

"You are a criminal."

Twenty-three, twenty-four. I saw the second burst through his window to my left. The Iraqi gunners had the range of the bus, and its speed. Turani was standing over the driver, bawling at him to speed up.

"Will you be more tyrannical than Shimr? Who deprived the family of the Holy Prophet of water in the desert! O Hosein!"

Six, seven, eight, nine.

"You are a criminal."

"They are are using gas shells, my dear. Do you want me to die helplessly by cyanide, like at Halabjeh, my dear?"

Fourteen, fifteen.

He reached behind me and deftly freed my hands. Against the back wall was a carton of bottled water, a gift for the Volunteers at the front, on which the sponsor had written Yaghma's lament for Kerbela: "Thirsty lipped we come to the Euphrates, O my sweet son!"

Seventeen, eighteen, nineteen.

Turani spun round. I had the case of Saboo water in one hand, and the boy's wrist in the other. Turani went for his side-arm and I heaved the case through the window, and followed it head-first. Twenty-four, twenty –

We landed in a rain of glass on the pressed sand. The bus was speeding away from us in a cloud of dust. In the Name of God the Merciful, the Compassionate . . . The bus came up on its back wheels, in the fashion in which a trained dog begs at table; teetered for a moment above its dust; and disappeared. There was a tremor at my feet, then a rocking. A balloon of earth and smoke inflated before me, dark red at its edges, spitting gobbets of fire and molten glass. It hung poised in air for a moment, turning scarlet at the tips; then burst in a cascade of scarlet. The wind picked me up and hurled me backwards, and I flew through a hail of stones and blood and steel and glass and burning cloth.

"O Lord Hosein! Hosein!"

"Shut your face! Turn round! Look at the horizon."

I walked forward through the drizzle of blood. The bus, still on its back end, was burning fiercely and ringing like machinery with loose ammunition. The smell of roasting flesh and blood, and the unspeakable fragments littered across the red desert caused me to vomit again and again and again. For this work, O Lord, may Thy hand not give Thee pain!

The heat from the burning bus was driving me back. I raised my wet face. Ahead of me was a foot, a decapitated trunk still in its uniform, and a whole person, greasy with blood, jerking spasmodically. In his hand, he was trying to get a grip on his revolver, which I took off him; and I wiped the blood out of his eyes. I suppose he had jumped from the front at the instant we had jumped from the back.

Turani blinked. He said: "Get it over, man." He was a brave officer, Turani, I never said he wasn't. "Nobody would want to live after that."

"I suppose not."

He blinked again. "All those children. So many children. I am going to fry in Hell."

"Where is my family?"

He looked baffled. He tried to raise himself on his elbow, but his face creased with shock: he must have broken his arm as he landed. His hand and fingers were limp. Slowly, the pain receded and he opened his eyes at me.

"Dead. I'm dead. You're dead. The whole world is dead."

The ground at my feet jumped. A bombardment had begun, from our side.

"Where is my family?"

"Well, now, let me see. Mum, well, she suicided in the Evin. And daughter, the one with the face, the one I fucked in her father's drawing-room, forgotten her name, she . . ."

"Yes?"

"Hanged with the whores in Ahvaz in '81." He could see I didn't believe him. He lost interest. "Look, they're dead. Everybody's dead. Get on with it, man."

I emptied his weapon and returned it. In the holster was a Form of Release, folded, smeared with blood.

I said: "I am taking the laissez-passer. Is it signed?"

"Of course. Not tempted by martyrdom?"

"No."

"No stomach for defending Islam and the homeland, have we?"

"No."

"You don't even have the guts to kill me!"

I turned round. The heat of the fire gusted at me. The horizon swam. I sensed that a part of my mind had shut down for ever.

"No."

I bent down and took him onto my back.

"It's your word against mine about my connection with Farameh. They'll believe me."

"Of course."

I stumbled and slid back to the boy. He was seated on the ground, trembling and keening.

"Why, O why did you do it?"

"Walk in my footsteps, soldier. Because of the mines."

Turani laughed.

"O God, why didn't you leave me to die! Hosein, Hosein, let me give my life for you . . ."

"Shut up, soldier," said Turani. "You'll have opportunity enough to die." Then he said into my shoulder. "Do you know why he hated the girl so much? Why he didn't care? Why he let you take her?"

I stopped dead in the track.

"Don't be tired!" said the boy.

"Because she wasn't his daughter!"

Of course. I am a fool and always will be. I stepped on.

"Then who is her father if not the General?"

"God knows. Ask the Frenchman."

At the berm, there was a commandeered Range Rover with mud smeared on its sides and windows full of red-eyed men. I tipped

Turani into the open back. Dazed, the boy tried to follow and got a rifle butt in his face.

An officer looked up from his phone.

"Survivors?"

"No."

"Bodies?"

"Not really."

He darted a glance at me, and at the bleeding boy.

I said: "Killing us won't bring 'em back, dog-arse."

He shivered.

"Permission to return to our units?"

"Go to Hell!"

As I strode eastwards on the track, churned up by tyres, the boy had to skip to keep up with me.

"May I come with you, sir?"

"No, young man. You must return to your family."

"I will be like a son to you."

"Be a son to your mother. Are you literate?"

"Alas, sir."

"Kindly repeat after me: In the Name of God . . ."

"In the name of God . . ."

"The Merciful, the Compassionate . . ."

"The Merciful, the Compassionate . . ."

"I have been released from active duty . . ."

"I have been released from active duty . . ."

"By order of the President of the Mobilisation Committee . . ."

"By order of the President of the Mobilisation Committee . . ."

"Proof-of-Islam-and-of-the-Muslims Seyyid Hashim Kola'i . . ."

"Proof-of-Islam-and-of-the-Muslims Seyyid Hashim Kola'i . . ."

"For acts of conspicuous gallantry . . ."

"For acts of constipuous gallery . . ."

"For acts of conspicuous gallantry . . ."

"Conspicuous gallantry . . ."

"In the face of the arrogant enemy."
"In the face of the arrogant enemy."
"Take this paper and don't lose it."
"God bless you, sir."
"Now go home and stay there."
"May your shadow never diminish."
We parted.

The door to the Russian Garden hung sideways on its lower hinge. Covering the right-hand garden wall was a drawing in wood ash of a man in European costume raping an Iranian girl. It had been done rapidly, in wide, bold strokes of a stick or finger, but so cleverly one could see the man's mouth hanging slack with desire, the girl's skirt and chador flying upwards, and on her face a look of pure despair. I thought: So the town knew about us all the time, and she knew they knew, and so she stayed and they left us alone; and I have learned nothing. Beside the picture was a smeared hammer and sickle, done in blood, and the initials of some Marxist-Leninist party of which I had never heard.

The windows of the upper story were stained with fire; but downstairs Ryazanov's office was untouched, except that the Shah's portrait as a Scout had gone and pride of place had been given to that of Stalin. The stairs had collapsed like match-wood, but I pulled myself up on my hands, into scalding sunshine and the long sea. Our bedroom had taken a direct hit, from a gunboat or frigate, which had blown a jagged hole in the wall and window traceries. In one corner was a pyramid of ancient shit, and the walls were daubed in slogans and obscenities and old blood. In the chaos on the floor of busted coral, spent cartridge cases, torn books, melon seeds, empty Pepsi cans, the ripped sole of a tennis shoe, dried blood and tissue, I saw the metal bowl which Shirin Farameh used when she shaved me.

As I passed through the rooms, I brushed against remnants of our life in the house, reticent as ghosts. An old scent, the sound of my feet on the coral, the way the sun had of falling in bars across the floor fluttered out of the strangeness. I sensed that to try to hold those impressions, to reconstruct my wife and child, and myself as husband, and the house when it was ours; to draw reassurance from recovered sensation; indeed, to exercise my will in any degree, would drive those phantoms away. In truth, what I needed was not the Shirin I knew but some other I did not know, who might have come here one day in the last fourteen years, and in her hurry and single-mindedness left some trace of her passage: not a message to me, no, but some involuntary evocation of our long honeymoon, such as a broken tile put to rights or a dead snake not yet fully decomposed or an over-grown shrub that she'd pruned out of habit.

Outside, the palms had been decapitated and trunks lay split and exposed at unexpected angles. In the dust and dried leaves of the tiled path, a snake was dozing in a coil. Beyond it was a litter of metal spheres, trembling in the sunlight. I had never seen the like of them, but I thought they were anti-personnel mines and I wondered what had possessed the ship's gunners to fire both high-explosive and such things. The gunners had, no doubt, to use what was to hand; and I trod carefully for fear there might also be defoliant or other chemicals of which I knew nothing. Nobody, I thought, will be coming here for many, many years, except those who know the place and have no fear. I whispered: "We will survive, Shirin, and be re-united, even if we have to wade through blood and stand on heaps of corpses, the whole world dead or dying, and just you and I to laugh at it."

At the far wall, by the ash-pit, there was a wilderness of pink roses. *Gloire d'Ispahan* had spread uncontrolled, and soon would top the street wall. The scent came at me like a wave on the beach, and I was filled with happiness that something of her remained, which must in the end engulf the place and all the good and bad done here. I whispered: "O snake, move away from here, or I will kill you." At the root of the rose bush, I scratched away the dust and came on a National Shoe box. In it were the rubies, Mr Ryazanov's Gardner dish, the passport blanks, and the gun and bullet. There was no message or writing of any sort; but in my disappointment, I extracted the consolation that she had been here, perhaps last year or the year before, after the Communists had been cleared out, and left for me the gun and things I could sell for money.

I took the dish, and the gun and bullet, buried the box, and went back to our bedroom to wait for nightfall. At midnight, I came back down the stair, walked through the dark garden and set off for India.

PART FOUR

❊ 22 ❊

One night in the spring of 1989, in the Hospice de Bon Sauveur in Pondicherry, India, as I lay in the cold desert of my bed, Shirin Faramch stood before me in reproach. She was clothed in a shift of blood and lime and her breast had been punched clean though by the firing squad in the Evin. Her right cheek and side and thigh had been eaten away by the lime-pit, and at her throat, her ruby necklace had fused solid with the collar-bone. Her head, nicked by the razor, lolled under the weight of a paper Persian crown with the word "SLUT" scrawled across it. Her greasy eye-sockets glared at me in listless rebuke. She stank of the battlefield.

I sprang up. I said: "I have looked forward to this moment, for I have seen the roster of humanity and it is blank."

She sighed. I bent down to kiss her ulcered lips. In her mouth, her teeth had been broken at the root. Her breath made me swoon.

"I had heard that love could survive death, ma'am."

"We are not dead, unfortunately. Remember your promise."

Our lips touched. I felt a tremor in her, and smelled the smell of roses after a rain-shower. Her breast pricked my side. Her heart started to pound against my ribs. Hair tumbled into my eyes.

She pulled back her head and laughed. "All it required was one kiss." I pulled her back to me. Against her palpable reality, her unmistakable Shirin-ness, India was a mere nightmare. I felt such relief that tears sprang from my eyes and ran down her cheeks; and such longing for her touch, that my clothes exasperated me.

"You are so hasty! Like a bachelor outside the ladies' bath house! Aren't you to enquire after . . ."

"How is she? Please tell me."

"Well, if I need to prompt you . . ."

"Don't torture me, Shirin!"

"Your daughter Layly, sir, is not bad. With her auntie. I thought, in the circumstances . . ."

"May I see her? After."

"After what, John Pitt?"

We passed the night in conversation. At some point, Shirin brought me my clothes. My little Layly was now an unwieldy teenager, furious and shy, all chest and feet and yellow hair in her eyes. I was shocked by her manner with her mother, and remonstrated with her and she howled into my chest.

"FERME TA PUTAIN DE GUEULE!"

It was not my daughter. I gently embraced the man's head and ground my gun into his ear. He went limp in my arms. Through the blind was the deep blackish blue of the hour before dawn. I was bewildered, for the face in my armpit was the Frenchman from Bushehr, Lachat's companion, the junkie, Fann. Or rather what was left of it. No doubt he robs all newcomers, clears out at dawn.

"Where is your friend?" My dream surged up in me, but I beat it down. Time for all that, later.

"It's cool, man. You were shouting in your sleep."

"Where is your friend?"

"Fuck you, man."

I covered his bony face with my hand, and pressed two fingers against his trembling eyes. He yelped with pain.

"Where is Lachat?"

I pushed him away so he could see me. His eyes revealed nothing but fear. It was as if his nature were an empty room. I thought: It's not me he's frightened of. He's frightened of Lachat.

"Fuck you."

I grabbed his scabby wrists and turned them over. He whinnied with pain. Across the dormitory, a man groaned in Tamil. I said: "Nous allons . . ." I had forgotten how to make a French sentence. "We are going to the beach."

"Fuck your arse, man. Fuck you, man."

"Please, be quiet."

I unlatched the door, and propelled him through. Palm trees were rattling on the esplanade. Across the dirty beach, breakers gleamed and sighed. Pieces of my dream still lay in corners of my mind, but I looked straight ahead at the sea.

"Now, Mr Fann, I'm going to throw you in the sea and shoot at you for a while, as you shot at me in the sea back at Bushehr all those years ago. But first you're going to tell me where he is."

"I don't know, man. We split, way back. That guy was fucking crazy."

"Walk on. It's not far."

The white sea tumbled and roared. Fann bent, crept round and leered at me. His eyes flickered up at the gun, and at my face. A breath had stirred the tatters of his mind.

"Recognise this weapon, do we, Mr Fann?"

I pushed him down in the surf. A wave thumped his back and knocked him flying.

"Jesus, it's wet, man. I'll tell you. I'll tell you!"

A wave broke over his shoulders, floated him, pulled his legs from under him. He raced away from me. He screamed. I put the gun in my teeth, waded in and pulled him back up the beach. I knelt down where he sat sobbing.

He said: "She just sat there in the bow, the witch, with the gun and that kid shitting and pissing on her lap. The captain had wanted to fuck her, but he sure didn't want to do that now, witch bit through his cheek, whipped out a gun. Lachat just sat in the stern, laughing and smoking the gear. Jesus, I thought she'd have to drink or sleep, but, No, she just sat there, putting the child to her tit, or washing its arse with sea-water. Then, the second night, we could see the lights of Dubai, this goddam launch, with a bright light and all these Irani guys in white, popping at us, I went over the side. I swear to God that's the last I saw of him, and that evil woman, and the stuff, Jesus, five kilos and two years in a goddam Arabic gaol. I don't want to think of it."

"You must. Then I'll take you back to the water."

His face glistened in the first wet light of morning. He had a look of profound cunning.

"Man, we were paid that goddam stuff."

I was still not accustomed to his values.

"Who gave it to you?"

"He went out of the hotel, Lachat, in the morning."

"Who did he see?"

"The usual guy."

"What was the man's name?"

"Jesus, how do I remember? His name was . . ."

"Yes?"

". . . Mr Qavam."

I burst out laughing. Shirin appeared before me, but I shooed her away. She stalked off with our daughter, and a nasty backward glance.

"All right, Monsieur Fann. Well done. Let's go."

"Where?"

"Into the sea."

I picked him up by his wet arm-pit. I thought: I've killed Iraqis, and they weren't my enemies.

"I have gear, man. You won't believe it. Grey from Chiang Mai. I'll lay it on you."

"Don't worry about that now." I led him into the brine. He struggled, but he simply had no strength.

"I'll tell you where he is."

"But I won't believe you."

"Goddammit, the guy said the gear was ours if we got that woman away from you and delivered her to Dubai!"

282

"Deliver to who?"

"How do I know?"

"Who?"

"I don't know, man. Somebody in the government. Lach didn't say."

He was out of his depth. I held on to his waist to keep him from sinking.

"But Lachat didn't go into the water with you."

"He was captured, man! By the Iranis. Only I and the captain got away."

"Well, that's one way of looking at it, Mr Fann. Another way is that he made a fool of you, took $150,000 worth of refined heroin and that evil lady onto a warship that may or may not have been Iranian. And you got twenty months cold turkey in an Emirates gaol."

"He's in Srinagar, man. Let me go, man!"

It is said that the Emperor Jehangir, as he was dying, was asked if he had any requirement. "Only Kashmir," he said. "Nothing else." Half of me was already there, stepping out beside the lake with the other honeymooners. Fann burst to the surface. On his face was a look of pure terror. I felt ashamed to be bullying a junkie. I picked him up, waded with him to the beach, knelt on his bony back to pump out a trickle of water. A crowd had gathered to watch us. The brine stung me in the early morning heat.

I said: "He will be well in fifteen minutes. Leave him alone. He has nothing in his pockets."

I rode north in surges of delight. Everything about me was tinged with sweetness: the jammed windows of the buses, the stench of diesel and woodsmoke, the mango trees and cattle and endless files of walkers on the roads, the paddy-birds standing motionless in the rice. All seemed mere expressions or appearances of my pleasure. I remember a man beside me lit one of the cigarettes they have in India, a little tube of paper tied with pink cotton and called a bidi; and I was on the verge of asking one of him – I turned to him, I came to it – before thinking better of it. I decided: When we are together again, I will smoke, to keep her company, and because it will not matter any more.

Beyond Jammu, the Public Carrier ground to a halt and the driver put chocks under the wheels. Before me, a line of trucks and military vehicles stretched up and round and up, and no doubt repeated itself at ever higher elevations as far as the tunnel into Kashmir. I slid down off the grain, pulled my parcel from the hold, and began to walk. At the Nasry Nallah, a bus of the Border Security Force had become embedded in the mud to its axles. I walked on and up, past vultures feeding on a bloated mule's carcass – the stench was like a wall – and families of green monkeys that chattered on the parapet, or pelted me with gravel. I helped a Sikh driver fix his starter motor, and he gave me some milk, for I was thirsty. Below me, above the foaming Chenab, the vultures lazed in the air like Russian tea-trays.

It was not that Fann's tale had prolonged their lives a day or two; or even that Shirin, in the boat, had behaved precisely as I could have predicted and thus remained the Shirin I knew even when I was not there to witness her. It was that the sensations of my dream, of pain and yearning and happiness, were authentic, had been reserved from the Russian Garden, survived in my secret self and were available to me not at will, alas, but in some pattern of circumstances which had occurred once and so may occur again.

At sundown I came to a high village, just a row of tea-shops and the last petrol pump before Kashmir, which was the cause of the fifty-mile traffic jam. I drank some tea, and ate a pound of apples from the Valley, the like of which I had never tasted. I slept in the tea-shop because it was cold, rose early for the same reason and was at the tunnel at dawn. A Border Force major shouted at me, so I squatted down by his tent, Indian-style, till he went for his breakfast and I walked into the darkness. The tunnel cascaded with water, and the trucks bellowed past like cattle and scorched me with their exhaust. About a mile in, I became dizzy from the diesel, and pulled myself up onto the backboard of a Public Carrier. The light at the mouth of the tunnel made my heart ache. It was bright and immense, as you would expect among such mountains, but softened by the mild colours of habitation, green pines and yellow rice fields, autumnal plane trees and tin roofs flashing through the willows. The light sparkled on the rinsed and shining vehicle. Tumbling and curving down the steep road, floating on the driver's exhilaration, I felt a sweet and delusive nostalgia, as though I were returning to a place I had never seen.

Srinagar disturbed me with faint echoes of Iran. I was drawn to a mosque that looked as if it had been designed in Isfahan and fabricated in Tibet. Below it was a still and filthy canal, and I found a place to sleep on the bow of a boat called a doonga, for five rupees a day. In the morning, I went to a tailor on a levee above the River Jhelum, and waited in the sunshine under a colossal plane tree while he made me a pair of black trousers and a white shirt; then I presented myself at the Burn Welch School for Boys in Park Road.

The headmaster was a Christian priest from south India. Behind his head was a long shelf with two small silver cups at each end. A watery light lapped at the room.

"We have no vacancy at present."

"I also teach classical Persian."

"Heavens above, John! That's the last thing I need! In this situation!"

"In addition, I am a skilled motor mechanic."

That intrigued Father Peter. "Unfortunately, John, I cannot pay you what you would expect in U.K."

"My family is not with me." I glanced at the cups above his head. "I am considered a useful rather than first-class cricketer."

He looked down at his empty desk. "Church of England, of course?"

"Shia Muslim."

"But you're British!"

"I have an Indian passport." Several, actually.

Father Peter gave up. "Welcome to the staff of Burn Welch School, John. *For Friend and Country!*"

"For friend and country."

The class was so big I broke it into two, forty in each division. My problem was truancy. Each evening, after nets, I took one of the boys over the bridge into Old Town, to pick our way between rotted cliffs of buildings, trailing a crowd. I sat over tea with old men in karakul hats, while women and girls stood in the doorway, saying their piece. I said, If you don't make him come to school, quite soon you won't have a grandson, which caused the women to shriek, but the old man would shrug. The lad thinks this. He thinks that. I was exasperated by a society that so fawned on its young men.

My best student, when he came, was Javed Khan. He batted third wicket down. One Friday noon, I followed him into the latrines by the cricket square. He was reaching into the cistern.

"Give that to me, please, Javed."

He sprang down with the gun at my belly. I could see he loved to hold the weapon, but was trembling on the brink of a thought that was quite unlike any he had ever entertained: Do I have the courage to kill my teacher? If I can kill my teacher, I can kill anybody.

"Give it to me, Javed. I will return it to you at the gate. I will not have you bringing a weapon to school. You must give me your word, as a Muslim."

He swaggered towards me. As he passed me, I disarmed him. Of all that I have done in my life, I want that action back.

At the school gate, I said: "Javed, you cannot hope to defeat the power of the Indian republic. You are a good student when you attend. If you do a stroke of work for once in your blessed life, you'll do well at Engineering College, and you can play for J. & K. State. With your looks and a double century at Minto Park, you'll win the heart of some doctor lady from this side of the bridge."

"You don't understand."

"May I keep you company?"

He shrugged in his First Eleven sweater.

As we came to Gupkar Road, he said: "Mr Khomeini was Kashmiri."

I had often heard that.

"His grandfather came this side, dealing in shawls. He is buried in Seyyid Hosein mosque."

"Yes, Asif showed me." Asif was the only Shia pupil.

We passed the National Conference headquarters. On the lawn, politicians in white suits and fur hats were squatting in circles on the lawn, transfigured in the evening light. At Polo View, Javed plunged into the dry fruit wallah's and brought some dried Ladakhi apricots, which we shared. Some boys tried to join us, but Javed spoke gruffly to them and and they drifted away.

At last, he said: "We know it is impossible to fight India. We are doubly sure of the might of the Indian Republic and our own meagre resources, but we are also sure our sacrifices will resurrect the dead issue of Kashmir in international forums."

He took a deep breath.

"You see, for four hundred years, we Kashmiris never fought, we were always under some form of oppression. We were submissive, non-existent creatures. After Partition, some armed groups arose but never managed to operate. This time it will be different."

"Why?"

"The time has come. Look at Romania, Berlin, Czechoslovakia! The common people can see on TV that all these oppressors are being driven out by an angry populace."

"The time has not come, as you would know if you'd lived as long as I have. You are just playing into the hands of the Pakistanis."

He looked at me sideways. "We have no illusions about Pakistan."

"Look. I've been there, you haven't. And to Iran as well. You must understand that the Iranian Revolution was not the beginning of something, but the end; not a revival of political Islam but its swansong. The effect of the Revolution has not been to revive religion in Iran but to make it hateful to all but the portion of the population that has a material interest in it, that gets its bread and water from the mosque. Without the war, the revolution would have lost its vigour long ago and its power to persuade. It survives only through control exercised on the minds of the living by the blood of young men and children who went singing to their deaths. Two hundred thousand boys died to prove that Islam could not be exported even to Iraq, home of one of history's most tyrannical despotisms."

I was surprised by my speechifying.

"Javed, you say that you want freedom, but it is not freedom you want but control. You and your friends want to close the hotels and the cinemas . . ."

"Yes. Life here is immoral. There are illicit liaisons . . ."

"Rubbish, Javed. Kashmiri girls are very chaste."

He trembled. I could see I had gone too far, for he hated his inexperience and I had made fun of it. He stopped. I looked for the last time at his flapping trousers and short-sleeve cardigan. I knew he would not come back to school.

He said: "People will not give their lives to see Layla Deep in a film at the Gulmarg cinema. They will fight and die for salvation in Heaven. In a year's time, just you see, we'll be the talk of the town. Women and girls will be singing songs about us. Nothing will happen in the valley but that I say so."

"In a year's time, Javed, you'll be dead."

"I am ready for martyrdom."

"There are so many ways to die, my dear, why do you add to them?"

"You will never understand. You have no country, no family, no religion, no friend!"

"You're right, Javed. If you don't come to school, I will inform the Headmaster and the J. & K. Police, as I am required to."

"Go to Hell."

The next day, I called on the Border Security Force at Misry Bagh. I was late for my appointment, but escorts were waiting for me at every crossroads in the barracks. At the office of G2 (Intelligence), a trim officer in dark glasses was talking gently, like a father, across his desk to a Kashmiri boy. The boy seemed about fifteen years old. I was distracted by an operations map on the wall over which the curtains had not quite been drawn; and when I turned, the boy was gone. He haunted the interview like a phantom.

I said: "Col. Ravi, I can give you the identities of the Haji Group."

He took off his sunglasses and looked at me. "And I can and will put you in Tihar Gaol. Where the hell did you get that passport?"

"I'll tell you when I am better acquainted with you and your methods. Meanwhile, are you interested?"

"What does that bugger Bateson think he's doing? Sending up a boody illegal. Isn't it enough for you fellows that you left us with this situation, without coming back to fish in troubled waters? You British make a point of leaving a festering wound when you go: Jammu and Kashmir, Palestine, the white governments in Southern Africa . . . "

"I have no connection with Mr Bateson or the British S.I.S. and never have had. Now, if you aren't interested in my intelligence, I am sure the I.B. or the Task Force will be. Or the Rashtriya Rifles."

"Where are the boys?"

"The last of the group passed over to Pakistan by the Baramulla road last night or early this morning."

"So what the hell is the use to me of their identities?"

"It occurred to me, Col. Ravi, that if you wanted to kill them, then maybe you could bomb the Muzaffarabad training camp over there."

That evidently corresponded to something he knew, for he said: "We pay 650 rupees for information. Including family addresses."

"I'm not interested in money."

He smiled. "Are you thirsty? I could get some drinks."

"Whatever you like, Col. Ravi. Maybe later. For this intelligence, I need Lachat."

He shook his head.

"The Frenchman."

He shook his head. He said: "I have given all my life to my country. I've served in the Nagaland, Miso Hills and Punjab; and our experience is that these militancies will last about ten years before they tire themselves out. Well, of course, some people will be embittered for life, if they have lost a son or a brother or a daughter, but in general it will take about ten years."

"Why do you use him?"

"Bear in mind these fellows are Kashmiris. We're not talking here about the Tamil Tigers, who steal an army manual and study it, and because they see that soldiers are trained to take cover behind a tree or in a culvert they put the improvised explosive device there . . ."

"Why do you use Lachat?"

He flared up. "I don't use such people."

I glanced at the chair where the boy had been sitting. "All right, that boy was tortured. He gives us bazar gossip, who said what to whom and where. It's better than nothing. Who do you think we learned it from?"

"I have Indian citizenship."

"Like hell you do. Patrick Lachat is in quite another category altogether. When he broke out of the Tihar, he cut a girl's throat on the Agra Express, some poor Australian girl, who had a mother and father back in Melbourne, just for her travellers' cheques."

"Have you children, Colonel?"

"Yes. I have children. Shall we have some drinks?"

"Why do you let Lachat move freely between here and Pakistan?"

"Did Jim send you up here to ask me that?"

"No. I have no connection with Britain. Why do you tolerate Lachat here?"

"I don't, damn you!" He paused. "If it had been my decision, he'd still be sitting in Tihar Gaol." He looked down at his desk. "Drugs have changed the nature of the conflict. We had no idea that heroin had such a power of concentration: that it could draw so much money, so many men and weapons and concentrate them in a single place. All the governments of the region are poor. The Paks need Lachat because they need money. We need Lachat because the Paks need him."

I stood up: "Will you think about my offer, Col. Ravi?"

"How can you do it? Those boys, the Haji group, whoever they are, trusted you."

"Just bugger off, will you, Ravi, or I'll go elsewhere."

"You know, John, what all people need is justice. If the government gave the Kashmiris justice, they'd throw their weapons at its feet."

After the game, which was won without Javed, I got drunk with Ravi at No 5/6, Extension Colony. His family were in Chandigarh. His eldest son had started at a stockbroker's in Bombay, earned more in a month than his father in a lifetime. His daughter was at college in Dehra Dun and he was bitter about not being invited to address her speech day. Every now and then, Ravi would squint at me and tell some story of Bateson or his predecessor. I didn't mind: it did me no harm that he thought me more than a schoolteacher with a grudge against a Frenchman.

The next day, I was walking with the Eleven down Dalgate, on our way to Neshat Bagh for a practice picnic. At the corner, there was a traffic jam, for the policeman had vanished from his stand in the middle of the road. I felt the boys slide away from me, like water off a pitched roof. Two young men in Kashmiri clothes were running up the pavement at me. I fell down at their feet and pitched them into the lake, for they were light. Neither could swim, and I had to go into the water and fish them and their brand-new Chinese pistols out. The houseboat-wallahs jeered.

I said: "I want you to tell Javed that I have given his identity to Ravi. The Government of India's offer is that if he and Hamid and the others hand over their weapons and give their parole, they will be resettled in All India, anywhere they like, at Civil Service Level ll/c; or they can stay in Pakistan, if they like that country so much. What they may not do is come back to the Valley and cause a commotion, for they will be killed and I will not be able to save them."

"You will be dead. Javed has sworn by God to kill you."

"Well, that's that." The team was drifting back, heads hung in shame. "Will you join us on our picnic?"

The boys were proud, as proud as Persians. "Damn you!"

On the night of 31 August, the boys advertised their return from Pakistan, exploding seven petrol bombs in Lal Chowk. Two days later, four off-duty air-force officers were shot from a motor-rickshaw at the bus-stop in Rawanpura. There was nothing at all glorious about Javed's choice of targets then or later – a Hindu journalist at All-India Radio in Dalgate, a lady doctor kidnapped from outside the hospital at Maharaja Bazar, a series of I.B. officers attached to the police stations – but by the autumn the Government of India was running in all directions. It was as if Javed had pushed at a door and it had fallen open. The Valley Hindus panicked and left for Jammu in government buses. There were fewer tourists and then none. The lake front hotels filled with soldiers and civil servants whose homes could not be fortified. Balconies flapped with khaki underclothes. The Home Office furloughed all the Muslim officers and sepoys in the Jammu and Kashmir Police; and that, I guess, gave Javed his recruits. Passing the smoking beams of a burned cinema or liquor store, I thought: Everywhere I go, Iran wounds me.

I moved first to Ishtibagh, I suppose because the plane trees there, which must have been planted in the time of Jehangir or earlier, reminded me of Isfahan; and when that became unsafe, to a houseboat at Hazratbal. The houseboat-wallahs, thin and unshaven and poor as rats, were happy to have my custom. The boat, which was called *Sweet Sixteen*, was joined by a long plank to the vegetable gardens which I drew up at night. I hired an old boat man, named Wasfi Kahn, with a punt gun and a pair of tourist's binoculars, and together we strung a maze of barbed wire fifty yards out into the lake. He took me to and from the school landing, the gun resting across his lap as he paddled. My students no longer came, but Father John would not sack me, so I worked on the vehicles and the plant. At night, I sat on the stern of *Sweet Sixteen*, drinking Peter Scott from a teapot and listening to the boats slipping across the moonlight, while boys shouted my name or songs floated down from the willow villages at the head of the lake . . .

Lord Javed came down from Sonnamarg . . .

Often, in the early morning, I would climb the extinct volcano called Takht-e Suleiman or Shankaracharya Hill for its prospect of the valley. At the top was a granite temple guarded by a platoon of armed police. From its rampart, I liked to look down at the Jhelum coiling its way between the wooden buildings, under the nine bridges, past the famous mosques and the fort of Hari Parbat, and thought: Lachat is here, or Lachat is there. In the smoke from the breakfast fires and the fog of army diesel from the boulevard, looking down at the sickly bloom of green and purple that was spreading out to cover the lake, I thought that a great amphibious civilisation was coming to an end.

As Ravi's spy, I was now worse than useless. He had but a single counter-insurgency tactic, which the people called the "crackdown". For days the roads would be full of vehicles, and then, in the small hours of the night, he would throw a cordon of wire around a district of ten thousand people and put men into every single house one by one. As I passed Javed's house at Masjid Jama, his aunt and sisters were unbinding their hair and pulling at their chemises so they could show the newspaper reporters they'd been dishonoured by Ravi's Sikhs. When they saw me, they set up a keening and spitting. Beyond them, I heard somebody speaking English and then the clatter of army feet. I ran down the alley in a hail of women's obscenities.

There was a canal in the middle. I bent down and slid off my shoes. I didn't want to corner him, so he'd turn and I'd run onto him. From in front of me, I could hear the rhythmical clatter of the soldiers heels, and the jingle of their rifle slings. On the roofs, there were whisperings, the crack of a broken tile, movement, people scampering to get away. I thought: I've got myself into a trap. If Javed or the other boys are up there, they can jump me.

I turned a corner and burst out into the open space in front of the Shah Hamdan mosque. Before me, by the light of pitch torches that blinded me, two three-tonners blocked the street and with them a curtained white Ambassador saloon with its engine running and Lachat's hand on the passenger door. Against the green railings of the mosque, half a dozen boys were being beaten with lathis across the face. At the road block was a Sikh officer of the J. & K. Police whom I knew.

"Captain Singh, stop the European! He's a Pak agent!"

The European turned. His long hair was tied in a pig-tail, and on his half-raised knee was a briefcase which evidently contained all that was important to him. Fifteen years vanished. He smiled at me and then, raising a finger, as if to say, "Will you wait just a moment" or "Un instant, monsieur!", whispered something to his escort. The man raised his rifle and shot at me. The world slowed to a snail's pace. I thought: That bullet is going to hit me in the waist. I tried to turn, to reduce the target by half, but of course I hadn't time. What hit the flat of my hip had the force of a speeding car. It threw me across the square. Even as it did so, I knew I would live. I landed hard on the paving stones, gasping for breath, saddened beyond all words. A second bullet passed over me. The car started and disappeared. I thought: You must be careful at the Bone and Joint Hospital, even if the doctors agree to fix you, which I suppose they will, what with their Oath, you'll need a guard by the bed. Also: You are a weakling. Why do you let him do these things to you?

On January 15, on the first day of what the Kashmiris call the Cold Forty, the lake froze. At ten that evening, a rocket-propelled grenade hit the bow and broke *Sweet Sixteen* in two. I watched from the ice with Wasfi, the shikara-wallah, as she burned merrily and then came down on her side. The boat was hypothecated to the J. & K. Bank, and the owners treated the mishap as an act of God.

"It's better than you deserve," said Ravi.

"What do you know about it? You're just a third-rate policeman!"

"Somebody has to protect the Union and its freedoms, even if we are not now appreciated. You betrayed your goddam pupil!"

"At least I didn't set fire to the bazar in Sopore and burn fifty shopkeepers and their families . . ."

"Get out! You bloody British bastard! Orderly! ORDERLY! Shoot this man! He is a dangerous militant."

"You're drunk, Ravi."

"So are you. Bugger off, soldier! Can't you see we're drinking?"

"Yes, sahib."

"Ravi, if you tell me where he's gone, you'll be free of me."

"You know these Afghans, John. They've been fighting Russians for ten years and are frightened of nothing. They sell their lives so dearly! They come down off the mountain during the night, set up their ambush, then shoot up an officer and his driver at breakfast. In the end, I have a thousand men running after them, and when we finally get them, they have four or five of our boys dead around them. What can you do with people like that? People who like dying! The Kashmiris are absolutely terrified of them."

I struggled to my feet. "Goodbye, Ravi."

"John, you won't make it to Kabul. You won't even make it to Peshawar!"

"Maybe not."

"I am warning you. The entire length of the Line of Control with Pakistan is manned. If you're interdicted crossing over to Pakistan, you'll be shot."

"Naturally."

Javed was killed on 30 March, 1990 in a routine clearance operation at Maisuneh. I didn't go to the funeral, which turned ugly. For a day and a night the army could not get across the bridges, but huddled behind sandbags and grenade netting on the approaches. Later, when nobody was there, I went to the martyrs' cemetery. It was at the place called the Festival Ground, where people came to sacrifice their goats on the last day of the Pilgrimage month. At the entrance was a sign in English saying: "Do not shun the gun / My dear younger one / The war for freedom / Is not yet won."

Javed's grave was the last in the front row, and on it were two framed photographs. One showed him as a fugitive on the last day of his life, exhausted, unshaven, dressed as an electrician, heading for Pakistan. The other, taken a few hours later, showed Ravi and his men posed round something wrapped in a bloody shawl, like hunters round a stag. Ravi had on his dark glasses, and was raising a glass of some dark liquid in toast.

I have always disbelieved in martyrdom, and in plastic flowers. But I thought: Was it worth all this to be no nearer to Lachat? It would be better to be dead than to go on with this treachery.

Each morning when the drunkard wakes, he praises God for bringing him safely through the night. As he comes up out of his sleep, not knowing who he is or where he is, or what occurred that he should be he and not another and in that place and not another, he suspects that it is God that brought him through the night, and alone recollects it; for the drunkard does not remember, and because there can be no identity without memory, but for the record kept by God and his angels, the drunkard would cease to be.

The drunkard dies each night and comes alive each morning. Every event for the drunkard is without precedent and he learns nothing from it. He feels the cold sensation of light across his blanket, sees a curved shiver of glass a-tremble in the window frame and pieces of blue sky on the concrete, hears thunder reverberating round and round his room, and those things appear to him marvellous; as yet, he cannot reconcile the sunshine and the reverberation and the broken pane, except by the agency of God. For without memories of glass and thunder, and how they act one with another, he can attempt no explanation of his own and must fall back on the limitless self-sufficiency of God.

It is in these moments, as the drunkard's memory begins to stir, and with it the beating in his skull and the desiccation of his body, that the room bursts a second time. The executioner's glass shivers, falls, splinters on the floor. The golden samovar tinkles. An empty bottle teeters, tumbles on its side and rolls toward the bed.

A shot-silk curtain detaches from the door and floats down like a baldaquin. Now, the drunkard remembers what connects the noise and his popping ears and the broken glass and the open door and the floating silk and the whirling snow and the bottle just coming to rest at his feet, and also this morning with the last morning and other mornings in winter. It is what he calls in his mind the sadopanj, which means "one hundred and five", and is used in the town about a .105 millimetre gun that is mounted on Sherzerwardah Hill, and each morning, for as long as the drunkard can remember, at about eight o'clock, has fired between six and ten rounds of phosphorus high-explosive into the bazar.

In his daily outing, the drunkard passes twice through the bazar: on the way to the Polo Ground for lunch with Dost Mohammed, an elderly antique seller and by general supposition the richest man in town; and, after that, to a place called the Kharabat or Ruins, a street of wine-shops where, if he has money, he buys a bottle for the night (though, no doubt, not for much longer). On each occasion, he is astonished by the sponge-like character of the place, its boundless capacity for injury. Picking through the puddles with their scabs of cracked ice and shit, he passes a tea-shop where, that morning, eight Hazara men, who had brought sheep to the butchers and were taking their breakfast, had been blown into pieces; and yet now other men are having their tea or eating kebabs of rancid mutton fat under a gunny roof; the blood has been partly scrubbed away and the morning is forgotten until the drunkard, careless and elated with the package beneath his coat, sinks into a puddle to his waist and comes up crimson.

The drunkard does not say his prayers, for he has become careless about the prescribed observances of religion. God is very merciful, says Abu Navas, so it is an error not to sin; for it is to doubt His mercy and to squander His gifts.

The drunkard lights his samovar, fusses with charcoal and tea. There was a time he remembers, when he used to take his breakfast in the kitchen across the courtyard. It was warm from the cook-stoves, and he liked to talk to the reporters and answer their questions and help them with translation, as if mere company had the character of warmth, but they'd all gone, and the cooks, and the tea-boy, everybody but the drunkard. Yet picking up the silk, which is patterned with a cypress tree, and tacking it to the lintel, he sees a loaf of bread in its polythene bag laid on the threshold, which stirs a memory of yesterday morning and other mornings before that. The drunkard thinks that if one morning the bread isn't there, that is the day the battle will begin.

A clap of thunder bends him double. As the exhaled air blows back again, he feels the tremor of an anxiety that is more than merely the protest of his returning personality. He knows the anxiety has to do with the coming day, some task or appointment that does not belong to his routine and might expose him to strangers, a departure from his daily outing, whose boldness and novelty alarms him; and beneath it, a shame so irredeemable that for a moment he buckles at the knees.

It has do with a visit I had, about this time of day, but yesterday, or the day before that, from a French doctor. The International Red Cross had sent a container of medicines from Peshawar, which had been held up by the Seminarians, the driver stripped and beaten, and could I do anything to help? I, or rather Dost Mohammed, could.

Someone was standing in the sunny door.

"Wakey-wakey!"

He stood in the incandescent doorway, bulky with clothes and yet shivering out of control. I had noticed long ago that many Indians, even intelligence officers, simply cannot begin with cold weather.

He called out in English: "Sorry to knock you up so early, old bugger."

He could not stop shivering. He said he was leaving, the Chargé had already left, everybody had left. He looked wetly up at me, and got his business over in a matching official tone: the Indian Union could no longer be held responsible for my safety. I felt sorry for him and made him some tea. I felt sorry for his shivering and the rattling of the glass and sugar in his saucer, because I knew it arose not from fear for his own life, but from the cold and the filthy slush and the wild gunnery and the high air raids and the typhoid fever and the women stoned to death and all the utter and irremedial barbarism of this country, killer of Hindus. I also felt sorry for myself, for I sensed the phantom outline of a plan or idea taking shape, which would disrupt my life, and though I beat the phantom down, I sensed that it was gaining in materiality with every moment and must soon be accommodated in my consciousness.

"I think I'll wait a bit longer, K. B. Remember me to Ravi, will you?"

"What the hell are you waiting for?"

I saw him to the courtyard arch. His jeep engine was running. His escort had fanned out and taken up positions straight out of the manual. They broke apart and mounted the vehicle in just as good order. As I trudged back to my room, I said to myself: I am waiting for the Seminarians. I am waiting for an assault that by its comprehensive threat and violence will drive every inhabitant of the city, and especially one particular man, from his shelter. I am waiting for one of two things: that one morning I'll wake and will not be myself: that as I come out of the world of ghosts, I will be one of them and not the man that fell asleep the night before. The other is that one morning, at about eight o'clock, an artillery round will pass through the paper ceiling of this room and blow this sodden body and its worthless property straight up to heaven.

Dost Mohammed's shop was a mud and timber building that occupied half the street that looked on the snowy Polo Ground. His apprentice opened the door, and showed me up a wooden spiral stair to a long smoky room with tiny windows caked with snow. In the middle of the room, hemmed in by bales of stock, was a large red satin quilt and under it any number of men warming themselves from the stove beneath it. No day passed but I thought I'd doze my life away under the crimson quilt, lulled to death by the charcoal- and tobacco-smoke and the conversation of the other men.

I'd known a time when each day brought some novelty to the quilt: two dealers from Santa Fé in America; a wiry Englishman with many questions and lovely, old-fashioned Persian; a newspaper reporter from Delhi whose English I was happy to translate; and even some European ladies, the wife of the Italian Ambassador and her sister, who were as witty as they were beautiful. They had all gone now, and it was just dealers who owed money to Dost Mohammed and sponges of rice and fat.

The host sat always in the same place, speechless, quilt up to his beard. I loved him for his restraint. I had been astonished the first winter I stepped through his door and looked around the dark and dirty shop. On one wall, clumsily tacked and rolled at the bottom, was a curtain of shot silk and cotton dyed with the pattern of a green cypress tree and a red field. It had been some years since I'd seen anything so beautiful. I turned from it, and saw an old man sitting, quite still, beside a small table. He was wearing a plain white robe and a turban of yellow silk.

I said: "You are a fortunate man, sir."

He inclined his head. "Only since you brought light into the room."

"I believe, sir, this weaving was made in Isfahan at least two and a half centuries ago."

"You have a right to your opinion."

"Are you familiar with the city of Isfahan, sir?"

"Alas."

I gave up. I said: "Thank you, Dost Mohammed, for permitting me to see this beautiful object."

"It is yours. The lad will wrap it for you."

"Sir, I cannot accept your kindness, for I have no property and can make you no equivalent present."

"Then I shall keep it. Shall we expect to be honoured again soon?"

"I do not wish to be a bore."

"As you wish."

My visits were at first rare, then once or twice a month, and then, with the start of the siege, daily. I loved his slit Mongolian eyes, his silences, and his indifference. I learned he was now the city's only banker, discounted cheques and banknotes and sent them down to Delhi overnight by armed taxi; sold weapons for opium and refined opium for money; transmitted subsidies from Peshawar and Tehran; but such operations did not employ his affections. He had no wish to part with his rugs and Nuristan wood and Turkoman saddle-trappings and Bokhara jewels; and if anybody wanted such things from him, he must offer so much money that it became tedious to refuse. He had ceased even to receive the brokers, who fawned on his apprentice. I don't know how much Dost Mohammed received for me from New Delhi, but every month or so he would give me some banknotes or something from the shop on which my eye had for an instant lingered.

"Ah, now the circle is complete! Peace be on you, John! Come and warm yourself!"

Today, a bore was under the red quilt. Generally, such men stuffed their faces and took their leave, no doubt to take a second helping at home and ensure their wives did not get lazy; but this man picked the mutton fat from his teeth with a matchstick, leaned back and asked for a cigarette. He was dressed in European clothes. I think he was a teacher at secondary school, though the pupils were on strike and had been for years.

He tried to speak of politics; but the men of the stove took no interest in the persons that, at any particular time, were oppressing them for it brought no pleasure or profit. Rebuffed, he turned to me:

"In your opinion, sir, who are the finest poets in the world?"

302

"Of the traditional school, Shahriyar. Forough among the moderns."

"Forough Morough," said the apprentice, picking up the plates. "We have no such gentleman here."

"Lady. She lived an irregular life, and died in a motor accident, in Tehran."

The quilt absorbed this treble justice. At length, the secondary-school teacher spoke up: "Women can't write poetry."

There was a murmur of approval through the smoke.

I thought: God has given you the most beautiful language in the world, a religion that anybody can understand, a land such as He himself would choose to live in, great monuments of architecture and all you can do is spit melon-seeds, mutter gibberish, mortar one another and mistreat your wives. I said: "Permit me, gentlemen, to tell you a story of this country in olden days."

There was a sighing and a shuffling and an extinguishing of cigarettes. They liked stories.

"In the Name of God the Merciful in the year 506 in the town of Balkh in the street of the Slave Dealers in the residence of Prince Abu Said Jarreh, there was staying at that time Master Omar Khayyam and Master Muzaffar Esfazari and I went to wait on them and in the middle of the company I heard that seal of the truth, Master Omar, say, 'My grave will be in a place where each spring the north wind will scatter blossoms on it,' and I thought: What a preposterous statement!, and was amazed that a man such as he should talk such nonsense until in the year 530 I was in Nishapur and it was four years since that great man had drawn the veil of earth across his face and this world below had been orphaned of him, and since, you see, he was my guide in the search for Reality, one Friday I went to pay my respects to him and I brought a gentleman with me to show me where the grave was and he took me to the Hira cemetery and I walked round to the north and found his grave at the foot of the cemetery wall, and just the other side of the wall were an almond tree and a pear tree which had shed their petals on his grave so that it was buried in their flowers and I remembered the story I'd heard him tell that day in Balkh and I wept that in all the wide earth and all four inhabited regions I would never see his like again, God bless him and grant him grace and favour in the gardens of Paradise and farewell."

I stood up.

"My friend, It is early yet."

"Dost Muhammad, permit me to trouble you no longer."

"Shall we expect to be honoured again soon?"

"I do not wish to bore you."

I disentangled myself from the quilt, bowed to the company and took my leave. Dost Mohammed accompanied me to the street door. He had never showed me such condescension.

I said: "Dear friend, where is the Frenchman?"

"What can I say?"

"Is he here in Kabul?"

"What can I say?"

"Who is protecting him?"

"What can I say? India, Pakistan, America, Iran, England, Russia. More than one at any time, never less than one. Thus can an unscrupulous man exploit the jealousies of governments!"

"Dear friend, if by chance you see him, will you do me the courtesy of saying to him I have business with him at his convenience?"

Dost Mohammed shook his turbaned head. He said: "You will not be able to prevail against him. He has friends and you are weakened by drinking alcohol and living alone. Even so, your command will be obeyed!"

"May I give my life for you, sir."

I pushed open the curtained door, and snow played with my face. I inhaled a burned smell, which was new to me, except within it was the smell of roasting meat.

"The Lane of the Tyre Retreaders," said Dost Mohammed. "Direct hit." He turned back to the shop door. "I dislike war."

I was startled by this intimacy. "We do not presume to advise you in matters of commerce, my love, but should you not consider moving your stock, I mean to a place outside the bombardment?"

He bowed. "Of course."

As the slush infiltrated my holed boots, I thought: The day Dost Mohammed ships out his stock is the day the battle begins. O, that that could be soon! Why can't these people get their fighting over and return to a life of peace! For God's sake, engage!

There was a black cloud that promised more snow at sundown. Veiled women scuttled home through the mud. The wind cut through my second-hand overcoat, and water seeped through the newspaper I used to fill the holes in my boots. I found after a while, that I was walking to the strangers' cemetery: for no reason, except perhaps to delay my appointment. It sat beneath a windy ridge to the north of the city, surrounded by a high mud wall, topped by leafless almond-trees. It had a stout wooden door and a heavy old-fashioned padlock, but I don't suppose either deterred the religious fanatics as much as the protection of the British Embassy. Now that had been withdrawn, I did not expect it to survive much longer. I pulled myself up and sat on the wall.

Under the snow, the graveyard looked forlorn. It was not so much the monuments of the nineteenth century, with their veiled women and Christian angels, that distressed me, as the rows of unmarked little humps: European junkies, I suppose, who had risked injecting Afghan morphine before the war or starved to death during it. I tried to connect the monuments by something other than their Europeanness. In truth, the connection was only their deadness, for these men and women, though they might not have known it, had come to Kabul to die. What other conceivable purpose could there be in a place so ruined and spoiled, a place revelling in its own puerility and cruelty and ignorance? It seemed to me that these little hummocks, mere disturbances in the snow, were the outcrops of an immense and subterranean misery which extended far beyond a single person's mental reach, preceded me and would succeed me. I saw that I had come here, for the same reason I had told the true story of Khayyam, which is that I wanted to mourn, but I couldn't. What I knew was that I was not going to any other place and would leave my bones here under the snow.

The British have a kind of soldier, from the mountain regions of Nepal, extremely ferocious, to guard their property overseas. These men come from villages high in the mountains, where their great-grandfathers served the British in the last century, refuse to learn foreign languages and, though said to be mild in their ways at home, address all problems with a curved knife they call a kukri. I won't say that Afghans are frightened of these fighters, who are called Gurkhas, but I was told that in the early days, when high-spirited young men used to pick fights with them, they were killed unless they could use treachery. I had no such illusions. The anxiety that had been with me for several days crystallised into a question: Have the British left some of these men at their Embassy?

Beside the iron gate, the striped sentry boxes were empty. The gate was chained with a brass notice in English and Pushtu saying the offices were closed. Inside, a group of men in thick quilted coats were seated around a brazier. I guessed they were gardeners who did not know where to go. They were waiting to gather their courage and their numbers to loot the ambassador's house.

"Go away! Go away!"

I sprang over the gate. They began to stir.

"Not here! Closed! Holiday!"

I walked past them towards the preposterous house. It had been built by Curzon with a colossal portico that looked, not on fields and streams and woods, but on the Hindu Kush. Partridges strutted around me under weeping mulberries cloaked in snow. One of the men came steaming and pounding after me. I stopped and turned.

"Yes?"

"We are owed our arrears."

"Don't you lie to me, brother. If you aren't out of here at once, I'll punish you. If any man approaches the building while I am conducting my business, I shall shoot him."

"Yes, sahib. Sorry, sahib. God bless you, sahib."

I walked under a sort of arch, built I suppose so that carriages could let down their passengers under cover, and up a broad flight of stairs. From the top I could see a scattering of houses in white and black timber, like the house of Shakespeare's wife that I once saw as a child in England. I pushed against the sunny door, which opened. In the hall was a very large carpet of the kind known as Ushak, made in the seventeenth century. It was missing its border, which was no doubt why Dost Mohammed had left it where it was. I took off my boots and rolled the carpet up to protect it from the sunshine. As I did so, scraps of French kept coming into my head and going out again, from my conversation yesterday with the French doctor. I said out loud: "I have a liking for deserted residencies."

In the sunshine, I was haunted by scents of the past. Beneath the smell of Afghanistan, of sweat and jasmine and excrement, was something that tugged and snatched at memories of my life in England: furniture polish, I think, and paraffin and cigar- or cigarette smoke. I found myself in a huge cold kitchen, scrubbed clean, and in the cupboards were objects of whose existence I had quite forgotten: cocktail cherries, pickled walnuts, toothpicks, Saxa salt. In the drawers were sharpening steels, knives, peelers, scrapers and skewers, dishes and cosies whose individual function in the hierarchies of British hospitality I had forgotten or had never known. I lit a candle and went down a short flight to a dark basement full of wine bottles, some of which I took. I said to myself, in extenuation of the theft, that they were already lost to their owners for the Seminarians would wheel them off to the National Stadium and smash them in a day or two. I sensed that the spirit of the house, its Britishness, was receding or indeed was already gone; and that even if, by some miracle, the Seminarians created a government that was recognised in the world

307

and conducted diplomatic business with other powers, even so the British would not bother to return. In the corner of the cellar were two children's bicycles and that vestige of a family existence pained me. I resolved not to stray from the public rooms.

In the Ambassador's sunny office, I found a safe with a combination, but its heavy door hung ajar and in truth I no longer believed I would find any information. The desk had been emptied of papers. The man was evidently a reader of books, or at least the office he filled was a bookish one, for all four walls of the room were covered in books, many in Persian. There was also a book in English, nicely printed and bound in London in 1992, entitled: *King and Courtier: The Secret History of Iran's Royal Court, 1958–78* by Prince Sadrullah Qavam, whom I had the honour of knowing. It was in the form of a diary, much indexed and footnoted. I took it and a bottle of wine and sat down in a patch of orange sunshine on the Ushak. The wine, which had no label, was dark purple and very sweet and contained a sediment which I allowed to settle in the cup. I had an idea it was port or madeira and I wondered if Curzon had liked those wines. Later, when I'd finished the book, and slept and woken to another sparkling day, I wanted to look again at two entries. The editors used Gregorian dates. The first was for 6 July, 1974:

I was still pre-occupied by my charming visitor of last night. Her only hope is the Empress, but H.M.Q. is sure to smell a rat, especially if she comes from me!

The second entry was for 2 June, 1975:

Audience. H.I.M. out of sorts. He got on to his generals, always a bad sign: "Not one of them has an ounce of guts, except Farameh and he is vile." Then, quite out of the blue, he said: "You know, Farameh's daughter and the English boy are living quietly in a house in Bushehr." I almost fainted: my beloved Shah knows everything! I made a joke of it, said I envied the boy, who is called John Pitt and was just a little teacher in Isfahan when Farameh was DG (I.I.A.F.) there, for she is said to be quite a beauty. "Nonsense! Bushehr is far too hot for any of that." I asked if I should inform Nassiri (Director-General of the Savak). "What on earth for? They're doing nobody any harm, except Farameh, and he's getting far too big for his boots. Leave them alone. I was madly in love with her mother when I was the boy's age. Farameh is a good officer but he is a brute. I dread to think what he and my sister Farahnaz get up to!" What a relief, and all the more surprising, considering how hard H.I.M. has been on his daughter Shahnaz. H.I.M. has a good heart, and always does the right thing, even if he is sometimes badly advised. The rest of the Audience passed pleasantly, in reminiscence about this and that, mostly girls.

The editor had added a footnote to our names.

John Pitt or Pect (b. 1956?) and Shirin Farameh-Qajar (b. 1958): Eloped from Isfahan in 1974, and Pitt was charged with her "murder" in his absence. The case was the subject of much speculation at Court at the time. Both are believed to have perished in prison in 1980 or 1981.

I lay down on the carpet and called up the ghosts of Imperial Iran. I summoned jewels and caviar and horses and prisons and money and girls. Qavam and Zahedi and Madame Claude paraded before me. I tasted again that *Iran Bonheur* of embassy and Court that had taken a capricious shine to me, and was now obliterated. I knew that the monarchy had persecuted and imprisoned me; that it was violent, cowardly and vulgar; that it created its destroyers, its Khomeini and its Kola'i; and yet how could I not regret the passing of an age, whose spirit one cool afternoon had infiltrated the bedroom of a house in Isfahan and whispered: "Go with him, yes, now, dear, for we see no solidity in this world or the next, and we are all going into the night"?

Yet in this reverie, in the icy mountain light across the Ushak, in which I sought to abolish myself as a person, to reduce time to history and personality to a piece of print, I felt a tremor of intellectual doubt. There was something missing from the passage, of which the editor had not been aware or not enough so as to delay him in his work; and of which perhaps only I of all readers could decipher or relate. It was not so much Mr Qavam's interest in us, but the case he had adduced to illuminate, like the good courtier I knew he was, his sovereign's state of mind. What had Shirin to do with Princess Shahnaz? Were they both, for the purposes of those men in 1974, indistinguishably unruly children who defy their parents? Yet, as I'd read, Qavam had often interceded for Shahnaz and finally brought her back into her father's favour.

All the while, as I reasoned in the style of the book I was reading, an obstinate memory was pulling at its trace, broke loose, rose, and bobbed on the surface. I sought out another passage, that I had read at the beginning and forgotten, and that made no mention of us. It was for 10 November, 1957, and described an audience the morning after a dinner Qavam had attended at the house of the then Queen Mother:

> Reported Mrs E's goings-on last night. Although she never once mentioned the word "divorce", she made a very significant statement to the effect that her daughter had not been brought up to luxury – implying that H.M.Q. could easily do without it and divorce would not cause her material discomfort. "Bollocks", said H.I.M., looking distinctly uncomfortable. After much debate, we agreed that that bloody girl ... who started all these rumours must be found a husband posthaste. Then, with a bit of improvisation on her part, nature can take its happy course. No prize for guessing who will undertake this match-making!

And so at last, the dam broke. My history disintegrated and reformed in a shape both barbaric and authentic. I saw at last the power of love on earth, its utter recklessness, its delight in smashing the world to pieces. I heard my interrogators whispering "Where is the slut?", over and over and over again. I saw my wife seated, filthy and exhausted, in the dust of the path in the Russian Garden. I saw her mother, in a skirt of grey silk in the style of her young days, inhaling smoke from a cigarette as if her life were at the tip of it; and Shirin lifting her head to tell a lie to her father, except he wasn't her father and that's why he hated both of them to death. And as for her actual father, how could he abandon her and then kidnap her away? How could a king behave with such caprice?

🏵 24 🏵

Each evening, as I drink, I remember. I cannot find those memories in the day or indeed till the next evening, when the action of drinking and certain formalities of my room – the stove-light on the samovar, the smell of woodsmoke and wax – revive the night before. It is as if I put on my remembering self at nightfall, as other men their sleeping clothes. I have heard men drink to forget, but I am not among them, for I drink so that I may remember.

"Psss. Mr John? Are you awake?"

It was the bore from Dost Mohammed's.

"No."

"John! You must be awake if you can speak!"

"Not in this case."

"I don't understand, Mr John."

There was a commotion and another voice and a touch on the door. I knew from the touch at the door, and the grumbling of the man, that he had somebody with him that he couldn't command.

"Merci, Monsieur. Ça y est. Au revoir, Monsieur. Au-re-voir-Mon-sieur."

I waited for the footsteps to drag away. I stood up straight and breathed in.

It was the French doctor, Catherine LePage. She stamped her boots in the snow and struck a pose. She was wearing a hat of fur. She said: "May I come in?"

"It is better that you don't, Dr Catherine. Your position as a foreigner and a woman is delicate. That man is a notorious busybody. I'll call him back."

"Damn him. I *am* coming in. I'm cold."

I stepped back to let her pass. She leaned against the stove, and looked about her in alarm. She lit on the door curtain in the stove-light. "Ach, que c'est jolie, ça."

"Catherine, I have a wife and child."

"How fortunate you are. Can I have some of your whisky?"

"Yes." I was not used to company, and had but one glass. Also, her femininity filled the little room and turned me into a fool. I splashed some whisky into Mr Ryazanov's bowl and held it out to her. I felt broken, overrun by her independence and wilfulness; and recognised in horror that that, too, was ingratiating: that my very caution and shyness had brought her across the town in the cold and curfew and into my room, sat her down on my bed with her coat round her shoulders, cupped her hands round my Gardner dish, turned her glassy blue eyes up at me.

"Tell me who you are."

She needed something from her pocket: cigarettes, perhaps, or hashish or something else to mitigate the awkwardness. Her coat slid off her shoulders, and as she caught it, Mr Ryazanov's bowl began to teeter, spill and slide from her wet left hand. I sprang and, from the air, I watched it fall between my hands; and heard a crack like a pistol shot that reverberated round the room, round and round and round; and saw the broken pieces on the ground, close to my face where I lay sobbing.

"O c'est pas normale."

I curled up on the cold ground and howled like a dog. I could not tolerate my humanity. The vessel of my life, that I had kept intact through these twenty years, had shattered and the shatter would go on ringing in my head for ever. Alien sensations flooded the vacuum. It seems I'd known that I was nothing but my fidelity; and now I'd betrayed my wife and friend, there was nothing left to me but pieces.

"It's nothing! I have seen them all over Kabul."

I looked to the head of the bed. Catherine had her knees to her chest. I could see she was frightened, and this was how she expressed her fear. Her face and curly hair, her strong neck and shoulders, were hard, defiant, masculine. I thought: It's neither her fault nor her business.

I rose, turned and lit a candle, scooped the wet china pieces into my hand and placed them on the sill. I was trembling from the gunshot. Now she saw that I wouldn't hurt her, Catherine was sorry for herself: to be here, in this bitter, dark room, with this madman.

"Objects have in themselves no power over us. Sometimes, Catherine, we invest them with more power than they can bear. Let me give you this glass."

"Who are you?"

"I'm a student."

"A student?" She looked perplexed. It occurred to me that I must seem old for a student.

"At the university of . . ."

I had forgotten its name.

". . . in . . ."

"Do you want to make love?"

"No thank you, Catherine. As I said, I am married."

"She isn't here. I am."

She raised her bare arms and shook off her tee-shirt in the way women do and I'd forgotten. She had on underclothes of a dazzling whiteness: I had never seen clothes so clean and shop-new, she must have brought them in their wrappers from Paris. I was astonished by a civilisation that could produce something so sweet and secret and insinuating.

I suppose I'd known all along that love would be the death of me: that what had survived a prison and a battlefield could not resist a Frenchwoman's yellow hair and alabaster shoulders. In all these years I had learned nothing, or rather I'd forgotten nothing, which is the same. I was no stronger than a babe in arms, ruled by my prick, wounded and trembling under the touch of her fingertips and mouth.

She undid my shirt and, then, as she took it off, slid onto her knees on the floor. I saw that action arose not out of passion, but confusion: an unswept piece of the busted bowl, so to speak, so I lifted her up and sat her down on my lap. I remembered this was the best thing in life and wondered what had caused me to renounce it.

I had not expected her to be so pretty. I had expected a certain reserve. Instead, she was single-minded in pursuit of happiness. Yet, as the room closed in on us, flickering with shadows on the cold wall, becoming not my smoky cell but the glimmering tent of our privacy, I saw it was not mere sensation she sought but reassurance: she was scared clean out of her wits. She had seen something here, in Afghanistan, for which nothing in her education or doctor's training had prepared her. Her breast, her hips, her mouth were rigid with fright.

"Puis-je loger ici ce soir . . .?"

"Of course you may, Catherine."

She was so pretty without her clothes. I thought: She's done me another kindness, which is to end this deceitful and cowardly life. Tomorrow, I will set off for Herat and Mashad and go back into the prisons which are waiting for me. For there is nothing to preserve now. It is not that Shirin will not forgive me for what I'm doing now, though she won't, but because I now understand that I do not forgive her; and that as I have done this act of violence to her, for all that I have suffered for her sake, so she has done the same or similar to me to pay me for her suffering. Our story is coming to an end.

"Jusqu'au matin . . ."

"Please."

Catherine recovered her softness. Reassured, she had passed into the realm of which she was undisputed queen, where she could require and dispose. One by one, she was inclined to overlook my several weaknesses, or found in them a certain sweetness; opened her mouth to tell me something, and then forgot it; remembered a man she'd loved very much at fourteen years of age; and remembered me; delighted in the flicker of the hearth and wished to see it every night . . .

"Jolie . . ."

After we had made love, Catherine LePage lay back on the quilt to permit me to admire her in the candlelight. I felt her filling up with questions.

"Why do you live in this shitty place?"

"Don't worry about that, Catherine. Go to sleep."

"I'm not sleepy." She winced. "I want to make love to you again."

"You can't. I mean, I can't."

Sulkily, she slid under the blanket and turned to the wall.

"Tomorrow, I'll buy you another dish, better than that one. I know the best shop."

There is nothing so precious that it cannot be made tiresome.

"Don't worry about that, Catherine. It was a present, that's all."

"From her?"

"No."

"Can I come and live here with you? The hospital . . ."

Why not? Why not spend a while with this pretty woman: help her with translation, keep an eye on her during the battle, make sure the Seminarians don't insult her. I said: "No, thank you, Catherine. As soon as the Jalalabad highway thaws, the Seminarians will attack and take the city."

"La bataille de Kabool aura lieu." The journalistic phrase sat oddly in her mouth. It occurred to me that doctors, who appear so in command of their patients, once away from them are quite unworldly.

"Yes. Once in control of the centre of town, the Seminarians will not permit you to practise your profession, because you are a woman, and they will subject you to indignities. I think it would be better if you returned to France, while the airport is still open."

"I must do my duty."

The idea of home appealed to her: clean sheets, decent food and working conditions, ordinary men. Away from this hell-hole, she would not need the likes of me. It occurred to me that the old notion of love, that I had learned as a child in England, and that had prepared me for its Persian incarnation, selfless and fatal, had passed out of fashion in Europe; or perhaps had never taken root in France. As I held her sweet warm waist, I tried to think of love as something purposeful, for pleasure or recreation or comfort or even, at its purest, for money. Yet beneath it all I sensed something half-hearted: that, in truth, she didn't really care for anything, didn't really feel anything except what we all feel, which is fear.

"Is there a Frenchman here?"

Her skin went cold. I held her tight.

"I didn't mean that, Catherine. Who do you think I am?" Or you are, for that matter. "I believe there is a Frenchman here that owes me something, that's all. If you could look out for him at the hospital, that is, if it's no trouble . . . "

"There is Dr Habibe."

So, that's that for now. I must learn in this new school of love. In the morning, Catherine, as you spring up, pull on yesterday's smoky clothes, experience cold as you have never known, you will regret admitting me so far into your life. Because the sky will be bitter blue, and the sun yellow and meridional, and people crunching back and forth between the craters in Gibbet Lane in quilted silk coats, you'll think: It's not so very bad, I'll get by. The man is nice enough in his way, but clumsy, and not so young, best not to get involved. Or make the best of it now.

She turned in bed. "Why are you so shy?"

"I was a soldier. I'm not any more."

"Ah," she said. "That explains this." She touched me softly on the scar on my hip. "Have you had counselling?"

"I don't think so."

* *

The next day, as I walked with Catherine LePage to the hospital, she was light-hearted. The anomaly in her station, as a woman without a man, had perhaps irked her; certainly, the passers-by now looked on us with an unctuous satisfaction; or perhaps it was the warm sunshine, which was the promise of spring. As I took my leave of her at the gate, she said: "Shall I see you after my shift?"

"No, Catherine. I am leaving Kabul."

"Because of the battle?"

"I have business in Iran."

"You are a coward."

"Yes, I am."

She turned and ran up the steps, my "God-bless-you" turning to vapour on my lips. One of the swaddled loafers at the gate unpicked himself from the group and moved towards me. Everything but his eyes was covered against the cold. He pulled down the scarf from across his mouth. He said:

"Are you Mr John of England."

"Yes."

"I have a message for you."

I took a deep breath, and blew it out again as fog. "Is he ready to meet me now?"

"Who?"

"No matter. Please give me the message."

"It is very important."

"If it is important, it will be rewarded."

"Come away from here."

We stepped out and stood in the slush in the street. The man was scarcely out of his teens. He said: "At the beginning of the disturbances, my father sought asylum in Iran. We were in Isfahan. My father worked for a building company, my brother for a sandwich shop, and my mother as a cleaner in the women's section of the prison on the Shahqord road."

"When was this? When did you return to Kabul?"

He looked at me cleverly.

"How long have you been here, lad?"

"Last New Year. No, I make an error, two New Years ago, I came back here to keep an eye on our property. My brother, who had stayed here when we were Iranian, had appendicitis and died, may God rest his soul." He looked to the sky. "This information is very dangerous."

"It will be rewarded."

"How much?"

"More than you imagine. Please continue."

"Mother, as I say, worked in the ladies' prison. One day . . ."

"When, for the love of God?"

". . . one day, as I say, a few years ago . . ."

"Was Mr Khomeini alive?"

"Oh no. One day, as I am trying to tell you, two ladies stopped her at exercise and gave her some money, very little, one or two tomans, but my mother was a religious lady, God rest her soul in His mercy, to give a message to Mr John outside."

An incoming round burst a street away. There was a chatter of answering fire, of every calibre. A mounted recoilless rifle came swerving into the street, firing in the air to clear the traffic, though there wasn't any. I drew the man to the side of the road.

"Please try and remember when this happened."

"I know! It was my last year at school, the year of the presidential election."

"Which one? How old are you now?"

"Just twenty."

Oh, thank God, who is very merciful! The election of 1993, just three years ago.

"How much will you give me?"

"A thousand U.S. dollars."

His eyes popped. I know Shirin must have given the crone a lot, so they would look for me, in the hope of more: but a thousand dollars was going it. He turned his eyes to heaven.

"Please, again. I can't hear you over the guns."

"They ask: 'Since you went away we have no news from you and people say things and our nights and days are dark and our bread and water always tainted with uncertainty since we could get no news of you by any means, your wretched bride is alone and the child says, Why is Dad's place empty? – what answer can we give? – and so we send different messengers in the hope that one will reach you, we beseech you by God and the Prophet and the Koran and by all that is holy that you write us two words in your own hand that you are alive and that is enough for us'."

"Thank you, young man. Take this key and go to the boarding-house at No. 4, Gibbet Lane, at the crossroads with Moscow Street, where you will find my property. There is a valuable old curtain across the door and a pure gold samovar. Take them to Dost Mohammed at the Polo Ground, say I sent you and he will give fifteen hundred U.S. dollars against them."

"He's not there!"

The other men had drifted up to join us. "I saw him this morning, with two army three-tonners, piling up his carpets. They say he doesn't like the Seminarians and has gone to Peshawar."

"Well, you must content yourself with my property."

The boy had a knife out, but I kicked his legs from under him and he fell with a crack on the frozen street. I picked up the knife and broke the blade against the street wall. The other men backed off a step. I pocketed the broken knife and walked away. A stone hit me in the back, but when I turned, they had no wish to fight.

As I walked westwards, the bombardment sounded heavier than usual. From the bursts over the bazar, I could see the Seminarians were firing phosphorus shells in the hope that a warehouse might catch fire. I thought: I shall go to Mazar-e Sharif, where Dost Mohammed will be with his trucks, sitting things out: he never goes far from Kabul. I'll pick up a heroin convoy that needs a mechanic down the Helmand, get off at Quetteh, get on the whisky run to Birjand in Iran or steal a Land Rover and go straight west where the border isn't even fenced.

It is hard to leave a city in which you have suffered greatly. The narrow twisting lanes were gilded to glory for me by the noise, and the pall of smoke and the running feet. Perhaps, too, I am wistful because I am leaving Catherine LePage when I might help her; and because know I will never drink whisky again. It is as if the drink in my blood is singing to me: How can you leave her and us? One more time, the best and the last, and then we'll go our ways. I found an open grocer's, and bought tea and bread and matches for my supper.

It was dusk when I came out into the cold fields. The bombardment had stopped or did not carry on the wind. I left the road and followed a track between knitted hawthorn bushes, to find a shelter for the night. The track ended in a village with tumbledown mud houses scattered with half-finished concrete boxes. On the other side, beneath a government anti-aircraft emplacement, a crowd was shouting at something in a field.

"O sir, you are a kind man, please bring her back to me!"

"What? Please excuse me, I am a stranger on my way . . ."

The crowd parted and a woman came howling towards me. She had pulled up her veil and her cheeks were scratched and bleeding.

"Please be calm, ma'am. I can't understand you unless you are calm." Beyond her, something was swaying in the snowy field.

The gunner threw up his barrels, and came prancing down through drifts of spent shells. "Good evening, sir! The lady's daughter is in the field. Unfortunately, she stepped on an anti-personnel mine."

I shielded my eyes against the orange sun. Scraps of sound came on the wind, high-pitched, girlish, sobbing.

"When?"

"At lunch-time."

Even my friend Dr Catherine could not have saved her. I shrugged and made to go.

"She is just fourteen. Please bring back my darling for me, you are a kind man."

"Give me the map please, soldier."

"What map?"

"The map showing in what arrangement you sowed the mines!"

"Oh no, we don't have a map, sir."

"Well, what in heaven was the lass doing in the field?"

"Her goats, sir! Her goats strayed into the field."

"Who sowed the mines?"

The soldier looked downcast. "Dostom Khan, sir. He is in Russia now. God damn him in Hell-fire!"

"I am afraid, ladies and gentlemen, that we must leave the young lady to God's mercy. It is wrong to sacrifice two lives for one."

"My Lord, help me for I have no other helper. Help me, My Lord, for God's sake! You will bring her back to me. You are a kind man."

"Where are her male relatives?"

There was no answer. I understood then that they had long ago despaired of the girl. They wanted something else to happen, someone else to die, a stranger, to assuage their sorrow and helplessness. I looked at them and they lowered their eyes. Only the girl's mother continued to pull at my sleeve.

"Please be cheerful, ma'am. I will go and with God's help bring your daughter safely back to you."

The crowd shrunk away from me as from an apparition. I turned to the soldier: "Have you petrol?"

"Of course."

"Have a truck ready for us here. Turn on the lights so as to light my tracks in the snow for the way back. Also, I need some water for the young lady."

Water they all had. I took a bottle, and stepped through the crowd. I thought: I will go, but not for reasons that you will understand or I can explain. I am stepping into the clean snow, because I hate my life and it is a delight to me to end it. I have been looking for

322

my family for twenty years, and long ago gave up hope of finding them; and now they are delivered me, alive, not three years ago out of that twenty, I haven't the courage to go back into prison to find them. Ten years ago, I made a secret promise to myself that I would never go back to prison in Iran; and that is the only promise, of all the promises that I made, that I shall, in the end, honour.

I have heard, God Almighty, that this is the state of mind most prized in your religion: the absolute and unconditional surrender to Your will. In truth, you will preserve me or blow me into a thousand suffering pieces. I have no concern in my life. I do not even look down at my feet, lest I slip Your hand from them. For reasons only You understand, and can understand, You took away my parents and my friend, my wife and my child; my good name, my gaiety, my courage and my loyalty. You made me a coward and a thief and a drunkard and a killer. And now You have taken my will, my last remaining shred of personality, so that in truth I am already dead: just a corpse, as my wife used to say, in the hands of the washer.

And now at last I see with Your eyes. I have grasped the scale of Your conception, which is not of human scale, but another, which must be devilish or divine. You did these things to me because only a man so treated would consent to walk through the mines and bring this poor girl back to her worthless family. Only a man who has no hope nor love of life could walk, as I am walking, laughing through the mines. I can see the girl well now, in a dress of red Moscow chintz patterned with irises, swaying at the waist. O God above, You took away her legs!

I stumbled, teetered, came down on my right hand and knee. Beneath the heel of my right palm, I felt something harder and colder than the hard, cold ground. I was trembling out of control. I pushed back my weight onto my knee, and then, gently, lifted my hand and covered my eyes. I counted to five. Then without putting my hands down, I came up onto my heels.

I recognised the mine because the Iraqis had sown them in a

four-kilometre strip the length of the Central Front in Iran. It was a Valmarra 69, Italian, that had somehow migrated to the surface, perhaps as an effect of frost and thaw and frost again. It was what Capt. Toloui called a "bounding" mine, for it springs a metre in the air and then bursts, pouring twelve hundred steel pellets into the groin. In '88, Kamran had bled to death before we could evacuate him, and so with the girl now.

I craned my head round. In the gloaming, the crowd had gone.

"The lights! Turn on the headlights!"

"Headlights," the girl muttered.

"Turn on the godforsaken truck lights!"

My shouts echoed round the snowy field. I screamed and screamed till I spat up bile. There was no movement in the gloaming. "Why are you shouting," the girl said.

"Miss, I have come to take you back to your mum."

There was no answer. I could just see her, about ten steps away, beneath a parapet of earth made by the exploded mine. I thought: In five minutes, you won't even be able to see that. You must go now. You will die tonight, and so will the girl, and that is just too bad, but at least you will be able to comfort her as she dies and, not to put too fine a point on it, she you. We are going on a journey, which is better not done alone. The bridge across Hell, they say, is finer than a hair and sharper than a razor. Come now, my man, throw your heart into the sea! What happened to the philosopher of five minutes ago! I took a step with my right foot. If every step could blow us up to heaven, we would ensure we took some delight from life. I stepped with my left and something wriggled under it, as if I'd trodden on a snake. I closed my eyes and counted. Then I sprang into the crater.

She was seated, separated from her legs, swaying at the waist and looking wide-eyed into the gloom. Her legs were still covered in trousers of chintz but I could not look at them. I took off my coat, to cover her modesty. Her touch was cold as metal. I said: "It's all right, my darling. I'm going to give you a drink of water and then take you back to your family. Unfortunately, it is dark now and I cannot see my track back through the mines. Have you any kindling which I can light?"

I slapped her face, but she was gone a long way out into the gathering darkness.

"My darling, I have water with me!"

I hugged and kissed her, tried to put some warmth in her. She shivered.

"Your what? I have some water with me."

"My animals."

"Safe. Don't worry about them. Have you anything I can light?"

I felt around where she lay. I found a brass bowl tied in a shawl, which must have contained her breakfast.

"We must wait until dawn. It is not long. As soon as it is light, I can see my track in the snow and can take you back to your family. What's your name, my darling?"

I felt something a cold splash on my cheek.

"Please tell me your name."

I put my hand to my cheek. It was wet with snowflakes. I looked up and snow was floating down around me, was lying on my coat and the girl's hair and the earth thrown up by the explosion and would quite soon cover all my tracks home.,

"Tell me your name!"

I hugged her close and lay down in the snow.

I woke to an earthquake. The anti-aircraft battery was pouring metal into the dawn sky. Cupful after cupful of clean white liquid fire splashed up against the vault of heaven. High up above me, way up in the indigo sky, beyond the reach of any weapon I knew of, among the receding stars, I heard the drone of an aircraft. Surface to air missiles crawled up to it like supplicating hands, but it was way, way up. I hugged the girl and recoiled from her touch. She was stiff and hard as a shirt left in the frost. I reached up to her face, to close her eyes, but I had no flexibility in my fingers. I covered her face with her shawl. I said: "You are gone to heaven, my dear, where all that you lost will be restored to you. Your beauty will be yours again, and your sisters and the husband that you never had and the child you will love. In heaven, there is no sickness or staleness or bitterness . . ."

The ground came up to me. An intolerable force pulled us apart and threw me in the air. For an instant, I thought I was back at the Front in Iran, and was puzzled by the spouts of clean snow about me. A hail of ice and stones rang down on my shoulders and my covered face. Slowly, I lifted my arms from my ringing head. From a vast crater, smoke and sparks were rising to heaven and, held up by them, fluttering this way and that on the hot gusts, was a scrap of red Russian chintz. All round me were fountains of snow, and the soft reports of the mines. They're destroying each other! The bomb, all half a tonne of it or more, has set them off! They've been sown too close, the silly pricks who did it, and they're setting each other off! I laughed and laughed: it was like listening to a foolish quarrel in a foreign language. I laughed as the fraticide continued to its close. Then I ran through the hot snow towards the anti-aircraft battery.

The Kandahar road was clogged with people. They were trotting, like driven calves, weighed down by clothes and possessions. A bus swayed past in a wail of its horn, its metal invisible for people. A Hazara man in an immense orange turban staggered by me, bent past the double by the Chinese refrigerator on his back. The people pushed past me, or halted in frustration, till the stream parted around me.

"Where is the European man?"

Women, covered tip to toe in their veils, lurched blindly past with baby children.

"Where is the other European?"

"Gone. Gone. The Seminarians are coming!"

Ahead of me, I saw the bore from Dost Mohammed's, in a thick coat of shot silk, harrying a shapeless woman. He tried to pass me.

"Where is the other European?"

"Sir, this is very bad. Pakistan have sent their air force to kill us."

"Don't be so ridiculous. It is a Russian mercenary flying at ten thousand meters."

A bomb burst a hundred yards from the road. The crowd surged and scampered past me.

A young boy was tugging at my sleeve. Beside him was a little girl, barefoot, with a dirty face.

"He is at Mustafa Street, packing his belongings."

"How many with him? How many people?"

"None. All run away."

I took a breath. "What are his weapons, my good boy?"

"Kalashan and grenades," he said. "May we come with you?"

"Alas, I have no money to give you."

The boy and his sister glided away from me and were carried away in the stream. A little later, I looked back and they were talking gravely together, like senators, while the adults scuttled past them.

Lachat was packing a Toyota jeep in the empty street. His actions were careful and methodical, indeed more so than was quite natural. I thought: He has the lost the habit of doing things for himself, is in a hurry, doesn't like the Seminarians, can't work with them, is exasperated by them. He had on a leather coat, such as the militia commanders had liked during the Russian years, and an automatic rifle hanging at his left shoulder. He had shed his hippie air. His hair, tied into a pony-tail, was striped with white. As he looked up, I sensed the force of time and mortality: that even Lachat was more than half-way through his life, was not as strong or light of heart as he was in Bushehr, or Srinagar, was subject to death. I thought: This does not matter greatly, for we must both die sooner rather than later.

"I have no space in the vehicle. Excuse me."

He continued tightening his nylon ropes. In the waistband of his trousers was a handsome revolver.

"I'm not looking for a ride. I have business with you."

"What? What? I can't hear what you're saying."

"I have business with you, man."

"Another time."

He continued with his back to me. He wanted to express his contempt for me, and to remember who I was, if he could, but more than either of those things, he wanted to finish with the Land Cruiser. I felt a small reinforcement, a flicker of superiority. He needs to be out of here more than I do. Slow it down, my lad, slow it down.

"Where is she?"

"Another time."

"Where is she?"

His back trembled with irritation. I saw that he was not a normal human being, that he could not tolerate the smallest frustration, that he felt himself a victim of the pettifogging irritations of the world. With fathomless generosity, he gave me a second chance.

"Get the fuck out of here, creep."

"Where is she?"

He turned and lifted his eyes to my face. I saw that he had given me my chance and I had squandered it. I saw that he was trying to slow himself down, to put the Land Cruiser to one side a moment, to concentrate on the matter in hand, which was to kill me.

He smiled: "I've fucked so many guys' women, that I don't know which one you mean."

The transition was without friction. A man who, seconds ago, was wholly concentrated on the task of packing up and getting out of town, was now just as single-minded in provoking me to attack him, so he could kill me.

"Where is she?"

I heard my voice as he heard it, scared, ingratiating, and tedious beyond toleration; and I knew that I was stirring something, as a child stirs a muddy puddle with a stick. In the depths of his nature and of his headlong, uncontrollable career, there was something that pained him, that he did not wish to think about.

"Where is she?"

"Well, I think I made a cut in her throat, not big, but big enough."

This is the beginning of death: things are said and done which cannot be carried back into life. This is not to frighten me, or to make himself brave, but to summon the authentic atmosphere of Hell for my murder. Who cares now about the packing and the bombardment and those mad Seminarians, when there's a murder to be done! Yet I sensed he was distracted by the irritation: that she and I were teetering on the edge of his memory . . .

"Where is the Shah of Iran's daughter?"

His eyes went black. It was as if a cloud had raced across the sun. He shook down his rifle in a reflex that was not quite under control: as if he needed his weapon as protection against a painful and unjust memory.

"How should I know, monsieur? One grew tired of her pestering."

I felt an immense force, like a wind, poised to knock me to oblivion. I felt the last shred of something, that I had kept secret up to now, some fragment of faith in her, of trust in her as she was and hope of her as she would be, vibrate and then crack into pieces. I thought: Not long now till everything is over.

"And the child? Where is the child?"

He shivered. Something had crept up on him, a thought or memory, then it struck him and his fury was uncontrollable. He was rising on his feet – that goddam bitch in the boat, she fucking got away with the gear! – and shrieking like a little boy; and as he sprang I felt pure joy – such gusts of aerial joy – that I would see my wife and child again and in this world . . .

I fired and the world turned red. Lachat was on one knee, his face drenched with blood. I felt satisfaction and also loss, as if something precious had gone from my life. On his face was a look of utter perplexity. He rose to a crouch. His bloody face opened on white teeth, black gums, a blue tongue. Without taking his eyes off me, he reached down to the snow for something.

It was my gun, to which my hand was attached.

I knew I must die of fright. I knew my heart must stop from fright or else must pump my life into the snow. Fright swooped at me and roared at me; and with it at my foolishness, that after forty years on earth I'd used a gun not fired for a century.

"You know I brought that gun from Isfahan . . ."

Another thought dislodged it, which I wanted to live to complete. It was that I was not so terribly unfortunate: that had that killer gun been fired in the boat in the Gulf, it would have blown my wife and child to kingdom come. I had a glimpse for the smallest instant of the world as if from a height, from a distance so great that good and bad were not to be distinguished, nor honour and shame, nor happiness and sorrow, nor any of the pairs by which I had arranged my existence. I began to laugh my life away.

Lachat looked troubled. Down on one knee, he reached for my right hand. I suppose his fault was a certain frivolity. He picked the hand up with two fingers; but it was greasy with blood, slid, dropped to the snow. His glance flickered down, so he never saw my torn boot in his face nor, a moment later, the broken knife in his eye.

At one time in the night, I woke howling for a blanket. I remember my teeth banging together and I prayed for death to keep me from shaking to pieces. The orderly thought the wound was infected, and the Seminarians picked me up and threw me out in the snow for they needed the bed for one of their comrades, but Catherine LePage came looking for me at the end of her shift and had me brought me in and laid on the floor of the kitchen. Even as I shook, I knew it was not from infection and fever but from relief and that I was only shaking now because it was all over and I could go home. I remember waking and Catherine was lying beside me, in her scrubs, curled up like a baby: I guess she'd been operating all night and all day

Her eyes opened. She looked aghast, sat up, pulled at her under-linen, shook out her hair. Frowning, she examined my dressings and glared at me.

"I had to cut it at the shoulder, John. There was severe trauma to the upper arm and chest."

May your hand not give you pain, Doctor.

"Don't try to speak. You don't deserve to live, but you proba-bly will."

May you live for ever, Catherine.

"You were right. They won't let me work, and Dr Habibe has protested that people will die but they just shrug their shoulders, like this. So we are setting off for Peshawar this afternoon and must leave these poor people to their sufferings! How can people be so foolish!"

I don't know, Catherine.

She glanced round, kissed me on the face, got to her feet and walked out.

I woke some time later and the boy and his sister were sitting on the floor, knees brought up to their chins. I thought I had dreamed them, but when I woke again, they were still there. Between them was a clean metal dish and a glass of tea-leaves. No doubt Dr LePage had fed them.

I said: "You have his weapons and the Land Cruiser and what-ever's in it. Now go and God protect you."

"We wish to come with you to Iran. We are orphans."

"I know. But I have nothing to give you but my blessing."

"As you command. We have the cadaver in the jeep."

"So let's go."

They helped me dress. In the jeep, brother worked the steering, and sister the foot pedals. We went to the strangers' cemetery, and the children punched a hole in the mud wall to get the body through, and broke the hard ground with the snow shovel for a grave, and said the opening verses of the Koran. With the body, I buried my right arm, so Lachat would be satisfied, and not trouble me or the children in our dreams.

✺ **25** ✺

I came back to Isfahan by way of Faisalabad. It was a beautiful spring day, windy and bright. Larks danced beside me as I walked between the triangles of green wheat, or soared high above me to sing their songs. At the Castle of the Girl, the vault had been repaired, with care, and then let go to the sun and weather as if by a race of technical spirits. An old and dirty man had been appointed or had appointed himself custodian. He said the palace had been built by the legendary Jamshid. The matter of snakes and buried treasure came up. After a while, he showed me something that intrigued him, a name cut with a pen-knife in one of the stone pillars:

H. M. STANLEY

1871

Beneath it, there were three lines of the beautiful Persian script called shikasteh, the broken one, which the man pretended to read, moving his lips; but he couldn't read it, because you can't read shikasteh unless you know already what it says. Its purpose is to convey not meaning, but ornament, not a message but a doodle, a conversation with the lonely self that has not fully given up hope. It said:

> If you come to my house for me my darling
> Bring a lamp and a window-pane
> So we can see down into the happy crowds.

Beneath it was the Iranian year, 1374, which is the year before last. So

I went down to the pool to bathe, and the old man walked away in disgust; and while he was gone, I went back and carved with difficulty in my left hand the first three lines:

> I speak from the depths of darkness
> and the depths of night
> and the depths of darkness.

And the day's date.

I tipped the man all the money I had, not that it would do any good, and then walked into the wind to town to pay my respects to Madame Qoyunlu who had, after all, forbidden me ever to return. At the petrol station by the Revolutionary Guards, where the young men were waiting to fill up their laden Land Rovers, I learned that madame had been tortured to death in the Adelabad Prison in Shiraz. She is said to have said: "I knew Reza Khan and he died in misery, and Mohammed Reza likewise, and Gen. Farameh likewise, and you mollas likewise will die in misery." Also that her sons were under house arrest in Tehran; that the two boys who'd saved the situation with their jokes had fallen in the fighting with the Revolutionary Guards in 1980; and was it really true a family member had put a kitchen-knife to the widow lady's throat?

No, it wasn't true. I was happy, there in the sunshine and the petrol stench and the wind snapping the shawls of the laughing women, while this ancient legend ramified and ramified; and I felt safe, as I had not felt for many years, for even the Revolutionary Guards wanted to hear it. I was happy to accept a ride with one of the families to summer pasture, for on the main road I knew I'd be arrested; and so I rode up to Maymeneh, two and a half days of bumping and bleating, and from there took my leave and walked the last eighty miles to Isfahan. I have been here ever since, but for one visit by Pullman to Bushehr; for I heard that the Russians were building a nuclear power station down there, and feared they might re-occupy their old consulate, where I had hidden some of my wife's property twenty years ago. I stay in a hostel run by the Martyrs' Foundation by the bus station, and do odd jobs in return for the bed. When the bus comes in from the villages, the place fills up to overflowing. Beside me is an old drug addict, who is no longer allowed to have his opium. Often I wake before dawn, and he is swaying cross-legged on his blanket, sobbing and burning his fingers or wrists. So I make him a cigarette, and light it for him, or rock him to sleep in my arms.

Isfahan is twice as big as I remember, and not so quiet or provincial. The river-banks, where once I'd run through the esparto grass to Mr Ryazanov's house, are now laid out in parks where families picnic together at weekends. The city has marched east and engulfed the Shahrestan Bridge, which now seems a small thing, not worth keeping really. The highway has to make a jink to pass Mr Ryazanov's garden, and the mud wall is crumbling.

Mr Mo'in is dead, God rest him! He was gaoled in 1979, for drinking alcohol and dealing in old-regime baubles and consorting with foreigners, and my heart bleeds for him in those days, howling among the opium addicts. He was sentenced to seventy-two lashes, but he thanked His Honour the judge and begged the favour of seventy-two more, so he might celebrate his liberty that evening with a drink. In the end, the sentence was commuted to a fine of a million tomans, which he didn't have, so he paid what he did have, thirty thousand tomans and his leasehold and stock, and starved for a year on a stone bench in the Meidan (which is now called the Meidan-e Imam), enraged, blasphemous and morose. On Fridays, he would shout to the worshippers hurrying to the Mosque of the Imam the couplet from Omidi:

Your Seminaries that rise so high will soon be brought to ruin
But the wineshops will flourish as they have always done.

Once, in Chahar Bagh, the Prayer Leader fluttered by and behind him, a large lady encumbered by children. She lost the rhythm of her step, looked down, scolded her chicks, then swept on haughtily, and I thought she might have been one of my pupils, perhaps Mlle Bordbar; and once, in the same street, I saw Mr Jamalzadeh stop dead, then raise his hands in triumph over his head, as if to say, "Now I can have no legitimate complaint!" but I signalled to him, and crossed the road, and he went on his way, out of breath.

I knew that we would age and die and be forgotten, yet I must have believed the scene of our occupations would endure. I now see that was an illusion: that the Isfahan of 1974 was in itself the last phase of a world that was dying, of a precious architecture, the shreds of British and Russian intrigue, of a cult of love and gardens, of an ironical view of history, that was even then falling out of fashion and is now incomprehensible. Yet there are moments, at the bridges at nightfall, or turning onto Abbasabad from the brightness of mid-afternoon, or passing the house where my wife was brought up (now the Isfahan branch of The Foundation of the Dispossessed) when I am visited by a sensation of 1974. It is as if I still wear a blindfold, which slips off at moments I cannot select or predict, and I see the place of my young days. This old town exists only because of me. Without me, it must be obliterated under the parks. It holds onto existence only by a thread, just as I hold onto existence only by a thread which she spun in this city a quarter century ago. I am still strong and can preserve my life and with it the city, for as long as it shall be necessary.

> Luck and Joy and Grief and I
> Set off together into the world of existence.
> Luck lay down and Joy ran off,
> But Grief and I go wandering on.

I am fortunate to live in a town in which to be poor and a cripple is no offence. At times of late, crossing the traffic in Chahar Bagh, or walking on the river shingle, I am blinded by certainty, as if by the light of an exploding shell. Yesterday, I pitched onto my hand in the sour cherries of Abbas Agha's shop. I tried to call for help, but I could not work my jaw to speak, till Abbas saw me, came rushing from the till, wiping his hands, cried at his apprentice to help me. I cannot speak, but my head teems with a sensation of the rightness of existence, that there is no evil nor suffering, for all is good in the eye of God. I fear that Molavi, damn him, was right after all: that it doesn't matter whether you love a woman or God, it comes down to the same thing in the end, for you make your peace with existence and go laughing to the other world.

The apprentice pours water down my throat. After a while, I come to myself. I can work my mouth and legs. I think: You must eat more, for you are growing weak and mad; maybe you were gassed that day at the Front. Shame on you, man, not forty years old and you're packing your valise. And the people look at me in a kind way, and yesterday a little boy ran up, gave me some apricots of the New Year, and then scampered off to his escaping mother.

Today, as I was sitting in the park of the Eight Paradises, at the point where the House of Language used to be, while the crows strutted about me, I looked up into the furious face of a teen-aged girl. Behind her, Mr Jamalzadeh waddled towards us through the pines. I stood up. Mr Jamalzadeh sank gratefully onto the bench. The girl continued to glare at us.

"How goes the search for wisdom, dervish?"

"It continues."

"God should know better than to answer our prayers! We thought back then: Good, well, we tried F-4 Phantoms and they brought nothing but headaches, so let us try something different, why not The Rule of the Jurist until the Second Coming! You know, dear John, people now blame the Shah not for his cruelties, which are bucolic when set against what we have done to one another without him, but for his weaknesses, in not protecting us from ourselves. We used to blame the outside world, the Russians, the English and the Americans for our misfortunes. We said: Leave us alone! And we will be happy! So they left us alone and we are wretched! At least," he sighed with pleasure, "we may now regret our Revolution at leisure."

"This is just a moment, Mr Jamalzadeh, which happens to coincide with our lifetimes. All this rage and anger, sin, virtue, Radicals and Moderates, plots and conspiracies will be forgotten in a year or two."

"Poor John. I remember when you came into my office at the school, so thoughtless and long-haired and what we call spoiled . . ." He caught his breath. "One of the little-remarked features of the Victory of the Revolution has been the utter and irremedial breakdown of paternal authority. Iran is now run by women and young people, particularly young girls. We wrap them up in cloth from head to toe, and then spend all day worrying what they are thinking under all that wrapping. My daughter has something she wishes to say to you."

I smiled at the angry girl, and invited her to sit by her father. She took a step back. I sat down.

"What she means, but is too reticent to say, is that she would be honoured if you were to come and live with us. She spares nothing to look after her poor father and she says it is no more trouble for her."

The girl looked mortified.

"And I confess, John, that I am dull and lonely since they took away the school and would delight in your company."

"Thank you, dear friend, and please thank the young lady for her kindness. In truth, I am obliged to continue my life as it is. Do you remember Attar?

'I would rather pass my life in inconsequential fantasies,
Than give my heart to home and shop'."

"You will become ill!"

It was the girl who spoke.

Mr Jamalzadeh stood up. "Now, now, Saira, these are private matters that are not our concern."

"If Miss Saira wishes to honour me and my family with her kindness, she could give a home to this parcel until such time as my daughter Layly should come to her and ask for it. I would ask her kindly to show it to nobody and keep it safe, for I have nothing other to give my daughter."

The girl took the parcel. It was only as it disappeared in her shawl that I recognised how the rubies had oppressed me; and I felt such relief to be freed of my last piece of property.

"I'll bring ice-cream," she said and walked away.

I am spending too long in the Friday Mosque. I used to sit against a pillar in the doorway of the Gonbad, and look at the courtyard and imagine the whole world reconstructed on the basis of faith as pure intellect; and sometimes some boys would come and sit with me, and we'd read some passages in Attar's *Memoirs of the Saints* of which I have become fond. Lately, some girls have been coming, and sitting separately, and they are ambitious and want to read Bayazid and Hallaj and the early masters who are quite beyond my understanding. While we were talking yesterday, about Rabieh, how on her pilgrimage she became tired and fed up and prayed to God to bring the shrine to her, which He did, with somewhat bad grace (which was embarrassing for Hassan al Basri, who had spent eighteen years on his way to Mecca, since he stopped to pray at every step, and was now in sight of the Ka'aba, or would have been if God hadn't done as Rabieh asked and moved it two hundred leagues to the east) – at that moment, the Imam of the mosque came by and gave me a vicious look. At the end, there was whispering and then someone asked me if it is permissible for girls to ride bicycles; the Militia are saying that it is a crime against the Blood of the Martyrs, and I said that I saw no connection between the two parts of the statement, but they should seek advice from a recognised expert in the Law. And I told them the story of Mohammed Baqir Majlisi from *Distinguished Men of Isfahan,* how he appeared to Ihsan Abulkheir in a dream, who asked him: "How goes it with you in that world and how have they

339

dealt with you?", and how the great Molla answered: "None of my actions profited me at all, nor all the Traditions I collected, nor the thousand lines of Commentary that I composed each day, nor all the men and women I condemned for deviation, except that one afternoon in Jubara I gave an apple to a Jew and that saved me."

In truth, I have always hated teaching. So tomorrow I will not go to the Friday Mosque of Isfahan, nor the next day, nor ever again, God willing.

I get so tired: tired from walking, and looking for my family, and also from the paralysis, and from the anticipation of it. This morning, I had a sip of tea, and tried to eat a piece of the cake that one of the girls had brought me in the mosque, but I couldn't finish it. I think I really must have been gassed at the Front. And I have such a sensation of blessing. I think that my self is gone, and what remains is merely my frame and a promise I once made to a girl of this town. That is the needle of Jesus, as they say here, whose weight keeps me pinned to the earth. So I push off my blanket, and make some tea for poor Gholam Hosein and boil the water for his medicine; and coax the orphans through their Arabic for half an hour – O how Ali beats Zaid through all the oblique cases!– and then step out into the sunshine.

I imagine the heart, like the other organs of the body, does not reconstitute itself after its early years; and the pieces of it that I have scattered through this town will not be restored to me. Often at nightfall, I walk past Mr Ryazanov's garden to the Shahrestan Bridge, which was built by Great Alexander, they say, though the river has been diverted and it has been engulfed in town. I remember an evening in spring, how the river thundered beween the piers, and from the tea-shop the roar of a gas-lamp and the click of backgammon pieces and the rattling of the willows each side, and the smell of fruit-skins, sheep's blood and excrement. That memory is masterful, because it is true. It obliterates the new highway and the half-built lunapark, because it is beautiful; because by some formal process, which I do not understand and nobody understands, and perhaps just for that windy evening in 1974, it achieved perfection. That bridge I reserved from the ancient regime in Iran, inspect without shame, carry to the grave.

I am happy in this glorious spring under this indifferent blue dome. Willow cotton blows down the river shingle as I pass. There are boys selling damsons in polythene bags at the roadside and I stop a time with them and listen to the nightingales from the apricot gardens. I return to town in a rain shower. On days such as this, I believe that I shall see my family again, and we'll be reunited, and I'll go to Geneva and sell one of the rubies and we'll buy Mr Ryazanov's garden from whoever the successor of the Soviet Union is and now owns it, they'll be happy to have our money; and I'll sit with my wife in the summer house in the evening, and she'll read to me from her verse romance of *Amin va Karulin* and we'll remember our friend who gave his life for us.

I believe it will happen soon, God willing; perhaps today, God willing; here on the Bridge of Thirty-Three Arches, where I am standing this morning. It will happen like this. I will be walking, as I am walking now, on the narrow pavement over the bridge, and two boys are running at me, as those two boys are running at me now. They will be students of mine from the Friday Mosque, as these two are. They will shout, as these two boys are shouting: "They're here, sir! Your family is here!"

And I see, through the traffic, at the end of the bridge, two women in black who have been too much in each other's company, exactly as these two. The taller of the two strides on, the other drags her feet, like certain widows who fear to leave their husband's ghost behind. A little further back still, and occasionally breaking his step to keep up, is a fat young man with a beard and a mobile telephone and an uncertain relationship to the ladies, a wholesaler's Number Five son by the look of him. Heavens, Shirin, you could have done better than that for her, but I don't suppose you can be that choosy, being princesses of the ancient regime.

The taller of the two will halt, stutter, shake, as if insulted. Then she is running, her shawl is flying off her head, God Almighty, she's fair-haired as I was at her age, and strong like her mother, running through the Guards, who jump aside.

"Shame on you, girl!"

"He's her father, bollock-eyes, come back with his wounds from the war. Leave them be."

"Cover, you harlot!"

"Leave them be, arse-eater!"

"Hey, semen-teeth, leave them be!"

"Leave them be."

"My soul my life my darling may I give my life for you, may I give my life for your handsome face and my life for your strong stature, let me kiss your hands, what has happened to your hand, I will be your right hand, O my father. Don't recoil from your loving daughter, O my Dad, O Dad of mine!"

"Do you speak French, miss?"

"Yes, sir."

"And Arabic?"

"Yes, sir. And Turkish, and Russian, and English and . . ."

She lowered her head.

"Excuse me, Layly."

"There is nothing to excuse! Granny and aunt didn't make it. God will forgive them, but mother never for one moment doubted that you would finish your business and with God's help come back to us. Not for one instant of an instant!"

"Are you married, my darling?"

"No, sir, but . . ." She pulled herself straight. "NEVER!"

"Kindly, wait for me here, dear Layly. I have business with your mother."

"Don't be angry with her, Dad! You don't know what . . ."

"No, I don't."

* *

I walk towards the lady on the bridge. Slowly, she lowers her chador, so that I can see her hair has been cut off; better get it over with. I suppose they thought they could take away her beauty, silly pricks. There is no sound now. The traffic has gone. The greybeards and the teasing boys have gone. Mr Son-in-Law-for-Cunt-and-Kebab has gone. The city itself is gone, leaving only the river and the bridge that spans it. In that moment, sound and air and warmth and light dissolve in the Isfahanian blue, which is not indifferent, but full of sensation, teeming with sensation; and time unveils at last and it is only memory, the memory of beauty, which is also the promise of beauty and sustains us in these agonies. Everything you lost, madame, I found and kept for you. Everything you sold, I bought and kept for you. Everything you broke, I pieced together and repaired for you.

I stand before the lady on the bridge, and her eyes come up with a start, full of old things, – trash, sour pickles, pain, sorrow, vomit, prison-yards and women's teeth and men's fists and fingers, interminable Friday sermons – which are themselves passing away in the river below us, which now brings something new, that lane she reserved from her girlhood, with a stream running down it drunk with the scent of acacia flowers, and grandmother's chador askew in the door-frame, dissolving in the sensation of light; and a pool in the desert and a ruined palace; and the orchard where two lives joined, split apart, then joined again, this time and for ever and for ever, O Master of Time and Lord of the Two Worlds!

Shirin Farameh laughs and offers her mouth for a kiss.